The Magic Fairy Rose

in the Lowland of Scotland

The Battle with Good and Evil

BOOK 2

BY A.E. FORTIN

THE MAGIC FAIRY ROSE IN THE LOWLAND OF SCOTLAND
The Battle with Good and Evil

Copyright © 2025 **A.E. Fortin**

ISBN (Paperback): 979-8-89672-201-4
ISBN (Ebook): 979-8-89672-202-1

All rights reserved. No part of this book may be used or reproduced by any means, graphic, electronic, or mechanical, including photocopying, recording, taping or by information storage and retrieval system without the written permission of the author except in the case of brief quotations embodied in critical articles and reviews.

Because of the dynamic nature of the Internet, any web addresses or links contained in this book may have changed since publication and may no longer be valid. The views expressed in the work are solely those of the author and do not necessarily reflect the views of the publisher, and the publisher hereby disclaims any responsibility for them.

Printed in the United States of America.

PROMINENT
BOOKS
EDGE

5830 E 2nd St, Ste 7000 #9983
Casper, WY 82609
USA

TABLE OF CONTENTS

Prologue: Rosemary in the hands of evil.   v

Chapter One: Saving Eleanor and Rosemary   1

Chapter Two: We found our brother's bodies.   19

Chapter Three: The power of the Fairy Rose.   34

Chapter Four: On their way home.   54

Chapter Five: A nightmare at the hunting cabin.   71

Chapter Six: A new family came to town.   83

Chapter Seven: Time to Say Goodbye.   101

Chapter Eight: The Eagle's cry out.   119

Chapter Nine: The Roses New Home.   136

Chapter Ten: Pregnant Horses & A Town to Save.   153

Chapter Eleven: Time to Clean out the Higher Killers.   168

Chapter Twelve: Albert is in the Highland's   201

Chapter Thirteen: The battle of good and evil.   220

Chapter Fourteen: The young boy.   232

Chapter Fifteen: Garret helped Albert.   239

Chapter Sixteen: Meeting the women.   257

Epilogue: About Kenyon and Raiman   265

Rosemary in the hands of evil.

ELEANOR WAS ABLE to see the sunrise; what a beautiful morning it was. Until she felt evil was near, she knew the man in black was there. *"Thomas the man in black is here, he has Rosemary. Why does he have to pick her? She is to be married to your cousin. I can't let him have her, she is the one who is keeping his mind sane. It's been hard for him after losing his twin. I must save her from him; he doesn't care who he hurts."*

Thomas heard Eleanor's thoughts; "Damn it…, William the man in black is in the Highlands. Eleanor is trying to save Rosemary; the two women had struck him three times with a big log. He won't stay down, and he is coming on them fast."

Eleanor cried out. *"I'm sorry Thomas…, I had to try. I don't think we will make it. Why is he doing this don't he know he's cursed, and no woman could give him a son. He keeps killing the women, don't he realize no woman could give him a son. Because a man chooses the sex of the child. He must think, the witch couldn't curse him. He had killed her daughter because she didn't give him a son. This imbecile still thinks a woman has the power to choose the sex. Satan…, must be disappointed with his son, the man in black."*

He had dropped his hammer. "William gathers your sword, we have two women to save. I'm going to use the spell that the storyteller told me to do."

Thomas could feel the fear coming from the two women. As the man in black was getting closer. *"Honey, we need your help, please I don't want to carry his child."*

CHAPTER ONE

Saving Eleanor and Rosemary

THOMAS AND WILLIAM were working on the wagon; everything was going quite well. Until he felt Eleanor, she was in trouble. Evil was in the Highlands, he could see it was the man in black. William heard the hammer drop, quickly he went to his side and saw he was having a vision. He heard his wife was in trouble. With a wave of his hand their swords were by their sides. Together they held onto Eleanor's hair as the two men thought of her. In a blink of an eye the two men were just a way from the two women.

William took out his sword, he prepared himself for a fight. Thomas quickly took out all the things he needed to use to cripple the man in black. With his magic he took a magic rose petal and turned it into a dirk. Once it was ready he took aim and threw it at the man in black. The dirk hit him, and it followed his blood stream, it went down toward his loins. Thomas and William stepped apart they we're ready to fight. Eleanor and Rosemary Road between them, the two young men watched the man in black stop. Here they saw him waying out, to fight or run. He took to run it was too much to stand and fight with these two young men.

Once again, they took hold of Eleanor's hair. They thought of her and went right to them.

William helped Rosemary down from Lady. Once she was on the ground, she went right into his arms. She couldn't help herself and burst into tears, Thomas went to lift Eleanor off her horse. When he put his hands around her waist, he could feel her body shaking. She wrapped her arms around his neck. He then pulled her to him and rubbed her back. He was speaking softly to her; he held her until she started to cry. When their eyes met, he kissed her deeply. Then he picked her up and carried her to Grana's place. William had done the same. Both women had their arms around the men's nick. When Rosemary stopped crying, she passed out on his shoulder. Thomas whistled for Lady to follow them.

There was no one in the streets to see what had happened. Rosemary was going to the bar to help set up for breakfast, she was one of the barmaids that work there. Thomas had knocked at Grana's door, when she saw Thomas and William. There were questions running through her mind, he sat down with Eleanor. William laid Rosemary on the table so Grana could check her over. She had given William a hug then turned to Thomas. "What is wrong with Rosemary?" It was Eleanor who told her what had happened.

Rosemary had come around, at first, she thought it was nighttime. As she started to remember she began to cry. Grana then said. "Ye are safe here with us, tell me what he had done to you so I can help ye. William had stepped out of the room; Grana had gone right to work checking her over. She had given Rosemary something to make her sleep.

When she came out, she could see Eleanor had her head on Thomas' shoulder. She was holding on to him for dear life. "Eleanor, do ye need anything?"

William looked at his grandmother then said. "Grana that had scared her to high heaven."

Then she knew a way to change her mind. "Eleanor, I found this book of magic roses." Quickly she went to get the book for her. "Here it is, there are three magic rose bushes that have magic. When the Fairy Queen and her Wizard died their magic went to the roses. She will have magic ones she breathes in the scent of the rose."

Thomas looked at Eleanor, he was worried about his love. "Grana, my wife has magic now; she can do insignificant things. It's funny ye can read that book, the ones Eleanor had found would show her just a little then went blank."

Then Grana went and read the rest of the story. "The two of them who take care of the roses will have great powers through the rose petals. After she finds the first rose bush, she must plant it in the garden that they take care of. The other two magic roses; ye will plant them in a different place. After the one rose bush blooms the man must breathe in the scent of the rose. Doing this will tell him how deep his love for her runs. It will also strengthen any gifts he has; then he will present the rose to her. She will find out how deep her love for him runs. After that, any gifts that she may have will become stronger.

* * * * *

Rosemary was resting now. Thomas told William to go back to the barn, he will be there after Eleanor is safe with his parents. William said goodbye to Grana and his sister.

Thomas waved his hand and William was gone. "Grana I have found out that Michael is alive. I know he is married and has children. We have found our brothers and will be coming home soon. Grana Eleanor is going to wait for us after the fight. Eleanor was coming for those things. She needs supplies for healing. I must go now to get Eleanor to the castle. I will see ye when we are back for good."

Grana watched him as he picked up his wife. "Thomas my boy, ye have become a strong and handsome man. These magic roses will be going to the new world; their magic will be necessary. This man will die but will not go to be judged by the Lord. Your brother will be fighting him in the heavens."

Thomas just looked at her, he was so tired. That he didn't see Grana give Eleanor something to drink. It was getting bad that he didn't remember what his vision had told him. "Grana do ye mean Michael is going to fight him somewhere in the Lowlands?"

She looked at Thomas. "My poor boy, no… It will be Ronald who fights the man in black. The fight will be in the heavens. This will go on until the demon calls the man in black. As this goes on, Ye and Michael with William and your uncle will fight the demon. This demon takes care of Albert. Ronald is keeping the man in black busy. Until the demon is ready for him to go into his new body. If ye can stop the demon and the locket from going into Albert's chest.

"Eleanor has been having dreams of Albert. Talk to her about this one's ye are back at home. Don't worry there will be someone to help ye to take down the man in black. If this happens. His master will punish him for not taking down the MacGregors. Another Thomas will have to fight him again in the new world. Like ye have done, he will also have to do. Make sure your journal tells that ye came from a far place to save your love."

He took a deep breath. How would she know something like this? "Grana how do ye know this? I have just found out yesterday of all that ye have told me."

She gave Thomas a big smile, she went over to touch his cheek. "Ye brother told me. His spirit is waiting for ye. My boy, your brother, has watched over ye all this time. He knew about the magic roses. Your brother Ronald had set it up. Michael had placed their bodies in that church yard. Your two brothers had a list for Father. This would guarantee their bodies will stay there until ye get here. "Rodney would send word for ye to see Father. Then come to the pub where he tells his story. Ronald knows ye to will my boy. Afterwards, ye would ask where to find a rose bush. He knew ye would have a vision of Eleanor riding hard to get to ye. My boy the Lord has sent your family to take this man down."

Thomas didn't understand. Eleanor was still in his arms. "Grana did Ronald know that he was going to lose his wife and child?"

She looked at the boy she had brought into this world. He stood in front of her holding his wife. He is a strong man now; she could see the pain in his eyes. "No…, your brother didn't know about anything what was going to happen. The Lord came to him the night after he buried his wife and child. Ronald set up everything, after the six of ye take down Rodney and his men. Ye will have to fight again. The Lord has plans for Ye and your brother's. Like always William and your uncle will be by your side. Thomas, go now and get your wife home. I gave her something so she will sleep for a bit. They need ye back in the Lowlands."

He gave Grana a kiss goodbye. She gave me the things that Eleanor would need. With a wave of his hand, he was on his land. I want the fireplace done now; it took a thought and a wave of his hand. Then Thomas had made their fireplace and cellar to their new home. He thought of William's home and did the same to his place. He took his time and rode down the path to the castle. Eleanor started to move; it was time to get her in bed. He waved his hand, and her horse was in a pen eating.

With a thought and a wave Thomas had her in their room. He was thankful that he had the magic the Lord gave him. His wife's lips called him. Gently he laid a kiss on her lips. Then he laid her down on their bed. On the table was a list of things to pack. With a wave of his hand everything she would need was there. On his knees he kissed his wife, he wished that he could lay down with her. He ran a hand over her face. "I love ye so much be safe my love."

He went downstairs to talk to his parents. Thomas had to tell them what had happened to Eleanor and Rosemary in the forest. He let them know that Rosemary was safe with Grana, that the two women were sleeping. It was time for him to get back to the Lowlands. He gave his parents a hug, "Tell Eleanor I love her. I will see her at the hunting cabin." Then he was gone.

* * * * *

Thomas was back in the Lowlands. William had just finished the top that goes over their brother's. The barndoor had opened he looked up. He had noticed his friend looked tired. "So how is my sister?"

Thomas had given a yond. "Both women are sleeping. I had told my parents what had happened. Grana is going to make sure that one of the men will walk Rosemary to the bar. Everyone is back from town. We have something to oversee. Grana had told me something my brother Ronald is going to do. William, I need a nap." He yond again. "Everything looks good." Thomas made a wave of his hand, if there was something wrong it would be fixed right off. The two young men looked around where done. "I think I will also take a nap; this had been a hell of a day."

* * * * *

Thomas was thinking about what Grana had said. As he closed his eyes, he found the dream took him to the future. At first, he thought he was looking at Eleanor when they were younger. One thing was missing. Where were his sister and Eleanor's brother? What were they wearing? The place wasn't in the Highlands. Where was he? It was nighttime there were fancy lights that lit up the yard. Two teenagers walked holding hands. They stopped in front of the lights. He was wondering if this was his grandson.

Tom had touched her face. "Ellen there is something happening to me. The two of us won't be together very much longer."

Thomas then thought that the next Tom and Ellen would have it harder than they had. It looks like he's been in love with her all his life. He told himself that he been in love with her.

Ellen took hold of his hand; she laid her forehead on his forehead. "Tom what do you mean. If you're not going to the same school. Then where are you going to be?"

Now Tom was touching her lips with his finger. Ellen noticed he was studying her face as if he were going to forget her. "On weekends I live in the Highlands of Scotland. I will go to school in the Lowlands and live there also. Ellen, have I told ye I'm in love with you?"

When Tom said that her eyes went dreamy with hope. She was a very smart young woman for the age of fourteen. For a long time, she has been in love with Tom MacGregor. "Could you tell me what kind of love are you talking about? I need to know that. There are all kinds of love."

She was tall like Tom was, her body was filling out nicely. Everyone thought she was older. Her mind and body looked like every part of her was strong. "Ellen, do you trust me?"

She looked at him and wondered where he was heading with these thoughts. "Tom, you know I do. You have always been there for me. Tell me, is it the kind of love for a man and woman? I hope it's not love for a sister. The first Eleanor had to go through that not I. For I don't think of you as a brother."

Thomas was watching this young man that looked just like him. It looks like those two will go through what we have been going through.

Tom needed a little more than touching her face. "Come with me, I need to find out something right now."

Ellen nodded her head, she felt different inside. Her mind was wondering if he loved her as a girlfriend, for she thought of him as her boyfriend. Please she thought not the love for a brother. He had taken her to the side of the garage. Tom had put his back against the wall. "Will you let me kiss you? There are strong feelings for you, I'm hoping that when we kiss. It will be clear to me; it will tell me what kind of love I have for you."

Ellen put a finger over his lips. The love stories she read told her what to do. Now she stepped into his arms. She closed her eyes as he drew her into a kiss. When he pulled away from her. He looked to see if she was afraid of what they were doing. "Tom, are you going to kiss me again?" He nodded his head. This time she was against the wall, his tongue moved over her lips. Ellen opened and he deepened the kiss. This time the kiss drew the passion out of them. Tom pulled her into him, she felt his warm hands, on her breast. In his mind he heard her say. *"Tom what's happening to us."* He felt her hands and nails pushing into his bottom, she was moving him closer to her.

Tom's head had popped up; he understood that his body wanted her. All this time I didn't know what I was feeling for her. He found them breathing hard now. "I heard you in my mind, Ellen I'm glad you said something. For you would have had my finger in your heat."

Ellen knew that was the first step of making love. "Tom, you love me as if I was a woman. My body feels different; it wants what you would give me. But my mind tells me that I'm not ready for what you would want to do to me."

She watched his hand run through his hair. Now she wanted to find out something for herself. Ellen went over to Tom she had put her arms around his waist. Her hand wanted to feel his heat. Slowly she moved down to his beltline and stopped. "*It's all right to touch me Ellen,*" she heard him say. She had dropped her hands, she didn't know what to do. Every part of her body wanted something from him. She knew that she could get pregnant if they went too far. Her body was changing faster than girls her age.

Then he heard her say. "*Tom these feelings were having. It's making us want to do something I'm not ready for.*

Tom thought back when he was younger his mother told him. When he was two years old, on the day she was born he fought with a demon. His mother told him he could have die that day. "I love you Ellen I would die for you. I know when we meet again. I might not know who you are. With your IQ it will be a year before I see you again. I know you and I can go to the dream world where we can be lovers. You will be twenty-one and I will be twenty-two. I wanted to touch you to give you the feeling of what it would be like with me." Ellen knew she was in love with Tom. She found her body was reacting to him.

*   *   *   *   *

Thomas watched the two of them. What was happening he thought, their age was when he fought the bear. What if that bear was Marcos, was that a test to see how strong his love was for Eleanor? He wanted to see if the bear could kill them. Aye, the bear didn't go after the cooked food. Damn it that was Marcos. I will kill that demon and make sure he goes back to hell.

*   *   *   *   *

Then the scene changed Thomas saw Ellen at a waterfall. There was a pool of water that she was standing in. Across the other side there was a big rock. This time she couldn't see Tom. There was something wrong, it was all black. She could feel the evil that was across the water. Then she heard laughter from something that was in print on her mind. The stories of an evil man from the past his name was Marcos. Ellen knew Tom was in trouble in the dream world.

What was this trying to tell Thomas. Could Marcos get into their dream world? Then he saw her change as she called for her powers. Now she was twenty-one and Tom couldn't change. Right then a beam of light came down to her. Thomas watched as that beam of light ran through her and into the darkness. He saw Tom change into a man of twenty-three. Thomas heard the name Garret. Ellen was calling for her powers and Tom's powers.

Wait who is Garret. Right now, he does not know any Garret. He's the one to give her his powers. How did he get into their dream world?

*　*　*　*　*

Then Thomas heard his uncle calling to them. "Thomas and William, it's time to eat get up my boys we need to have a family meeting. We must get ready for the battle; our weapons need to be ready for us to fight. Your guns cleaned and our swords sharpened. Ye dirks must be the sharpest for close fighting."

Thomas was rubbing his eyes he remembered the dream he just had. Now what was that all about? This dream was from the future. Ellen felt Tom was in trouble then he heard her call to Garret. Who was Garret? Could evil get into their dreams? Thomas had heard a man's laughter he had to find out what happened to them. Eleanor has been dreaming of Albert. Could it be this, Marcos? What would it take to find out what happened to them? Will it take a rose stem to investigate his dream?

*　*　*　*　*

At the table Thomas and William told them what had happened today. "The man in black was in the Highlands. Eleanor saved Damian's girlfriend."

At the table Duncan slammed his hand down. Donald understood why he did it. He knew Damian was in love with Maryann. If I get my hands around that man's neck, he will be dead."

Then Donald spoke up. "Enough my boy. Just be thankful Thomas and William stopped him from getting the women. Thomas are ye telling me both of ye went home?"

He looked at his uncle and smiled, aye, that we did. Now do ye remember what Meghalaya told me to do. I made the rose petal into a dirk and through it at him. I made sure it went down to his loins. When he tries to take a woman to rape her. He will find it very painful to do so."

Thomas looked at both men. He was very thankful they had gotten the roses. "Aye… We were working on the wagon when I heard Eleanor. I took out Eleanor's hair. William came over to my side, with the wave of my hand we had our swords. Then we went where Eleanor was riding. She had ridden between us as we stood apart to engage him in a fight. At least we were able to turn him away from the women. Eleanor, said he had a hard head. Both women hit him hard with a log.

The men smiled now their women will have someone else to talk to. Thomas looked at his uncle. "I have more news for ye, we have talked to our fathers."

They both have their vests. I will tell Eleanor when ye leave with the bodies. "Uncle after William left and came back to the Lowlands. Grana had given me news about Ronald. I don't know what to make of this. She said that Ronald knew about these roses. He must have heard the story about them. This part is confusing to me. Grana told me that the Lord came to Ronald, after we buried his wife and son. She said that this man in black will fight Ronald in the heavens. I had a vision about this. Eleanor also had visions and dreams of this young man.

"She had the sweater on that I gave her. Then it changed the voice wasn't the same. She had told me that she heard a young man pleading for help. He said his name is Albert, she saw a locket going into his chest. The demon with him has put him a sleep. If I'm right, we will be fighting this demon who has black magic. At the time Ronald is fighting the man in black. The time isn't now. We have time to get the bodies home.

"I believe when Michael went for the bodies. He had killed these men but missed the man in black. He must have hit him close to his heart. The demon that was with him, he must have taken him to be heel with black magic. If he was near death, he must have given his soul to the devil. I believe this man will have black magic. If I'm right, the Lord made it possible to get these roses. I know why Father Sinclair is coming with us." Thomas waved his hand and there were small crosses on the table. "I want these crosses on are weapons with the rose petals on them. Thomas stood up and waved his hand again and six shields showed up. Before we leave, we will have Father to bless them with holy water.

"I don't know why I had this dream. It's about Ellen and Tom in the future. These roses that I have on me. They are telling me that evil can come into our dreams. Ellen called for Garret magic, who is Garret? When she called him, she said Marcos was in the dream world. That he is trying to kill Tom in his sleep. We need an idea to stop this from happening. Grana said when we are home there will be another battle. That battle we have time to prepare for; we must prepare for this one. Tomorrow, we go for our brothers."

At the table he heard Eleanor's voice. Thomas told them what she had said. "They were leaving for the hunting cabin. They should be there in the morning. Our fathers will be resting for an hour. Then they will head out for the ferry. They will also rest on the ferry to make sure there ready to fight. I told them safe travels." Thomas looked at his brothers. "I don't like this part. I feel they're not going to get enough sleep. I'm going to try something outside. Please excuse me from the table."

*　*　*　*　*

Thomas went outside to talk to Eleanor. *"How do ye feel my love?"*

As Eleanor rode, she said. *"She was fine. I wish this were over with my love. It will be nice to finish our home. Please be careful our lives have just started."*

Thomas looked to the heavens. He thought he would try to send them closer to the hunting cabin. He closed his eyes and thought of the six of them riding. He wanted his father, and her father rested. From memory of the road, Thomas waved his hand. He had brought them closer to the hunting cabin. They were an hour out of the cabin. Then he heard his wife. *"Honey our fathers want to know if ye had done something. For the road looks different to them."*

Thomas, smiled to himself. *"Aye… that I did. Now, ye can rest all night. Tell dad to sleep and start out the next morning. Rest again on the other side of Lock Ness. They can wait for the bodies there."*

Then Thomas heard his father in his mind. *"Thomas can ye hear me?"*

With a big smile on his face. Thomas answered his father. *"Hello dad. This is good that ye can call me. I want ye to rest before the battle. Now that ye can call me, I will let ye know where Rodney is camp. Thank ye for doing this for us. I love ye dad. I haven't told ye this in a while. I'll let ye know when we have our brothers. Rest easy tonight."*

With a wave of his hand the crosses were on all their weapons. Then he sent rose petals to the crosses. He needed to send rose petals on the weapons to kill the demons. He will have Father bless all their weapons with holy water. The battle he got out his wide leather belt. It had a frog leather strap near his kilt. He will wear his best kilt into battle and home. All his thoughts went into the journal. I must find out what happened to Ellen and Tom.

Things were ready. He had looked over everything they had done. It was time to go to sleep. The two men were outside. "Tell me if ye were able to send our fathers to the hunting cabin."

Thomas smiled at his friend. "So ye knew I would try to get them there sooner."

William laughed. "Aye… Ye wouldn't put our fathers in danger. Now that ye have magic, ye would use it to help them. Thomas now that I can go to Catherine. Would it be all right if I do so now?"

Thomas had to laugh now. "If I want to pull my wife to me. How can I say no to ye? Go now I know my sister will wait for ye. Right now, sex is strong with us the need to be with them. To be as one with them is important to us. I can't get enough of your sister, my wife. So, go ahead. Ye must get some sleep also." Thomas waved his hand and William was gone.

Then it was time to call Eleanor to his side. "Honey would ye, like to be with me tonight?"

At the cabin Eleanor was cleaning up the dishes. Their fathers had just stood up to go outside. It was her father who asked if Thomas was going to call her. Then Eleanor smiled and spoke. "He just asked me if I like to go there tonight."

Both fathers laughed. "What are ye waiting for, get out of here. Just remember to go sleep to after would."

Eleanor's face turned red. To hear that from her father was too much. Then she called back to Thomas. "Aye… pull me to ye my love. Before my face gets any redder our fathers are laughing at me."

With a wave of his hand, she stood in front of him. Then Briana and Duncan came out of the house. It was Briana that spoke "Hello, Eleanor it's nice to see ye, I heard that that evil man had Duncan brother's bride to be…"

Duncan laughed to see Thomas had Eleanor in a deep kiss. Now both of their faces were red. Thomas brushed it off quickly.

Briana smiled at Eleanor. "Don't mind my husband. There have been times Thomas caught us in that kind of kiss. We can talk at the cabin."

Eleanor smiled at Briana. "Did Catherine check your baby out?" Briana shook her head yes. "At the cabin I will check ye again after your long trip. Don't forget to bring food on the ride there. I know Damian won't stop for ye to get food. Be prepared for him, to be a pain-in-your-nick. He will worry about everything, also ye will talk and he will not hear a word ye said."

Briana smiled, she was happy to hear there were more people to take care of her. "I didn't even think about care for me and the baby."

Then Eleanor looked at Briana. "Have ye done much horseback riding?"

Briana smiled. "Now that Flower came to me, I have. She was Peter's horse."

Thomas smiled he had looked at Duncan then said. "Honey for two years all their brother's horses were here. It didn't hit him until William, and I got here. I can see why he didn't notice."

Eleanor laughed. She smiled at Briana. "I can see that happening."

Then Thomas took her into his arms. "My love does ye remember that a man has two brains?"

She couldn't stop smiling. "Aye… I do remember ye saying that to me."

Right then Donald came out of the house. "I thought that I heard women's voices. Hello Eleanor. It's good to see ye. So, my boys are married. This is good to see, has William gone to see his wife?"

Thomas looked at his uncle. "Uncle would ye, like to go see your wife?"

Donald thought for a moment. "No but I would like to talk with my two friends. It would be good to be with them. We have everything done, is that right."

Thomas understood we had our wife with us. He would like to talk with his friends. Now that he has magic it has helped everyone out today. "I will let my father know ye will be joining them tonight." In his mind he called his father. "Dad, Uncle would like to be with ye two tonight. Would that be all right with ye?"

Thomas then heard. "Aye…, that would be fine with us. Tell me do ye have any Scotch we can drink?"

Thomas just started to laugh. "Wow Dad! Us young men go for sex. While our fathers go for Scotch. Not bad." Thomas waved his hand and gave his uncle a bottle of Scotch. "I guess when your young sex is on your mind. Being older Scotch helps with all that we have put our bodies through. For tonight ye can sleep inside and talk about out time. I hope ye three get the sleep ye will need. See ye tomorrow uncle." With a wave of his hand Donald went to be with his old friends. The three of them will be fighting with us the next day. It was time to rest in their own way.

*   *   *   *   *

In the morning, the women fix breakfast for the men. Thomas had sent the food for the five men to the hunting cabin. Today they would pick up their brothers' remains. Hopefully, Father Sinclair won't be ready to go yet. They had to put their bodies in the one wagon first. Then place Briana's things on top. They would have to keep Father in the dark. He must not know what was also in that wagon. Then he wouldn't have to lie to anyone about the bodies. Thomas watched the three women working together. He could see they were becoming good friends. He had pulled his sister and William to the farm for breakfast. The women were enjoying being together. Now this was good to see all of them being as a family. His magic couldn't do everything; they had to fight that battle. He couldn't just wave his hand and bring his brothers to the Highlands. Their group here had not talked about what was coming. Just of the plans when they get home. Thomas knew he had to send the girls back after kissing their wife goodbye. He sent Catherin home then Eleanor to the hunting cabin. It was time to bring his uncle back here to the farm. He went outside to think if he had miss anything.

When he sat down off in the distance. Thomas could see there was a fog slowly rolling in. Then a thought came to him, if only this fog would grow thicker. This fog would be the cover they needed. It would let them go into town without anyone detecting them. Just a little more fog, which is all they would need to make sure that they're not detected. He thought the roses seemed to know what he needed. Then again this must have been the Lord's work, he knows just what we needed. Thomas then went to the barn to get the horses and wagon ready to go into town.

His uncle came out looking for him. By that time, the fog was getting thicker. "Thomas, ye have everything all done. It was good being with my friends. I know the women enjoyed working together. Did ye ask for this fog."

The wagon was ready with the coffins; Thomas led the horses out already saddled. "Don't look at me like that, I didn't ask for the fog. It was the Lords doing. I'm glad he thought of it for me."

Then the rest of them came outside. William spoke. "Thomas ye should have asked me for some help."

He looked at his friend. "William ye were talking with Briana and Duncan. I need this time by myself. I was glad ye four got along. Your home is between us by miles."

Briana was smiling, knowing she would have two midwives to look after her. "I was happy that Eleanor told me to get food for myself."

Thomas told her what catherine had said. "Hay cousin my sister said she better double it, she could be eating for two."

She looked at him. "What is he talking about."

Duncan hit his head. "I forgot we have twins in the family. Sorry honey."

Briana took a deep breath. "I see my horse is ready for me. I will ride with my husband then I will use my horse to get our food for the trip. She had overlooked what Thomas said. "Wow! The fog is getting thicker."

In the yard the fog was thick Thomas couldn't see too far. "We better get going this is just what we need to get the bodies from the churchyard. I have this canvas to go over the coffins. With the help of the fog, we can slip into the churchyard to get our brothers. Then we can slip back out. We can be back here to place the bodies in the other wagon. What do ye say?"

Donald looked at his family. Time has gone so fast these two years. When he got to talk with his friends, he could see how time has slipped away from them. "I say it's time to ride the fog isn't going to lift any time soon. When Briana goes to get the food Duncan ye can go with her. We will get Ronald up first then Jonathan will be next. When ye get back he will get Peter's body next. Now it's time to head out to the churchyard."

The thick fog made the ride into town slow going, the four men didn't care. For they were heading to the churchyard under cover so they could claim the bodies of their brother's. Up to now everything the four of them had done will seem like child's play. This would be the hardest thing the three young men have ever done.

Thomas wondered if everyone was thinking the way he was. When we dig up their bodies what emotion will he be feeling. It's one thing to bury brothers after they have died. It's another thing to dig them up just to rebury them somewhere else. Could he deal with the emotion, this time? He tried to picture what it would be like. Eleanor heard his thoughts. *"Honey don't think of it now. I believe ye should use your magic. Don't look at them now, do it at the farm. Get in there and out as fast as you can. He will be with ye when ye see him again."*

Thomas rode up to his uncle. "Dad, what if I use my magic. Get in there and out as fast as we can. This fog is good cover for us. What do ye think of doing that? No one will see us putting them in the other wagon. This way the dirt will not be disturb."

Donald smiled at this strong young man. He was now one of his sons: now Thomas has two fathers and more brothers. "Aye…, that's a good plan. Let the others know then we can say goodbye to them the right way."

At the cabin Eleanor wondered what everyone thought. *"Honey did everyone like that idea?"*

Thomas smiled, she always had clever ideas. *"Aye…, that's the plan now. I think I will be all right. I have seen him once as a spirit. He said it was just the shall of his body was once before. Ye, are right I do think too much on that subject. I know I will deal with this once it happens."*

Thomas felt better hearing Eleanor's voice. *"I just want this over with, there is a thick fog here today. We should be able to get into the church yard without anyone knowing. I'm hoping no one will see Briana and Duncan getting the food. I feel better hearing your voice. Now I'm looking back at what happened. With everything on my mind, it had overwhelmed me. It was when his son died. I had looked into Ronald's eyes; it had scared me. Death took a whole new meaning when it was my brother's son. Michael was right behind me. I jumped when he touched me. Eleanor, I was worried that ye thought I was a coward. All of this made me fear what ye thought of me. I was scared what would have happened if we married. That's why I made ye go to those parties.*

"Right now, I going to use my magic. Dad said he will keep Father busy; I couldn't get them in the coffins quickly. The priest, even said the gate would be, unlocked; just a wave of my hand and think of each one. William and I can get the letter from each of our brothers. Father can see once we have them, he can bless them again. We can go back to the barn, then place the bodies within the bottom of the other wagon. When we arrived at the hunting cabin. We will place them in the coffins that we made. Then we will make are way to their last resting place.

"Eleanor I'm glad that I went for the roses. For I wouldn't have been able to marry ye. I've realized from the first day I kissed ye. I knew I would make ye mine. Now that's your mine. I have enjoyed making love to ye. Each time I join with ye I find that I can't get enough of ye. To watch what I can do to ye makes me want ye right now."

Eleanor was feeling his hand moving over her body. She could feel his hand on her breast as he ran his hand down to her heat. When she felt a finger inside her heat. Her body reacted as she came. She had to lay down and cover herself up. *"Thomas ye are scaring me?"*

He didn't know if he could do what he was thinking. *"Honey, I need to be one with ye. If only with are minds. Don't be afraid of what I'm doing. Use your mind and touch me."*

Eleanor pictured Thomas as she moved over his heat. She heard him say. *"Honey that's it. I'm picturing my heat sliding inside ye. I can feel ye as ye come, that's it. Honey can ye feel me coming?"*

Eleanor felt Thomas was with her right now. She had felt the weight of his body and everything he was doing to her. When she got up, she felt something running down her leg. *"Honey how did ye do that?"*

Thomas had felt so much better now that he had relaxed. *"So, I was able to come inside ye, without being with ye. I'm glad ye are on something. Or ye would be with our child as much as we made love. I had to relax so I could get through this. How do ye feel now."*

Her mind thought of him as her lips kissed him. In his mind he felt her lips deepening that kiss.

CHAPTER TWO

We found our brother's bodies.

THOMAS HAD FELT nervous until his wife helped him. Now he felt relaxed, time has gone by fast. It was just four days ago. Uncle Donald had found out were the location of our brothers resting place.

I shouldn't be afraid of my brother's body. His spirit has spoken to me, and I wasn't scared of him then. Ronald knew I had to grow up. The time of his death evil wouldn't allow us to bring him home a hero.

William and Thomas had opened the gates. In the churchyard we went to their brother's graves. There we placed the wagon near the graves. They brought the coffins over one by one, quickly they took off the lids. With a wave of his hand, Thomas had placed his brother Ronald's in his coffin. He made it look like they had dug his brother's body up. He had to get the others in their coffins. Jonathan was next then it was Peter who was place in his coffin. Donald was pleased that Father Sinclair didn't come out until now. Father went over to give them their blessing for safe travel. They told Father we will leave after 10:00 today. The grounds now restored Thomas made sure of it. This had pleased Father. They took the stones with them;

Thomas was going to change the wording on the stones. It was good timing because Briana and Duncan were riding up. While the three men came out of the churchyard.

*　　*　　*　　*　　*

They must get back to the farm, there's still time to retrieve the letters. The fog was still as thick when they had left. At the farm it was time to get things in motion. The men brought the coffins to the ground. It was time to look upon their brother's. Thomas took a deep breath to get hold of himself. Slowly he knelt beside the body and reached for his dirk. He cut two of the ropes and placed his dirk back in the frog. With loving care, he pulled away the cloth to view the face of his brother. His hair was long and so was his beard. Then Thomas felt a hand on his left shoulder. There before him stood his brother. He was a spirit from God; There was a heavenly light that surrounded Ronald.

The magic of the roses had given them the sight to see their brothers. In Thomas' mind he spoke to his brother. *"There ye are my brother. I wish ye were here in the flesh not as a spirit. Ronald ye knew I would marry Eleanor. The first time I received my magic was by a book. With the petals from the magic roses, Eleanor has her magic. The rose petals have made us stronger; there are petals on all are vest. I give ye one and Micheal and his son. He can see ye with his vest.*

Thomas waved his hand and Ronald, had his vest. Then he thought of Micheal and his son. *"Micheal, I have given ye your vest that has the magic roses on them, ye son also has one."*

Then he put three rose petals on Ronald's hair and put it in his sporran. Then he called Michael. *"It's time to head home Michael, I will see ye there God speed. As ye know, the three of us will have to fight. This time our father's will be able to take these men down with us. I have a feeling ye know all about this."*

Thomas saw Ronald nod his head. *"Well done little brother. Ye do know that ye will always be that to Michael and me. We knew that ye would find are graves sights."*

Thomas smiled at his brother. *"That was a clever idea for those questions for Father. That man Rodney he enjoyed telling us that story. I knew he was the one to stab men in the back. The fool didn't realize he had told us more about himself. He liked it when he got a reaction from me. If Duncan didn't put a hand on my shoulder. He would have gone down with my hands around his neck. William did damage to Rodney's wrist; he was going to throw his dirk at me. Uncle gave him an ear full; he told him if he was one of them to kill his family. He will be coming after him.*

"When we burned a rose stem. I saw everything those men had done to ye. If ye like to wish dad good hunting. He will be waiting for ye on this side of Lock Ness; he has his vest on. We will take care of those men with dad's help. Our father's will have the chance to kill the ones that killed their son. With my new magic and the rose stems. I will be able to tell Dad where Rodney will be. Then Thomas placed a rose petal on his cross and a hole rose in his sporran. I know that ye will have to fight the man in black.

"This should give ye power to help our father at times. This vest is to keep ye safe from demons. I had a dream before I went for the roses, I saw ye fighting the man in black. I know his name now, it's Marcos, he was fighting ye in the heavens. I see that ye have your weapons with ye."

Thomas placed a small cross on his sword and petals on the blade and cross. *"The Lord told me in this dream to help ye with everything I have. I give ye magic from the roses. For Marcos, he has black magic. He will be using Albert to have a new and younger body."*

Thomas saw Ronald smile. *"I knew ye could do this. I watched over ye while ye was here in the Lowlands. So ye know that the Lord sent me to bring Marcos and his men to be judge."*

Thomas was glad his brother was with them. *"Aye… Ronald do ye know he's in the Highlands; he had Damian's bride to be. Eleanor heard Maryanne cry out for help. She had freed her by hitting him with a big log. But Marcos has a hard head, three times they hit him. She called me for help he almost caught up to them. William and I went to save Eleanor and Maryanne. We wish that we could have cut him down. At least we were able to turn him away from them. Ronald Ye will like this part; Meghalaya told me to take three petals. Then make the petals into a dirk, throw it at him. She said that the petals will go into his blood stream and down to his loins. When he takes another woman, he won't be able to do anything. She told us it will give him pain for what he was doing to women, just a little pay back."*

Ronald smiled with that thought and nodded his head. *"I knew that ye would pick that out quickly. For the man in black, Eleanor had met him as Albert. She had seen evil in his eyes; he is the man in black as ye know. He used Albert face ye must already know all of this. Eleanor had a dream; she showed that locket going into his chest. The pain he was in as he fought to dig it out of his chest."*

Ronald was pleased with his brother. *"Aye… it is true that Marcos has black magic. I saw that magic comes easy to ye. Thomas, I'm so proud of Ye. After this is over with. Ye will have to find a way to use magic when ye must. I will be there with ye in spirit. Give that letter to dad for me."*

Thomas nodded his head yes. *"Ronald, I have found a way to do just that. Your cross will give ye magic, ye can have fire come out of your sore. It's blessed with holy water. I place the rose petals on your cross. Ye can now help when ye see your needs. I gave the locket to Eleanor. I have placed a cross with a rose petal on it. The dream I had told me to do just that. Without the vest I can use these powers when I need them."*

Thomas used his magic to wrap the three bodies back up. He had them placed in the other wagon. He places the roses at each of their brother's feet. The top of the floor, was over the bodies. The coffins were back on the other wagon. Now it was time to put everything on top of their brothers. Thomas used his magic to make sure everything fit.

*   *   *   *   *

It was 10:00 they had everything packed and were ready to go. An hour later, Father Sinclair arrived at the farm, he rode up on his horse. The fog was still thick out. "This is a good sign from God, around us the sun is out. All the way here the fog was thick. Here I see the fog is starting to close in on us, are we going to use this fog to hide under cover?"

Donald had his horse ready to ride. "Aye…, that is what we are going to do Father. We are leaving right after my son says good-bye to his wife. Also, could ye bless these crosses for us. These other two is for my two friends."

Thomas had the rose petals on the crosses. "I will place the cross on ye as I bless ye and the cross together."

Father had given everyone a cross, even Briana, he had waved his hand. He had to give Father another cross with the rose petal on it. "Here Father we need two for Damian and his brother. We had sent word to them."

Then he said. "Uncle don't tell Damian about Maryanne. We will tell him when we get home."

Father Sinclair watched everyone, and he saw that they were all family. "So ye three are going to make sure that we get through first. I can't tell ye the number of men who wanted those bodies. The one who brought them to me. When he told me what they were going to do to the bodies. I understand now why he gave me that list. I will pray over both wagons." Then Father said a blessing to all to get across Lock Ness safely.

Thomas looked at Father Sinclair, this priest understands more then he likes us to know. Donald went over to his son; I will make sure Briana is on the next river boat. Then we will be joining ye three, Ye see Father I am going to be a grandfather. My son wants me to make sure his wife gets to the Highlands."

Father smiled at Donald. "Your son is wise and brave, I've known of young men like the three of ye. Ye have a job to do, the Lord be with ye."

Thomas and William could see that it was hard to let his wife go, Briana was trying not to cry. He kissed her deeply and lifted her onto her horse. "Dad it's time to ride, the fog is staying thick for now. Before it lifts ye should leave now, ye must be there by five to get the last river boat across Lock Ness."

Thomas William and Duncan would leave two hours later. They will have to camp and cross in the morning. He prayed the fog would hold long enough for Uncle Donald to get out of town. It was Thomas that said three hours is too long. Let us leave in two."

*   *   *   *   *

Just before sundown the three of them made camp near the waterfall. They will make there stand here with his two best friends and his brothers. By the fire, a wagon stood, there were three coffins covered by a tarp in the back. Five hours ago, Thomas prayed that Father Sinclair, Briana, had crossed Loch Ness. He hoped his brothers were in the Highlands, who were hiding in the special wagon, and were safely across Loch Ness. He was glad Donald went with Father Sinclair. Thomas knew there would be men watching for the coffins or any wagon that came along. If those men whoever they may be would check the wagon. They would find Briana's things on top. He hoped they wouldn't start looking at the floor of the wagon if they looked too hard. Those men might find out what we did to the floor, where it started and ended wouldn't look right. Thomas felt right about the decision to make that special wagon. Once they heard the story, Rodney McNeill confirmed Thomas' idea.

On that day, his uncle cried out. *"If ye were involved I will kill ye myself for doing what ye did to my family."*

The information that Rodney had shared with them. Thomas had felt comfortable telling his uncle about his idea. It had led him to believe Rodney killed Eleanor's brother; he told them it was dark out. He had seen one of the men stabbed a tall thin man in the back. Thomas remembered that the pleasure had danced in his eyes. Rodney said that the man laughed when the knife went into the man's back. When he told us about the man in the tree, that he cut two of the men down I saw anger in his eyes. They were trying to burn his brother alive.

Thomas was watching as a thick black cloud covered the moon. The darkness carried evil as it lurked through the shadows of the night, he could sense that death was nearby. The presence of evil was upon them; it blew through the camp riding on a frosty wind. Thomas prayed they would survive until morning; on this night men will die. It won't be the six of us, we will take down evil tonight. He swears this on his nephew's grave; whoever sent these men wanted us dead. These men were professional killers, who would kill just for money. He knew the men were coming for them. As he watched the fire dance over the log.

Thomas cried out. "Where are ye Rodney, tonight, ye will meet your maker."

The Lord strikes evil

They had five miles left before crossing Loch Ness. Donald was leading with Briana riding next to him on Flower. Father Sinclair had to stop the wagon; five men came out from behind a group of trees to block the road.

Donald spoke. "What do ye think you're doing, let us pass ye have no right to block the road.

He recognized one of the men from the pub. "I know ye, you're the man from the pub, well now! We meet again, now where's Rodney your boss. I know he's here, come on Rodney show yourself or are ye a coward. I know ye like to stab men in the back."

Then a man rode out of the trees. Rodney spoke. "So ye saw my man at the pub."

Donald place Briana on the other side of him. Then he was closer to Rodney. "There ye are! Aye… I saw him follow right behind ye. Your man should have waited before he left the pub. What do ye want? The coffins are not here."

Rodney shifted in his saddle. "I can see that for myself. Father Sinclair what are ye doing here?"

Father sat tall in his seat. "I'm going to the Highlands to start a church there, let us pass. Ye are interfering with God's work, are ye here to do the devil's work tonight. If ye are, ye men are killing for Satan. They told me that ye wouldn't let the bodies go to the Highlands, is this true."

Rodney didn't like that he was there. "Father this is our job we make our living this way, stand aside and no one will get hurt."

Father stood up. "Stop…! Can't ye not see there are no bodies on this wagon?"

Rodney didn't like him questioning him this way. "I still have to look Father."

Donald spoke. "If ye break anything on this wagon ye will answer to me."

Rodney looked Donald in the eyes. "Ye can try old man."

He gave the orders, and the men went to check the wagon. Each of the men grabbed something to throw, one by one they howled in pain.

Rodney then spoke. "Get those things off that wagon now."

His men turn to him and spoke. "No…! I don't know what's on this wagon, it just zapped me. I didn't like the kind of pain it's giving me."

Rodney looked at his men. "What are ye talking about, Ye men fear Father. He is a man just like ye and I."

One of the men spoke. "Father Sinclair is a man; but he has strong magic. There is something here that zapped us, I didn't like the pain it gave me."

Rodney got off his horse and went to grab one of Briana's things.

Briana screamed. "Don't break that, that crib is for when I have my baby. My father made that when I was born."

Before Donald spoke. Father Sinclair then turned toward him and shouted. "Stop right there…, Ye have no right to touch her things. Be gone Satan…, the Lord is protecting this wagon. Go now before he strikes ye dead."

Rodney got back on his horse and gave Donald a dirty look. "All right Father, this wagon may pass, the other wagon shouldn't be that far away…, let's ride."

Donald got off his horse and went to call for Rodney. He desperately wanted to fight him. Briana went over to him and spoke. "No…, it's not your time to fight, my baby lost one grandfather please don't make it two. Duncan left my life and his unborn child in your hands, I know those evil men will be judge tonight. They will pay for what they have done to your son, it's not your time to fight yet. Thomas and William's father are not here; I believed that they would be coming off that ferry. Please Donald…, ye must help us to get across that river, pray for what Thomas had said, so it may come true. Only then ye may go and fight, please do it for your unborn grandchild. If ye kill Rodney now the other men will kill ye."

He was pleased with his daughter-in-law. Donald thought here was a strong woman. "Briana my son needs a strong woman like ye. Ye are going to be a good wife for my boy. Ye are right, let's go."

*   *   *   *   *

At the hunting cabin, Daniel told Gallivan to stay there with Eleanor. Ye must help her to get ready for any men wounded.

Eleanor spoke. "Uncle I would like to go and fight beside ye and my brother and father."

Daniel said. "No…! Ye must stay here, I need ye to protect your cousin's wife. If something happened to Eleanor there would be no one to take care of the wounded. Without her the wounded won't have a chance. Do ye understand what I'm telling ye?"

Gallivan spoke. "Aye…, uncle I will do as ye ask of me."

Eleanor cried out. "Dad, I wish that I could go. Thomas told me to stay and be safe for him."

Then her father spoke. "Daughter I'm glad that ye listen to your husband, we don't know what we are going into. They could kill ye or catch ye and hold ye so we will give up, then kill all of us after we do. Thomas wouldn't be able to keep his mind on what he was doing."

Eleanor went over to them; she gave them a big hug. "Please be careful, it's time to catch the last ferry over to the Lowlands, it will be leaving soon."

Daniel, Theseus, and Damian got on their horses and rode hard to catch the last ferry.

Evil was on the ferry

The ferry for Loch Ness had docked on the side of the Lowlands, there would be one more for the night. On bord the ferry was a black buggy with all their window shades drawn. Inside no one could see what was happening when the drawbridge came down. It had covered the sound of a thump and a cry for help from a young woman. The driver of the buggy had led his team of horses off the drawbridge. Once he cleared the drawbridge, he hurried to the top and gave the command for his horses to take off. The evil man told him to push his team of horses hard. Two miles down the road they heard a team of horses coming fast down the road.

Donald had motioned for Father Sinclair to move over quickly. They had seen the seal on the door, he knew that seal, right then it didn't mean anything to him. He had to get to the ferry, that buggy had just got off. The ferry will leave again and be back in an hour. If he's not there the next one will be in the morning, they got there in time for the ferry to arrive. Donald was checking over Briana's things from her father and mother, the water of Lock Ness was sometimes rough. This wagon had to make it across safely.

Briana spoke. "Donald how far do ye thing Rodney and his men are from Duncan."

Donald spoke. "Don't worry Briana, he's a way from him he won't attack until it's much darker."

Then they heard. "Dad..."

Donald swung around and saw his son and friends. Damien Daniel and Theseus were leading their horses off the ferry.

He could hear Daniel call out. "Donald, we made it, did everything go as plan."

Donald had to brace himself for his son was running right into him. "Aye…, ye son is set up right now, can ye let him know you're here."

Damien ran over to his father and gave him a big hug. Donald then turned and introduced his son to Briana, his sister-in-law. "Dad…, my big brother is married."

Donald spoke. "Aye…, he's going to be a father in eight months."

Damien just looked at Briana then spoke. "A father in eight months at last, we will have little one. It's nice to meet Ye Briana. Dad, does she know that we have twins in the family?"

Briana looked at Daniel. "When ye said it before it didn't hit me, but the way I'm eating makes sense."

Daniel smiled a little happiness before we fought. Then he spoke. "Donald so ye are going to be a grandfather. I'm happy for ye old friend."

Then he introduced her to his best friends. "Briana this is Thomas's father Daniel. This old friend is William's father Theseus."

Donald went over to Father Sinclair to introduce him to his friends. He then asked Father if he could lead the horses onto the ferry. "He must talk to his son and friends it was important."

Father spoke. "I understand my son. Before ye leave I will bless the three of ye for battle, the Lord will be with ye."

Then Father placed a cross on the two men. Then spoke. "Ye are going up against evil tonight, your son asked me to place crosses on ye. God speed my sons…!"

The three men told Father thank ye for what he has done for their families. As Father led the wagon on to the ferry.

Donald spoke in a whisper. "Damien ye can't go with us. Ye must protect your sister-in-law and the child she cares for. Your brother's body is at the bottom of the wagon that holds Briana's things, this is what ye must do. I want ye to take them to the hunting cabin and wait for us. Go now and take care of everything until we return. Son, Father don't know about the bodies keep it that way."

Damien nodded his head yes. "I understand Dad, I will protect Briana with my life."

Donald turned to his friends. "We ride; Rodney has five men with him. He's about five miles ahead of us. They believe the coffins hold our sons. I'm thankful Father Sinclair was there. I have a feeling that with Father and the magic roses. Rodney couldn't take anything off the wagon. The man in black, gave him orders to burn the bodies and kill our other boys. Daniel have ye told your son ye were here?"

He looked at Donald. "Not yet…, I will do it now."

Before they left Briana ran over to Donald and gave him a hug. "Thank ye Donald for getting us to safety. Ye must leave now to be able to fight with your sons."

The three men wave goodbye to them. Daniel said. "Thomas knows we are on are way. He's going to let Eleanor know that they are crossing now. Well old friends…, it's time we ride; this time we fight evil again. So let us ride into battle to join our sons."

The men got on their horses and took off down the road.

* * * * *

Thomas called Eleanor. *"Eleanor my love. Dad said the wagon is on the ferry and they are starting to cross Lock Ness."*

She smiled when she heard her man. *"Ye did it my love. When the fighting is over, let me know if ye are all right."*

Thomas could see Eleanor in the fire. *"I will. Our brothers are under Briana's things. Like I thought Rodney tried to take things off. I don't know if it was Ronald, or the magic rose or Father. Dad said Rodney's men didn't want to take anything of that wagon. Father had seal it when he told Satan to be gone. Dad told me that Damian told Briana that there are twins in the family. She said that makes sense why I'm always hungry. He was shocked, the first time we reminded him of that. Honey, do ye think we can get your delicious food, in a bit? William and Duncan are looking around; they will be back soon. I can send three bowls to ye."*

Eleanor smiled and she was glad he liked her cooking. *"Any time ye are ready my love."*

Thomas had sent the bowls. *"I will call to ye when they are back."*

He had to know how far away Rodney was. He needed to see where their fathers were, this time when he gazed into the fire. Something happened that didn't happen the times before. Deep red flames shot up and black smoke surrounded the flame. Thomas could see Rodney had five of his men with him. He had made camp somewhere down the road. He must have seen us before the cloud moved across the moon. "Well now…!" Thomas thought. Rodney and the man in black came after my brother with six men. Ronald had two men with him; this time it will be different. He will let his father know where Rodney is. Then there will be three for our fathers and three for us. That will do nicely. "Dad, Rodney and his men's camp down the road from us."

Daniel was riding hard with his friend when he heard his son. He came to a stop; in his mind he heard his son. *"Dad…, Rodney is two miles from ye."*

Quickly Daniel took a breath. As he slowly let out the breath, he cleared his mind. *"Son…, I hear ye, are ye all right?"*

Thomas smiled and told his father. *"Aye…, we are all right. Dad the three of ye must close your eyes so I can show ye something."*

Daniel then told Donald. "They're all right! We need to hold hands to see what he wants to show us. The three of them close their eyes. *"Son, go ahead, were ready."*

Thomas spoke. *"As ye must know there is six men to fight. They are camping near to us; my brothers and I camped around five miles from Lock Ness. Where near the waterfall, Rodney has his camp by one of the streams. Ye looked like the three of Ye are two miles from us. Let us get ready and ye can catch your breath."*

Thomas then showed his father what he had in mind. He laid the idea out to trap Rodney and his men between them. *"This way we can put them between us. There are three of us and three for ye. We fight fare. They didn't fight fare for my brother. Tonight, these men will meet The Lord."*

*   *   *   *   *

William and Duncan were watching Thomas and knew there was something happening. They waited for him to stop staring at the fire. When he lifted his head and started to rub his eyes, they knew it was time to talk to him. With a nod from Duncan's head, the two men placed a hand on each of Thomas's shoulders at the same time. They were sitting down beside him, he thought he was going to jump out of his skin and went for his dirk.

Duncan smiled at William then spoke. "Tell us what ye saw."

When Thomas finally caught his breath. He spoke. "What are ye trying to do to me, I could have cut one of ye."

The two men laughed, and Duncan spoke. "No… why do ye think we grabbed your shoulders. It was a way to make sure ye wouldn't be able to get to your dirk. That way we would be ready to grab your hands if ye tried it. Tell us what ye saw and heard."

He looked at them. "Everyone is safe, I saw Rodney's group of men, they are nearby."

William asked. "How far do ye think they are?"

He then tried to picture how far they were. "Ten minutes from us, there are five men in Rodney's camp. I thought I saw one man coming this way, he is waiting for two of us to go to sleep."

William spoke. "Do ye know if they can see us."

Thomas looked at the sky. "Not yet…! I believe Rodney has sent a man to find out just that. His man will only be able to see us by the light of the fire. They don't have the moonlight and can't see much of what we are doing. If the moon stays covered and we let the fire, go low. I don't think they will be able to see us. I have a plan that may give us the edge for what we are about to attempt."

William spoke. "Ye were able to see all of that."

Thomas smiled then spoke. "Aye…, and there is more."

William looked at his friend then spoke. "You're magic is quite strong in ye. The old woman didn't say anything about this, could these powers be all new?"

He smiled at his old friend then spoke. "William the more I use the powers, I find that I can do other things. What I know is my great grandfather had strong magic like his wife. Ones Eleanor and I bring the roses back home, the gifts we have inherited will get stronger. Thomas then told them where their fathers were going to be soon. "If we could time it exactly right, our fathers could close them in. The six of us could take them out tonight, they will see The Lord. Tell me if ye two are hungry."

Duncan looked at his cousin. "Aye…, I wish there were something good to eat. Now that I have a wife that can cook, I'm spoiled.

Thomas smiled and asked William if he was hungry also. "Aye…, what do ye have that is good."

Thomas then called his wife. *"Honey, can we have some food."*

Eleanor had cut more meat. She knew that the men would be hungry soon. "I have a bowl ready for one of ye."

Thomas waved his hand, and a bowl appeared. "Here eat up."

Then he heard Eleanor. *"I have another one for ye."*

He waved his hand, and another bowl appeared. He handed it to William. Once again, he heard her say. *"I have yours ready, my love. I miss you be careful honey."*

Thomas waved his hand, and his bowl appeared. *"Thank ye, it was getting hard to think. The guys said thank ye for the food."*

Then he pictured kissing her, Eleanor felt dreamy. *"Any time my love."*

As the men ate Thomas took a stick to draw out the idea in the dirt. Duncan spoke. "Thomas ye have also the gift of planning. Dad said uncle and your brother had good fighting skills, I think it could work. Let them think we are sleeping. The three of us could circle around them and take those men by surprise. I like the way ye think, Ye have what Ronald and Michael have."

William spoke. "Then what are we waiting for, with our fathers on their way. They will help close these men in for the kill. The way they did to our brothers, an eye for an eye. Then and only then will our brothers rest in peace. I will keep watch, while ye two get the decoys ready to take our place."

Thomas looked at his friends. "Hang on, tell me have ye had enough food."

The two of them nodded their heads, he had the bowls clean and put them away. Then he waved his hand and there were three decoys, he called his father. "Dad the trap is set."

Daniel heard that the trap was set. *"Son, I see them moving in, get ready my boy. When ye see them call me. We're all set here, ye just tell us when to go."*

CHAPTER THREE

The power of the Fairy Rose.

AT THE HUNTING cabin Eleanor heard a wagon and the voice of Gallivan, and Damien. She ran out of the cabin to see Briana. Eleanor watched the boys treat Briana like she was glass. She almost started to laugh. "Hello Briana. I see that the boys are being overprotective with ye. Forgive them Gallivan, and Damien, this is the first time having a sister-in-law. Damien hasn't been himself scents he lost his twin brother."

Briana eyes looked to be throwing daggers at them. Finally, they stop fussing over her. "Hello Eleanor. Can ye call these boys off? Damien got it into his head; I'm going to lose Duncan's baby. I tried to tell Donald I was hungry. I understand that we had a deadline to meet the ferry. I thought I brought enough food; twins could make me eat that much. We just had to keep the wagon going to get there in time. Damien wouldn't believe me that I was hungry. That's because I got sick on the ferry, he thinks I'm going to lose his brother's child. When they are born, he is going to babysit them. Babies don't hear what anyone says. That is what Damien did, he didn't hear me. See what I mean, I ate all the food I had, and I brought extra. What's this I hear about twins, is that why I'm so hungry?"

Damien spoke. "Eleanor ye must help Briana, she got sick on the ferry, and she feels she might lose her baby."

Eleanor just gave him a stern look. At first it was funny, to her not now. Damien helped Briana into the hunting cabin. Gallivan had looked at Eleanor's face, he noticed she was getting upset with Damien.

Briana spoke. "Damien why did ye say that? I didn't say anything like that, just emit it. Ye are the one who is scared I might lose ye brother's child. I'm hungry and tired riding for so long, if ye was pregnant ye would be hungry, I want food, do ye understand that? I got sick because of ye, we didn't stop after getting off the ferry. Don't ye remember I told ye I have to eat because I was eating for two?"

Then Eleanor couldn't help herself. "That is a sign that ye may have twins."

Damien had noticed Gallivan was staring at Briana and Eleanor. He didn't hear what the two women had said. He went over to his brother and punched him in the arm. "Why did ye do that."

He then went and looked at his brother. "Will now my brother could feel that punch. Do ye think he could hear that she is hungry? Brother Briana told ye she was hungry. Clean out your ears. These two women know each other. Catherine had checked her out before they left. I hope when ye get married ye will hear Rosemary when she talks to him. If not, she will make you hear her."

Eleanor looked at Briana then she got a bowl of food. Then it hit Briana. "Eleanor did ye say that is a sign of twins."

She smiled at her. "Don't worry ye will do fine, Thomas's father was a twin, he had lost his brother when they were in a battle. That's what happens with Damien, it took a bit for it to hit him.

Eleanor brought over the bowl of food for her. "Briana set down this food is for ye. One question any pain any where's?"

Briana had a mouth full of food. "No… I'm just hungry."

Eleanor shook her head. "Ye can stop worrying about her losing her baby, so far it looks good. I talked with Catherine, and she thought ye were doing good."

She went over to the food and filled two bowls, one for father and another for Damien. "Here is a bowl for ye and one for Father,

Ye two go help Father out. Damien for her to lose her baby, something had to hit her in the stomach to make her bleed. It would have to be a hard hit to do so. Like what happened to Ronald's wife, I hope ye remember. Don't do this to your wife when ye get married."

Briana spoke. "Damien, I hope ye are happy. I had told ye that I wasn't going to lose Duncan's child. I just got a little seasick coming across Lock Ness. I never said I was afraid I was going to lose my baby. Ye were the one that had said it… not I. Now go help Father. Be careful with my things and what is inside the wagon, your twin brother is home. With the cross and rose on ye, have a talk with him.

Then Eleanor said. "Give us a while after she eats; I'll check out Briana."

Once she had enough food, Eleanor went to work checking out Briana and her baby. It's been hard for the brothers. "Briana ye and the baby checkout find. Ye could be in your second month, Ye are a strong woman have ye had any morning sickness?"

She looked at Eleanor, "No, I haven't, I don't like to get sick. That's about right Duncan and I have been married for over a year. We got married after my father died. He stayed with me three months afterward. Duncan knew my father was dying and he stayed with me until the end. Ye could say he was courting me at that time, which was five months in all. Donald had sent him to find a place for them to stay. It was mostly for Thomas and William; Duncan came back to me quite often."

Eleanor then checked Briana sides they were tight. "The pain ye had that scared Damien, it was from when ye tightened your muscles. While ye were getting sick that is why it hurt ye. Ye must have gotten there in time for the last run to the Highlands."

Eleanor brought over a cup of tea for her. "Aye… there was no time to get any food. All the food I got I ate on the way; Donald had got us there just in time. We caught the last ferry across to the Highlands.

Rodney had stopped us he wanted to look at the bottom of the wagon. I don't know if it was the roses or Ronald who zap his men. Ones we were going again then a black buggy all most ran us over."

Then Eleanor looked at her. "Did ye say a black buggy, would ye say it was an English stile buggy?"

Briana shrugged her shoulders, she just didn't know about that. Eleanor fixed herself a cup of tea, she was going to put something in hers. It's been hard knowing that her men were going to have to fight. She knew that it would be getting dark out soon, that was her family of men out there. "I know our men will be all right. Thomas didn't tell me that he saw Ronald, I just knew he did."

The two women was talking about the vest when Gallivan came into the cabin. "Eleanor what do ye mean that it will keep them safe, it's just dear hide."

She looked at him. Then spoke. "Thomas had given me this piece of hide that had the magic roses on them. Gallivan take your dirk and try to put a hole into it."

He had looked at her funny like. "Why should I do this, my dirk will go right through it."

Eleanor knew that it wasn't going to happen. "If ye think ye can, then do so."

Gallivan had taken his dirk and thrust it into the dear hide, try as he my it didn't make a dent. "What the hell is going on."

Damian and Father came through the door. "Brother see if ye can put a hole into this hide."

He had taken it and looked at the hide, all he did was shake his head. "Your dirk is dull; I know my dirk is very sharp."

Gallivan just watched his brother try to put a hole into that dear hide. Father was watching the young man. "I know my dirk is not dull, this is not just dear hide."

Then the women watch Father take out his dirk. Gallivan saw this beautiful handle on Father's dirk. "Wow…! Father that is a beautiful dirk."

Father smiled when he took his dirk out. "Aye… it was the time I fought in the war. This dirk saved my life, what ye like me to cut in two."

Ye could see it was very sharp, after he had tried to put a hole into it. He then spoke. "What is on this hide?"

Then Eleanor looked at him. "Father have ye heard the story of the magic roses."

Father was looking at the hide now. "Aye…, I've heard it told by Meghalaya when I went to have supper. I did that when Father Ben was cooking, he does not know how to cook. Are ye telling me that there are rose petals on this hide?

Eleanor took out a rose petal. She then placed it on the hide before their eyes it disappeared. "Aye… that is just what I'm telling ye. All six men have the rose petals on the vest."

Damian had said. "I know my dirk isn't dull, Ye said that there are magic rose petals on this. Then are fathers and brothers will be safe."

Eleanor took three cups out. Father would Ye like to have some tea and a little bet of Scotch in it. "Aye…, that I would."

The young men open the door to go out. Gallivan spoke. "There is a storm coming, we will be coming back in when it starts. Thank ye for the cup of tea and Scotch."

Eleanor asked. "Could ye try to put something over Briana's things."

Damian answered. "It's already covered up; we had help Father to do just that."

Briana watched Eleanor as she took sips of her tea. Then she spoke. "Ye, see we had found the valley of the Fairies. The king told us the story of a Fairy called Marcos. A demon raped his mother; she died giving birth to her son. The demon was Satan himself; Marcos lived in the valley during that time he had killed the King.

Thomas and I went to the valley to save the roses. When Catherine and I got back home from are trip. We found that something was killing the roses. We found out it was black magic, even in the land of the Fairies. Marcos wanted a son; the Fairies women didn't want anything to do with him. Out in the world he tried to start a war, so his father could have a great amount of souls."

*　*　*　*　*

The door open and the two men came in. Gallivan had placed the bowls on the sink. "That was tasty food Eleanor, Father helped us bed down the horses. We had taken off Briana's things and covered them up, as ye already knows. We had two tarps and put one on the wagon also. Father had asked me about the wagon; I told him to ask that question to Ye or Briana.

Briana spoke. "What would Ye like to know, Father?"

Father looked at Briana and asked. "Before we got on the ferry, there was whispering about the bodies of your brothers. I thought I heard one of them say our brothers are now safe. They are under the floor of the wagon. If this is to be true, I know why The Lord stopped those men from taking Briana's things off. What better way to get the bodies to the Highlands, Ye made sure that I didn't know. Then I wouldn't have to lie to those men, thank ye for doing that for me."

Briana spoke. "Father, forgive us that was the only way we could get the bodies home. Thomas knew those men would be waiting for us. Duncan had a dream; in this dream he saw is father died. Thomas believed Donald must bring their fathers to the battle. To show Rodney he was taking his daughter-in-law to the Highland. When Rodney man grabbed my crib as ye know I told him it was for my baby."

Father Sinclair nodded his head and spoke. "My children your brothers are not in the wagon. All that is there is just their bones. The Lord was with us; it was The Lord that didn't let those men touch anything on that wagon. Could ye not feel the power of The Lord."

Eleanor looked at Briana and shook her head no. "Father all I can say there was a great power there. I've heard that the three rose bushes, are with the bodies. Ye said that ye have heard of the roses, Father ye said that The Lord was with them. Then would ye say he had made the rose so my man would be able to get them. Would he also get my man the power to take down evil."

Eleanor thought how I could tell him about the roses. "Father, I know that The Lord was with ye all. Is it not true that The Lord made everything."

He nodded his head, yes. "I tell ye that there are magic rose petals on that hide."

To show him she took a petal and placed it on the hide. The three men saw it disappear. "Ye saw this before, is this not magic, didn't the Old Testament say that Angels came from the heavens and mated with a human woman. Few of the Angels, became fairies, they had lost their way and became small. The other fairies are not little; they are big like us. For a long time, they stayed in their valley, there were no more children to be born. Until a Wizard came to their valley, the Queen of the Fairies sung a song for anyone with magic that heard her song came to the valley."

Father Sinclair looked at Eleanor. "My child does this have to do with the story of the magic roses."

Briana shook her head yes. "Father this magic is not evil. Did ye not place crosses on all of us." Father had to nod yes for that part. "What ye don't know the holy water ye gave Thomas he had dip the crosses in them. There is a petal on each of the crosses. Ye, had even blessed them, answer me this if we were evil, it would burn us all. Father Sinclair taken his cross and place it on the hide."

They all watched him as he placed the cross on the hide. Then he tried to cut it in half again. When he had no luck in doing that. He took his dirk and tried to put a hole in it. Father Sinclair took out the holy water and put it on the hide. Then he tried again to put a hole or cut it."

Father Sinclair then looked at the women. "Briana did Thomas go after those magic roses."

Both women looked at Father. "Aye… that he did. I wouldn't believe it if I didn't see the roses come from the ground. When the moon came out the snow melted. The vest that all six men had on has these roses on it."

Eleanor took out the rose petals. "Father Sinclair ye have watched as they disappeared. Would ye, like to try a piece of ye robe? Here are four rose petals, try to see if they are evil. If it's evil it wouldn't go on your robe, ye can place holy water on first. Take your dirk and try to cut or stab it."

Then the women jump with the loud crash of thunder.

*　*　*　*　*

It was time to put their sweaters back on, Eleanor closed her eyes. She had remembered Thomas said with the roses on her she could see him fight.

It was dark out, with a speck of light. She saw men coming toward her. What she saw came from Thomas's eyes.

Thomas had looked at William then at Duncan. She could see men making their way to a campsite, the fire was down low. She heard Thomas say there taking the bait. He watched the men get to the dummies; each man had his dirk out. Quickly he saw the man grab one of the dummies head and cut its neck.

In her mind she cried out. *"Thomas be careful, I know ye can do this."*

Then she heard his voice. *"Thank ye my love, I will be with ye soon."*

When she opened her eyes, they were all looking at her. "The battle has started; they had set a trap for those evil men."

*　*　*　*　*

Father Sinclair quickly did the test, all he said. "What The Lord has made let know evil take it down."

Then he gave the young men crosses that had holy water and a rose petal on it. Father then gathered his group together. Then Eleanor told them, when ye close your eyes think of who ye like to see the battle with. If ye believe in the roses and your brothers, ye will see your father and brother fight those men. These roses have powers that no one knows about. Briana and Eleanor had their sweaters on with the rose petals.

Then Eleanor spoke. "Father, I understand ye was in the war, ye have the roses on ye. Ye already knows what a battle looks like. Maybe if ye asked The Lord not to let ye see the battle."

Father Sinclair spoke. "My child ye are right I know what a battle does to men. When the Lord saved my life, right then I gave myself to The Lord. If The Lord wants me to see the battle, so be it. I will pray for that man, who died by your family. These men souls if they asked forgiveness, for the sins they have committed. They only need to ask, and he will answer."

*   *   *   *   *

Eleanor nodded her head. "Briana if Father is right. I will pray for our men to come back to us alive; I know the power that The Lord and these roses have. I just don't want to use my healing powers; these men are my family."

Briana went over and put her arms around Eleanor. "I believe ye will do fine when the time comes. Is this your first time when there been fighting."

Eleanor wiped her eyes. "No…! I had to fix a man's arm; he had fallen against a big sword. The cut went down to the bone. The only thing that held the arm on, was a bit of skin and the bone itself."

Briana looked at her. "Did ye have to stop and think about what to do first."

Eleanor looked at her knew friend. "No…! There was no time to think, I had to act before he died."

Briana smiled at Eleanor. "Just what I thought when the time comes, Ye won't think about anything but what ye must do. Ye will only act first no matter who it is. Only after it is all over will ye break down and cry. Thomas told me ye are a strong woman. When the time is at hand, I know ye will do what ye must do."

*   *   *   *   *

Eleanor pulled out her locket, the women join hands with the men. The five of them knelt together, they heard a loud sound there was thunder overhead. Father Sinclair spoke. "Let us pray for the men that will fight evil tonight."

Eleanor closed her eyes. She thought of Thomas then she saw who he was fighting with. When the lightning lit up the sky. She felt as if she was fighting in the battle. Each time the lightning hit the sky she could see a little more. She thought of her father and wondered how far away they were. Up a head were the men waiting to join the fight. Her father had looked at his friends. Once again, they will fight evil. This time they will fight with their sons against evil. One of their Fathers had yelled. She knew who that voice was. It was Uncle Donald who cried out. *"Rodney ye are mine. Prepare yourself to meet your maker."*

They were riding hard toward the men who were waiting to join the fight. In the darkness men fought as the sky fought with darkness. Lightning lit up the sky and the grounds below. When the thunder clash darkness took back everything. It was hard to hear with the thunder clashing as their broadswords met their opponents. When the lightning hit. She saw Thomas jump up to block the dirk that was heading for Duncan's neck. She saw it hit his chest and bounced off, going into his arm. Before that happened, Eleanor had seen the black cloud change into a man's hand. It was pulling on the half sleeve and neck piece of Duncan. Then she heard laughter and a voice. *"I will hurt him some way."* She saw Thomas pulling the dirk from his arm. He through it back at the man's chest killing him out right. Duncan looked back at Thomas only to see him throwing a dirk at a man.

Briana had heard someone suck in the air. When she opened her eyes, she saw Eleanor biting her lip. There were tears running down her cheeks. All they could hear was the rain coming down. Then it was nothing but quietness. There was no thunder or steel clashing. They didn't know how long they stayed on their knees praying. Eleanor didn't know if her father or brother could hear her. "William check Thomas left arm. William can ye hear me. Dad can ye hear me."

When she heard Father say in Jesus's name we pray. Amen."

She heard Father saying those words. She was saying them also. "Please let my family hear me. In Jesus's name we pray. Amen."

*   *   *   *   *

Twelve men fought for their lives. Six men fought for goodness while the other six were evil. The wind raged recklessly through the battle-field. Fine needles of ice pricked at their faces and hands. Ye could hear the clash of steel against the thunder. The darkness fought with the lightning. Ye could see spider webs of light across the sky. On earth evil fought with goodness in the sky and on the ground. Each time a lightning bolt lit up the sky. Evil died a little more in the sky and on earth.

*　*　*　*　*

Rodney had thought his men would have and easy time to kill these young men. Tonight, would be easy money. What a fool he was to think these young men would go to sleep. These men knew they were coming after them. Rodney thought being young they didn't have knowledge of what would happen to them if they went to sleep. *"Aye, this will be an easy kill. Our boss will be pleased with us. We have the bodies of the older brothers. They will never make it back to the Highlands. We also have their youngest boys here. Their fathers were fools to let their only sons go after their oldest boys' bodies. This will kill their name.* He thought.

Rodney then sent three of his men to slit the throats of Thomas, William, and Duncan as they slept. He smiled as he sat on his horse watching his men sneak into the camp. Thomas had tricked Rodney. They believed that there were men sleeping in this camp. What they thought was a man's neck. They found dummies made with sticks and cloth in their place. The three men were upon them before they knew what happened.

In the darkness they couldn't tell a man from a dummy. Rodney was the dummy to think these young men were that dumb. Then he heard his man call out. "It's a trap…" Quickly they dismounted from their horses, as they went to help his men.

He could feel a strong power; it wasn't like his boss's powers. This power was of good…, then he heard a voice. *"Ye fool, there is a young MacGregor here tonight. He is stronger and smarter then ye. There are no bodies here there in the Highlands. Ye will be fighting the young's men fathers. They have strong magic with them. Ye better pray for your soul Rodney. For tonight I Ronald MacGregor will take ye to be judge by The Lord."*

When Rodney heard his name ring out. He knew his time here on earth was up. That voice was from Donald MacKinnon. Two other men charged Rodney's men. While Donald engaged Rodney in a sword fight. In the dark he tried to stab Donald in the heart; his dirk just bounced off Donald's chest. The dirk functioned as if it were rubber, it couldn't penetrate the shield that he wore.

Rodney cried out. "Die old man…, why don't ye die."

His other men were having the same trouble with the men they were fighting.

Donald replied. "Because ye are evil and tonight goodness will endure. We wear the shield of righteousness. Prepare yourself to meet your maker."

There was strong resistance that evil couldn't overcome. Rodney had thought it would be an easy job. What happened to his victory… Donald's dirk went through Rodney's heart as the lightning lit up the sky. "Ye had killed my son…, here I have killed ye. Tonight, ye will die and meet The Lord."

With the last man dead. The rain had stopped; the moonlight pushed back the darkness. The fighting was over all six of Rodney's men were dead.

Daniel went over to his two friends. "Donald was this the man who like to stab men in the back."

He looked at his friends and nodded his head. "Aye…, evil likes to fight in the darkness. Daniel, these are the once that ye saw in the fire who killed our sons. There is one that is missing, they call him the man in black. We have taken down his hired killers."

*　*　*　*　*

When the fighting was over, Thomas had felt Eleanor was upset. What could she be that worried about? When he closed his eyes, he saw his love ringing her hands. Thomas moved away from the fight area. He sat down on a big log, all at once he felt weak. When he closed his eyes, he saw her walking back and forth. Everyone was in the room; Briana had her eyes closed. Did he see a tear running down her cheek?

He wondered if she could be talking to Duncan. *"Eleanor my love I'm all right. What are you upset about? Those men that killed our brothers are dead. Ronald has taken their souls to The Lord to be judge. We will be leaving here very soon, honey why do I feel your worried about something."*

Eleanor let out the breath she held and sat down. *"Thomas it's good to hear your voice, tell me is your left arm hurting Ye? Honey when ye took that dirk in your left arm there was a black cloud over ye. I heard him curse ye for doing what ye did. When ye pulled it from your arm there was black goo on it."*

That question surprised him, then he felt that someone was watching him. He had opened his eyes; his best friend was sitting next to him. "All right Thomas what's up with ye, I haven't been able to talk with my sister. I can feel my sister is worried about ye, that emotion is coming in loud and clear. I don't know why I can't hear her. Everyone else can, someone will have to tell me what she says.

Then Duncan opened his eyes. "I can help ye with this William, Thomas ye wife seen what ye had done for me. Eleanor said the demon took your sleeve from your arm. She heard him say. He cursed ye for doing what ye did. When ye took the dirk from your arm, it had black goo on the dirk. Ye must have felt that evil was trying to take are shiels off us. Ye saved my life when ye jumped in front of the dirk. For he took off my neck piece, Briana told me that the dirk went into your left arm. She saw a black cloud over us. Then there was a hand, she saw the hand removing are shiels from us."

William got up and helped his friend out of his coat. They saw the deep gash in his arm; Eleanor saw it and spoke. *"Tell my brother to have dad bring over what I packed up for him."*

Thomas had told him what his sister said. She could hear her brother's voice. "Dad get the things Eleanor gave ye, bring everything here Thomas is hurt."

Duncan went over and looked at the gash on his arm. "Eleanor had told Briana that the dirk was going for my neck, that evil man had pulled my neck piece off. Not only would I be impaired, and not able to move. If the poison were on the dirk I would have and agonizing death. One way or other he wanted to hurt ye, for what ye did to him.

Thomas then spoke in a whisper. "Duncan stops; my father is coming. Don't say anything about that please."

William looked at Thomas. "That vision ye had when Eleanor was riding hard to get to ye. Ye told me that ye felt pain in his heart, that it scared ye. That's why ye went for the roses."

Thomas looked at William. "I saw the vision again; this time it was my arm. The dirk did go for my heart; it bounced off the vest into my arm."

William told Duncan to get the holy water from his bag. "I have two bottles of Scotch bring them also."

Thomas saw his father running over to him. "Dad don't run I'm fine; the bear did worse than the dirk did." Thomas tried to cover up how he was feeling.

When his father got to him, he looked at his son's arm. "Aye…, ye are right. We will get this clean up and let Eleanor sew it up for ye."

In Thomas's mind he heard. "Tell William to look at your gash, Ye are going to have nineteen stitches when ye get here. Honey can ye come here to me."

Thomas was worried about that, he had heard more then what Eleanor heard from Marcos. The voice that he heard was saying a spell. Then he tried waving his hand, nothing happened. "Honey I can't, Marcos said some kind of spell."

Eleanor was ringing her hands. "Tell my brother to put more cloth on it for when he wrapped it up. Now tell me what he had said."

Thomas looked at William, he smiled at him when he said. "William your sister said to put more cloth there before ye rap it, it could bleed a lot."

William laughed at that, he knew how bad it was. "She is not here but still is bossing us men around. I know she's worried, thank sis I will do just that."

Right before he wrapped it up, he noticed it was getting red. There was some black stuff coming from the gash, it was the black goo. "Thomas ask my sister could I rinse the wound with Scotch?"

He had told her that the gash was turning red just a bit. When Eleanor heard that she bit her lip. "Honey asked William if he would look at the gash."

Thomas told William she wanted ye to look closely at the redness. She wants to see what he saw before he wrapped it up. "My love, do ye have any more holy water with ye and two crosses."

Thomas looked at his friend, then asked him. Before he could speak, he took out two crosses from his pocket. "Ask her how we can make more holy water."

Eleanor looked at Father. "Father could ye bless the water after William pours it over Thomas arm. We have a black spell. He needs your help please Father help my husband."

Father then smiled. "Aye…, my child just tells me when he will need more."

He went quickly to see if there was any in his bag. "There is, thank heavens." He knew what his sister wanted him to do.

He handed Thomas the Scotch. "Drink up now, this is going to hurt ye a lot."

Thomas had two drinks then told his wife that they had some. William's going to pour it on now. He nodded his head, then there were some choice words coming out of his mouth. Thomas' eyes flew open, and he took another drink. Eleanor heard him and knew what kind of spell Marcus had place on the dirk.

When he had taken another drink. He had seen everyone was around him. "What the hell is going on son."

The evil spell

Then he looked at the cut. "Dad, Marcos is giving me a taste of what I had done to him."

Then he heard Eleanor, I have the spell. Grana gave me this book; I must be there for it to work. There are things I must do while I'm saying this spell. Tell William to put the holy water on each time he changes the bandage. Do ye have two small crosses. If ye do put it on top of the gash with a rose petal on it. The other one under his arm directly under the gash. Then ye can wrap it up. Tell William to be careful of the black goo. Take a stick and wipe it off his coat, don't touch it. Then burn it in the fire." Thomas told William what she had said.

He took another drink; all the men were looking at him. Duncan spoke. "I felt that neck piece come off. Did Marcos take the sleeve off at the same time."

Thomas didn't want to show them how he was feeling. "Get these things burned, after that is done, we must ride."

His father looked at him. "Aye, that we are my boy. He had put a spell on ye. Can ye ride, or should we make something to carry ye in."

Thomas shook his head no. "I will ride as far as I can. Can we get going now?"

Then William spoke. "Did any of ye touch any black goo."

The men looked at their hands, they all shook their heads. While the men took care of the dead, once that was done. They had helped Thomas with his horse. All the men knew without Thomas they would be dead. They all knew they owe him their lives. For if he didn't go after those roses, they would be badly hurt or dead."

William stayed close to his friend. Thomas told him to take one of his old shirts to make rags if he need to. His father rode on the other side of his boy. Duncan took the wagon seat; William had his hands full with Thomas. What Marcos did to him, it had taken his powers away. They move quickly down the road. Five miles seem a lot longer than it did to get to the boys. Finely they arrived at the ferryboat crossing. Six tired men led their horses and the wagon onto the ferry. Two years ago, Thomas William and Duncan set out to find their brothers in the Lowlands. After a long hunt we were now heading back home. Soon the bodies of their brothers will be at their last resting place.

On the Ferry

Thomas was trying to get off his horse. He was thankful that he had back up from William. "Thank ye old friend." Quickly they found him a place to rest. With the wagon on the ferry and the horses. All the men went over to where Thomas was. They were all there when William cleaned his arm again. This time he had something to bite down on.

After it was done, he looked at them with their sad faces. "Will ye stop looking at me like I'm dying. What I did I would have done for my brothers and for my three fathers. Ye…, must understand I have three brothers; I also have three fathers. Duncan ye are now my brother, William ye have been my best friend. Ye are my brother and my brother-in-law. I have lost a brother and now I have four brothers. I can't wait to see Michael. Dad, your friends have been there all the time. I was just one of ye sons. We six are family now and we are brothers in arms. I find that when ye must kill it takes a bit from ye." Thomas had taken the words that his father had said to him. He could see his father was very proud of him.

* * * * *

He was watching the sunrise; William had gotten done with his arm. Now he looked at the sky, he was thinking about what Eleanor had written to him. It was about this man at the party she went too. Then he remembered the vision of the woman that she saved. It was the man in black he needs a son. Thomas thought what he had done to this man. "Uncle how was the trip down here; I know that Rodney gave ye some trouble. Did anything else happen."

Donald thought for a minute then spoke. "Come to think about it, this black buggy almost ran us over. I had asked Father if he knew that seal on the black buggy. He had said it belongs to the Duke Marcos Huascaran. I then told them the man at Eleanor's coming out party was Albert's Huascaran.

A feeling came over him, his brother was heading home. Thomas looked at his father. "Dad, I have a feeling Michael is on his way home. We have two homes to build and one to finish. It's funny the home Michael was building for Ronald. He was really building it for himself. That is why Ronald had taken Michael's spot; I would have to say aye."

Thomas laid his head back. "Son how do ye know Michael is coming home."

He thought for a bit. "Dad, I think Father had sent word to Michael. When I gave Ronald his vest, I had sent Michael and his son vest. I had put three rose petals on Michael's wife's hair in his sporran. I told him we have the bodies come home. We took care of six of the men that came after Ronald. There is six men still missing. I believe that Michael may have taken care of them. Unless Michael can't find these men. I know where that black buggy was heading. Just outside the Lowlands, it's not over yet dad."

His father looked at his son. "Thomas do ye think Michael will come home to find out what ye know."

He then nodded yes. "Aye…, that is just what I think. Dad must be getting dangers for his family. Michael is a family man. My brother was close to our brother; he would like to say goodbye to Ronald.

Thomas smiled at his father. "Son does that mean your mother and I will have grandchildren in the castle."

He felt the love his father had for his son's. "I believe so Dad, at last the journey is all most over. There is so much to do to get those homes ready for us."

William had come over to Thomas and his father. He spoke, "How are ye doing old friend. Could I look at it, we will be getting off the ferry soon."

Thomas had nodded yes. The redness was trying to move around the crosses. William couldn't clear out what Marcus had place there. He had given him something to bite down on. Then he had a thought to place the magic rose petals on the cloth where the gash was. They had four miles to go to get to the hunting cabin, after they got off the ferry.

Thomas's father watched him place the petals over the gash. "I know what ye are doing, Ye are fighting magic against magic. I will be glad when we get there, I hope Eleanor can get it out of his system. Do ye think that Father would help her."

William then sat down next to Thomas. "Aye…, he is a holy man, he gave me more holy water. Father believes in the roses; Eleanor showed him what the magic roses have done for us. Dad, I want to thank ye for telling me that story about momma and ye. I've been remembering back if I didn't make the move, I know she would have. Dad, is it wrong to want her? To be able to hold my wife and kiss those lips of hers, I just want to go home. It's been hard on all of us."

William looked at the two of them. "Thomas, I know how ye feel. I too…, want to go home. To hold my wife and start living my life with her. Thank ye for going after those roses."

Thomas looked at his father. "Thank heavens for that vest."

His father had felt the same way. "Son those feelings go through all of us. You're lucky to have your woman there waiting for ye."

He knew his father missed his wife. "Dad, go and try to talk to mamma. Tell her where all doing well. If ye can help it don't tell her about my arm yet."

His father looked at his son and nodded. "Son ye know that your mother already knows. I will not lie to her if she asks me. With this vest, she will hear me, get some rest son."

Thomas watched his father go back to where his friends were. His father was right, he does feel weak; rest is just what he needs.

He couldn't stop thinking about this man in black. Thomas thought once he is dead, he will come for us. If Albert does have that locket going into his chest. We must stop him. That vision told me he will go after Tom to get to Ellen in the future.

If he did make a deal with the devil. Did his wife say his mother mated with a demon? His father had his soul, what if he didn't get his part done. I believe he will be coming back to earth in the future. What Meghalaya told me. He could go after the next McGregor in the new world. If this is true, I need to put everything to the last thought in this journal. I think after this is over with, I think William and Michial

Thomas then called Eleanor. "Honey I'm going to get some sleep for now."

Eleanor heard him and called back. "How do ye feel my love."

He closed his eyes to look at his wife. "William put the rose petals on the cloth, to go around my arm. Marcos is working had to get the redness to go around my arm. The rose petals are fighting even harder to stop him. I need to sleep now, love ye."

On their way home.

AT LAST, THE ferry was landing in the Highlands. The tall ramp lowered, six men led their horses and the wagon off the ferryboat.

William helped Thomas with his horse. Theseus spoke. "Duncan will ye take William's horse with ye. Son, ride Little Foot to the cabin. I think it would be a good idea for ye to head home. With Duncan's two brothers, they can get everything ready for us when we get there."

Daniel looked at William. "When ye are home tell the women, we need food and drink. Have the family met us by the riverside in four days? I know ye will help your sister with Thomas. Ye won't leave their side, until ye knows he will be all right. At least get some rest before leaving."

Donald spoke. "Duncan makes sure Briana's things are off the wagon."

Then Duncan spoke. "Father and my brothers took everything off the wagon already. Father knows about the bodies. He asked Briana and she told him, he heard ye talking."

Then Daniel spoke. "Son, do ye think ye should ride. We can make ye something to lay down on."

Thomas looked at his father. "Dad I would like to ride, I will be all right."

Ones Thomas was on his horse. William rode up to Thomas' left side, Duncan was on his right side.

William spoke. We have his back." The three men took off at a good pace.

*   *   *   *   *

Thomas made it to three and a half miles; he called his wife. "*Honey I'm not doing that good. I'm dizzy, and I can't see straight. I believe I'm going to pass out. The pain is beyond my ability to stand. Where about half a mile out? I'm going to tell Midnight to get me to the hunting cabin. Go to Eleanor. I love ye honey. I'm still fighting this; don't think I'm giving him this win.*"

William and Duncan heard what Thomas told Midnight. They saw him tuck his hands under the saddle. Then he leans forward. "Go as fast as ye can Midnight, take me to the hunting cabin, to Eleanor."

William yelled. "I got Thomas, let my horse go stay close to him. Then William whistled for his horse to follow them. Midnight felt his master go limp; he took off at a full gallop. He was going as fast as he could, the men stayed as close as they dare.

*   *   *   *   *

Eleanor ran to ask Father to bless a pale of water. "Father, he's coming in fast the poison has worked its way to other parts of his arm. Could ye help me with this black magic? William saw the start of an infection. I saw a black cloud over Duncan and Thomas as they fought. He had taken the shields off Duncan's neck and Thomas's arm. Thomas jumped to take the dirk; it bounces off his vest into his arm."

Father looked at her. "My child the roses showed me what had happen. We will fight evil tonight."

Eleanor told Father about Thomas's vision, that a dirk was going to the back of Duncan's neck. He had jumped to take it with his own body. We women place a shield to stop what was going to

55

happen. That black cloud turned into a hand and ripped their shields off both men. My brother has two crosses on his arm. To try to stop it from going up or down his arm. He also put rose petals on the rag to fight evil with goodness. Father, I need ye to bless everything that I'm going to work with. I have a spell to dilute the spell that was put on him. I need ye to cast it out of him, as ye pour the holy water on the gash. Please help me Father we are all he has. The black magic Marcos had cast, was spoken in latten. I can't speak latten, could ye speak those words?"

Father looked at her. He had seen what the roses could do. He knew that they were not evil, so be it he thought. He made the sign of the cross. The prayer he had said, didn't come back to him in a bad way. Even though he didn't want to see the battle. The Lord showed him what Eleanor was talking about.

Eleanor thought of William. Through his eyes she saw that Thomas's head was on Midnight's neck. They were riding hard down the road; tears ran down her cheeks. She called for Gallivan and Damian. "Ye must take care of the horses there coming in hot. Thomas is hurt."

Then she opened the door and told Briana that her husband was here. Then she thought of Thomas, she could feel he was very weak. She must stop that bleeding before she loses him. First, she had to get evil out of his body. When Thomas called her, she had placed rose petals on both hands. She was hoping it would help her to feel what was going on with her husband.

*　*　*　*　*

At last, they were at the hunting cabin. Eleanor whistle for Midnight to come to her. Then he slows down and went right up to her. "Thank ye, ye are the best Midnight, ye brought him home to me." William and Duncan had jumped off their horses, they went to his left side. Eleanor went to his right; he was still alive. She nodded to her brother and the two men gently brought him down. Duncan grabbed his legs, as she went to open the door. "Put him on the table."

Eleanor moved quickly to cut the sleeve off the coat and shirt. She had put the sleeve of his shirt on the fire. Father took the coat sleeve with black goo on it. The boys took his coat and shirt off; he had lost a lot of blood. She looked at the spot where the dirk went into his arm, she saw the black goo.

Father Sinclair had put the coat sleeve in a pale; he had told everyone to leave it where it was. "Father here is what I saw."

He came over to look at the black goo, he turned to Duncan. "After the horses were bed down, have your brother's dig me a deep hole. I need another pale to catch the bad water. Eleanor, don't touch the black goo, anyone helping her don't touch it. This man called Marcos, he is hoping ye are not that smart. The magic he used on Thomas, was to kill as many persons as possible that he could.

"William have ye touch that black goo before. "No Father, I always try to use something to help me. To take the bandage off his arm I knew it was evil. On the ferry I used the last bit I had; Marcos was pushing hard to make it go pass the cross. I use the rose petals on the bandage, to keep the goo contain in one place."

Father looked at the young man, he nodded his head. "Aye…, this family knows what evil looks like. When the bandage is off, throw the rags in the fire. Briana ones that's done, I want ye to pour holy water over his hands.

*   *   *   *   *

Eleanor found out that Father had cleaned the table with holy water. They sat him down to take off his coat. She had everything she needed near her. William had burned what was left in the fireplace; they had laid him down on the long table.

Without Father knowing she had put rose petals on her hands. Eleanor went over to Thomas's right side. She had checked his eyes and placed her hands, on the side of his head. Eleanor called him in her mind. *"Honey, hear me. Tell me what Marcus's doing to ye."*

Eleanor closed her eyes; her thoughts had to go deep into his mind. Then she heard a weak voice. *"Honey I'm here, he's trying to kill me. He's in my mind, the weaker I get it's hard to fight him."*

Eleanor heard Marcus in his mind. "Father evil is in his mind, could ye place holy water in the sign of the cross. I'm going to place two rose petals over the cross."

Father came over to him, he had blessed his forehead, ears, lips, and heart all with holy water. He had noticed a strong power on his forehead. Father knew it wasn't evil; she must have heard the evil inside his mind. She checks again and heard nothing.

Eleanor took some of the holy water and did something to help him fight the blackness. Her brother held his head as she told Thomas. *"Honey drink what I'm giving ye."*

Thomas was getting very weak. When she checked his heart, it was getting stronger with what she had given him. Eleanor spoke the words of the spell in Gaelic and Father spoke in latten. It was casting out the blackness from the demon spell. As he spoke the words, he poured the holy water. They saw the black goo come out with the water and blood. Father had kept pouring the holy water until it was just water and light blood.

The two crosses were removed, and one of them went into the water of darkness. I will take care of this evil spell, do ye need any more help."

Eleanor looked up. "Thank ye Father ye were right, The Lord needed ye here with us."

After the door closed, she went and laid a kiss on Thomas's lips. She had felt just a bit of his lips move. Then she cleaned the spot, with holy water then dry it. She went to work sewing the gash up. She had poured holy water over her stitches to clean them. Then she placed ointment afterward.

Evil was killed

Father picked up the two pales, at the hole that was dug for him. He had placed a cross in the hole to kill the black goo. He ran the holy water over the coat sleeve. He held both ends and put it into the holy water. He took a stick and put it inside the sleeve to hang it up to dry.

Where the goo was, he looked for it again. Then he placed a cross inside the cut and left it to dry outside.

*   *   *   *   *

Eleanor had finished with the nineteen stitches; she then wrapped it up. Once again, she tried to get Thomas to drink some more of what she made for him. In her mind she told him to drink. *"Honey ye got to drink this. Please listen to me, just drink ye have lost to much blood."*

Then she started to cry, a tear rolled down her cheek. It had dropped onto his face, then he spoke. *"Honey don't cry; I will try to drink the rest of it I love ye so much."*

Thomas had drunk all of it, then William picked up his friend. He had laid him on the bear skin. "I know sis your man has a strong willpower. He let ye know what was happening with him. Thomas had no time to say anything to me, but I did hear him tell Midnight to go quickly to the hunting cabin. To go to ye."

Then in her mind she heard. *"Honey I'm still here with ye please don't cry; I love ye. Let me get some sleep, what ye gave me is working."*

Eleanor looked over at Thomas, she went down to her knees and kissed him. *"I'll try not to cry, now sleep my love.*

She got to her feet. "Let me get ye some food, and we can talk outside. He always knows when I cry."

*   *   *   *   *

William took his food and the two of them went outside. "Sis ye left a tear on his face, it brought him back so he could drink more of what ye made him. He tried so hard not to pass out. Thomas has been my best friend for a long time. I've seen him do things that amaze me. He has strong willpower; I know one thing he loves ye with all his heart. Sis I'm glad ye gave me a lot, I'm hungry."

Eleanor had watched her brother down the food. She saw Duncan coming up the little hill. "Tell Duncan I will be bringing out the food for him and Briana."

Inside she got two bowls out and put some food it them. She heard him say. *"Honey can ye come and lay down with me."*

He had moved over so she could lay with him. *"Aye..., let me talk to my brother and gave this food to Duncan."*

Before she could bring the food out, her brother came in for more. He had taken the bowls out to Duncan. When his bowl was full, she brought it out to him. Duncan was heading down the hill.

William looked at his sister. "Ye should go lay down with him. That will be enough to help with the heeling, is there any more food."

Eleanor looked at her brother. "Aye..., are ye still hungry."

William smiled at his sister. "No..., dad and they must be resting. They will be hungry when they get here. Ye, know that Thomas didn't let them know how bad it was. Sis this is good, and now I need some sleep."

Eleanor had watched her brother go down the hill. She went back inside to clean the bowl for the next hungry person. Then she went over to Thomas, she had laid a kiss on his forehead. He was cool to the touch. She ran her hand through his hair, how she missed him. Now she had to check his bandage, she knew he was a fast heeler. For the bandage was dry, there was no blood going through. Then she heard his voice. *"Lay down with me, my love. If I could make love to ye. I would, now come here and lay down with me."*

Eleanor had felt the pull to be held by her man. Her body was running out of energy, all that was left was her willpower. She gave in to him and lay down. When she laid her head down on his shoulder. His arm pulled her into him; she heard him take a lazy breath and let it out. The two of them went right to sleep.

*   *   *   *   *   *

William made his way down to the wagon. As he walked closer, he saw Ronald. *"How is Thomas."*

He heard him in his mind. In his thoughts he answered him. *"He's much better, it took Eleanor and Father to pull him out of it. That goo was bad stuff; those rose petals are very powerful."*

He saw Ronald nod his head. *"Get some sleep and thank ye for taking care of my brother. What ye had done for him right off. It had saved his life that was a strong spell. The spell was made to kill him. But it would have been a painful death. What Thomas had done to Marcos, was a god sent. The name Marcus was his fairy's name. It had stop him from raping women. The last woman he had taken. He had gotten mad and through her out of the buggy.*

She had found Rodney's horse; the body fell off. The horse came up to her, she is now heading home. Also, before ye leave, tell your sister that Michael is on his way home. He's bringing his wife and children. Ye are now an uncle, don't tell Catherine. Let her find out herself."

* * * * *

When Damien rode over to William, he had said hi Ronald and Peter. "William, I was talking with my brother Duncan. He asked me to go ahead of Ye and Gallivan, he knows how tired ye are. He said that ye should rest for an hour. I will set up camp around sundown. Before it gets too dark out ye should have caught up with me. I will have some food ready for the two of ye. What do ye say?" Then he stopped and turned back to see Peter. He looked at William and spoke. Tell me ye see my twin there on the wagon with Ronald.

William smiled and then couldn't stop yawning. "Ye brother knows me quite well. Tell me, if he is lying down with his wife, that is what I would like to do. I'm going to get some sleep, then head home to my wife. *Peter, thank ye for all that ye did for all of us. Ronald, I know I will see Ye again. I will do what ye ask of me."*

William headed down to where his bed was going to be. "Damien talks to them, ye have the rose petals on ye. Speak to him in your mine, he liked to say goodbye to ye. I'll see ye later."

* * * * *

Gallivan was coming to get William. "There ye are, I'm glad I came up here to get ye. You're walking as if ye were drunk."

William smiled it had been a long and dangerous day. "Just show me to my bed. Afterward go and make sure Damien has left. He had gotten talking to someone. Do ye still have your cross on?"

Gallivan helped him to lay down. "Aye…," He was going to ask him something, but he was already a sleep. Then he made his way up the hill, he saw Damien was on top. On the back of his horse was Peter. He had to rub his eyes. When he heard a voice, *"Gallivan you're not seeing thing, those two need to talk. Damien needed a companion that knows him, he had to ask him about something that only his twin would know."*

*   *   *   *   *

William got up slowly. "Gallivan, I like to thank ye for making me a bed. Your brother was right. I believe I would have fallen off my horse before I could have gotten down the road. Have ye seen Eleanor outside."

He was getting their things ready to go. "It's going to get dark out soon."

While ye are doing that, I'm going to check on my sister and Thomas. When he opened the door, he saw his sister getting up. "I know it ye were going to be drawn to lay down with him."

Eleanor went over to her brother to give him a kiss. "He's doing well, there was no more bleeding, and he don't have a fever. I must make some more of that drink. It had done a good job of heeling him. Then she went into his arms again, I'm so glad that ye saw that redness. If ye, didn't I would have lost my man."

William held her in his arms. "Sis, we do what we can. I have his back, and he has mine. We are more than just good friends. He had said it best; we are brothers-in-law and now brothers in arms."

Then the two of them heard Thomas. "Hay old friend can ye help me to the table. I could eat a hold deer, will at least a lot."

William got him to sit up, then he got behind him and lift him to his feet. He went under his right arm and got him to the table.

When Eleanor turned, she had a bowl of food. There was that drink she had made with the holy water. She had a big smile on her face. "Ye are a very strong man."

Thomas looked at her, he had this little boy look on his face. "Are ye going to feed me or hold it and look pretty." He looked at her, then he put his hand out for the drink. She watched him drink it down. "Can I have some food now."

She went quickly and gave him his bowl of food. "How do ye feel right now."

Thomas looked at her and spoke. "Right now, I'm hungry talk to me after I eat, more please."

William smiled at the two of them. "I'll see ye when ye get home."

Thomas had finished his food. "Honey, could ye come here to me, I like to see him off."

Once he was at the door he thought of where Damien had camped. Then he waved his hand, and the two of them were riding into camp.

Both men looked at each other. William spoke. "I see he has his magic back."

Gallivan just looked at William. "Are ye telling me that Thomas has magic?"

William laughed, he saw Peter was smiling. "Tell ye what I'm going back to sleep while ye three talk."

*　*　*　*　*

Eleanor watched her man eat his food. He ate as quickly as William had. Now she was looking over his chest, his neck was bigger than before. Her eyes moved over his arms they were so much bigger. His chest had more hair for her to play with. When she looked up, her man was looking at her.

Eleanor had seen all his body before. "Honey, can I have some more please." She was so pleased that he was hungry. She had brought over his food; he did what her brother did. Eating the food and going back to bed, she went over to him. It was time to change his bandage. She found that Thomas was sound to sleep.

When he was eating, he acted not to know her. Right now, she must change his bandage. With everything in hand, she brought it over to him. Eleanor went down to the floor setting cross legged. With his arm in her lap, she took off the bandage. As she cleaned his wound, she was checking for any redness. Why was her mine drifting, she had to make herself finish what she was doing first. She had to put more of the ointment on then bandage it back up.

When that was done, she took his hand and kissed the inside. They haven't even had a real kiss yet. As she sat there, she remembered the battle. Tears ran down her cheeks. She told herself he's going to be just find, all right stop it. With her eyes close Eleanor found she had his hand on her breast. His hand was warm and felt wonderful to her. She had placed his hand on her cheek. Then she felt his hand move to the back of her neck. Eleanor opened her eyes and looked into her man's eyes. "Come here." She let him guide her to his lips. His kiss was just what she needed. He made love to her mouth. She took all that he could give her.

Then she heard. *"Honey let me heal and get stronger. Ye saw what happen to me didn't ye."*

She felt like a little girl that got caught. "Aye…, the four of us did, I'm sorry I don't know what came over me. I love ye so much, forgive me ye need your rest."

Thomas opened his eyes. "That maybe so but ye did need more of my kisses."

He had pulled her to him giving her a little more of himself. "Will that hold ye tell I can get stronger."

Eleanor found she was touching him. "It scared me so much, honey that spell was to kill ye. William talked to Ronald he said, ye had stopped Marcos from raping the women. The last woman he through her out of the buggy. She found Rodney's horse; he had fallen off. She didn't see anyone, so she took the horse and went home. I know that ye don't like me to cry, I'll go outside."

He was so tired, but he knew she needed him. "I guess I wouldn't melt with your tears, come here and let me hold ye."

Everything that was held inside her came out. He knew there wasn't much he could do right now. He let her cry and held her in his arm, her tears were warm to him, he knew she loved him. With her fingertips on his chest, he could feel a strong power healing him. His mind was clear, the power ran through his body, it was giving him strength. Still his body made him shut down. Thomas had no more control over his body, she saw it demanded sleep.

Eleanor had fallen asleep with him; he had told her that he loved her. When she woke up her hands were hot. She had sat up and ran her hands over her face, head, and neck. Then she placed her hand over the bandage, she felt her hands get hotter. From his shoulders she ran it down his arm to his fingers. What was still left ran out of his fingertips. It was time to make some more food. This time she will make some muffins. Eleanor felt so much better; she was humming as she worked. Soon their fathers should be here, she took some more meat to cook up. She had given Damian some stakes to cook for them. As she cooked, she was thinking of everything that happened to her and Thomas.

She hadn't told anyone about the dream of Albert Huascaran. It was his eyes that kept coming back, the face didn't match the eyes. At the party he knew she had an idea what he was. What was he trying to do, his eyes were older she knew in her heart he was a demon. I've had this dream a few times so far. Even the voice didn't match the man. He was trying to scare me. Then again, the dream was in two parts. One part he needed help calling for the demon hunter. I didn't know what that was all about.

While the meat was cooking, she checked on Thomas. His arm was dry no more bleeding. Eleanor went and sat next to him. Softly she brushed his hair with her hand. She had closed her eyes and thought of all the things she would tell him later. How would she tell him how she felt?

She thought about starting it. "Honey I'm so glad that we married, it's been hard at times with my mother. Ye wouldn't believe how many times my mother lost her voice. At nighttime, my body demands your touch. It helped when ye came home for a bit. Do ye know I couldn't find anyone to even hold a candle to ye. The men I did know I found them a wife.

"As I set here, I know ye has been the one for me. It's funny to think of this. Without thinking ye were shaping me to be the woman ye will need and want. When you're stronger and were by are self. I want to just touch ye, no that's wrong. I really want ye to touch me, how about we touch each other.

"Your mother seems to know when something is bothering me. I had to tell her that my mom still pushing men on me. She talked to my mother. It helped at lease my feeling to have sex with ye has slow down. Each time I had to compare ye to the other men. Made me think of ye hard, of the times ye made love to me. Then I wished for ye to be with me. So ye could quiet down my hunger to make love to ye. That demon who was inside her, had done some damage to her mind. When ye are home, we will have to enforce that I'm your wife."

She didn't remember at the time he could hear her thoughts. There have been times thinking about ye, my body got worked up over ye. I did what ye told me so I could go to sleep. It only happened when I was sleeping in your bed, which was every night. There were times I could picture everything that ye did to me on your land. Honey, I got it bad for ye. I don't know if ye felt my eyes were looking over your body.

"One day I was cleaning the roses, your father had taken his shirt off. I thought of ye, I told myself, that will be ye when you're his age. I wouldn't want to go up against him in a fight. Ye looked just like your father. Your mother is a beautiful woman. I had watched her go down the hill to her man. She had something for him to drink. After he was done, he put the glass down on the ground. He took your mom into his arms and kissed her deeply. They disappeared after that. It didn't help me in the way I was feeling. I had thought this isn't fare; my man is not home yet.

Eleanor didn't know he had woken up; she had fallen asleep. With his good arm Thomas pulled her down to him. He had set up what he wanted her to feel by talking to her. Now they were on his land. The two of them were playing like they did near the pond. Honey ye must watch out for my arm. So ye been hungry for me. As she slept her mind went along with the story. In his mind he asked her what she wanted him to do. Her thoughts told him to touch her, he had asked. *"Where would my love like me to start."*

She had told him to kiss her. Then run your hand down to my heat. Let me feel when your hand moves up my leg. When ye find my heat push your finger inside me. Thomas did as she asked. He found her body wanting this. As his hand slipped between her panties. There was the hunger she told him about. She tried to push his finger inside. He wouldn't let her; in his mind he called her. *"Honey looked into my eyes, I want to see what ye are feeling. Let me see your hunger for me when I push my finger into ye. Honey opened your eyes."*

Eleanor opened her eyes and saw it wasn't a dream. Thomas moved his fingers between her wet pussy lips. He watched her eyes as the pleasure washed over her. Her legs lifted as he pushed inside her. "It's not a dream, I'm home honey. Picture that my heat pushing inside ye. He felt when she came his mind picture his heat was moving inside her. Now he brought her up again. Then he felt her body come and his body had come with her. His magic was back; she felt his seed pumping into her. He stayed where he was until her body stopped quivering.

Eleanor watched him take his prize as he tase what they had done. She had seen the hunger in his own eyes. "There now will ye kiss me, I can't wait to have ye any time I wish. This will have to do us until I'm stronger."

Eleanor had a rag and had to clean herself. "Your magic is back, ye came inside me. I can't wait until ye can do it yourself."

Thomas laid back down. She got up to look at his arm. "Honey do ye think that ye pulled anything in your arm."

Thomas noticed she was a healer now. The pleasure was gone from her eyes. When she was pleased with what she found. The pleasure was back, and she wanted to kiss him.

He smiled when he said. "I saw that hunger of yours, I like what I saw."

Eleanor's cheeks got red. "I know ye did and I saw your hunger also. The next time, I want your heat there in person. With your friend moving in and out of my pussy."

She saw the pleasure in his eyes, he smiled, he was pleased with himself. "Because I've been just as hungry for ye, are ye still on that stuff. I would want ye a lot, until we wanted a child."

She smiled and nodded her head. "I knew ye must be just as hungry for me as I'm for ye. I've been feeling this way for the past two weeks, aye…, I went back on it. Being in your bed I could feel your own hunger for me. I knew ye was coming home soon."

He was smiling now. "We've been close for a long time; I'm glad dad told me to cross over. That day, ye jumped that horse, honey it scared me. For a long time, any time ye came into my arms. I didn't want to let ye go, I was glad we did it that way. I was able to grow up more, this way your body is stronger, my toys that ye have are bigger. When we have our children, I'm going to enjoy them a lot, until then I'm going to enjoy getting there. I would like to start to try for our first child, when ye is going to be twenty. I want to play with my toys for a while. To make love to ye as much as ye let me. When we go to our land. To plant those two rose bushes, I will want ye when these stitches come out."

Eleanor looked at him. "I have seen Grana; she has given me a check up to see if I was ready to have a child. My body for that part is a go. Before we start trying for a child, I need a week to go off it."

Thomas wet his lip it hasn't been that long that he made love to her. "When these stitches come out, I can have ye again on our land. I know ye want my friend inside ye. I'm feeling stronger, may be to night I can made love to ye."

Eleanor closed her eyes. She had pictured herself making love to him on the grass near the pond.

"I just want ye. Now how about some more food? Is your arm hurting ye."

Thomas wanted to take his time with her. He wanted to run his hands over her body. Just lately they with going to fast making love. "Honey what are ye doing to me. Ye had to say ye wanted my friend inside ye. Now he has put it on my mind. Tonight, will ye help me with my friend."

Eleanor looked over at him. She walked over to him then got on her knees to give him a kiss. "It's time for ye to eat, come on let me help ye get up. I have more of that drink that will help ye with the pain."

Ones he was setting and started to eat. She took his arm to see if he had any fever. There was nothing that she could feel, she let her hands get hot. Then she started at his shoulder and ran down to his fingertips, his arm started to glow. Thomas was hungry, he didn't even feel what she was doing. Then he drank what she had for him; it was Scotch.

Eleanor went quickly to get things ready. "Honey, I need to go." She helped him outside so he could do his business in the outhouse.

When he was done, she took him back in. "Come here so I can kiss ye." He waved his hand, they were up against the wall, her skirt and his kilt was up. "Would ye put it in for me. Honey I'm home, as she guyed him into her."

She had asked him to lay them down. He had laid them on the bearskin with her on top. He wanted to take her breast and suck on her nipple. He had to use magic to help them both. She had another idea to ride him until they came. Eleanor felt herself come. His magic brought her breast to his mouth. She tightened her girlfriend muscles and rode his friend hard. This time she felt his friend pump his seed into her heat. "Aye…, ye are home with me, honey that felt so good."

He wanted to touch her breast. He pulled her to him as his tongue made love to her mouth. Eleanor took as much as she gave. She found she was just as hungry for him as he was for her. His hand moved over her nipple to make it hard he brought her down to him. There he sucked on her nipples. Thomas thought it was a good thing he came home. Eleanor was really built, know wondered the men wanted her. She moved her hands over his chest. She knew what she gave him was going to work soon. "Ye feel so good to me. With my heat inside ye, it felt good to come. Ye are my wife the one I would give my life to save ye."

Thomas looked into her eyes he wet his lips. He took a deep breath before speaking. "I know ye gave me something to sleep. Honey when ye took me inside ye. I watched your eyes." He waved his hand, and a wet rag appeared in his hand. "This is all I can do for now." Eleanor took the rag and cleaned herself. Then she cleaned him and put down his kilt. In her mind she heard him say.

"Honey, I like ye to know what war is like. Ye are in hell. Men have died from my hands. It made me feel as if I was dead inside. Only the thoughts of ye kept me going. I would remember the way ye looked. Ye must think of me as an animal. That I'm just out for one thing. There are men like that who would say sweet things to ye. Just to take your virginity. Not I. Do ye think I'm an animal."

She looked at him. She knew killing was hard on him. "Honey ye are a good man. Those men were evil. They were the animals not ye, I saw ye fight. Ye were fighting evil. I felt everything when ye fought these men. It's time to let go and sleep."

*   *   *   *   *

Eleanor went to prepare the food by adding more meat to what she had there. This was for her father and the others to arrive. While the food was cooked, she went to lay her head down on the table.

In minutes she was fast asleep. As she slept, she could hear a man's voice. "Help me he's using my face to get to the women, be where of his eyes. He had taken blood and hair from them and put it in a locket. I didn't know it was a spell to take over my body. The Locket is going into my chest; I can't stop it. Once it is fully in my chest, he will take over my body.

Then he will send my soul to his master. "A witch put a spell on him; the spell was for him to be unable to have a son. These women he takes can't give him a son; he keeps killing all these women. Please help me, the demon hunter is the only one who could save me. He has two brothers that will fight with him. The demon hunter has strong magic, Ye are his mate, tell him if ye stop him now. He will come back in the future. Be where of his eyes.

CHAPTER FIVE

A nightmare at the hunting cabin.

IT WAS A beautiful day out. Thomas was selling one of their white Quarter horses in town. Eleanor was making her rounds to the sick. It was getting harder for her grandmother to do rounds herself. From the day that Eleanor had that encounter with the man in black. Thomas had been riding with her on her rounds. There hadn't been any sign of this man.

In town the two of them had to go different ways. "Honey, meet me by the stable when ye are done."

Eleanor found herself in another dream. She spoke. "I will see ye there my love."

It didn't take her long to make her rounds. As she rode toward the stable, she saw a man talking to Thomas. The closer she got the more the voice sounded familiar. Flashbacks of a man with blond hair came from her memory. Then it changed and it was the voice of the man in black. She knew she was having a dream. What was her dream trying to tell her. Could it be because he sounded like that Englishman. The closer she got to the man the worse the fear became. Her first thought was to run to get away from this man.

Then the scene changed again. Eleanor found herself on the ground under the man in black. There was one thing I noticed about his eyes. He had a malevolent glare of true evil. At one point they turn red, the sign of a demon.

This voice was from the party an older voice. "I know you. You're the girl from the party. You took that woman from me; I'm coming after you. You're the one that will give me a son."

Eleanor saw her grabbing his arms. She held on to him as her hand burned into his skin. He thought she couldn't go anywhere. "Never…! Ye will die from Ronald hands, his is Thomas's brother. No woman can give ye a son. You're a stupid man; all those women couldn't give ye a son. It wasn't our fault the witch put a curse on ye, because your seed will determine if it would be a girl or boy. Get it through your head the women do not determine sex of a child. The men are the one."

Briana had just gone into the cabin. She heard sounds coming from Eleanor. She went right over to her; he got her off him quickly as he screamed in pain. Eleanor still had the rose's petals in her hand.

This time the voice sounded was of a woman. "She ye got to wake up. It's only a dream, come on wake up. Ye are going to wake Thomas."

Eleanor sat straight up and quickly looked around. When she saw Briana, she tried not to yell. "Eleanor it's all right, who were ye fighting with. Come with me and let's get some air before ye wake Thomas."

Outside she took a deep breath, that dream had made her a little shaky. She was trying to get hold of herself. "Thank ye I don't like having those kinds of dreams. This dream made me scared and angry at the same time. In the dream I had burned the man in black. How can that be Thomas made sure he couldn't have sex with any woman. For that reason, he tried to kill him."

Briana looked at her. "Come on, let's sit for a bit, I got to talk to your brother. He said the only time ye have any disturbing dreams is when something is about to happen."

Eleanor looked at her. "Briana, I heard a voice of a man, he was calling for the demon hunter. I knew the voice was of an Englishman.

He was asking for help; he told me to watch out for his eyes. That he was using his face to get these women. A witch put a curse on him so he couldn't have a son. He's taken so many women and rapes them, until he gets her with child. When the child is born and it's a girl, he kills the mother. This voice was softer spoken; this old man has powers. He used the face of Albert Huascaran. This soft-spoken man talked as if he were afraid, that this man was going to take over his body. He has a locket that's going into his chest.

"Then the dream change, it started to be a pleasant dream. Thomas and I were heading into town. He had a buyer for one of his horses. It was the Englishman at the barn. I don't understand my man always looks at the person's eyes, Thomas taught me that. He said ye can see what kind of person you're dealing with. That Englishman I seen him in Edinburgh near Berwick Upon Tweed. The party was at our cousin's home. This Englishman name was Albert Huascaran. I found out his name later because he was the only Englishman there. Mom's cousin learned they found her daughter dead. It was the day of the party. For some reason that man scared me, I had felt the evil within him. When I looked at his eyes that is what scared me. Briana that man was evil. He was only looking at the women with blond hair. It made me feel like he was a wolf on the hunt for his next victim. This keeps coming back to me, repeatedly. I don't know why, Albert is looking for my man. Something is going to happen, that is why he is calling for the demon hunter."

Briana looked at her. "Eleanor, I had brought Thomas saddle bags in with me. My husband told me that Thomas has a book he's been writing in. I think ye should put this dream in that book. To me Albert was asking for help. This Duke may have the power to get into dreams. He had changed the dream to scare ye, Ye know what he is. May be ye will get some of the answers of what he is doing."

Eleanor smiled at her then spoke. "Briana ye may be right. One thing in the dream is my hands burn his arms. That is how I got away from him. I didn't like feeling up tight like I do right now. Has ye come to get some food for your husband and ye."

Briana thought she was quite a woman. "Aye…, also for Father, Duncan said that your fathers should be here soon."

"Briana I'll take the food to Father. It's time I paid my respects to my family and friends. Ye know Ronald would have been my brother-in-law."

The two women went to give the men food. "Hello Father Sinclair, I thought ye like to have some more food."

Eleanor smiled at him. "Aye… my child that would be good. How is Thomas."

Father closed his eyes to say a prayer over is food. "After that spell was gone, he was quickly heeling. He needs sleep to get stronger; I used the holy water to give something to heal him. I also brought ye some Scotch to chase the cold away."

Father took the cup and drank a bit. "Thank ye my child, this helps a lot."

Eleanor smiled. "Your welcome Father, I'm going to pay my respects to my family."

When she went to the back of the wagon. There sitting on top was her brother and Ronald.

It had surprised her, but William told her that he had talked to Ronald. *"Hello sis. Now are ye going to scream."*

Eleanor gave them a big smile. *"Jonathan she is Thomas's woman. She had an idea she was going to see us. Ye are finding out these roses have strong magic."*

Eleanor took a deep breath. *"Aye…, ye are right Ronald, do ye know who this demon is. I don't like these dreams. I know those eyes; I saw them at the party. What scared me was the evil that almost took my breath away. I found that the eyes didn't fit the face."*

Her brother smiled at her. *"Sis ye always was a very smart woman. Albert asked ye for help, as ye know he is not the demon. Thomas taught ye to look at the person's eyes."*

Eleanor stood a little straighter. *"Aye… that he did, Jonathan who is the demon with the red eyes."*

She found she was missing her older brother. *"Sis this man is not a demon yet; his name is Marcos. Albert was his son, so he thought."*

Ronald then spoke. *"Eleanor Thomas will not fight Marcos. Thomas and Michael with William and Uncle Donald will fight a demon with black magic. They must save Albert from damnation. Tell my brother that there is a locket with all the hair from the women he has killed. Marcos is going to try to take over Albert's body with black magic. That locket can't be allowed to go into his chest. There is a man that will tell him all about this. Aye... Ye should go and write this in his journal. Eleanor ye do know that Marcos will try to come after ye. Use the rose petals on your fingernails. Also put the rose's petals on all their weapons, have Father Sinclair bless them.*

Eleanor then spoke. *"Ronald ye are going to fight him in the spirit world. Thomas felt there was more than one reason to leave this earth. Ye also knew Thomas had to see Scotland. If he had stayed, I would have been with a child, we weren't both ready yet. Don't worry, everything is on their weapons. We must charge it in the next moonlight. That goes for ye to. Ronald ones we take care of the roses ye should have the same magic as Thomas. Your sord can throw fire."*

Her brother spoke. *"Sis I'm proud of ye. Ronald ye were right. The two of them are a strong couple, I love ye sis. Tell William that I'm proud of him. Ye both turn out to be a strong man and woman."*

With tears in her eyes. She spoke. *"Thank ye for the high praise Jonathan and Ronald. Be for ye leave this earth. Talk to William, he misses ye a lot and so do I. I will make sure that the family will have a petal on them. Ronald if ye are going to fight Marcos in the spirit world. My man had figured it out before he left the Highlands. Could ye tell me how much time we have? I have a feeling that it won't be that long."*

Eleanor saw both men smiling at her. *Wow...! She just has a little magic. Sis when ye have the full powers of the magic roses. Ye will be a strong woman, ye married a strong man. Marcos won't know what hit him."*

Ronald looked at her. *"Eleanor ye have just until the second moon. Thank ye for placing those two petals on Thomas's forehead. I saw ye had place petals on your hands. That was a good move on your part. Now place them at your fingertips. Ye did good burning him. Next time mark his cheeks. After that is done place it in Thomas journal."*

* * * * *

When she went back to the cabin. Eleanor wrote in Thomas's journal. What was making her jumpy? Could it be thinking about those eyes of Marcos. It's because she will have to deal with that animal. Thomas was still asleep when their fathers came to the hunting cabin. She was about to go see if they were outside. Eleanor about jumped out of her skin.

When the door opened and there stood Daniel. "Eleanor, are ye all right? I'm sorry I scared ye. How's my boy."

She placed a finger on her lips. Eleanor pointed over to Thomas and the two of them went outside. "It's so good to see ye Daniel. Thomas is sleeping with my help. I had to give him something to help him go to sleep. The more rest he gets the stronger he will be.

"I have something to tell ye, we could have lost Thomas. I won't lie to Ye, before he got close to the cabin. Thomas had black out, the man in black not only did he give him an evil spell. He was also in his mind; I had placed rose petals on my hands. That's how I knew he was tormenting him. I had Father to bless him then I placed a cross and rose petals on his forehead. The best medicine that my brother used was holy water and two crosses. He said he also had petals on the rugs.

"With what he had done to his arm, that also saved his life. We would have lost him to the black magic. With the blood lost and that spell, it had made him black out. Thomas was half a mile down the road; he's a lot stronger now. Don't worry, he is not hungry, the food I made he had four bowls of it. If I didn't give him something to make him sleep. He would push himself until he dropped. So far, he has eaten every time he wakes up. The bleeding stopped and the black magic is gone from his body; he is now resting. Duncan is with his wife; he told them to make William rest for one hour. Gallivan's older brother, had given him orders which needed to be accomplished. William has gone to catch up with Damian. When Thomas had gotten up, he sent them to Damian. As ye know he had lost his magic with that spell."

Theseus smiled. "I'm glad that my son paid attention to details, daughter it was that bad. When I went over, I saw that he saw something the rest of us didn't. Then again Duncan had said there was a black cloud over him and Thomas. That it had changed into a hand and took off their shield. Your brother thought it was evil. When he saw it on Thomas's sleeve, he called it black goo. Thomas said he heard the spell, I knew he was trying to go to Ye it had blocked his magic.

"Duncan had my boys back, He knew when it comes to Thomas those two always had each other's back. He knew William would push himself until he dropped. Ye said that Thomas had a bad time with what happened to him. William wouldn't leave ye until it was over with. Duncan had made sure that William had gone and laid down for a bit. What a good idea to make sure he would rest."

He had looked at his daughter. "I'm glad he is doing better, I'm wondering if ye have any food. We have rested and now we'd like to eat."

With the bad news out of the way. She spoke. "I'll bring out the food to ye. I would like to make sure Thomas rests a little longer."

Eleanor looked at the three men, they were like their sons. I would say their sons are like their fathers. "Ye sound like a healer, he is in good hands." She smiled and went inside.

Aye... his son is strong, now if she told them he wanted to fool around. What would they say? What a day. First try to keep Thomas asleep. Then that evil dream. After that to see her brother and Ronald, they were able to talk to me. I guess being so jumpy is caused by these roses. Being able to see things that I shouldn't be able to see. I better get used to it; I can't get over seeing Thomas getting hurt. What if he didn't get to me in time, will I always see spirit, there I go again.

She had jumped again when his father came back in. "I'm sorry Eleanor I guess ye didn't hear me come in. I think ye are being overwhelmed with what has happened. Ye seem distracted in what ye are doing."

She could feel everything was coming to a head. For a minute she had closed her eyes. "Your right about that, he's a strong man like his father. I just want all this over with. I'm sorry I can't stop crying, I try not to cry in front of Thomas. It's got to the point where I can't get rid of all these feelings. I saw the battle and the black cloud with the hand that took off his shield. I also had a dream of the man in black. There is a young man fighting for his life, the man in black has a locket going into his chest. He has hair from the women he killed. I heard that he drinks their blood. Albert is calling for the demon hunter. After he took Damian bride to me Grana has all the women with crosses on them."

He looked at her, then his son. "Come here and let those feelings go. For a long time, ye have been my second daughter. I have learned when something is troubling ye. Ye may laugh. I fine that I can pick things that may be troubling ye. Before, your father could even do so. It's the same with your father and my daughter. Thomas feels helpless and doesn't know what to do. Ye must cry at times, when ye want to have a baby. If ye keep everything inside ye, your baby will be a jumpy child. Tell me if ye saw the knife go into his arm."

Eleanor nodded yes. "Aye…, that spell was made to kill him. With the dreams, along with the goo. I had to sew up my husband, it's been too much for me to endure. It scared me knowing it took nineteen stitches. He was out of it for a while. When he woke up, he asked for food. I was going to see if he could drink the medicine.

"I had used the holy water for what I made him. I'm still afraid that a bit got into his system. He didn't talk, just ate his food and asked for more. After he drank and ate his food, he went back to bed.

Eleanor thought she was going to jump out of her skin. When she heard Thomas's voice in her mind. She had been quite jumpy since all these things happened.

Every little thing she heard made her jump. *"Honey my father is right. I'm sorry if I'm not letting ye cry, have ye gotten some sleep."*

She looked at her man. *"No not when everything coming at me at ones."*

His father was looking at Eleanor. "Is my son a wake now."

Thomas was setting up. "Dad could ye give me a hand, I still feel so weak."

His father went over and lifted him to his feet. "Son ye are lucky to be alive what I understand from Eleanor."

She looked at her man. "Honey could ye make some more bowls and something to carry them on. We will need five bowls."

Thomas waved his hand, for what she had asked appeared on the table. "Thank ye my love, go outside and talk with everyone."

She had brought out their food and gave them their bowls. Eleanor went back in for her food and the Scotch and cups. Outside she handed them their cup with the Scotch in it. For Thomas, she had given him a glass with the holy water and his medication. "Honey here this will help with the weakness." Before she could sit down Thomas asked for more food. She had given him her bowl and went in for more for herself. Can I get ye any more for ye men? She laughed when all the bowls came back. Ones the bowls were filled again she went and gave them out. At last, she got to set down with the men.

Then his father pored some scotch for her and Thomas. "Son ye can have some of this. This is for Eleanor to take the edge off that she has been feeling."

After Thomas and Eleanor ate Donald had given them some Scotch. He put something in the Scotch so they could sleep. When she was done, he waved his hand, and all the bowls were clean and put away. She was listening to the men talk. The two of them sept on the Scotch until it was all gone. She found that she couldn't keep her eyes open. Eleanor went and laid her head in his lap. He was brushing her hair and remembering the time at the garden."

Thomas thought why hasn't evil been after me. Then he remembered what she had said. She had put two rose petals on his forehead. Thomas had done the same think for her.

Then he thought let only good be able to get into are dreams. "I think it's time my wife and I go and laid down. Where would ye want to sleep."

The men looked at the two of them. "We will go down by Father."

Thomas waved his hand and there were three beds of hay, and a fire for them. He spoke. "Everything is ready for ye. There is a fire also down there, I will say good night to ye now."

With a wave of his hand the two of them were on the bear skin fast to sleep.

The three men checked on them. Eleanor had her head on his shoulder; the two men smiled at their children. They found that they could eat more of her stew and gone on talking about Marcos.

Donald spoke. "Duke Marcos Huascaran will stop at nothing to get what he wants. Wait I saw the buggy with its seal on it. He must have found another woman to take. If he is using Albert's face, he must have magic now."

The spirit of Ronald came to where they were. "*Aye… he has powers now. Michael had gotten him with his arrow that night. He was close to death, the demon who takes care of him. He took him to this place to save him. It had cost him his soul; it cost Marcos's time here on earth. The devil is his father; he has given him his powers back for now. That is how he could use Albert's face. Albert had asked Eleanor for help. Marcos is trying to make him look as ruthless as he is. I've been told he is going to take over Albert's body. He found out that Albert is not his son.*

"How this came about Marcos's wife gave birth to a little girl. The rumor going around that each child that was a girl didn't live long. They found the child dead in its bed.

After the third child, they found women gone missing. It was always after ten months had passed; those women were found dead. When the women were checked, they found each of them had a child. Newborn baby girls were left on the church doorstep. The number of babies found alive. There were the same number of women found dead. Finally, Marcos had a son, and the killing of young women stopped. One of the women must have been with child. No more children were left on the church doorstep. This time the mother and child are together. Marcos needs souls if he killed the child like he had. The baby would go to heaven. The women will be sacrifice to his master. He has put a piece of her hair in this locket that Albert wares around his neck. Slowly the locket will go into his chest.

"On the council there has been four men killed. These men wanted the Highlanders to do things for themselves. They were trying to stop their land from being taken. Rumor has it, that the head of the group has sent

men to kill these men. It is Duke Marcos Huascaran. I will tell ye this Thomas will not let this man get close to his wife."

Theseus then spoke. "My daughter is a strong woman she will fight him; with everything she has."

The spirit of Ronald spoke. *"Eleanor's last dream she had fought with him. He found out that she had strong magic with her. When she got her fingers around his arm, she had burned him. Meghalaya had told Thomas to put rose petals on her nails. To mark him even when he is a ghost. As ye can see she has the bands on her wrist with rose petals. When Michael comes home his vest along with yours must be placed in the moonlight. All the weapons must also be placed outside in the moonlight. Father had blessed everything ones before. Now that it's going to be a new battle everything must be blessed again. Eleanor is a smart woman; she did what Thomas told her. To find out what kind of man he is, to look at his eyes."* Ronald also put that in Thomas's journal.

*　*　*　*　*

Now that Thomas had rested the bodies were placed in the coffins. The other wagon was loaded back up; it was time to head home. The family will be waiting for them. Gallivan had headed back toward the hunting cabin. He knew he would catch them on the road home. Their three fathers rode in front of the wagon. Father was driving the wagon with the bodies in it. Thomas Eleanor and Briana rode behind the wagon. Duncan was driving the wagons that had Briana's things. When Gallivan got there, he told his father that everything was ready. Then he went to take Duncan's place.

Duncan spoke. "Gallivan could ye put Briana's things in her new home. Ye don't have to place everything. Then take the wagon to the castle after would. The roses Thomas will take care of them. Then come back to the gathering."

Gallivan spoke. "We have everything all set up; Mamma told us what to take out. We have everything cleaned up and ready for her things to go in. I must go to the castle to get the food with the wagon. Aunty and mamma are bringing the food they will pick up Grana. They will be they're two hours after ye get there. They all did some of the cooking, the women thought to say goodbye to their sons first."

Donald spoke. "Son ye did well I'm proud of ye and your brother. Take the wagon ahead of us. Don't break anything by driving too fast. We got all her things here without breaking anything. Don't ye be the one to break something."

He nodded. "Dad it will be done, see ye at the gathering." Gallivan quickly went down the road.

CHAPTER SIX

A new family came to town.

A YOUNG MAN STOOD looking over the land, the sun was just coming up. The man who was driving the wagon, felt a familiar present. At the time no one was in the streets when a young family pulled up to Grana's home. The man with a reddish-brown hair got quickly down from the wagon. Michael knocked on the door of Grana's home. When she opened the door.

She found Michael standing in front of her. Twenty-three years ago, she had brought him into the world. Didn't Thomas tell her that he would be home soon? Quickly she went into his arms. "Grana, I finally made it home, I know that I upset my whole family. It had to be this way to keep myself and my family safe."

Grana wiped her eyes. "I know all about this. Thomas told me, ye were going to be heading home ones they had seen Father."

Michael was playing with his beard. "Grana is my brother home."

Then she pulled out three rose petals that Thomas gave her. "Do ye have some hair from your wife."

He knew that she had magic of her own. "Grana, is Thomas home now. How do ye know I was married? Aye…, I have her hair in my sporran."

She made a motion to see it. Michael took it out and she had placed the petals on her hair. "There that will keep your wife safe. Oh…, there is some on. Ye have the vest also, does your son have his vest."

Michael looked at her. "Aye…, I heard my brother voice he told me not to take this off. None my sons."

She was anxious to see the children. "They have the magic roses on them. Now will ye bring your family into my home. Then place the wagon out back. I will have Gallivan bring it to your home and put it in your barn. Just do what I have asked ye."

Michael got back on the wagon and placed it out back. Then he got his wife and children down. "Honey, I like ye to meet Grana. She had brought me into this world, after my grandmother passed away. She became a grandmother to us. Grana is my wife, Malinda. Here is our daughter Wanda and this young boy is our son, Ronald Scott. Afterwards, my brother and my wife's brother. They both died in battle.

Grana, how do ye know all of this? Ye said that Thomas told ye."

As his wife sat down Grana went to get them something to drink. "Aye… Ronald took me one day she was telling us about the roses."

*　*　*　*　*

Michael closed his eyes. He was remembering the story that Meghalaya had told them. Didn't she tell us about the next one, to go after the roses would have strong magic. She even placed a petal on his skin. That was for him to know when to go after the bodies. "Aye…, I know of the roses."

Didn't he see what Thomas and his father and friends went through in that battle? Then he heard a voice, ye are home at last my brother. The two of us have been through hell and back again. Michael called him. "Who are ye."

On the hill Thomas had his eyes closed. "Ye and Ronald made me work for the answers. I was upset with ye, it didn't last long. Ye and Ronald call me little brother."

In his mind he called back. "*Thomas, I was scared for ye. I saw the battle ye and our father's fight. Thomas are ye all right, I saw the black cloud with a hand. That spell was to kill ye, I miss ye I knew ye would find a way to get them home, will done little brother.*"

Thomas could feel a tear was trying to fill both men's eyes. "*I'm much better now. Are ye still wearing the vest for ye and your son? We killed all those men. The demon tried to kill Duncan. I took the hit the sild down and went in my arm. William helped me to get to my wife. Eleanor is a healer she saved me from the black magic with Fathers help.*"

Michael felt like crying. "*Aye..., we have them on. Is that why I can hear ye.*"

Thomas smiled. "*Aye... Ye can also talk to Ronald and the other two. It's good that we can say goodbye to them.*"

Thomas smiled at his brother. "*The rose petals are what saved us. Don't worry about your things. It's at your house; your horse is ready to ride.*"

Then he looked at Grana. "Do ye know where they were meeting."

She looked at the young man, who also had the whole world on his shoulders. "It's going to be outside of town where we will meet. They came in late last night. Gallivan been running crazy trying to get all of this done. William told me that this evil man with his black magic. Pulled Duncan's shield for his neck and Thomas's shield for his arm.

"Your brother had a vision that one of the men saw, that their dirks wasn't going through. They had placed shield s on their vests, that man in black took it off them. With his magic he made a black cloud turn into a hand. He heard his voice speaking the spell. For a bit that spell all most killed your brother. Eleanor his wife and Father got rid of that goo. She used the holy water to give his medicine."

Michael's wife Malinda touched her man. "Honey are ye all right."

He smiled at her. "I will be after this is all done. Then we can live our lives on are land."

He looked at Grana. "Would it be all right if my wife and children go with all of ye."

She smiled at him. "I would love it. Then I can say to your mother that I got to hold the baby first. I know ye want to talk to your brother. Michael, anyone that has a rose petal on them, will see their brother. It's about time; the women are going to be here with food and drink.

"Your mother and her sister-in-law Lindy. My daughter Bridget, along with your sister Catherine and William, her husband. We are going to meet the group at the end of town. They will be coming around 8:00, that should be any time. Michael, I would love to have them with me. Malinda, I hope ye don't mine if ye ride with us. This way we can get to know Ye and your beautiful children. It will be good to have children here in this family again."

She went and touched her husband's hand. "Honey we will be fine, it will be good to rest before we must ride again. This way I can hear all the stories about ye."

Grana spoke. "Michael we will be fine, if ye are going, then do so before your sister gets here."

She held the baby with loving care. Then she looked up at Michael and smiled. "It feels good to hold this sweet child."

Grana couldn't believe that Michael was a husband and a father at last. "Your mother and father will be needing them to heal. It's been hard for them after they loss their oldest son and his family. It didn't help when Thomas set out to find Ronald.

He kissed his grandmother on her cheek. Then his little girl went and kissed his wife deeply. "Michael if ye would like to talk with your father and brother go now."

Then he turned to his wife. "Honey I'll take Ronald with me. He always likes to ride with daddy, this will give ye a break.

Michael had grabbed his son. These women he loved with all his heart. As he kisses each of them goodbye, he knew he would give his life to save them.

*　*　*　*　*

Then he felt joy and knew it came from his mother. "Grana mamma knows I'm home. She told me one day that she knew when we were back in the Highlands. Come on son, let's go meet your grandfather and your great uncle. Your uncle and aunt are just going to love ye."

Michael and his son were out the door. He quickly got on his horse and rode away from town. He was unaware that his sister had seen him. Here in the Highland's, he felt safe to let his guard down. Even though he knew the man in black was here ones before.

Catherin could feel something was different. She knew that horse, and the man was her brother. Michael was home at last. William had told her that Michael wasn't dead. "Honey, I hope my eyes are not playing tricks on me. That man is my brother Michael; I would know him anywhere. Besides his horse gave him away, no man could ride that horse but him."

William smiled. He wondered if his wife saw the little boy with him. "Aye… that is my brother Michael. Come on, I know he wants to talk to Thomas Duncan and ye. After I get a hug from him, ye can go with him.

Bridget looked at Franceam. The two women knew there was something else going on. As Catherine and William rode off. Franceam's sister-in-law Lindy looked at her.

When the two of them were together. They always try to see if the other mother knew what was going on. "Franceam's what was that all about?"

The two women laughed. "Lindy Michael is home. Catherine didn't think I saw her brother riding off. Come on let's go meet my daughter-in-law and her little girl. I know my daughter will bring her nephew back with her.

Lindy was puzzled at first. Then again, she knew she had gifts like herself. "Franceam how do ye know that was Michael? Never mind about that part, how do ye know ye have a grandson and granddaughter?"

Franceam laughed. "Lindy come on, tell me how do ye know that your sons were coming back before the others. That your oldest had found himself a wife. Didn't ye tell me that ye had a feeling ye were going to be a grandmother? Right before Donald came home."

Lindy laughed. "Franceam ye have me there. Let's go meet your new daughter-in-law and her little girl."

* * * * *

After a bit Michael instinct told him that his sister was behind him. He held onto his son and slowed his horse. Then he turned quickly to meet his little sister.

Catherine yelled her brother's name. "Michael ye are home, honey it is him, he knows I'm behind him. He's slowing down for us; my god he has a son."

Then there was a squeal of delight. William saw that she was crying, he knew they were happy tears. "I'm and aunt and ye are an uncle."

Tears rolled down her cheeks. Quickly she pushed her horse forward to meet her nephew and brother. "Is it really ye Michael, I knew ye were not dead. I prayed ye would come home soon."

She looked at her brother. "Michael are ye back to stay."

Then she saw his face and bit her lip, saying that. Michael, I wish ye didn't have to go away. It made him sad with the look his sister gave him. "After I take care of a few lose ends. Then I will be back for good."

He gave his sister a big hug with one arm and a kiss on her cheek. Catherine noticed that her nephew looked like Ronald when they were younger. "Michael what is your son's name."

Then she stopped and looked at her nephew. She knew her brother would name him after their older brother. "No don't tell me. I already know his name it must be Ronald."

Michael saw the tears in her eyes. "Aye... Ye are right. When I saw little Ronald after he was born three hours after our brother passed away. My brother lives on…, with in my son. Sis, I would like ye to meet your nephew, Ronald Scott. Ronald, this is your Aunt Catherine, daddy's sister. The man with her is your Uncle William."

William smiled at the boy and thought. This is a good thing we will have little ones to help with the healing. "Hello little Ronald, it's good to meet ye. Michael, your brother, and I knew ye would be heading home. We knew Father had sent a word to Ye. It's good to have Ye home.

*   *   *   *   *

Michael had looked at the two of them. Here before him was two good looking man and woman. "Aye… it's good to see ye also William. I'm sorry ye and my brother had to go through that."

He was looking at his beautiful sister, who is now a woman, a married woman. Michael even though it's been two years. It's sad that they had to miss so much.

William spoke. "It's been hard for Catherin; she is a strong woman. She didn't like to hear about what Thomas had gone through. She knew Eleanor would fight to get him better. Father he was a live saver. With his help he stopped them from finding the bodies. Michael we will be speaking a lot about this."

He looked at his sister and gave her a smile. He knew it was hard for all of them. "Sis will ye take my son, it will not be a good place for him right now. The men will be talking about Marcos."

Catherin had smile back at her brother. "Aye… I know what ye like to do."

Michael had picked his son up to look at him. "Ronald I would like ye to ride with your aunt. Daddy must talk to your grandfather and your two uncles. I must find out what they know of this man in black, do ye mind sis. I should have left him with his sister and my wife."

Catherin smiled at her brother. "Michael ye know I love babies. That's why I'm a midwife and a healer."

Her eyes got bigger when she heard he had a little girl. "Michael did ye say ye have a daughter."

He laughed at that. Ye might get to hold her after she makes her rounds. With her grandmother and great grandmother along with her great auntie. "Aye...! that maybe so but I'm their aunty."

He could see in her eyes a baby. "How old is she?"

He was smiling at William. "She is three months old. Grana said she looks like our mother when she was younger."

Catherine looked at William and smiled. "Do ye mean I have a niece and nephew."

She gave a little squeal of delight. Catherine took her nephew and gave him a hug and a kiss on his head. Ronald looked up at her and back at his daddy.

Michael smiled at his son. "Ronald it's all right, your aunt loves little ones. Your safe with daddy's sister, ye can call her Aunty."

A tear rolled down his sisters' cheek. "Aye... we will be fine. Mamma will say, it's good to have little MacGregor's running through the castle again.

His sister started to say. William spoke. "Honey if I know Grana, she had told Michael all about Thomas and Duncan. Aye…, he is married. Aye…, his wife is going to have a baby. Honey why don't ye get going? Help your sister-in-law, she is the youngest there now. Go on and help her out." William went over to his wife. "In joy the little one, I love ye." He put his hand behind her neck and kissed her deeply. "In joy my love."

Michael gave his son a kiss on the head. He told him to mind his aunt. "Sis, go back and show mamma her grandson, take your time getting to the camp. Us men has a lot to talk about before ye come to the camp."

*   *   *   *   *

When Catherine was out of sight William spoke. "Michael your brother loss a large amount of blood, we were a half a mile out from the hunting cabin, when he blacked out. I was proud of my sister she kept her cool. I could see in her eyes she was scared for him. Once she saw he was still breathing, I heard the breath she held let go. It was good he was out; her and Father had to deal with the black magic.

She had seen what happen to her man. At the time he lost his magic and couldn't go to her. She had to put nineteen stitches in his arm, after the goo was gone. Thomas had been very weak; my sister was giving his medicine to him in holy water. She believes that evil man had a twist on his spell. When I left, he was up and eating and had his magic back. She told me the bleeding had stop."

The two men watch her ride away. "I see that ye have the vest on, along with your son. If I know Thomas, he knows that Ye and your family are here. He had told Grana to place those petals on his wife's.

William smiled at him. "Aye…, do ye think we would let them go to those parties unmarried. We will have time to talk about many things. We better get going. All right, the first time I did this Thomas took three rose petals. He told me to think of my wife, to close my eyes and think of her. Now we will think of being outside of camp. Close your eyes and wave your hand, think we will be outside of camp."

*　*　*　*　*

Before they could get away, Michael smiled to see one of his cousins. "Hello Gallivan. I see ye are very busy today. It looks to be moving day, who's things are these?"

Gallivan smiled to see his cousin was home. "It's Briana's things she is Duncan's wife. She is going to have a baby."

Michael laughed inward. He thought he was married and had a baby on the way. "So, your brother has found himself a wife. This is good, in the Highlands, there are going to be little ones running around. Gallivan ye must be having a lot to do."

His eyes got big. "Aye…" In front of the three men all the things were gone. Thomas called Michael. *"Tell Gallivan to drop off the wagon at the castle. I will send him there to save time. Tell him thank ye for doing this for us."*

Michael wanted to laugh. "Gallivan my brother is trying to help ye out. He is trying to get everything done for ye. He wants ye to put the two horses in the pens with food. The wagon next to the rose garden. Then ride to my place and put my two horses in the barn with food. Then ye can rest until the women are ready to go."

He didn't know what to say. Then he asked Michael a question. "I like to ask ye if ye seen any pretty lassies around my age. If ye do, will ye bring her home so I can meet her. Or ye can take me there one day.

Michael smiled, he thought the next generation was starting out. "Aye… that I will do for ye. Tell me has the spring fever been hitting on ye."

He shrugged his shoulders. "Aye…, a little. In a way, it has Damian has been eyes on Maryann that works at the pub. I still have some time left, if ye could do that for me it would help.

"Will ye tell Thomas thank ye for helping me. He must be feeling better, he didn't look that good when I saw him last night. I was told to ride with the women, making shore there going to be safe. We will be there close to 5:00. I don't think they will be going off without me. Now that William is going with ye."

Gallivan spoke. "When Damian left the hunting cabin Peter went with him. I see ye have a vest on ye, I have three rose petals on us."

William spoke. "Michael, Ronald knew that place was for ye. That was the land ye was hoping to get."

Michael had sadness in his eyes. "Aye… he told me that before he died. It's a bittersweet to get the land that way."

Gallivan looked at his cousin. "A lot has change here, that home is now done. Your father finished the house a month ago. Remember there are three bedrooms there. Tell Thomas I'll see him soon, ye better get going. The family will be there soon."

William spoke. "Your sister doesn't want ye to tell dad about your children. She wants to bring your children and wife to dad. It will mean more to him when he sees your family with mom and me."

Michael smiled at William. "So ye can talk to my sister now. Tell her aye… this way I can get all business out of the way. Then he can enjoy his grandchildren after that, that is a great idea. Tell Catherine for me, that she has turned into a beautiful and smart woman."

William looked at Michael and spoke. She said, "thank ye Michael. I missed having my brother's home."

They watched Gallivan, as he started down the road and disappeared. "I have a feeling that Ronald found a spell that took away Thomas weakness. His spirit has been around us. Eleanor got to speak to our brother with Ronald. Peter knew his twin needed him. He stayed with us until we had to go.

"Don't take off your vest. Tell your wife to keep that vest on Ronald. The man in black has been trying his best to keep Thomas weak. Ye see Thomas with his magic, the day the man in black when he came after Eleanor and Maryann. Thomas took three rose petals and made it into a dirk. He hit him in the heart the petals went down to his loins. Ronald told my sister; the last woman he took he had through her out of the buggy. He had stopped him from raping any more women. Are ye ready to go? Do as I had told ye." Both men thought of where he wanted to be. They waved their hands and off they went.

*   *   *   *   *

It was late when they got in. When six men and two women arrive at the spot where the family agreed to meet. Father was driving the wagon with the three coffins. This was his duty, he told the family. He will not leave these bodies until we've placed them at their new resting place.

Damian and Gallivan had already made camp for them. There were clean clothes and food waiting for them when they arrived. He brought hay from the ranch to make a soft bed for each of them. Father Sinclair stayed close to the coffins; not once did he stray far from the wagon.

Damian went over to the priest. "Father ye should come over by the fire to get warm."

He looked up at him then said. "No, my son I will stay here. Evil has tried to take them once before. This is my duty to tend the dead. I will be by their sides until we reach their last resting place."

This had touched Damian. "Thank ye Father for doing this for us. I'm going to make ye a fire here. This way ye can stay near the wagon, I'll bring ye some food."

It had been a hard day for Eleanor and Briana. The two of them were so tired from traveling. After they ate, they had both fallen into a deep sleep next to the fire. The men were talking about tomorrow and drinking something hot to warm their insides.

As they ate, stories of Duncan's home were told. "Duncan ye home is clean. Our mother had made me clean the place a month before ye was to come home. All the men had a good laugh over that story."

His brother went over and told the story about his place. "Duncan it won't be bad, Mamma had me take some of your things out. There up in the barn."

Damian went over to the fire. He saw Eleanor's arms were moving like she was in a fight. Thomas heard her say. *"Your using Albert's face. I know ye are an evil man. No woman can give ye a son. Only a man seed, choose the sex of the child. My man will save me. Ye come after me I will mark ye as a man that rapes women. Be gone Satan."*

Thomas had tried to get to his feet to go to her. That's when Damian came over to tell him Eleanor was having a bad dream. He had it with this weakness. "Damn it… that dream of that man has her again. I've had it with him if that man comes near her and tries to hurt her. He will be a dead man. No man will hurt the woman I love. No one!" His father saw the anger in his eyes. They knew he couldn't get to his feet yet. They watched him wave his hand and Eleanor was in his arms.

Eleanor knew he was the one touching her. He had called her in his mind. *"It's okay honey, I have ye my love.* Eleanor it's only a dream look at me." In a soothing voice he spoke. "Honey open your eyes and look at me."

Her eyes flew open and there were tears rolling down her cheeks. Her arms went quickly around his neck. Everyone heard her say. "Thomas, make this demon go away, he's a cowered to use Albert's face. Please keep him away from me ye are the only man I want; this man is evil."

Thomas didn't like to feel Eleanor's hold body shaking, she was angry and scared. Didn't he place rose petals on her forehead? He realizes the man in black use Albert to get into her dream. "This dream must stop. With his magic he places a spell onto this man. In his body were the rose petals. *"Ye can no longer use Albert's face again. Each time ye try, this spell will burn ye with in your body. Ye have the magic rose petals with in ye."*

Thomas kissed his wife. "Honey, I promise no one will touch ye but me." He was happy he had married her a long time ago. He knew this man will do anything to stop him. Through Albert he knows that he will stop him from using his body.

Evil must die, then through the fire he saw Ronald. *"Little brother I will deal with Marcos. Michael and Ye will take down the demon who is watching over Albert. Ye will see Michael in the morning. William is bringing him here with magic. Brother asked Damian to get a glass of water and ask Father to bless the water for ye. Place the medicine in the water. Then ye must place a rose petal also in the glass. Wave your hand over the glass, say these words. This is to take away the weakness. Eleanor was right that Marcos had added something to that spell. Ye will feel like yourself in the morning."*

Thomas quickly called Damian. "Could ye get me a glass or cup of water. Take it to father and ask him to bless the water for me. Then bring it back here to me." Damian did as he asked him. Father knew that Eleanor was using the blessed water at the cabin. He thought Thomas had found out that this evil man had add something to the spell. This time he dropped a cross in the water and prayed over it. Then he spoke. "Tell Thomas to do what he has to with his magic. Drink it with the cross in the holy water."

Damian went back a told Thomas what Father had said. Eleanor was up now and place the medicine in the water. Thomas had placed the rose petal also in the glass. Then he said the spell that Ronald told him over the glass. When he was done, he drank it down. "Then he took the cross out and told him to bring it back to Father and thank him for me."

Thomas knew this dream was just playing with her thoughts, trying to scare her. She knew right off this man needed her to fear him.

Their fathers were pouring them a drink. What they had done was put something in the Scotch to help them sleep. The two fathers had brought over a drink for the two of them. "Daughter drink this it will let ye sleep."

Eleanor took the drink then handed it to Thomas to drink the rest of the Scotch. Before he drank the Scotch, he looked at the two men. His father stared right back at him. He gave his son a nod of his head.

Then he knew they had put something in the glass. "Wow…!" I have gotten fooled a lot these past four days. This time when he wakes up, he will feel like himself. "Thank ye dad, I can feel what ye had given us is working. Before I fall asleep my wife and I will say goodnight to all ye. Also, dad Michael will be here tomorrow, I will see ye in the morning." With a wave of his hand, they were laying on the bear skin on the hay that Damian had for them. Thomas took them where they could be alone together.

Duncan had placed a blanket down over the hay for him and his wife. He had picked his wife up and brought her to their bed for tonight.

*   *   *   *   *

The next morning Eleanor and Thomas woke up. She had been lying on his shoulder all night. She was going to get up when she felt his arm rolling her back to him. Thomas turned his head and lazily opened his eyes. He had pulled her into him for a kiss.

It had felt good to have her next to him. Last night he knew he was fighting to sleep. Their fathers didn't put that much medicine in the Scotch. "Good morning my love. Did ye sleep all right last night?"

Eleanor went back for another kiss. "I slept quite well, I'm so glad ye are home. How did we get here? Thomas what happen last night."

He was trying not to laugh. "Don't ye dare laugh. What happen last night?"

He couldn't help himself; Thomas pulled her down for another kiss. "Ye don't remember falling asleep near the fire?"

She laid her arms and her chin on his chest. "No, I only remember eating. I felt so tired that I put my head down and fell asleep near the fire. Wait, I remember dreaming, it was about the man in black. He wanted me to run and fear him. I felt scared and angary all at once. He wasn't going to get the best of me. I was faster on my feet than him. I found something, picked it up, and hit him with it. I cried out for ye and ye were there. There was a fight and then ye were picking me up. Ye told me, that he will never touch me again. While ye are still alive no one will ever hurt me. I remember burying my face in your neck and falling back to sleep. Thomas, would ye do that for me."

He wanted to show her that he didn't have any more weaknesses. "Honey, do ye really have to ask that question? Haven't I proven that to ye once before." Thomas turned her over onto her back, now he was between her legs. He had pulled her skirt up and his kilt.

Eleanor was moving over his heat trying to slip him inside her. "Aye… that ye have. Ye didn't have to answer, I can see it in your eyes. I thought that it was true before. Now I know for sure that ye do love me and always have. Thomas, ye have always been there for me. Even before that bear attacked us.

He watched as he pushed his heat inside her wet lips. "Honey I will tell ye this. If the bear had killed ye. I would rather have died then to live without ye."

Her muscles took hold of his heat and he grown inward. She watched as he started moving inside her. "I tried to help ye I couldn't. That bear turned and hit me; it had thrown me into the rock. I knew I was going to black out soon. Before I did, I saw ye on top of the bear. Ye drove your dirk into his head."

It was getting harder to talk, he wanted so much to make her come. Still, they talk as if they push themselves higher. "Aye… ye had me scared, Ye didn't wake up for a long time. Being so young and blind to what I was feeling for ye. I didn't know I was in love with Ye.

Everyone knew but me. Eleanor, I need ye, never leave me. Honey, how about we start are family next year. By the time I get ye with our child. Ye would be close to the age of twenty-one."

Then Thomas gave her a deep kiss. His hand moved over her breast and down to her bottom. He drove her up until she came. Her arms held on to him until the pleasure stopped. He was already bringing her back up. He took her mouth into another deep kiss. Then she nipped and suck on his ear lobe. She was enjoying the pleasure and what she was doing for him.

Eleanor drove him up until he came. There was no weakness in his body. Her man was back, it felt good when he had come inside her. His lips kissed her neck and mouth. Thomas collapsed on top of his wife. He rolled her over on top of him. "I've been wanting to do that from the time I got back. Honey after we had married and all those things ye did amazed me. My eyes had gone wide with disbelief. Back then I was amazed that ye was able to do that to me. My sweet lover ye knew how to bring me to my knees. I thought back then that I had been blind all those years. I had my future in front of me all this time.

The two of them went over to the water to clean up. After that was done, she headed over to the firepit to fix breakfast for everyone. A cold wind blew through the camp; she could have lost her man that battle was roofless. Those men were out for blood, killing was the way they got paid, it was blood money. The man in black he was out for power and sex. Didn't her man take a way that one part.

Briana came over to help her. "Eleanor how can I repay your man. If he weren't there, I would have lost Duncan."

Eleanor had just put some dear stakes on. "Briana there is nothing to repay him back. Duncan is family, all Thomas wants is to be able to live his life out in peace. Those men didn't care if he was a family man or not. There are more men out there, Ronald said it's not over with yet. I believe the three brothers will end this, does Duncan know that ye saw the battle?"

She looked at Eleanor. "I see the weakness is gone from Thomas's body. Do ye happen to know what he is doing."

Eleanor smiled at the thought of what her and her husband had done this morning. "Michael should be coming here any time now. My brother is bringing him here. He's feeling as if the whole world is on his shoulder. He is trying to achieve his brother's last wish. Thomas was asked to fine their bodies and bring them home. Ronald didn't think that it could have kill him in doing so."

*   *   *   *   *

Afterward he stood looking over the land. He knew how Ronald felt about the land and people. Right then he could feel Michael. There was so much pain he could feel it pour out of him. At least he and his son have the vest on. He had done a few things for his cousin. I can see that William is showing him how to use magic.

Then the spirit of Ronald came over to him. *"I see that the spell I found help ye."*

Thomas felt so much better. *"Ye know Eleanor had a feeling that there was another spell with it. I couldn't make love to her the way I needed to. She tries not to cry in front of me. To relaxed she use sex, I do the same. Do ye know the hardest part of all of this, was taking what ye said and what happened to Eleanor and me. I had to take everything apart and look at it. The promise we had to only look at Eleanor as a sister. It would have taken awhile but I was coming around. It was as if she was made for me. At sixteen she came into my arms so easily, I didn't understand what she was doing. Until mamma made dad tell their story. I had to play that game of looking for a wife. Ronald, I couldn't send her to those parties unmarried. That woman can bring me to my knees.*

William felt the same way. "Ronald, I know ye have seen what was to come. Tell me how long I can keep Michael home?"

Ronald was worried about Michale. "Thomas until the next full moon, we must keep those vests on. Ye have done, a number on Marcos he can't have sex at all. Do ye know that are great grandfather had fought him before. I found out he was a fairy at one time. Those books Eleanor found can't be read until this is all over with. In the future they will have to know about him. The next Thomas called Tom, and his mate Eleanor she is known by Ellen, will need all of this."

Thomas looked at Ronald, *"I know what ye are talking about, I had a vision of what he was going to do to Tom in his sleep."*

Ronald spoke. *"Your child will go to great length to get to the woman he loves. Thomas Michael is going to need ye. The two of ye will need each other through all of this.*

Thomas, our cousin Duncan, didn't realize that Briana had seen everything of the battle. He thought it was only Eleanor. Brother, I think the one who has his head on straight is Gallivan. He had to ask Michael if he see a lass, who would be good match for him could he bring her home. I think it's time for ye to help Duncan out. Briana thinks that he owes his life to ye."

*   *   *   *   *

Eleanor had placed some more meat into the skillet to cook. Briana had gone over to pick Duncan's vest. As she held his vest her hand ran over the top of his collar. She remembered that Eleanor saw the cloud turn into a hand. She could see the strings where the sleeve was. The hand had pulled it off the vest. Then Thomas had come down the hill, Briana went over to him to look at his vest. She saw the dirk had slid off the side of the vest and went into his arm. It had lined up; she had seen the strings on his vest. Slowly she ran her finger over the mark, without this vest they would be dead. The men who fought at that battle with Thomas, were behind Briana listening to every word. Briana looked at Duncan, his eyes full of pain, she knew how close it would be. Without these rose petals on the vest, she would have lost her husband. He nodded his head at the truth of what Briana had said.

CHAPTER SEVEN

Time to Say Goodbye.

BRIANA WENT INTO Thomas's arms. "Thank ye for saving my husband."

Thomas brushed her hair. "Briana ye must remember this part. The six of us are our family, not only that we are brothers in arms. We were there to take down evil that night. To also take revenge for our brother's deaths. We all had each other's back. I'm glad that I was able to help my brother. What happened to me was due to what I had done to Marcos. He had taken his revenge on me, for what I had done to him. He was trying to help his men."

Duncan walked over to her and placed his hands on her shoulder to comfort her. "Thank ye Thomas I'm lucky to have ye as family and my brother. Come on honey let's go ye must eat, I don't want ye sick."

* * * * *

Thomas went over to his wife and put his arms around her waist. Eleanor had a vision it was the day of the full moon. She could see they were on their land. She saw herself placing all nine vests and weapons shields laid out on the ground. The moment the moonlight hit the vests she saw many rose petals appearing. Then disappeared after a few minutes later.

He had pulled her against his chest, with his arms around her waist. He knew she was in a vision. She was watching her man kneeling next to a big rock, there was a bare spot. Eleanor watched Thomas dig up a flat piece of stone, he had brought over some water for the roses. When the moonlight hit that bare spot, in minutes two rose bushes appeared. Once the roses had bloomed, he had cut them off as soon as they appeared. Thomas handed the roses to his wife. She also took rose petals to put on all Michael's weapons. She had seen Father bless them after would. It made it clear who he was going after, Ronald said he would be the one to take down Marcos.

Michael needed his family

Once again, the scene changed, and she saw Michael and her brother riding towards them. It was 10:00. Thomas was with her on the hill. In the vision she saw herself watching Thomas's face. He had let his father be the first once to greet Michael. She saw joy and tears in Thomas's eyes. The moment his brother jumped off his horse and ran into their father's arms.

Eleanor turned into his arms. "Both of are brothers will be here soon. But ye already know this. Honey, I don't think Michael is to kill Marcos. I have a feeling he is going to save a town from Marcos's men. There is a town just outside of the Lowlands. Honey can ye make Michael arrows that keep coming back. There will have to be many rose petals for them to take down demons. At the next full moon, the men's vest must have their names put inside with magic.

Eleanor's father was the one who went over to the fire pit. He had removed the pan from the fire to save the food from burning. "Well now we still have breakfast. It's been two years that Eleanor, hasn't burnt any food. Thomas has been back for just a little while and she almost burnt breakfast. The only time my wife burns food. Is when I have my arms around her waist nibbling her neck."

Eleanor looked at her father and gave him a little smile. She knew just what he was trying to do. When Briana started to giggle. Everyone knew that Duncan had done it to her a time or two. Quickly Briana and Duncan took a piece of the meat. "It isn't burnt.

It has a good taste to it." Everyone took some of the food and started to laugh.

*   *   *   *   *

Thomas took Eleanor by the hand. He had led her away from everyone. She had grabbed her bag to change his bandage. He had made her put her things down. With a soft touch he laid his fingertips on her cheek. Then round to the back of her neck, where he drew her in for a deep kiss. "Ye were seeing a lot of different things."

Eleanor looked into her man's eyes. "I knew I would have lost ye that day, that's why I'm finding out these things. I'm the mate to the keeper of the magic roses."

He pulled her into his arms and just held her. "Honey, I wish that ye didn't have to see the battle. I know Ye had seen what happened to me that day. When ye told Briana what happened at first, she thought ye must have been mistaken. When she grabbed Duncan's vest and started to look it over closely. She had found it was all true."

Thomas pulled her away from him, he looked at his wife. "What do I need to know about the magic roses?"

The two of them sat down. "Honey did ye know that the vests need to be recharge on the next full moon."

Eleanor grabbed her bag to change her husband's bandage. "Wait…, so that is why Ronald said that I have my brother until the next full moon. What else will I have to do."

The two of them sat down on the ground. Eleanor took out the things to rewrap his arm. "Did ye know that no one can use your vest. At the full moon when ye lade the vests out. Ye also has to say the names of the person who belongs to that vest. Then the name will appear at the top."

Thomas had the bandage, but he had put it down. He smiled and pulled her closer, he had started nuzzling her neck until she started giggling. When she stopped giggling, she told Thomas the rest of her vision. "Honey it was Michael that I saw, he is the only one I know could shoot an arrow with little light. He can hit his target every time."

Eleanor had finished wrapping his arm. Thomas spoke. "Aye… I saw Michael and what he had to do to save them from being burned alive. Then I saw him close to the fire holding Ronald. I watched it when our brother took his last breath. It was hard to see that happening. It must have been harder for Michael to factually feel when he took his last breath…, then died. I'm glad I went for the magic roses. Meghalaya told me that I should burn a piece of the magic rose branch or stems. Think of what ye like to know. That the power of the rose branch or stem will let me see into the past and future.

"When we went to see Father Sinclair, he told us about the man with his young wife. They brought the bodies to him. He was amazed by the way the bodies arrived at the churchyard. At first Father Sinclair was under the illusion that they were the dead men's family. The way the bodies were prepared led Father to believe. That the man--woman who washed, wrapped them with loving care was their family. He also helped dig holes for the bodies. They believe it was Michael with his wife and newborn son, because he knew the names of all three men. He had told Father that the last man written their first name on each of their chest in blood."

Eleanor gave a little shiver when she heard that. "Thomas when we were at the cabin. In my vision I saw the man in black. I don't know if ye remember what Ronald had told ye. He had appeared to all of us. That vision was Albert asking me for help. At my cousin's place Marcos used Albert's face. It was his eyes that gave him away.

"Marcos will be back here. Because Albert had told him what he was looking for. There is an old man that takes care of Albert. He is coming here looking for the demon hunter. Honey, I believe ye are the demon hunter.

"The next time Michael will be coming home. Ye will be riding to the pub, to get the beer for the party. He will take down one of the men that fine Marcos's women. The other man ye will kill he is a demon. When I saw Albert, he had a locket around his neck. The man that stays with him is a demon; he has black magic. Uncle Donald and Father Sinclair will be bringing all your shields and weapons to the pub. At that time, the locket will be deeper than it was.

"Marcos has magic black magic, Michael will see Marcos dead. After he couldn't have that woman, he went back to see if the last woman would give him a son. Marcos will burn everything, even his men. Inside the pub will be that old man with a story to tell ye. It is about Albert and his family; they will be looking for me to fine ye. Marcos believed that I could give him a son. In the vision I saw rose petals on my fingernails. There were bands on my wrist that had rose petals on them.

Ronald will be fighting Marcos in the spirit world. When it is the full moon, he will lay his own vest with the others. He will come to Ye when it's time to fight. In the vision for a moment. I got to see Marcos true face. It had change from Albert to an old man, those eyes were pure evil. The magic roses let me see what he really looks like. I believe ye are going up against black magic. In that room in the castle there are books on black magic. I will find spells to counteract those spells for ye.

"Honey, I understand why Ronald had ye leave the Highlands. He wanted ye to see what Marcos did to our people. He had sold many people as slaves; Marcos made many women to endure his touch. Right off he placed things over their mouth so no one could hear them. After he has them in his carriage, he has fun feeling them up. To get a young woman with his child, he must rape them many times. Until they are pregnant these women are nothing to him. Marcos has killed many of these women who didn't give him a son."

Thomas could see she was caught in the vision she had. "Enough honey…! Ye don't have to do this. Please my love…, I don't need ye to be thinking of that when I'm touching ye."

Eleanor opened her eyes. She wanted her man to have all the information that she could give him. "Honey I'm sorry, it's been a very long week."

Eleanor watched her man put his shirt back on. "Thomas, I hope ye take that shirt off a lot when we are at our land."

He smiled at her, with a twinkle in his eyes for mischief. He spoke. "So ye like having me without my shirt on. I will be happy to oblige ye, I could help ye to take off your blouse then I could rub my hands over your breast."

Thomas watched her eyes as they went wide with those thoughts. She smiled and wet her lips. He could see she couldn't wait to start their lives.

*   *   *   *   *

Then she stood up and looked just before the road that came into camp. Eleanor spoke. "I feel William is here they are using magic, can ye also feel Michael?"

Thomas put his arms around his wife. "Aye…, I felt him early this morning, I gave him a hand and brought him to Grana's place. He had just enough time to talk to her before he would meet up with my sister and William. I gave Gallivan a hand and Michael's things are in his home. Briana's things are also in her home. I let him take care of the horses and wagons. These two young men have been going all night. "Aye… for the past two years. William been my brother, my friend. I haven't been able to feel Michael's present. We've been too far away from each other."

*   *   *   *   *

Thomas felt a cold wind move around him. In the sunlight was his brother Ronald. *"Thomas, Michael needs to bare his soul to ye. This has been hard on him, I know ye saw the two of us. He will need his brother to just hear what happened that night. Drink with Michael and let him tell ye what he saw and how he felt. Thomas, he doesn't know how to let go of his feelings. Ye are a strong man ye know how to let go. If he doesn't talk about it, it will eat him alive inside. Can ye do that for me I used to help him; I must leave it to ye now."*

"Ronald, I got this. Michael and I will work it out together. I have his back as he has mine. I know it's not over with yet. Ye will be back after we put ye to rest. I know ye will be fighting Marcos in the spirit world."

Ronald smiled at Thomas then went to stand with his father. Thomas saw his brother and William ride in. He saw Michael get off his horse quickly and run to their father. Thomas turned to Eleanor. "Before we go down to meet Michael and William."

He pulled her into his arms and kissed her. "When we are at the castle, I will need ye to pick the one rose bush from the three. Ye must please them and give them food and water. After a bit, the one will show itself to Ye. Together we will plant this rose bush. Once this rose bush blooms, we can get all are gifts. I want to make love to ye as often as I can."

Thomas closed his eyes and gave a little laugh. "Are ye saying the sex will help us in bad times."

He pulled her to him and gave her a kiss. That is how William and Michael saw them. Michael was next to the wagon. He could see Ronald had his hand on Michael shoulder. Their fathers were with him they had their vests on. William could see their other brothers sitting on the wagon. Then Eleanor and Thomas walked down the hill. He let his wife greet her brother first. "Thomas how do ye feel."

He gave William a bear hug. "I feel like myself, after Ronald told me the other spell Marcos use on me. I had stopped him from giving Eleanor a hard time. He can't use Albert's face again without some pain.

Thomas smiled at the sight and spoke. "Aye… have ye spoke to your brother?"

William shook his head no. "Sis can ye see our brother Jonathan."

She nodded her head as a tear rolled down her cheek. "Aye…, that I do. I spoke with him and Ronald at the cabin."

Thomas saw Jonathan get down and go over to them. William took Eleanor into his arms. The two of them felt a cold hand on them. Thomas saw Jonathan talking to them. When he felt Michael's hand on his shoulder.

Thomas turned around and faced him. "I've missed ye Michael, it's good to have ye home again."

Michael took his brother into his arms. Thomas could feel Michael shaking a bit. When Michael looked up, he saw Ronald in front of him. Then he heard his brother say. *"Thank ye for all ye have done for me. I wish it could have been different for us. Now it's just the two of ye. Thomas knows I'm talking to ye. He hears what ye hear, the two of Ye wear the vest with the magic roses. It's time to let go Michael, I'm home at last."*

Thomas looked up at Michael, he smiled at his two brothers. Tears rolled down his cheek. "I have a feeling that ye know about the magic roses. Ronald helped me with the last spell from Marcos. Everyone will have rose petals on them. They will be able to see our brother and hear what he is saying."

Eleanor came over to Thomas. She had two glasses with a bottle of scotch in hand. She had given Michael the other glass with Scotch in it. She watched him down that Scotch. After filling Michael's glass back up. She gave Thomas the bottle and one glass. William came over to them with his glass. Then Eleanor gave Michael a piece of deer meat and one for Thomas and William. "Now ye men go do some talking. Ye don't need me there when ye have my two brothers and Ronald with ye. I will get more meat for ye and bring it to ye. Then I will help Briana with more of the food." They saw Duncan heading over to them. He had his vest on and a glass in hand.

Thomas kissed Eleanor then said to the men. "Shall we go up to the top of the hill."

Eleanor looked at Thomas Then spoke. "Honey, we need more Scotch and firewood. Up on the hill, ye can start a fire, down here we need more firewood also. Damian had taken a brake he fell asleep. Briana and I will bring the food up once it's done." Then Thomas waved his hand and everything she needed was there.

On top of the hill the men looked toured the beauty of the stream and mountains surrounding them. Once the fire started. They all sat down and started to tell Michael about Huascaran. Michael slowly understood that the rose petals had the magic of the fairies and the wizard. If the spirit of their brothers didn't want to be here, they wouldn't be.

From the top Thomas saw Eleanor bringing the food up. Michael had all the information he needed. Thomas had been watching Michael drinking the Scotch. He was slowly forgetting that Ronald was dead.

Ronald was looking at his two brothers. *"I've been blessed with two wonderful brothers. Ye two went beyond what I have asked of ye.*

Michael did Ye know if ye burn a stem from the roses. As it burns ye can ask anything to see pass or future. Thomas had asked to see how his family died. Michael Thomas saw us on that day, ye are not the only one living this nightmare. Ye came on time to save me from being burned alive. It's time to let go of me and that memory.

"*When ye leave here, it will be after the full moon. I want ye to go to this small town just passed England. This town needs your help, don't look for Albert. He's looking for Eleanor and the demon hunter. It's Marcos ye are looking for.*

"*Michael I will always have your back when I can. Ye have a beautiful wife and children. Thomas I'm glad that ye found out that Eleanor was for ye. Ye two looked good together. William Ye and Catherin are a beautiful couple. Duncan ye be good to this beautiful woman. She has family here now and they will have her back.*"

It was all most 5:00 when they saw the group of women. "*Michael it's time for ye to let go. I need to go see momma and all the women.*"

*   *   *   *   *

There were many kinds of food to choose from. Catherin had brought Malinda up to where the fire was. William had moved the table closer to the fire. The two women place the food on the table. "Eleanor this is Michael's wife Malinda. She has two beautiful children."

Franceam came over to Eleanor after placing the food on the table. "How's my boy doing. Your brother said that ye thought there was another part, to that spell. Have ye found the spell to get rid of it? I also heard that ye were giving Thomas his medication with holy water."

Eleanor gave her a hug. "He's doing well, Ronald found the spell and told Thomas what to do. That last part of the spell was to keep Thomas weak. What was going to happen, he wouldn't be able to fight. I had to put nineteen stitches in his arm. That black goo I was thankful that Father was with us. He helped them to get their bodies home. With the roses and Father's words by calling out Satan begone, had push Rodney away from the wagon.

Eleanor hadn't thought about it until now. Her eyes were watering up, as she went into her mother-in-law arms. "It had scared me to death; Thomas had passed out a half a mile down the road. In a way it was good for what I had to do to him."

She took a deep breath and stepped back from her. "Sorry I hadn't thought about it until now. Father had helped me with the spell Thomas had heard. At the time he lost his magic, so he couldn't come to me. There was this black goo, my brother's quick-thinking saved his life. He had placed two crosses, one above and the other below. Every time he cleaned his wound; he poured holy water over the gash. The last time he cleaned the wound; he thought they had a long ride ahead. He placed rose petals on the bandage; he said fight evil with goodness.

Franceam smiled then spoke. "I thought so. My husband said these magic roses been letting ye see things and do different things when needed."

She was glad his mother had trained her. "Aye… That they have. I have something for all ye.

Then her mother came over to them. "What's going on? Are ye all right Eleanor?"

She had nodded her head then placed a petal on her mother. "Aye… I think it's time all ye talk to your sons. Then Jonathan's wife came over to the women. "Am I missing something."

Eleanor went and placed a petal on her also. "It's time for ye women to see your loved ones.

The two-women hugged. Eleanor spoke. "When he couldn't get up by himself it scared me. He had to use his magic when Marcos had added another spell to that goo."

Catherin took her hands then looked into her eyes. "Stop my brother is fine because of the two of ye. William had high praise for what ye had done. Remember we were there when Thomas went after the roses. Have ye talked to your brother Ronald."

Eleanor looked at her friend. "Aye…, now have ye talked to your own brother?"

Catherin smiled. "No not yet, I'll let mamma do that first."

When the women turn torte the wagon, they saw Ronald Jonathan and Peter. Eleanor heard a gasp, as the women headed over to the wagon.

Malinda then said. "Has Michael seen Ronald."

Eleanor came over to Malinda. "Aye…, that he has. Thomas gave him a rose stem to throw in the fire. To see what Thomas had to do, he had told Michael about Rodney. Also, to tell each other that they did it together. Shall we bring some food to our men. Don't worry about your children, not when the family is together. Your son has a playmate, the two of them will be fine. Grana has the baby she is well cared for."

Malinda smiled at her. "Eleanor how far is your home going to be from us."

The two women brought food to their men. Eleanor spoke. "About a mile not that far. I would be happy to babysit for ye. Catherin and I are healers and midwives. I'm still learning things from Thomas's momma and Grana. How does it feel to have many women looking after your children."

Malinda saw that her son and his friend were eating. "Very different I was the one to have all the children from my sister. She's the oldest of the family, I had no time for myself. I hope I can have some time with Michael. He's been up tight, I'm hoping being home it will help him. The day that he brought home those men. He felt that he couldn't tell me they were family. I met Ronald and Michael a long time ago. I know Ronald MacGregor, he knows my father. One day he brought Michael along with him. I knew him as Michael McCabe. That was four years ago."

Eleanor looked surprised about that. "Ronald knew something was going down then. I wonder if Ronald told Michael everything. I believe he didn't know that Marcos was going to take out all the young MacGregor's. They took out his wife because they thought she was going to have a boy. He was right about that."

* * * * *

When everyone was gone but Thomas. Michael started to think about what Ronald had said. The feeling of Ronald and the other's not being dead was gone. "Thomas was that a dream or was he with all of us. I didn't see Peter was he here?"

Thomas looked over and saw Peter with his twin. "Damian has been having it ruff he misses his brother. Michael, you're not drunk or dreaming, your eyes weren't lying to ye. When I saw ye holding Ronald that day, tears rolled down my cheeks. I wish I could have been there to help ye, that was your cross to bear.

"My cross to bear was to dig them up and look at their faces. Here throw this into the fire and think of me looking at Ronald's face."

Michael did as Thomas asked. He now understood what Ronald meant. "My God ye saw everything I had to do. I know that ye and I had to do different parts. We took care of our brother together. Thomas still hurts, how did dad and ye be able to stand the pain."

Thomas saw that Michael's wife and children had arrived. Michael, we have our mates, I talk with Eleanor about everything. She is the one that keeps me grounded to earth, she knows when it gets too bad I have her to bring me back. Brother, we are all that each other has. I hope ye don't think of me as just your little brother. Here ye can see the six of us fighting. I don't want to kill; those men would have killed us and think nothing about it. That night ye were there to stop those men. They were evil and had to die, the same as us six. I think it's time for Ye to grieve for Ronald. I had to do the same if I didn't it would kill me inside.

Michael, being there was hard to watch our family cut down. Ronald was a strong fighter, it took Rodney to stab him in the back, this is a coward's way. When he told the story I almost went for his neck. William had my back, Rodney went for his dirk, he was going to stab me in the back. William almost broke his hand."

Then his brother started to talk. "I didn't see what happened to them when they were fighting. Ronald made sure I wasn't there. He had made me go across Lock Ness before them. It was tearing me a part; he told me to go home to my wife. I knew how long it would take them to get to their next camp. I tried to go to sleep, but the rose petals Meghalaya had place on my skin. When I did, I could see the fighting in my dream. Malinda knew there was trouble, I couldn't tell her about what I had to do. It was the only way I knew how to keep her safe. She was carrying our son at the time. I love that woman and the children she gave me. After we clean the bodies, our son was born."

Thomas saw that Malinda was now behind Michael. Eleanor was right, his brother's defenses were down. No one could come up behind Michael without him knowing. He didn't even sense his wife came up behind him. Eleanor poured more Scotch for them. She could see that Malinda had a glass of Scotch with her. "I tried to stay in bed as long as I could. The tossing and turning I was doing was keeping Malinda from getting good night's sleep. She didn't tell me she was in labor; I saw that they sent in more men in the dream. The way that madman was laughing, made me think something was going to happen to the bodies. It was that dream that made me get out of bed. I knew where the campsite was to be. There was a desperate need to get there. I had a wagon ready to go that night, as fast as I could I had that wagon going down the road. It felt as if it took me forever to get there. Halfway down the road I could see a raging fire. There was this smell of burning flesh. I had this fear of what that madman was doing to the bodies. In my heart I prayed that they were dead. I promised them to take their bodies to a safe place, until ye could find them.

"In the dream I saw nine men attacking our brothers. Three men at a time came after them. When I got there, I saw that man in black. He was enjoying having his dead men thrown into the fire. I could see our brother, all of them were dead except Ronald. Our brothers took out seven of their men. There were six of their men in the fire. The man in black gave the order to throw Ronald into the fire. At first, I thought Ronald was dead. I found out he wasn't yet. With the last of his strength, he drove his dirk into the man's heart. That's when I started to fire my arrows. I took care of the last man, who tried to pull Ronald into the fire. The man in black pointed his gun at that man. I should have taken out that man first, he took off with two other men.

I got down from the tree and ran to Ronald. I held him in my arms; he was slipping away from me. He told me this is the way Peter and Jonathan wanted to die. It had to be in battle, killing those evil men. I couldn't tell Malinda that they were my family. That I had lost my older brother, she knew. Right after we cleaned the bodies, she had our son. The two of us took them to Father Sinclair. In town a story went around saying there were six men who attacked them."

In his grief Michael had tossed back the last of his Scotch. "Thomas, I had enough with these feelings. It's killing me each time I must remember what happened to them. Ye may be the youngest but ye have learn how to let go. Thank ye little brother, I see that ye want this over with. That ye want to see our children grow up."

Thomas knew what he was going through. His own heart was braking to see his brother torn apart inside. Eleanor came over to Thomas. Michael saw what this was doing to Thomas and him.

Malinda put her arms around her husband and pulled him to her. "It's all right my love, ye did what ye had to do. These were his last wishes; come with me it's time to let go my love."

The two of them walked into the trees. Thomas felt his heart was breaking for his brother. Eleanor spoke, "Honey what the two of ye have done, is taking a toll on ye two. What ye had to do to save your own life. I stayed on my knees praying ye will be safe, I saw ye fighting with those men. I watched that black cloud moved over ye and Duncan. I saw it change to a hand and take your shield off ye both. That hand then had a dirk, and it was thrust into your arm. It was as if ye didn't hurt ye. The way ye took it out of your arm and through it at that man."

Thomas pulled her to him; all he wanted was to go home. "Have I told ye I love ye."

Eleanor touched his face. "No… not for a little while, I always love to hear those words."

He loved holding her in his arms. "Then I will have to say it more often to ye. When I went away for two years. I wished that ye didn't have to go to all those parties. It was bittersweet to see ye at Holy Trinity Church?"

Eleanor spoke. "I knew that was ye. I was looking out the window when I saw three men. My heart told me it had to be ye. I called to ye and ye heard me."

* * * * *

Thomas looked around and saw that his mother and father were coming up the hill. They had Michael's two children. "Mamma looks to be so happy. We are in a bittersweet moment. They will need these children to help them to get over this.

Eleanor saw Michael's baby. "I love little ones; I can help others with their baby. For now, we can have the enjoyment of trying to make one. I think we can try for a baby next year.

* * * * *

Thomas thought we will have to do a lot of practice making love. "Shall we meet our niece and nephew?"

Before long, his wife will want one of her own. Now it began, the two of them walked down the hill. "Thomas, I want to hold the baby first. Go and give your mother a hug so I can take the baby from her."

Franceam went over to Thomas, and he wrapped his arms around his mother. It was so good to be in his mother's arms, he felt as if he never left home. When Thomas opened his eyes, he saw a beautiful picture of Eleanor holding a baby. In that moment, it was their baby.

His mother knew all about what happened to him. "Tell me son, how is my baby boy feeling."

Thomas looked at his mother and she saw this once before. With their father and his brother. "I'm doing much better mamma. Now that all his evil spell is out of my body. I'm just happy to be home again. Before ye ask Michael has finally let those feelings go. He is with his wife.

His father had his grandson with him. "Papa, who is that man in Nana's arms...?"

The boy looked hard at Thomas. "That is my son, your father's brother."

The boy looked at his grandfather. He noticed he looked like his papa. "What do I call him Papa."

Being young he had to staired at Thomas. "Uncle Thomas."

The boy shook his head no. "I will call him Gunkel…!"

After a moment, the child knew he was safe. Little Ronald said. "I am Ronald Scott. Papa said ye are my Gunkel."

Thomas smiled at the sweet boy. "Aye… That I am your uncle. I like the name ye gave me Gunkel. Would ye mine if I hold ye."

Ronald looked at his grandfather to see if it was all right. "Ye can go to him, ye will always be safe in your Gunkel's arms."

Thomas's eyes filled with tears. When little Ronald wrapped his arms around his neck. The feelings poured out of him. He couldn't hold his older brother's child. Ronald looked at him when he heard him take a breath. He took his finger to catch a tear. "Gunkel why are ye crying, Daddy said big boys don't cry."

Thomas smiled at his nephew. "Like I told your daddy, it's all right for big boys to cry when he's sad or happy. Ye see when ye are very sad, the body needs to let go at times. Like now, Ye see little Ronald I didn't get to hold my oldest brother's child. He left this earth not long after he was born. I'm not sad, little Ronald. These are happy tears. For now, I can hold my other brothers' child. Your daddy is now the oldest out of three sons. We have lost our brother and his son and wife."

He looked at his uncle closely. "Gunkel did ye cry when ye got hurt."

A smile came over Thomas. "No…, I didn't cry then. When I lost a lot of blood I blacked out. I don't cry easily. Now that I can hold my nephew for the first time, I'm happy and sad all in one."

Little Ronald looked puzzled at Thomas. Then said. "Those boxes over there have your other brother inside."

Thomas smiled as his eyes filled with tears. He bit his lip. "Your daddy, name ye right. Ye are very smart like your other uncle. We may have lost our brother. What made him who he was. Ye have a little of him in ye. I love ye little Ronald, welcome to the family my boy."

Thomas threw him up into the air and caught him. He knew it was too soon to do that with his arm. Then he heard his mother and Eleanor say. "Thomas MacGregor don't ye do that again, your arm may start bleeding, I don't want to stitch ye up again."

Little Ronald saw his uncle bit his lip again. "Gunkel, it hurt ye."

Thomas nodded his head. "Aye… that it did. We will try that again in a month. How does that sound."

His little eyes had a twinkle in them. "Good I like that it was fun. I love ye too Gunkel. Don't hurt yourself like that."

Daniel smiled and looked up into the heavens. One single tear rolled down his cheek. A prayer went up, *"Thank ye Lord for giving this sweet boy to us Amen."*

*   *   *   *   *

Time went quickly for the families as they ate a feast in their honor and drank to their memories. They told stories about Ronald, Jonathan, and Peter. Stories of the three men made them laugh and cry right up to sunset.

Everything was brought with them. The camp was clean as if they were never there. Thomas took care of that part. They had walked to the cemetery, and tonight each of the three families buried a son. Father had gone to each of the burial sites. One by one they laid their son and their brother to rest. He had blessed each one of them before they laid them to rest. The last body to be laid to rest was Ronald. The sun was starting to rise. The men had placed the last shovel of dirt onto the grave. Then the three families heard two eagles cry out overhead. The women were laying rocks around the gravesite.

Michael's son broke the silence. "Daddy, look over there." As little Ronald pulled on his father's clothing.

Michael didn't know what his son wanted. "Aye…, son what is wrong."

He had wave to this man he seems to know. "Daddy there is your brother, he's standing over there. He talked to me before we left to come here. He said he was also my uncle; his name is like mine."

Michael was surprised how well his son was talking at only two years old. Everyone stopped and looked up. Right in front of the grave was Ronald.

The two brothers went over to their brother. "Ronald, I thought we had said are goodbyes to ye."

Ronald was looking at everyone. "Thank ye for bringing us home, I wish it were all different then it came out to be. Remember this isn't over with, ye have until the next full moon.

He looked at his brother, what he understood was Ronald in his own way. New we would turn to each other in times of need. "Michael it's been hard on both of us. How about we start as friends? Being brothers is the easy part; I didn't want to be the oldest either. I know ye always went to Ronald, as friends we can go to each other in times of need. I know ye will always have my back as I will have yours. I can't keep secrets from Eleanor. I found out that day with Ronald crying is not weakness. All it does is clear your mind. Then ye can deal with what ye must."

CHAPTER EIGHT

The Eagle's cry out.

BEFORE MIDNIGHT THEY enjoyed the stories about Ronald Jonathan and Peter, it made them laugh and cry. They had a feast in their honor; they drank to their memory. Just before the sun went down, they heard two eagles that flew around the three caskets. With all the stories and the food and drink were gone. Right at midnight, the three families broke camp. All signs of them being there were gone. The head of each of the three families where in front of the wagon. They will lead everyone to the cemetery. Father Sinclair will drive the wagon behind them. Their mothers will be next in their buggy. Their brothers with their brides will follow behind their mothers. Each of the three families will bury their son that night. In the cemetery each family had their own plot.

The McKinnon family plot was first. They laid Peter there next to his grandfather. His three brothers and cousins will lower him down, as Father said prayers over the body. Peter will lie next to his grandfather and grandmother. This family along with cousins will help to cover the hole.

The next plot was the family of the Heart's; Jonathan will be placed also by his grandfather. His brother and three of his friends will lower the body as Father said prayers.

Under the cover of darkness, the families buried their brothers and sons. They fought as heroes for freedom. At least their bodies were back in the Highlands once again. It took them until the next twilight. Ronald now lies next to his wife and child. In the sky the two eagles flew around the coffin, the cry from the eagles went out when the dirt went in the hole. Father said prayers as the last shovel of dirt covered the whole.

In stone Thomas had placed these words. "Here lases Ronald McGregor a man who is free at last."

By the tree three young boys were playing while the women had placed rocks around the grave. No one knew that Marian was helping them. Until they heard her say. *"Ronald McGregor my love. It is time to go home with me and your son."*

Everyone looked up there stood Ronald's wife. Then her husband stood by her side. *"Marian my love how I missed ye."*

It was Keith who cried out. *"Daddy…, I missed ye daddy."* Keith ran to his father's open arms.

Little Ronald was by his father's side; Michael had picked his son up. "Daddy Mick and I had fun with Keith. He was playing with us while everyone packed up. He asked me if I was his cousin. I said aye…, your daddy is my Gunkel."

Keith waved at Michael and little Ronald. Michael waved at Keith and his brother. Seeing Ronald with his family made tears come. Malinda, his wife, stood next to him. On the other side of Michael, stood Thomas and Eleanor, she was holding on to his arm. Ronald was looking at the once he loved. He saw his sister Catherin, she was coming up the hill with William. There was his mother and father, with his two uncles and their wives. These strong and beautiful people were his family.

Ronald looked around, he didn't know what to say. *"I stand here trying to think of the words to say. Michael, I put ye through hell. Ye stood by us in what we wanted to do, Ye saved our bodies so we could be here in the Highlands. Malinda ye are a wondaful woman a good mother too your children, the best wife to my brother Michael. Thank ye for what ye did for us, my two uncles and my father. Thank ye for helping Thomas get us home.*

"Thomas ye were the one to pull this off for us. William and Duncan ye three, found us. I think the two years ye found who ye are. Thomas and

Eleanor, the keeper of the Magic Fairy Roses. Don't stop believing in these roses. Eleanor Ye was always to be Thomas's mate. Remember our time on earth is short for the ones who complete their tasks. Love them with all your heart and keep them safe the best ye can. Uncle Donald thank ye for helping them, I wish this were over with. Thomas and Eleanor Ye are the key to all of this. Don't be afraid of your dreams, Marcos needs ye to be afraid of him. Ye know that he is using Albert. That is what he does, in the future Marcos children will help the next Thomas and Eleanor.

"*There is a demon that ye must take down. Also, there is someone who will need your help. Thomas Ye will be the one to help him. Make sure ye put this and everything else in your journal. Michael I must ask ye to go after these men who's left. Ye must stay here until the full moon. If I can... I will be back to help. Thomas believes everything Eleanor tells ye.*

"*All ye women has your own gifts. What I mean is, "Ye can see things in a dream or vision. There are others can be strategizing problems; there can be a large amount more gifts.*

Malinda, I'm sorry to take him on another journey. Aye... he will be safe with what my brother has gave him."

Malinda had tears in her eyes. To see a beautiful family wiped out like Ronald's. "Then Ronald I will do my part. I will always be there when he needs me. Please end this soon. Ye say we are strong women. I find I'm stronger when my man is with me. Our men will do what they must to take down this evil man. I just want to live with my husband and children. Then ye can rest in peace with your family."

She moved closer to her husband, more tears rolled down her cheeks. As they stood looking at Ronald's family. Everyone there had witnessed what Ronald had said, they could feel the strong magic.

Ronald looked at his old friend. "*Briana and Duncan, I'm happy that ye found each other. It took ye a long time to find Briana. The Lord had to send ye that storm to get ye to go that way. Michael had left the horses to let ye know ye were home. It was time ye have a family of your own.*"

Duncan wiped the tears from his eyes. "We've already started. I'll miss ye... rest in peace old friend."

He placed his hand on Briana's stomach and smiled at Ronald.

Ronald had a big smile on his face. *"Catherine and William, I knew, ye two were meant for each other. William, take care of my baby sister. I may not be here anymore. If ye hurt my sister, ye will have to deal with my brothers.*

William pulled Catherine into his arms. "I will always take care of her, I didn't know back then she was for me. Catherine is my love, my life. I loved her back then. I thought it was the love of a sister. Your sister… made sure that I knew that her love… wasn't for a brother. The feelings she had brought up in me. Well… it took me a while to realize she was the only one who could do that to me."

With that said he looked at his brother. *"Thomas I'm sorry I made ye grow up faster than ye wanted. I knew ye could deal with all of this and more. Ye are a strong man who found something wonderful. What ye have found… never doubt yourself or the power ye have from it. Eleanor, I always knew there was something about the two of ye. Ye was always there when Thomas needed help. I know now ye are his soul mate.*

"That battle we went through together it felt like we were in hell; without our fathers being there all of us wouldn't be here. Thank ye for saving us all when ye did. Your love for Thomas is strong. Take care of each other always."

Eleanor went into Thomas's arms where he gave her a kiss. Then turned Eleanor to face Ronald. With his arms around her waist.

She spoke. "I didn't do that much to help ye all. Thank ye Ronald for saying that to me. Aye… I do love Thomas with all my heart. I will always love him. Ye may be right about our love for each other. Thank ye for finding that spell, to free himself from that weakness he had."

Marian looked at her man. When a bright beam of light came from the heavens. *"My love it's time we must leave here. The family has much to do before ye see your brothers again."*

Each of them watched Ronald take his wife into his arms and kiss her. Keith put his hands over his eyes. With that it gave the families something to laugh and smile about. Keith peaked out between two of his fingers. His father had deepened that kiss. All three children had hied their faces in their father and mothers' neck.

Keith looked at his cousins. *"I will always remember the time we had. Thank ye… my two Gunkel's for playing with the three of us. I will remember ye all. Little Ronald I like the name for uncle as Gunkel. That name will remind me of ye."*

Before they left Ronald went over to his mother and father. *"Mamma and Dad. Thank ye for being there for my brothers and me. For your three sons. Ye two made us who we are today, not only ye taught us how to read and write. Ye showed us how to work together with are brothers and sister. The four of us can work together. Dad Ye showed us how to use the tools we use in fighting. Ye gave us the knowledge…, to be able to live off the land. We know what it means to be free, and how each of us must have paid for are freedom. The three of us men couldn't have done what we had to do without it. Mamma and Dad don't think I was a weak man. Ye wouldn't understand what I'm going to say. I couldn't do anything more here on earth. I gave my friend and cousin what they asked for. To die as men… before they were too weak to be able to fight in a battle. This way they fought for what they believed in. Freedom! I love ye both. Remember that always."*

His father looked at his son then at his wife. When she nodded her head, Daniel spoke. "My boy we understand more than ye think. Your mother and me never thought ye were a weak man. Everything your mother and Eleanor saw in their dreams. Ye three men didn't lay down and die. Ye fought to the end. Ye took out a great amount of his men as ye fought until they took your life. Ye three were fighting evil. What ye were talking about your going to come back to fight that evil man in the spirit world. What my three sons done took all your skills and willpower. When Michael comes home this last time. There will be another battle. This will be to end this evil man and the men who works for him. Son we will make shore that everything ye five men need will be there for ye. We love Ye and your family so much. All I can do is pray this will be over with soon. Then ye three can rest in peace."

Ronald went over to Father to help his family. *"Father Sinclair when Michael brought the bodies to ye. Ye had helped him with everything. Ye used the list he gives ye. For two-years ye look after us, as men tried to get our bodies. Then when the true family came ye understand why that list was important. I was pleased that ye came with them. Ye stop Rodney from finding out that the bodies were there at the bottom of the wagon. Ye didn't stop there, ye helped Eleanor to save her husband. Now that we are home and there is still more, we must do. I ask ye if ye will back the five men who must stop evil. There will be a young man who will need your help. He has a vessel going into his chest, it will be up to ye to remove that evil vessel."*

Father Sinclair was pleased with his words. "My son when it is time I will be by their sides. The Lord told me to come to the Highlands. Evil is trying to overrun the Highland's; there is The Lord's work that needs taken care of. I must help take down this evil man we are to send him to be judge. Go now for The Lord is calling for ye. I will see ye again my son."

Ronald closed his eyes and nodded his head. When he looked up, he gave them a big smile. He went back to his wife and son picking up Keith. Then he wrapped an arm around his wife's waist. Once again, the bright beam of light appeared in front of them. The three of them looked over to their families.

The three spirits spoke. *"We love ye all. Take care of each other until we meet again."*

They walked toward the heavenly light as it got brighter. The magnificent beam of light surrounded them, until they disappeared into the heavens.

*   *   *   *   *

Later that day when the family were resting or headed back to their homes. Thomas and Eleanor had to do something very importin before they could rest. They still had to take care of the roses. Hidden in the belly of the wagon were the three rose bushes. Gallivan had placed the wagon near the rose garden. It was time to find out if his love could find the right rose bush. "Honey when I lift this lid place the wood on each side."

Thomas took out the tablet with the wooden box and handed it to Eleanor. When she opened the box, she read what was inside. It read under this tablet lays three rose bushes. These roses are a deep cherry red. They come from fairy magic. See if ye can please them. Eleanor understood what the plants needed. She saw three bundles wrapped in canvas. One by one she took them out and brought them to the bench near the castle. When the rose bush was out, he lowered the lid. Thomas watched her take the last rose bush to the bench. Eleanor took off the lid to the barrow of water. "I understand what these roses need. What do ye think of your mother's rose garden?"

At first, he thought. *"Did I even look at his mother's rose garden yet. No, I haven't."*

What she had brought with them, when the two of them had fed the roses for the first time.

When he turned around all he could say was. "Wow Honey! What have Ye been feeding these roses? I haven't seen any rose gardens as beautiful as this one. Is this the same stuff that ye fed them the first time."

Eleanor took Thomas over to a barrel of water. "I've been working on the best way to feed these roses. Grana and I produced this formula and poured it into the barrel of water. It works the best on these roses. Let's see if these fairy roses still like what I had given them the first time."

With the metal vase near the barrel. Eleanor drawn out a pitcher of the water. She knew turning over a little bit of dirt would help that part; there wasn't enough dirt to do so. As she poured the water. It amazed her when the rose petals disappeared as they placed them on the vest. These roses are magical. The power these petals hold saved the men who fought with Thomas. Now she must make one of these roses appear to her. When Thomas had to do it, he had to make all of them appear. For support she took hold of her locket. She took a deep breath and felt her man's arms go around her waist. Then she poured the fertilizer into each of the plants. Thomas took the vase from her and put it on the bench.

He started to kiss her neck. "Honey it's going to be all right." Thomas then rubbed her neck and shoulders. "You're tight in your neck muscles all the way to your shoulders. Honey the rose bush will show itself to Ye. Don't doubt yourself, my love. Ye had save these roses and the ones at the land of the Fairy's."

Quickly she turned in his arms. "Thomas, I love ye with all my heart. What if the rose bush doesn't show itself?"

Thomas looked at his wife. Then he spoke. "Eleanor comes out from this cloud of doubt. It's not like ye to doubt yourself. Honey these past few days has been hard on both of us. We haven't had enough sleep. The two of us haven't been a loan much." Thomas took both her hands and kissed the back of her hand. "I would love to take ye to are bedroom and make love to ye."

He turned to look at the land. He ran a hand through his hair. Michael had come down the path to the rose garden. Eleanor spoke. "I'm so tired all this time felt like a nightmare. If my brother didn't do what he did. I could have lost ye."

Thomas had spun her around to face him. He could see she needed to cry. Then it was as if the flood doors opened, and the tears came pouring out. She had buried her face in his neck. In the back of his mind, he knew his brother was watching them. "There's my love, ye had needed to cry. Just let it out, I love ye so much. You're not going to lose me. Will make sure of that at the full moon. Look at me." He had brushed the hair away from her face. "You're so beautiful your eyes seem to bewitch me." Thomas lifted her chin up to kiss her. Her lips had a salty taste as he deepened the kiss.

After a moment Michael cleared his throat. "I'm sorry to but in on ye. How about the two of ye stay at the house? My children are staying with their grandparents. Then tomorrow Thomas Ye and I can work at your home. While Eleanor helps Malinda get our home set up for the children. Ye can use one of the bedrooms until…, we get your home built. I thought ye can stay with Malinda while I'm gone. What say ye brother."

Thomas looked at Eleanor. She nodded her head yes. "Aye…, That sounds like a plan."

Michael smiled at them. "Good… Thomas after ye plant the two rose bushes on your land. I wanted ye to know that our parents are going to have a party for the four couples. Father will bless our marriage then. Thomas thank ye for setting up are home. How about ye show me how to whittle a toy for my son? He loves the horse ye made him."

When Michael was gone Thomas guided her over to a corner of the castle. He had put his back to the wall and pulled her to him. With one hand around her waist and the other hand moved over her face. "Ye are so beautiful, in my travels I couldn't find a lass like ye. No other woman I saw could hold a candle to ye. Honey I will do everything in my power to come back to Ye. I will be all right.

He kissed her lips then his tongue brushed over them. When her lips parted his tongue made love to her mouth. Eleanor had her arms around his neck. His hands pulled her bottom into him. She could feel his heat pushing against her clothes. In a husky voice he said. "Honey would ye enjoy making love now or later."

He had lit her body on fire. "How about both."

Thomas loved her answer, as he turned her and put Eleanor against the wall. His mouth enjoyed her lips as he kissed his way down her neck. How he loved her blouse as his hand pulled down her top. His thumb rubbed over her nipple until it was hard as a nub. He held her breast his lips took her nipple and suck on it. Eleanor felt the pull that traveled down to her heat. That is all it took before they were one. He felt her hand tighten on his hips as her body push against his heat. There was an explosion inside her body. Her head had been buried into his neck. She went for his ear lobe, then bit it as she started to suckle it. Before it was over Thomas was bringing her back up. Her body bucked as the pleasure washed over her. There was another explosion inside her as the two of them came together. His mouth covered her lips. His thoughts went to her. *"Honey how I love ye."* He was against her as he tried to catch his breath.

While he had taken care of himself. She had fixed her outfit. Eleanor was a maze that her body was still tingling from what he had done to her. It was time to find out if the rose bush will show himself. Thomas came over to her. "Did ye enjoy what I did to ye."

Eleanor felt so relaxed when she went into his arms. "Aye… I still fill the tingling there. Kiss me my love."

I love being one with ye, when we have our home built. I like to do other things to ye. I want along sex life with ye. When ye are hot for me come after me. I will love to oblige ye." Thomas then kissed her and pushed her bottom into him. "I'll make love to ye as often as ye let me.

"Come on let us fine this rose bush. The roses had time to drink the water. See if they like some more."

How wonderful it will be, being a father. I hope that I know everything that my father knows. He said ones ye start kissing sex gets in the way. I can't go back to being just friends. Ye are still my friend. Now ye have become my lover and wife. After a while we enjoyed ourselves. When the time is right, we will enjoy making our child together. Then we will become parents. What do ye say to that?"

Eleanor had a big smile on her face. "Do ye think a year will be enough? We could go for a year and a half. What I'm doing will help us, I want to be there for Ye. To go anywhere ye like. If ye want me and no one is around so, be it."

Thomas had that devilish look. "Are ye saying I can have ye now. That we don't have to worry about getting ye with child?"

Eleonor laughed. "Aye… does that mean ye are going to have me a lot." When she had said that. Thomas faces turn red. "Ye were thinking that also. I think when we been lovers. We were both wet. When ye don't know what it was like and your dryness it will hurt. That is what I can tell are new brides. If their man take care of her. They will have a wonderful sex life."

Eleanor went over to the roses. "Honey, I guess life is a big lesson."

She poured more of the water into the rose bushes. "Thomas after we are done, will get are things."

He was watching her move, how he loved her. "Honey I've already sent everything to the wagon. We can go and play with little Ronald. Before we leave, we can see if the roses have bloomed."

Thomas was looking over the land. What Meghalaya had said about their children worried him. Thomas had waved his hand, and his journal appeared. "Honey Meghalaya told me that Marcos even when we defeated him. He will come back to the new world. She said that our children will have to take him down. The roses will go on because there is a son through my brother. That is why he was trying to kill off the MacGregor's men, doing so he kills the roses."

These days have been hard on all of us. Being at home is wonderful. What my brother had said. It scares me to know that the man in black will be looking for my wife. When I'm alone I will see what he will be up to. Thomas keeps writing so the next Eleanor will marry one of our sons. He wonders if my wife and I will be able to help them. I have a feeling the next Thomas will have to make sure he is stronger as a young man.

Your name Meghalaya said could be Ellen and Tom. If ye need to find out what is coming don't forget about the roses. Ye will have to use the rose stem to see what Marcos is up to. For in your time may be different than ours. Use the rose stem or branch to find out what ye need to know. Good luck my child.

*　*　*　*　*

Eleanor was looking at her man. Something was wrong. "Are ye all right Honey?"

Thomas had brushed a hand through his hair. "Aye… what would be wrong. I have a beautiful woman that is my wife. Why are ye asking me that?"

Eleanor had a bad feeling about what it might be. She had to take care of the roses first. May be he would talk to her after they fined the one rose bush. She had turned around to see if the rose was going to appear to her. "It's okay, Thomas will ye dig a hold for this rose bush?"

He looked down at the garden to see if there was room. He needed it to be next to his mother's first rose bush. Eleanor went over to the three bundles to see if they needed more water. She could see that the roses hadn't shown themselves yet. Two of them were still dry. The one in the middle was moist. She got more water to pour in all three of them. She felt the rose bush that was wet, she ran her hand over the trunk of the rose bush and found it. Slowly she worked her way up the trunk until she came to one of the branches.

*　*　*　*　*

Eleanor followed the branch, until she ran into one of the thorns and cried out. "Ouch… that rose bush bit me."

She could see a drop of blood left behind. It looked like it was hanging in the air with nothing to hold on to. Thomas went over to Eleanor and looked at her finger. He wiped the blood away and placed her finger in his mouth. She just stared at him. Thomas was watching her eyes, as he moved her finger in and out of his mouth. "Thomas why is my heat throbbing again. Honey, I don't understand this. How could something like this make me want ye inside me." All she could do was close her eyes and let those feelings wash over her. He drew her into his arms and kissed her deeply. When he pulled away, she looked into his eyes.

Eleanor found that it was also making him hot for her. "I think when were on our land I will have ye again. I will make love to ye by the water." When Thomas looked up, he saw the blood on the thorn and went over to the rose bush. "Well now, this must be the one."

He rubbed the blood into the trunk of the rose bush. When he had done that the rose bush appeared to him.

Eleanor clapped her hands. "Honey ye have done it, now we can see the rose bush."

Thomas had the rose bush in his hands. "No…, I wasn't the one. Ye were the one to find the right one. The rose bush needed your blood to see if ye are my soulmate."

She was watching what he was doing. "Thomas did the rose bush bite ye."

He looked puzzled. "I don't remember. What if you're the key to all of this? I was the one to take off the stone from the roses. I had to pick up each of the roses before ye could put the petals on the vest."

Eleanor looked at the rose bush. "Did Meghalaya tell ye to put the rose petals on ye."

Thomas looked like he was going over what she had told him. "I don't believe she knew but then again. In her story she said that his daughter was putting rose petals on his clothing. Meghalaya told me to put rose petals over my heart just before the battle. We are going to have to see if those books ye found will tell us the rest of the story.

"Let's get this rose bush planted. Then we can play with little Ronald for a bit. Will come back and see if a rose bloomed yet. Make sure we have the plant food for the other two roses. When it is the full moon. We will make sure my brother has all his weapons ready for him.

Thomas finished the hole for the rose bush. It had brought the memory of Keith and little Ronald when he was playing with them. Michael son loved his cousin. Why did they have to killed Marian and her son Keith. Eleanor could hear his thoughts. She felt the raw pain he was feeling and brought more water over the hole. They put the rose bush into the hole together. This time one of the thorns bit Thomas. She made him rub the trunk of the bush with his blood. She had cleaned his finger off and put it into her mouth. He watched her and brushed her hair from her face. He had pulled her up to him for a kiss. As they buried the rose bush, she felt he had to get up. Eleanor knew it brought the memory of burying his brother back. She didn't dare to speak because his mine was going over everything that happened. He wouldn't hear her even in his mind. His raw pain was making her cry. The tears rolled down her cheeks and onto the rose bush, it soaked up into the plant. Where the tears had landed a small bud appeared. Thomas had bent his head in prayer. *"Lord, I don't understand why things happen. Ronald had so much to live for. A beautiful wife and child on its way. This man name Marcos had her killed. In the blink of an eye, he lost everything.*

"The spirit of Ronald and his family. Their spirits came down to staying with us until we buried Ronald. He had asked Michael to take down those men. Thank ye for letting them stay with us. Lord, I had used the stem of the rose. I saw Michael hit that man in black with his arrow. The young man with him waved his hand and they were gone. That means the young man has magic. If Marcos lived, then he must have given his soul to the devil himself. That young man with magic, we four will go and take him down.

"Eleanor's dream told her that Marcos was using Albert's face. She said Albert was asking for help. What she saw was a locket going into his chest. He's been trying to dig it back out. Albert must be the young man that Marcos wants to take his body over."

He's tried to scare my wife; he's angary with her for taking that woman from him. I must keep Michael's wife and children safe along with my wife. I heard her say she likes to have one or two things made from wood. Then we will put the rose petals on them afterward."

Eleanor heard what he was saying. When he stopped praying, she spoke. "Amen!"

She had gone over to him and put her arms around his waist. She started to kiss the back of his neck. She could feel his body relaxing. "Honey you're going to put me a sleep doing that. Ye heard me didn't ye?"

Thomas had brought her to face him. He knew that he needed her to make him feel whole.

He knows that he will not sleep without her anymore. "Honey with what we went through I need ye. Please make me hole, I feel so lost right now."

Eleanor had pulled him down to her mouth. This time she was the one to make love to his mouth. As she kissed him, she said in her mind. *"Aye… let us go now, I need ye also. It's been a long-time sense ye been on our land together."*

From Thomas window Daniel and Franceam watched them. "Honey, I wish this were over for them. Michial is hoping to live there with his wife and children. Eleanor showed me how bad that gash was, that man wanted him dead."

Daniel could almost feel his son's pain. Michael wants it over with also. "Aye… Ye are right. I know that our boys would like her to be able to get their gifts from the rose bush.

Franceam was watching the rose bush. "Dear do ye see what I see?"

Daniel had a big smile on his face. "There is a rose blooming, no…, there are a larger amount of blooming. He must see if one of them will drop into his hand.

Franceam was worried about a dream she had. "I've been having dreams of two men.

One of these men is old his face looks evil. The other is young; he looks to be fighting with a locket. This is especially important to the man who looks evil. There is two men with him. Every time he is fighting the locket. This young man puts him a sleep. Honey, I could see the locket was going into his chest. What does this mean?"

Thomas and Eleanor came into his room. The two little ones were sleeping, he then said. "The evil man is Marcos; he wants to take over Albert's body. He's been calling Eleanor for help. Marcos has been trying to scare her. He's been telling her when he gets his new body. She will be the first woman he has to give her a son. If he doesn't get a son from her, she will die. I'm hoping the roses will bloom before we go to our land."

Franceam looked out the window and saw the rose bush fully bloomed. "Son come over here and look outside my boy."

At last, the roses bloomed, and the two of them went to the garden. Thomas went over to the rose bush. She had given the two roses more water. Still the dirt was dry, the roses must be like what she put in the water. In the garden Thomas went to the new rose bush. He placed a hand under one of the roses and thought of Eleanor.

"In his mind he saw her at the age of ten. He smiled at the memory of her being always underfoot. It never felt like a job teaching her things. Eleanor always made it fun to be with her. Then the memory changed to when the bear came after her. He remembers the fear was grate, that he could have lost her if he didn't do something quickly. Could that have been when he fell in love with her? It was right then when the rose dropped into his hand. His cousin Meghalaya had said this would happen. His eyes opened and he took the rose and breathed in the sweet scent.

In Thomas's room his parents watched their son fall to the ground. Eleanor had just turned around to see him fall. He was on his knees and went backwards. She got to him quickly and went to her knees to take him into her arms. He was out for a bit.

Franceam was getting worried about her son. "Daniel something is very wrong with our son. He's been out for a bit. We should go and help Eleanor with him."

Daniel turned to his wife. "No, my love, this is only for Thomas and Eleanor. Our son is at the magic rose bush. Didn't ye see the rose drop into our son's hand? They had said the longer he is out it means his loves for her has no boundaries."

Franceam had looked back out the window. She saw that their son was on his feet. "Aye… He had breathed in the scent of the rose."

Daniel kissed his wife. "This will tell them; how much, they love each other. That's why we could see the rose drop in his hand. Donald told me the story about this magic rose bush. Didn't ye see your son breathing in deeply of the scent of the magic rose. This rose bush will tell Thomas without a doubt if he really loves Eleanor."

Franceam knew her son was in love with her. "I hope he will not question his love for her again, we know he loves her. He was willing to give his life to save her when the bear attacked."

Daniel smiled. "Aye… he would also do it for his sister. If ye remember he thought of Eleanor as his little sister. When he across over he knew he would marry her before he left. He knew she was his soulmate. This tells them their love can endure challenging times, that they can weather out any storm.

Franceam looked at her husband. "Aye… Honey he would let ye take his sister into the castle. With Eleanor no one could touch her until he laid her down on the bed."

Daniel turned; his wife toured the window, his arms around her waist. Franceam thought my young son has the one he loves. They watched the two children who grew up together.

"Eleanor knew from the time the bear attacked her, that he was in love with her. Her man was out for quite a while. She knows how deeply he loves her. His love for her has no boundaries. The magic gives them the gift of sight; she is the key to all of this. The magic rose will strengthen any other gifts they may have. We three men were riding hard toured the battle. Our son had called me. I know he could talk to his wife, from far away through his mind. What is happening to the two of them, this is only for them. I think we have seen enough."

*   *   *   *   *

When Thomas awoke Eleanor was holding him. Then she kissed him deeply. The two of them had gotten to their feet. She noticed he still had the rose in his hand. Thomas looked into her eyes. He knew now why her eyes bewitched him. It was the love he had for her. With his hand open Eleanor took the rose from him. With his arm around her waist. She breathed in the sweet scent and fell into his waiting arms.

Thomas scooped her up; he took her over to the long bench. There he sat and waited for her to wake up. He knew her love for him had no boundaries. Her senses will be stronger, their love for each other will last forever. When Eleanor woken, he drew her in closer where he gave her a deep kiss. Afterward she opened her hand there was the rose he gave her.

Thomas smiled. "We must take one of the petals and place it into the locket."

A cross appeared behind the roses. It was on both sides of the locket. "I love ye my sweet angel. Ye are mind and I'm yours. Our love is strong together we can do anything. Let's take the two rose bushes to our land. Once we plant then I will make love to ye as if it were our first time together."

CHAPTER NINE

The Roses New Home.

I T WAS TIME to plant the last two rose bushes. The place Thomas had picked was near the rock. This is where he first found out how he felt about Eleanor. The two of them set off toward their land. What Thomas didn't know was that Eleanor had a surprise in store for him. While he was gone, she had the trees he cut downturn into bords. They had cut down more trees for their home. Daniel had the logs made into bords for the barn. The money to pay for it came from Eleanor being a midwife. There was also wood inside the barn for their home. This was Eleanor's wedding gift to him. When Thomas took her off her horse, he was so pleased with what she had done for him.

That kiss lasted a long time. "Honey this is my wedding gift to ye. I know we have been married for a while now. It was Daniel and Theseus with your cousins Damian and Gallivan who built the barn. On the days I wasn't doing my rounds I helped them. These four men built two barns one for us and the other for William. Catherin helped also. Before the work started, we did a drawing to show what ye two wanted the barn to look like."

Thomas couldn't believe his eyes. He had a barn on their land. "Honey do ye like it?"

It was the place. "I'm going to have to thank them. I have something for Ye. I hope ye like them?" Thomas took out the two horses he made. They were wrapped in paper, "Here open them I had learn how to work with wood. What do ye think?"

Eleanor saw her horse and his. "Honey these are beautiful they look so real. You're going to have to make toys for your nephew and our children. I think I'm going to make our niece a doll."

Thomas went over to the barn. She had everything the way he liked. "Honey ye have the barn the way I wanted. I see ye got a large amount of rocks left over. I know what I will use them for; he waved his hand there was another place we can cook outside.

"Michael and I have enough wood to start building. Honey let's get those two rose bushes planted."

Thomas closed the barn doors. He took Eleanor by the hand, the two of them had grabbed the rose bushes. They headed towards the water, to that rock that was high on the hill. He went down on his knees. He started to dig the hole for the rose bushes. She had plant food and a pitcher to get water with. She poured the plant food into the water. Before Thomas buried the roses she had poured them in the water. Then Thomas put the stone over the roses. He had put more dirt over it. The patch of grass was put back where it was before.

"I love ye so much honey. Tell ye what, after Father bless us at this party. We will enjoy are self for three days. I will take ye to this waterfall. There we will camp; I will make love to ye in and out of the water. Would ye, like that it will be our honeymoon."

Eleanor was so happy. "Honey, it sounds so good to say ye are my husband. I didn't like not being able to tell anyone I was married. Thank heavens, I will go anywhere with ye. We must tell my mother; she keeps throwing men at me. Ye must take off that spell before the party, I have brought food for us. Let us get our food and the bear skin."

*　*　*　*　*

They took off only the things they needed from their horses. Thomas placed the bear skin down on the ground for them to lay on. She knew they weren't hungry for food but for each other. "If we had a party, we would have food and drink."

She had a small glass of Scotch that they shared. Eleanor fed him a bite of food, and he had done the same for her. There was some laughing as he tries to put a piece of meat between her breast to eat. Afterward she had started to put everything away. The last time they were here he teased her with grass.

She needed the fun and passion to come out. As before, Thomas took a long piece of grass. This time he moved the grass over her face. Then down her neck to her breast, she had given a little giggle.

With everything put away. Thomas thought it was time to start as he took is shirt off. He could hear her voice say. *"Wow…! Honey your all mind."*

She had followed his lead and took her blouse off for him. "Aye… that is just what I wanted ye to do."

He moved in so they were hip to hip and face to face. He watched her run her tongue over her lips. She saw that his breathing was shaky. When his hand cup the back of her neck. He drew her to him where is mouth claimed those lips of hers. Her hand was between his legs so close to his heat. She was trying to hold herself up, she let him feast on her breast. She had found her breathing was also shaky. He went back to her mouth as his thumb made her nipple hard. It was the moment when he sucked on her nipple where she took hold of his heat. His head popped up and his eyes went wide. "Are ye telling me ye want my heat my love."

Eleanor looked at him and she ran her tongue over her lips. "I guess I am."

Thomas smiled, tonight he will treat her as if it were their first time together. "Then let go of me. My love tonight ye will mate with the keeper of the roses. My magic is now yours so ye can use it."

Eleanor wet her lips in a sexy way. His eyes watched what she did. "Your lips are driving me crazy." He pulled her to her feet and against him for a deep kiss. She thought why I haven't noticed his body before. Because he had gotten hurt.

When he broke away, she watched him take off his kilt. His body was rugged he had a small waist and strong arms to hold her.

She notices his heat had matched the rest of his body. Slowly she unbuttoned her skirt and let it fall to the ground. His eyes went over her breast down to a small waist. He saw nice hips and strong long legs. Thomas pictured those legs around him. She could make him do whatever she wanted. Thank, heavens, he married her before he left. He moved in quickly to put his hands around her waist. Eleanor felt the strength in his arms as he lifted her up. He used his foot to brush her skirt away. Then he scooped her up into his arms and lay her on the bearskin. He went quickly between her legs.

Eleanor watched as he moved her legs farther apart, his heat in hand. It was long and hard, as he moved over her heat. Thomas played with her clit it was driving her crazy. He found when he went farther down, he slipped inside her. Then lay down on top of her, as he took her mouth into a hungry kiss. Slowly he moved inside her a bit.

He felt her nails on his bottom as she cried out. "Honey don't tease me, I need ye inside me."

Eleanor looked into his eyes. She saw the hunger for her had matched her own. For she lifted her bottom his hands cup her hips. In one smooth movement he pushed deep inside her. He took her mouth in a deep kiss.

Suddenly she wonders why her chest would burn. Then it was gone, his tongue was making love to her mouth. Until he felt her take hole of his heat. His head popped up and looked into her eyes. She saw the moment he lost control when she did it again. Eleanor moved with him until she felt the explosion the moment she came.

She held on to his back until the pleasure was gone. Why does this feel like our first time together? Then he brought her up again. This time when she came, he came. Eleanor felt the power as his heat pumped his seed inside her. She was aware of everything that was happening to her. It had taken all his strength as he dropped on top. His lips kissed her neck then went to her mouth, as he rolled her over on top of him. When she lifted her head to look at him. She found her locket stuck to him.

Thomas took her locket from around her neck. "Your locket burned me, ye don't have to ware this anymore if ye don't want to.

His mind took him back to the rose garden. He was going over every-thing they did. There was something he had felt when he closed the locket. Then he remembered there were two small crosses. Now they were gone. "Honey did ye feel like ye were burned for a moment?"

Eleanor thought about it, she had placed her hand where she had felt it burned her. "Aye that it did. How do ye feel?"

Thomas looked at her, the moment of the crosses burning them was gone. Now he was looking over all his toys. "I don't know if I need any more medicine. All I know what I have here is the best medicine I could take."

Thomas was going to throw her locket. "Honey, give me my locket. I have a feeling this locket will be very important in the future."

She grabbed her skirt and put the locket in the pocket. Eleanor looked at her husband as he moved his heat inside her. She could feel little quakes inside her heat.

His hands love to feel her firm breast, it's as if he wanted her again. Thomas went to the spot, where they were as one. It's no dream he was home and on their land. He felt her body wanted to come again; he kissed her again. "Now we rest."

Eleanor looked at him. "There will be no resting if ye don't stop those little quakes."

He felt her move over him until she was able to come again. Eleanor's body relaxed after she came, she had let out the breath she was holing.

He smiled and knew he had quite a woman who could match his needs. "I'll do better next time. I know what ye need now. Honey my body is so relaxed because of ye. Ye been my childhood friend, my soulmate and now my wife. We are one in mine and body; it's time to rest. Lay here on me and go to sleep."

Thomas covered them up. He rubbed her back until she fell asleep. The moment she relaxed he had joined her in the dream world.

The sun was high in the sky when Eleanor woke up. It was time to wash up. Thomas woke up the moment she tried to get up. He grabbed her arm and pulled her down to him. His mouth took her into a deep kiss. "Where ye going my love."

She smiled at her man. "I was going to wash up at the pond. Come with me and join me in the water."

Thomas nodded his head. When she was off him, he picked her up and went into the water. She didn't notice how deep he went. Eleanor thought to have some fun with her husband. She splashed him with water and started to laugh. Then he dropped her into the water. A squeal escapes her lips when she gone under. Thomas quickly pulled her to him.

He laughed. The look she gave him told him he was in for it. "Now ye know I can't get my arm wet."

He drew her to him. Thomas found he couldn't stop kissing her. Her wet hair was over her face. "I thought of ye a lot when I was away from ye."

He took the wet hair from her eyes. "I could picture ye with me when we were at the waterfall. I've been so hungry for ye to touch ye. I love to suckle these firm breasts, after I get your nipple hard. I have a dream of this day. To lay ye against that rock and have ye again."

Eleanor knew he needed her. With her hand she cupped the back of his neck. She pulled him to her mouth and made love to him with her tongue. She wanted him to pull her legs up, so she could wrap her legs around his waist. "Honey takes me to the rock, do what ye like to me. I want to feel something knew."

Thomas was walking over to the rock, as she moved over his heat. "Ye knew ye could get me hot again. So ye want something knew, all right."

He laid her down on the flat part of the rock, her legs over his shoulder. "Honey do ye remember what Midnight did to Sunshine."

He didn't wait for her answer, his tongue plunge between her lips. His finger moved inside her as his tongue played with her click. She didn't think she would like this, she found out that the pleasure was over the top. "Aye, ye are sweet."

He didn't keep going because she might not let him do it the next time. He had stood on this rock that was under him. It made him high enough to come inside her. He went in slow she felt him go deeper, he stopped to play with her breast. She took whole of his heat; he went to lift her bottom up. Slowly he moved inside her. Now he put her legs around his waist. "Honey move, that's it."

The two of them came together. "Woman ye are just what I needed. Is that new enough my love?"

Thomas put a bubble around the bandage. He pulled her to him and let himself go into the water together. He thought of his pour wife. "Honey I'm sorry, I haven't let ye rest much. Ye just got up when I grabbed ye. Here I'm back inside Ye tell me, is this a dream. I hope not, I can't get enough of ye."

He pulled her up to him and buried his face into her neck. There were things about which he was thinking. He had told her not to think about that man. "Why are ye thinking of what ye told me not to think about. You're not that evil man. Ye didn't kill those men just to be doing it.

"We grew up together and before ye left. Ye had showed me what kind of man ye are. I was glad that ye married me before ye left. I didn't want another woman to trap ye in marriage. To feel ye inside me back then was wonderful, and now it's even better. My body is ready for ye honey ye are everything I wanted. I'm just as hungry for ye. I could see in your eyes that it was my body who made your hunger come out. I knew when ye came home our bodies would be different. I know that after I have our baby. I won't want it as often as now, we will have to see.

"Honey, I played the game looking at the men. No one could hold a candle to ye. Now from here out, I will tell ye if it hurts. I will do something else to make ye come. I love only ye. When we have enough of just making love with each other. Then it will be time to have a child. I want this time to have ye when I want ye. I'm not ready to take care of our baby. I have my man, and he needs me as I need him. Stop worrying if ye hurt me. I need this raw sex that we been enjoying."

Thomas found their bodies and mines were like one. He was thankful she knew just what he needed. She went down to lay on top of him. Thomas was thinking of when they were children. Back then they would never think they were heading for this. Now as man and woman this is where it had led them. Just today was he trying to wash away the killing, we had to do with sex?"

*　*　*　*　*

In the castle Malinda was putting her children down for a nap. "Franceam's thank you for taking care of my little ones. Michael and I haven't been away from are children for a while. He wants to help his brother get the frame up. Our home is not that far away from them. I'm going to have Eleanor help me sit up at our home. This way we can talk and get to know each other. I'm going to bring some of their clothes with us."

Franceam was looking at her daughter-in-law. Malinda smiled; Eleanor told me she loved Thomas so much. She turned around quickly. "We were telling each other stories of when they got married."

Franceam had a big smile on her face. "Catherine is also married. We had to help the four of them. Her mother gave them so much trouble. She can't keep a secret. There were times when she gave Eleanor a bad time.

Thomas had to make it rain because her mother wanted to come here to the castle. The weather was bad, but it was a beautiful wedding. Both fathers walked them down to the fireplace. The only person that doesn't know is Bridget. She would tell everyone, Thomas made Eleanor go to those parties with Catherine. As the boys said we must play the game of looking for a mate. Michael's older brother knew a lot more about this them he let on. He didn't know that man was going to kill his wife. It will be good for ye to talk to them."

*　*　*　*　*

Michael was getting the wood that his father told him about. He had the wagon in front of the barn doors loading the wood into the wagon.

Daniel had come down to help his son. "Are ye going to help Thomas?"

143

Michael watched his father as he had picked up some wood. "Aye…, he went to plant the two roses. I saw that they found the one rose bush. There are flowers on it already. Dad was it hard to believe in the roses?"

Daniel looked at his son. "No! Not when your brother was talking to me in my mine. I see ye have your vest on. Ye will see that Thomas may have his shirt off, but his vest is still on."

Michael saw that his father had his vest on. "Aye! Thomas told me not to take it off. Dad, I knew about these roses. Ronald also knew about them. I've heard the story from Meghalaya where she placed a rose petal on me. That's why I was able to get to Ronald so quickly."

Daniel had brought out more wood. "I've knew about them also. At the time we didn't need them. Thomas needed them, Michael if William didn't think quickly as he did. We might have lost Thomas. On the day of the battle, Thomas had the week before a vision that a dirk was going to Duncan's neck. He had put shields on his neck and Thomas's arm. Ye see Eleanor saved a young woman. Thomas and William came to save them. Your brother has magic now. Meghalaya told him to make a dirk out of three rose petals. He through it at him, and it went into his skin. Thomas said he made it go down to his loins. He had done that to stop Marcos from raping these women. Then killing them because they didn't give him a son."

Michael looked at his father. "Dad to tell the truth I'm scared. I know there will be another battle coming. I was close to Ronald; I had a strong bond with him. Now it's just Thomas and I, how can I get the bond with Thomas?"

His father stopped and looked at his son. "Son the bond is there, ye are having trouble because ye are the oldest now. Thomas had that same feeling, ye are afraid to try to fill Ronald's shoes."

He looked at his father. "Dad that is what Thomas had said to me. He told me let us be friends first, being brothers is the easy part."

He smiled at his son. "For a long time, him an Eleanor was close to each other. When that bear almost killed them both. All his feelings got locked up, until the list of the suitors, along with the promise to William got in the way.

He was in the library getting a book the title on it was. Ye have--cigam. He had seen the word in the mirror. It had said ye have magic. He went upstairs, got change and thought about Eleanor. He told us that he went to see her. At the time she was washing herself naked. He then told us she was bonded to him. As he was bonded to her. He wanted to marry her at the end of the week. We had Donald marry them. With his magic he sent a gift to William. What Thomas done William had done. The same with Catherin and William."

He's been married for two years. Thomas found out that just a kiss from Eleanor had set his blood on fire. Your brother and sister are both married. Eleanor asked your mother for something so she wouldn't get with child."

Michael smiled. "I should have known that he wouldn't put her in danger, in a way I did the same, I went under a different name. Dad, Thomas, and Ronald are going to fight this man in the spirit world. He through a rose stem into the fire. To show me what Marcos is doing with his son. Marcos is going to use his son for something very evil."

Daniel went into the castle with his son to pick up his wife. "Son that is not his son. Eleanor found out with all these women he raped for a son. All he gets is girls, the woman he took was married. She was going to have a baby."

There were more things to load onto the wagon. "I see Mamma got something together for us."

Daniel smiled at his wife. "There is nothing going on that your mom doesn't know about. Now that she has those rose petals on her, we can't get away with anything."

Michael smiled at his mother and went to give her a kiss on her cheek. "Thank ye mamma for taking care of our little ones."

His mother looked at her son. "Michael make sure ye let your brother know you're coming. Remember the two of them went through a lot this week. They may be caught in the moment. Almost losing her man and him with all that killing. Sex is one way to wash away what happen to them."

Daniel had called Thomas. "Thomas your brother has more wood for ye. He will be coming there after he says goodbye to us. Will that be all right?"

Thomas smiled, he looked at Eleanor. "That will be fine dad. Eleanor and I have the frame up for downstairs. Thank ye for telling me. Tell mamma we are fine; I could feel her worrying about us. Love ye both."

Daniel told his wife what Thomas had said. Then he spoke. "They have the downstairs frame up."

Michael looked surprised. "Wow they had that much done."

His father looked at Michael. "Son, he likes to work with wood. He wants to make a shop for the winter to make things. He also likes to make knives or dirks, and shoes for horses. He's waiting on ye. I told him ye have food for them."

*　*　*　*　*

After their love making. Thomas and Eleanor went to work putting up the frame. He needed more wood for the frame for the roof. There was a place under the house to keep food. Eleanor had gone to get her husband water. He had the well dug three years ago. After she got them two cups of water to drink. That's when the two of them heard a wagon coming down the road.

"We have company coming it's my brother. I didn't realize I had missed Michael this much. The two of us were close when we were younger. Did ye know that the land Ronald built his home on? Michael wanted that piece of land for himself. Him and I with dad's help build that home. Ronald took the idea that Michael had for the home. I wonder if Ronald always knew he wouldn't live in that house. I have a feeling that Meghalaya, had let him see into the future.

Eleanor looked at her man. "Honey with the things going on. I too wonder if he had an idea know."

Michael yelled. "Hay could ye use some wood for the walls? I even have more for the frame."

Thomas smiled and yelled back. "Aye…! Does this mean you're going to help me get my home built?"

It was good to have his brother home. "Aye…! Ye have me for two weeks."

Malinda called out. "Eleanor do ye think ye could help me get my home ready for my family? Franceam said ye were free until Grana needs ye. If so the four of us can stay in our home, what do ye say."

Eleanor smiled and yelled. "That will be wonderful. Thomas said "Ye have food with ye. Let's eat then we can get the house set up for us."

When the wagon stopped and the four of them were close. Michael said. "This way ye can sleep with your wife."

Thomas stopped and stared at his brother. "Michael, I've been sleeping with my wife when I could get away from the Lowlands. Did dad tell ye I have magic."

Then he took the wood out of the wagon, with his magic. Michael looked at what he had done. Then he spoke. "If ye can do that why do ye need me."

He looked at his brother. His face had sadness in his eyes. "I didn't show ye that to upset ye. Aye…, just a wave of my hand the wood was on the ground. I like to create things with my hands, like with wood, iron. I would enjoy doing things with my brother. That's if he would like to help me."

Michael had seen the sadness that he brought on. "Thomas I'm sorry about that remark. I would love to help ye. We have a lot to catch up on. Dad told me. Ye like to make a shop for making things."

Then Thomas gave a big smile and waved his hand. Near the barn he put up a workshop. "Now if we need to make things for our homes, we can do so."

The two men went to look at the things inside. Michael smiled at his brother. "This is great, I worked in a shop also. It brought in money for us. I like to make new things for are home. Mamma said there will be a party when I come home. Once I come home after I help this town out. Father will bless the three homes and are marriages. When we are ready, he will have the licenses for us. Did William also work with wood?"

Thomas smiled and then spoke. "He likes to make bigger toys. He's been trying to whittle also. I like to make tools up for all of us. We can teach these young men to work with wood. It's a dream I had. I have friends that live about halfway down from us."

The two weeks went fast. With the help of their father and Gallivan. Thomas's home was going up fast. Inside Eleanor will also have a place to cook. He waved his hand; the item had been made with iron.

When he was gone for those two years. He learned how to do blacksmith work and woodwork. He found he was good at both. He had fixed Malinda's cooking spot along with his mother and sister. Ye could say all the women in is family had one. When the winter hit, he was going to work in his shop. He had a blacksmith shop on the other side of the barn.

*   *   *   *   *

On Friday there was the full moon. Thomas had everyone bring his vest to his land. The sky was clear, and the sun was slowly going down. There was food and drink because they had been working on Thomas's home. Father Sinclair came to see what kind of magic these rose petals had. He remembers seeing the battle. He also saw Ronald, when everyone was gone, he talked to him. Father had seen the petals on his clothing a pear and disappeared, when the moonlight hit it.

Near the pond there was a fire started. Thomas had them open their vest and lay them down one by one. Inside he printed the names to whom they belonged with his magic. Then he turned each vest over and left them on the ground. This was the first time the whole family would see the magic rose petals in action.

He had noticed that he placed the rose bushes, where he could see the mountains in the background, he felt this was meant to be. He had found the rose bushes in the same setting. There were mountains and a stream running nearby. The night was warm the heavens were beautiful. With the moon lighting the heavens, ye could see each of the stars adding its own light.

Michael and Malinda watched as the rose petals reappeared on each of the vests. It hard taken a long time before the petals disappeared once again. Father Sinclair was nearby; he was watching what Thomas was doing.

* * * * *

Michael spoke. "Thomas where are these roses ye were talking about. The moon is out, where are they."

He laughed when he took off the stone. "Michael they are right here, the reason ye didn't see them is that there is a magical tablet over them. That kept the roses hidden from the world. When I take off this tablet only then will ye see the roses. I will let Eleanor read what the words say on the tablet."

Thomas lifted the tablet off the roses. Everyone could see the roses when the moonlight hit the spot. The ones who still had their vest on, saw Ronald place all his things on the ground. Father went over all their things placing holy water on them. The brothers knew trouble was coming. There weapons had the cross and rose petals on them.

Thomas cut and past the roses to Eleanor. She had taken and placed the rose petals on Michaels weapons. As she did the petal seemed to have been pasted on the vest and weapons. Malinda took his weapons and lay them down, so the rose petal hit the moonlight. It took a bit for the petals to disappear because the roses were being charged up when the moonlight hit them.

Then Franceam had brought the things for the women. Thomas made his brother's arrows case with a larger amount of rose petals. Then his arrows when he shot them, another one came in its place. When Father blesses his arrows, he said if there is a demon the part of this arrow will turn into a cross. He had poured holy water on the rose petals. "Michael these arrows will take down demons."

Thomas spoke. "Eleanor been having these dreams. I'm going to give ye everything to bring ye back to us. We will be keeping your children safe. The women will be with me when I work on my home. Will that be all right with ye."

Michael looked at his brother. "Aye…! I'm going to leave on Monday. I wanted time with my children and my wife."

Michael had placed his son's vest on him, then he put on his own vest. He saw that his wife had her scarf on. *"Malinda can ye hear me?"*

He smiled at his wife. *"Aye…! Ye better check in everyday with me. I will do the same."*

Thomas walked over to Michael. "I don't know if ye know this. A Wizard and Fairy made these roses. Their son, our great grandfather, was part Wizard and part Fairy. He was a twin, his magic was strong, they were MacGregor's. What I'm trying to tell ye is see if ye have magic."

Michael had called his wife. "Honey could ye come over here. Thomas will ye take care of our children for a bit?" He smiled at his brother with his arm around his wife. He waved his hand like his brother does and thought of their bed. Thomas knew right where he went. *"Brother are ye home,"* he asked him. All he heard was laughter. Before they left, she had asked Eleanor to watch her son and daughter. At the time Franceam had the baby and Daniel had his grandson. He smiled when his brother and wife disappeared. "Honey, I think it's time to pour the Scotch for the men and women."

While everyone was talking Father went over to the rose bushes. He had brought with him holy water. Father blessed both rose bushes. He poured the holy water into the ground. He then placed his cross on the rose bushes. Before his eyes four rose petals appeared on his cross. Quickly he made the sign of the cross. When he did that, his cross started to glow brightly with the moonlight. Then the two rose bushes also glow brightly. Father bent his head and spoke. *"I believe Lord."*

At the time no one had seen Father do anything. This was only for Father's eyes. When he put his cross in his pocket Father Sinclair felt different.

Thomas saw his brother and Malinda pop back in. They looked happier as they walked back to the group. He knew what they had done. He looked at the heavens and said a prayer that Michael would come back to them safely. He saw that they stopped and gave each other a kiss. Malinda went over to the women, she enjoyed being around his family. Michael had walked over to his brother. "Thomas these rose petals let me call to my wife. Ye knew what we wanted to do. How far can I go and be able to talk to my wife? Before ye tell me thank ye. I know now if I keep this vest on, I'll be safe."

The three brothers together in the moonlight

Thomas felt good inside. Then he saw Ronald put on his vest. The two brothers walked over to him. "Ronald ye have your vest on now. Michael has his magic, ye should have magic also. When Marcos had that hand take off are shiels, he had to have magic. Ye are going to need that magic brother."

Ronald smiled at his brothers. *"I knew about the powers. I just wished that."*

Thomas looked at his brother. "Listen to me, I believe if ye don't use those powers with your weapons. Marcos will try to wipe ye off the face of this earth. He was a Fairy when this started. He was taken down by the twins, it's our time to take him down again."

Ronald looked at Thomas. *"So, the two of ye will take turns being a big brother to each other. All right, I will use everything the Lord has given me. Michael's meet me at the lowest part of the Lowlands. It's a small town outside England, just think of that. When ye use your magic, I will see ye there, Michael I will help ye when I can."*

On Monday Michael had to leave. The four of them rode with Michael for a bit. When they were on the other side of town he had stopped. Michael gave his son to Thomas after he kissed him good-bye. He went over to his wife and baby girl and gave them a kiss. In his mind he said. *"I'll be back my love. Take care of yourself until we see each other again."*

Michael is calling his son, little Ronald. *"Son do ye hear daddy. I love ye my boy. Help mamma when ye can."*

His son was jumping saying. *"I hear my daddy in my mind."*

Malinda called back to her man. *"I'll be fine now that Eleanor and Thomas will be staying with me and the children. The two of them love us very much. The MacGregor family takes care of themselves. Thank ye for bringing me here my love. My family is not like these people.*"

He was going to leave after he said goodbye. Michael smile and spoke, "I will call to ye to let ye know I made it."

Thomas rode over to him. "Before ye leave I have something for ye." Thomas took out a deer hide it was a little bag. Everyone watched as he placed three rose petals in the bag. Then Thomas handed the bag to him. "Ask for some money for your wife." He did what Thomas had said. Michael took out the money and handed it to her. "Just ask for what ye need. All ye must do is think about it. Good hunting, come back safe. Remember at the next full moon place everything out so the moon light can charge it back up."

Round up

Thomas and his father were in one of the pastures rounding up the pregnant horses. His father was with him when they saw one of the horses stop. "Dad, she looks as if she's in labor. We are going to the castle now. I'm able to take care of her at my place. I'll call Eleanor to go to the castle. I'm getting Malinda and the children and taking them to the castle. With a wave of his hand all the pregnant horses were safe in one of the pens.

CHAPTER TEN

Pregnant Horses & A Town to Save.

ELEANOR WAS WITH her last patient for the day. She could sense something was wrong near their home. Thomas was concerned there were too many pregnant horses. She knew that they were rounding up all the pregnant horses. With her eyes closed she thought of Thomas. She was now able to see what was happening. After giving the medicine to her patient. Eleanor road quickly to the castle, Franceam was there to greet her at the door. Malinda and the children were staying at the castle, until all the pregnant horses had their babies. Briana and her mother-in-law were also staying.

Damian was helping his father and brothers with the round up for both families. When he saw wolf tracks, he went back to his father. "Dad, I saw wolfs tracks, there close to the herd."

Donald was pleased with his son. "Will done son, now go and take out that wolf pack."

The two families helped each other out. The MacGregors barn was perfect for taking care of the pregnant filly. It was the biggest among the families, it was set up for pregnant horses. Catherin was helping William's family they were farther away.

Eleanor looked at Franceam. "My last patient told me the wolves have been going after the newborn horses. Damian was on the hunt for a wolf that looked like he was following the group of pregnant horses.

Franceam smiled when she saw Eleanor. "I know that Damian will get that wolf. Go now I have clothes upstairs for ye. There is a horse that looks like she is in labor. What the men thinks it could be twins. This will be a long night for both of us. Daniel had found that there was quite a larger number of pregnant horses. Two of the horses are going to give birth tonight, they are in the barn right now. Thomas had to use his magic to get them here, he's with her now.

"Go now and change. I must go and help my husband with the two that are also giving birth tonight. I have a feeling there may be another going into labor, Thomas has the twins."

Malinda had put her two children down for the night. Briana stayed with them because she was due to have her baby next month. Her mother-in-law was helping inside the castle. Their men were rounding up the horses. Two female's horses where given to the oldest sons if they had their home built. Their sons had each a male horse, this way they could have a small heard.

They had it planned out that there would be pregnant horses every two weeks. Someone had gotten to four of their horses. There were four females in labor tonight. Briana was helping to make food for all the men. The two youngest men their horses couldn't mate yet.

Eleanor went up the stairs quickly to their old room. It was going to get messy delivering those babies. She headed down the hill to the barn.

She had seen Daniel bring in another horse. He spoke, "I'm glad ye are here, Thomas will be needing ye. She is quite big for a young horse. I don't know how she got in with the group that we set up to get pregnant. When ye were heading home did ye happen to see Damian.

Eleanor saw he was riding down a path, it looked as if he was hot on the heels of that wolf. The sun was starting to set behind the mountaintops. Daniel was guiding the last pregnant horse. Then they heard a wolf, there were two shots that echoed through the valley.

Eleanor went over to Thomas; she knew that he didn't like the sound of the wolf. "How is she doing honey?"

Thomas shook his head. "Not good, she been in labor for a while. This filly is too young to have twins. Someone mated her with another horse, our males had no marks on them. This young horse was from the herd that was too young to mate with.

So, he used his magic to make sure they all got here. He found that it was just in time before two of them went into labor. I'm glad ye are here. Coming down the hill did ye see any wolfs around."

Eleanor shook her head no. She saw the other horse that was due this week. They are going to have their hands full. "No but Damian had seen some tracks he was following them." Then they heard gun shotes. "That sounds close to our home."

She looked around before going into the barn. "Franceam and Malinda will be here soon. They said they will be here after they change."

"I'm glad that Malinda is coming with my wife. We have three horses in labor. To be able to get four of the fillies pregnant at the same time. That stallion was horny, I believe there must have been another stallion. Someone made it possible for another stallion to have these other two horses. Our stallion doesn't have any marks on him. I know that he would have fought with the other horse. Ronald's horse, was down here with small amount of females of his own. I saw Thomas took two other females along with your horse."

Eleanor was wondering if that wolf was looking for that one with twins. "How far away was Thomas from our home when the mare went into labor. Thomas wasn't that far from your barn; he decided to bring all the horses quickly to here with his magic.

Eleanor spoke. "That was a good thing for that wolf is looking for that group."

She noticed that the filly was lying down, she heard her whinnied the young horse was scared. "Hang on girl I'll be right with ye." She gave her husband a big kiss and ran to the barn.

The town Marcos took over

Michael sat in the back of the pub drinking Scotch. It was good that he got here fast. He knew that he would have to get home soon. Ronald told me to only look for Duke Huascaran. Ye can find him in a small town just before England. Only to find out he wasn't in England but on his estate in the country. When Michael rode into town, he took a room over the pub. This way he could ask questions. He needed to find a horse that was all black with one green eye and the other blue. The people quickly made the sign of the cross. They couldn't get away fast enough from him. He thought this must be the place.

Michael thought he had better not ask any more questions about this horse. Even the name Duke Huascaran. The people thought of this horse and the man as a demon. Why would the color of the horse's eyes make any difference? He could see about the man as a demon.

Once again Michael was back undercover. He had to dress as the English did. This time he knew whom he had to find and kill. *"Ronald, I had enough with all of this. I want to go home; I miss my wife and children."*

Michael took a sip of Scotch and saw a man coming toward him. "Are you a Scotsman from the Highlands."

He looked up from his drink, there stood a tall man like himself. This man wasn't afraid to ask questions. "Aye… which I am and proud of it. Ye must be an Englishman from England."

The man looked at him, it felt as if he was sizing him up. "You're quite aways from your homeland. I see that you have one of MacGregor's horses. Since you sign in as Michael McGee, you're not a MacGregor. You must have money to have one of those horses. Why are you asking about Duke Huascaran horse? I hope you are not going to breed Terror with one of the MacGregor horses."

Michael laughed. "Ye know where my horse came from. Ye didn't know that my horse was a stallion. Who are ye to ask these kinds of questions may I ask. Are ye a bobby or a friend of this Duke Huascaran?"

That question had the man upset. "Hell no…, to both questions. I am not a friend of Duke Huascaran, are you?"

Michael looked him over. "No…, I don't know the man. I have personal business with him, do ye work for him."

The man gave a laugh. "I don't work for that evil man. All right; I'll turn the question back to you. Michael McGee, do you work for him? The reason I'm asking there have been a large amount of men looking for him. These men come to the pub and ask for Marcos. The town found out that these men are all hired killers. They all wanted to work for him, are you a hired killer who wants to work for Marcos."

That didn't please Michael. "As ye said hell no…, I told ye that I have personal business with him. Are ye telling me that all those men were Scotsmen. Is that why ye think I may be a killer. Who are ye and what do ye want with me."

Norward wondered if he could be a man that could help them. "No there not all Scotsmen. You must understand the Scots are the best killers. I work for the owner of this pub. He also owns where you have your horse bedded down.

"My name is Norward. I help keep an eye out for men that would work for Duke Huascaran. The people of this town have heard about a Scotsman called Hawk. They have said that this man came upon the MacGregor camp. There was nine men going after MacGregor's four. That Hawk killed two of the other men who try to burn the MacGregor. Since you have a horse from them, we like to know if you are that man."

Norward had stopped talking when the room started to fill up with people. "Rest easy I don't work for Duke Huascaran. Tell me what ye want from me."

In a whisper. "I'm sorry if I offend you, we'll talk later. The town needs your help to find Hawk."

*　*　*　*　*

That night Michael came downstairs. He went to the back of the pub taking a seat at one of the tables. There he could watch people come and go. A bar maiden came over to take his order. "I'll take a pint of ale and your special to go with it."

Michael had been watching for the man called Norward. He was hoping to speak to him again. This man knew his family's brand and recognized it on Shadow's rump. No one else had ever confronted him with this before. Why would it happen now when he was so close to finishing the job? Does this man know more about the MacGregor horses, than he is letting on.

When his food came, he thought back when his father gave his son a black horse. From that day when each horse was born from a different female. The boys grew up with his horse. Their father made sure that each of the horses knew his sons. Each son was able to tell their horse where to go or come with different whistles. Then there was loud talking that snapped Michael out of his daydream. He saw two men coming into the pub.

One of the men called out. "Johnny, give my brother a drink, keep the Scotch coming until he tells you to stop. That evil horse Terror tried to kill Jargon tonight."

Michael finished his meal and took his plate up to the bar. He went over to one of the corner stools with his pint of ale. There he could hear and see everything that the man said and did. Johnny could see that Jargon was scared. He asked Jargon what had happened to him.

He was trying to slow down his drinking. "Jargon where you hurt in anyway."

He didn't speak; he just kept drinking. His brother Whitley did the talking. "That damn horse should be killed just like his master; Johnny was almost hurt because of Terror."

He stopped drinking. "Enough Whitley be quiet the walls have ears. I don't want you killed for saying something like that."

The man was really scared for him. "Jargon that horse could have killed you. The owner of Terror laughed at you; that's not what I saw."

Jargon looked at him. He said that that's why I quit tonight and took my things to your house. Duke Huascaran doesn't care what his horse or his son does."

Jargon was drinking slower now. Michael could see he was getting foxed. Jargon may be he will talk freely.

Whitley his brother spoke. "Jargon, do you think he will let you live now. You know too much."

His hand shook with those thoughts. "If he's going to kill me you will know why. Did ye know that Terror fears snakes? That crazy horse loses his head when he sees a snake.

"Tonight, he almost killed himself trying to get away from that snake. I heard Terror, I could tell he was scared. I was hoping a big animal was attacking him. Then I thought better of it, I ran out of the bunkhouse before Terror woke the boss. Terror is a monster, his master made him that way."

Jargon laughed and took another drink. "He is just like his master. They're both monsters."

He laughed again. "They say, Marcos's father made him that way. Do you remember when that dog ran up to Terror barking? Terror reared up and killed the small dog."

His brother said. "I remember what Duke Huascaran did. He shot the dog's owner when he took a stick to Terror for killing his dog. Marcos let his horse maul the man and the dog until there wasn't much left to bury."

Jargon took a drink and went on with his story. "I hated to work for that man; the hate goes for his horse as much as his master. You would think that Terror wouldn't be as terrified of snakes."

Jargon laughed. "When his master is a snake himself. The town people thought that Terror and the man in black should die, for what they have done. Four long years that horse has tried to kill me. There are men before me that Terror killed, I'm lucky I have lasted this long. At the full moon that horse goes crazy, I always stayed out of Terror's way. Marcos at the full moon goes a little crazy himself. He keeps himself locked up in that house, but you hear him yelling. The only day he comes out is on a Saturday. He rides his horse on that same trail every week.

"I've heard stories about him when he was a young man from the housekeeper. When he was young, he killed just to see a man bleed. Marcos took land from good people and killed everyone; he puts the land up for rent. If these people couldn't pay, he kills them. He's hard on his horses to insure he has a black horse. Marcos had to find white horses with blond mains. He lets his horse have his way with the young horse that he has found. He believes there is a black horse after she gives birth to. If there is one that has green and blue eyes. He would not die; he had sent Albert to Scotland. Albert must look for the woman in his dream. Marcos told him to breed his horse with one of the Andalusians. Tell me do you think that sounds a little crazy,"

Jargon was fox, as he talked. He was jumping from one subject to another. Michael thought Albert was in the Highlands. He will be going after their family's Andalusians. Then he thought didn't Eleanor say that he is using Albert's face. He had said that Marcos was in the Highland just nine months ago. If that was true, then the family would have a horse that Terror sired. He must tell his brother; they will have their hands full.

Jargon went on talking. "Do you know who that man in black is. It was Marcos up to two years ago. Albert took his father's place as the man in black. Can you guess why Albert can't have a son? An old woman put a curse on Marcos because he raped her daughter. If he does have a son.

"Wouldn't his blood have the same curse? How did he get around that curse, I don't think Albert is Marcos's son. To tell the truth, Albert doesn't look anything like his father. I believe one of the women he took was already with child. Albert's wife is with a child now, they are saying she's going to have a son. There are seven daughters; this is true we will see if he has a son. If he does have a son, then he's not a Huascaran. There is one thing that doesn't make since to me. How is it that father and son are never together."

* * * * *

Then Michael called his brother. *"Thomas, do we need help with the horses."*

Thomas looked up when he heard Michael. *"Aye…, Fredrick is getting old to do what he is doing, why do ye ask. Before I answer ye, did one of our Andalusians get pregnant?"*

Thomas thought about what he was saying. *"Aye…, she had twins last night."*

Michael thought about what the man had said. "Tell me does any of the twins have one eye blue and the other green?"

Thomas was wondering where he was going with this. *"No…, but one of the female twins has green eyes and the other female has blue eyes."*

Micheal smile with that. *"This man needs to get out of here. He has been talking about this horse called Terror. Marcos must have taken one or two of our horses, he had let Terror breed with them.*

Thomas then spoke. *"Now that makes sense, both females look just like their mother. He took the ones that were too young to be breed with. We had our hands full with them. Tell them to look up to us.*

Micheal smiled. "I will send them to ye, he took care of Terror the demon horse. He has information about Marcos, ask dad what he thinks."

Then he heard from his father. *"If the man needs help from Marcos, do ye believe he is a good man."*

Then Michael moved away from the bar. *"Dad, he is a good man. Anyone running from Marcos must be good. We have no choice for whom we work, everyone needs to eat. Right now, the two men must get out of town. I will get back to Ye. I need to do a big clean up, for this town. How is my wife and children doing?"*

His father smiled. *"They are doing just find, there in the castle. We have our hands full with the two extra pregnant horses. Sent those men are way, be careful my boy."*

Michael was happy to hear everything was all right with his wife and children. *"They will be heading your way soon."*

*   *   *   *   *

Whitley put a finger over his mouth. "Quiet brother. If Marcos hears about this, you will be dead before nightfall."

Jargon spoke. "Another drink Johnny and give one to my brother, I know about Marcos. On his land, there is a building out back. One day I followed Marcos and found the building. This building is where they took the young girls that Albert raped until they are with child. Albert needs a son, or the money from his father will stop. It's because of Marcos's father so they say. His will and testament say, no son no money that is final. That's if it is true about the will and testament. I believe they like what they do. Power goes to men's heads; this man had killed women around here. These women they all had blond hair. The housekeeper said that Albert is not like his father. He didn't like going out back to the little house. The cook told me that Marcos in his youth needed a son. He took young women to get a son from them. There has been a large amount of women he had to go through. In that building there were dreadful things that went on. What I heard and could see no man should put a woman through."

Jargon had just downed the last of his drink when the door of the pub flew open. It was Norward and he moved quickly to close the door.

He went right over to Jargon and Whitley. "You two must get out of town. Marcos's men have been looking for you. You know what that means. Marcos had given orders to take care of Jargon. If any of you men know anything about Marcos's business. They will kill all of you. Don't speak of what you have heard here tonight. Let's get you men out of town. You must go now, or you will die. Now move it."

Cleaning up time

Norward didn't see Michael leaving the pub. He thought that it was time to take out these killers. When he was out of sight, he waved his hand, and he was in his room. Then he will find a snake to take out Terror. That's if there is no one around. Michael then would have a present to give Marcos after Terror is gone.

The wolf

The night came quickly. Thomas could hear the wolves in the hills. Eleanor had her hands full she needed another set of hands.

She yelled for help. "Thomas, help me I need ye to help me. One of the colts is coming, now the umbilical cord around the baby's neck.

Thomas went quickly to her side. "What do ye need from me."

The two of them worked quickly to save the little colt. "Hold the baby's head so I can get this cord from around her neck. I almost got it off, there…, let's pull her out. Then it will be time to get the other one out."

It was rough going but Thomas and Eleanor were able to save both colts. He was glad that she was home sooner then she thought. Her hands were able to pull the cord from the colt's neck. Both colts were female one had green eyes, and the other colt had blue eyes. Their markings were just like their mothers with golden brown hair. With the colts and their mother taken care of. Thomas and Eleanor went to help the others. "What a night, I think we need to wash up."

Thomas was looking at all the new colts. He went over to see if anyone needed help. "Dad has Michael got back to ye."

His father was making sure that the colts were feeding, after the mother cleaned them. "No…, not yet he said he must go to work. There is two men coming our way."

Thomas looked around and their two were doing good. "Dad if it's all right with ye. I'm going to wash up at our pond, that's if ye don't need us."

His mother came up behind her son. "Go on we got this."

Thomas smiled and with a wave of his hand. The two of them were in the pond and were naked. He was enjoying soaping her up. She was also doing it to him, then he put them under the water, their hair and bodies were clean.

Eleanor walked over to the rock that Thomas was leaning against. He pulled her against his bare chest and kissed her deeply. That kiss warmed her all the way to her toes. His skin was so warm against her that she forgot about the cold. She didn't notice she was the one against the rock. He moved his hand down toward her heat. His finger found her womanhood and there he dipped inside. "Thomas, I don't want your finger, I want ye inside me."

He smiled at her. "But honey I like their sweetness."

Eleanor through up her hands. "Are ye going to do that every time?"

He had a boyish look on his face. "Don't give me that look,"

At that moment, he was inside her. Tonight, he will have her more than once. The pleasure surrounded her she felt his heat moving deep within her. He drove her higher until they both came. The moment she came Eleanor felt Thomas's body stiffen, she felt his heat pulse inside her. He was kissing her with everything he was feeling for her. He took them under the water where he rinsed them off. "Come on we have to get out of this water and back to the horses."

He pulled her into his wet body and kissed her deeply. They had a blanket, and he laid her down on it. "I can't keep my hands off ye. I saw your stomach big with are child growing inside ye. Ye were so beautiful and still ye wanted me inside ye."

She touched his face as she brought him down to her. "Honey do ye want me now? Thomas nodded his head yes. "Aye…, that I do."

Eleanor watched her husband part her legs and come down on top of her. She felt his heat slip inside. She knew her body needed him as her fingers dug into his bottom. He knew just what to do to make her come. To feel her fingers pushing him down brought them both up until they came together.

Thomas helped her up. With a wave of his hand their clothes were dry. "Come on let us go check on are two colts." Another wave of his hand, they were back at the big barn.

Inside the barn they checked on the two babies and their mother. It was a good sign to see the babies nursing. They gave all the mother's food and water."

Eleanor looked at the two colts they help into the world. Their eyes looked different than the other colts. "Thomas, I don't know who's the father was. Now of are males has these eye coloring."

Thomas came over to her. "Micheal had called me; we have two men that is coming are way. It seems like Marcos let Terror mate with our two females. His horse has one blue eye and the other green. I knew about his horse; Rodney made it clear about his eyes."

Eleanor quickly looked at her man. "That's why I had that vision of that Englishmen at the barn in town. He was looking for a black horse with one blue eye and one green. He needs another horse. It didn't work this time. I believe he's going to be mad about that when he finds out. Thomas ye do know if ye didn't bring in those our pregnant horses. I believe we would have lost the two of them."

This young horse would have died. "I wonder if Michael had called back about that man he was talking about."

Thomas was looking at the two colts. "I haven't heard anything yet. Dad told me that he had to go to work. To me that meant there was Marcos's men was after that man. It was time to take out the hired killers.

* * * * *

Then they heard his father's voice. "Thomas, how is all our newborns doing."

Daniel came over to them. "They are all doing fine, the babies are eating now. Eleanor and I just figured out who the father was. While I was in the lowlands, Rodney painted a picture of Terror, his black horse. Marcos believed this horse with one eye blue and the other eye green, he wouldn't die. Terror must be getting old like his master. When he was in the Highlands, he went looking for a certain kind of horse to breed with Terror. That's why Marcos picked a white Andalusian with a golden mane. One colt has blue eyes and the other has green eyes. It fits the timeline when he was here. There both females and look just like their mother. We thought we were going to lose the two of them. My wife and I needed four hands to save the first colt. That colt had the cord wrapped around its neck."

Daniel looked at his son. "The two of ye always work good together. Your brother must have his hand full of those men. I'll go and check on the babies, their mommas. "Dad, we checked in on all the mothers and colt. We all had a colt to bring into this world tonight. It's good we had enough hands. How about the two of Ye rest up? I can stay to wash over the colts and mothers."

Damian and Hamish came into the barn. He had just got back from the hunt for the wolf. "I was able to get that wolf. I stopped by to check on the other pregnant horses. Right now, all is quiet for now, I didn't see any that was in labor yet.

Hamish had brought water for the horses. Thomas spoke. "We been thinking about hiring another hand. Tonight, with Eleanor's help we had saved twins colts. There is a man we heard about. Michael is sending him are way. I would like ye to teach him are ways. Hamish, now that the family is growing, we think it's time for Ye to have help. With all that ye must do, help is in big need. There have been four houses that have been going up. That means two female horses for each house. On breeding day as we bring are stallion's fillies to breed with. When they give birth, we have been having are hands full.

Hamish smiled and he nodded his head. "That's a great idea, if we have more horses, that getting pregnant there will be horses for the little ones to grow up with. Ye go into the castle and rest, I'll stay with the colts and their mothers."

The three of them went to the castle to sleep. "Good night, Hamish see ye in the morning."

*   *   *   *   *

The next morning Eleanor was helping to get breakfast. She was cutting bread up, when she heard a scream, it made her drop the knife. The vision hit her hard, she had to grab on to the table. Then she saw a young man, it was the face of Albert he was crying for help. *Please someone get this locket out of my chest. My father wants my body; he is going to give my soul to his master. I don't want to die this way. He had told me he was my father, who did this to his son. He will be here soon,"*

Eleanor saw him fighting with the locket. He was trying to dig it out of his chest. She thought this was black magic. She said the words; she closed her eyes. She tried lifting the locket a bit out of his chest to buy them time. Then she saw a tall young man around eighteen there, he had the look of a demon. She had felt her hand push away from Albert. Then she felt a strong power pushing her backwards. *"Please ye are the mate to the demon hunter. Hawk is in the town where the man in black is now. Thank you for your help I can grab it now."*

Franceam saw that Eleanor was trying to help someone. She went over to her when her hand was slap away, from what she was doing. She was behind her when Eleanor was thrown backwards. Her mother-in-law had to call her to wake her up. "Eleanor come out of it right now. Don't fight with that demon."

When Franceam had touched her shoulders, she was able to hear and see what Albert was talking about. Just before that man hit her hand away. Albert cried out; Eleanor heard him in her mind. *"He's trying to take over my body. If this locket goes into my chest like it is. He can go into the locket, which is how he will take over my body. He will give my soul to his master. Please Lord sends me the demon hunter and Hawk."*

Eleanor opened her eyes up. She had to sit down after that had happened. From outside Thomas called her. *"Honey what are ye doing. Why did I feel a strong power."*

She had taken a breath to com herself. *"I'm all right my love. Albert is looking for Ye. He knows Hawk. He also knows I'm your mate. But he doesn't know who we are. Honey, do ye remember Ronald will fight Marcos in the heavens? Marcos, the man in black will have to die. To be able to fight Ronald in the heavens and take over Albert's body."*

Franceam looked at her daughter-in-law. "Don't tell me Thomas felt it also. Albert is the victim and the man in black must be Marcos."

Eleanor looked at Franceam. "Did dad get anything more from Michael."

She smiled at Eleanor. "We need help, and this man called Jargon, and his brother just came here. Jargon and his brother didn't know what happened to them. It was Jargon who asked if he needed help. Daniel acted cool and went along with what he said. He just told me that we have a knew hand. Hamish was so happy to get more help here. Last night we had two colts born. He went along with Daniel."

CHAPTER ELEVEN

Time to Clean out the Higher Killers.

AFTER THE MAN was gone Michael spoke. "Johnny will ye show me how to get into the house without being seen."

Johnny was looking over at Michael. "Tell me this, are you going to take care of Marcos."

Michael was trying to see what kind of man he was. "I'm going to try to get Mena and her mother out of that house."

He shook his head no. "I'll go with you. Michael Mena knows me."

The two men was staring at each other. "No… Ye will get in the way and get yourself killed. Just draw me where the entryway to the tunnel is."

Johnny slammed his fist down. "Look here Michael. You can't tell me that you can get those women out of that house without my help. I know my way around those tunnels. I can get the women out and into the woods. You need my help Hawk."

Michael just stood there and looked at Johnny. "I would think you would be surprised but you're not. You are good at what you do. This is my place, there is not much that gets past me. When the man came into the pub to tell me that they were going to hang Norward.

I saw you got off the stool. When I went outside, and the first man fell. I could see it came from the pub. After it was over with. I saw a man going into your bedroom. Michael, you are the man called Hawk, you can walk in the dark. I can't do that. I own the building, and I always bump into things."

Johnny smiled at him. "All right why didn't ye say that ye didn't see anything."

He was determined to go with Michael. "At the time you didn't need my help as you do now."

Just then Dias came downstairs with Michael's bow n arrows. She also had her husband's gun. "Dias where did ye get those weapons."

She almost laughed at the look he gave her. "Michael this is our home and business. Do you think I wouldn't know where I could hide things."

Michael shook his head. "Dias ye two are just like my parents. I thought that they were the only ones who could catch me doing anything.

Michael had a worry look on his face. "After Marcos is dead, and we have taken care of his men. I must head home because I know where that demon is taking Albert. If I'm right my brother will need backup. One of my brothers will fight Marcos in the heavens. Eleanor found out that Marcos will use Albert's body, there is a locket going under his skin. That's why he was digging at his chest.

"Johnny, I hope ye can ride. We need to ride hard to get to Marcos's place. I don't want Marcos to find the women in the house when he gets back. I got a bad feeling there going to die tonight."

They looked at him with a puzzle look on their face. The two men rode toward Marcos's estate. Without Johnny knowing he waved his hand, and they were at that rock he told him about. Michael found out that Johnny was right saying, he needed help getting the women out.

The rock they had to move was quite hefty. Michael waved his hand as they pushed the rock out of the way. It must have taken a team of horses to get the rock over to this spot. "I take it all back Johnny. Ye, were right about needing your help. My family has moved large rocks in our time. I could have moved it if I had time to do so."

Michael looked at Johnny. "Michael are you a MacGregor."

This wasn't the time to talk. "Johnny asks me this question when this is all over with. Now put ye back into it and help me move this damn rock."

Johnny chuckled when he started to help push the rock aside. "I hope you don't mind spiders. If you do this, it won't be any fun for you. The last time I was down here. There was a grate quantity of spider webs."

Michael thought of a memory, where he had placed a spider on his sister's shoulder and gave a chuckle. "No spiders don't bother me. I hope the women don't mind."

Johnny gave him two sticks. It was the right time to see if he could use his magic. He thought of a spell. "That's why I'm going to have you clean as much of the webs out of there way with this stick."

He grabbed two sticks after he lit his torch. Johnny was right. There was a great quantity of spider webs everywhere. When they stopped, they started to explore each of the peepholes. They need to find the women's room. At last, they found only one man in the house along with the two women. He could kill the man but when Marcos got back, he would know the girls were gone. *"Not yet Michael."*

Through the peephole Michael saw his brother. He was standing in front of the man guarding the women's door. Did that man see Ronald and know who he was.

In a whisper Johnny spoke. "Michael, this way."

The two of them moved over to a wall. In front of the entrance Johnny moved a tall board. Behind the board was the way into the room. "We're in luck… they placed the women in one of the bedrooms that led to the tunnel."

Slowly Johnny opened the door and saw Mena talking with her mother. Quickly Johnny placed a finger over his lips. Mena ran into Johnny's waiting arms, and they embraced. When Johnny went over to Leanna, he saw what Michael had been telling him. He understood now why Declan looked the way he did. Marcos was poisoning Leanna and Declan. Back inside the tunnel the men helped the women down the long tunnel. Leanna was too weak to ride by herself. Michael picked her up and placed her on his horse. "Johnny, we have one stop to make. I know there are herbs around here that could help her and Declan.

Michael saw that Mena could ride quite well. If the herbs helped Mena's parents. Then they could bring her to the highlands. He thought that Mena would like to meet Gallivan, his cousin. The thoughts of Albert in Scotland had made his mind up. To keep Mena here until it was safe for her to come to the Highlands.

Johnny looked at Michael. "Where would we find these herbs ye are talking about."

He had brought them to a place he knew about. "It's not here we need to go a little farther away from the house."

There in the clearing was Declan. "Daddy."

Mena got off her horse and ran as fast as she could into her father's arms. "Mena, how did you get free."

Michael had waved his hand to get the herbs. "It was Johnny and Michael who freed us."

Then he saw Leanna in Michael's arms. He was bringing her over to the fire. "Leanna my love I failed you and our daughter."

Leanna looked at her husband, she had tears in her eyes. Michael spoke up. "Declan Ye have not failed them. Give me a minute and I will make ye something to stop what ails ye."

Michael moved quickly to get everything he needed. Declan had a pot of hot water with tea in it. Michael asked what kind of tea was in the pot. It wasn't what he wanted but it would help until he could get the right things to give them. He had waved his hand over the pot. "Johnny, give them both a cup. Don't stay here long, I don't want to bring them backout for a second time. I want ye to drink all that tea up. The faster ye drink the tea the faster it will work."

Declan had just finished his tea when he spoke. "Michael, where is Hawk."

For a moment Declan saw Ronald. "Thank you, Michael, for bringing Hawk here to help us. Michael where did Hawk go…? He was just there."

His daughter answered that question. "Daddy, there is just Michael and Johnny here with us."

She looked at her husband. Then spoke. "Mena I too saw that man. He was big like Michael. Johnny you must have seen that man. He looks like Michael."

Johnny shook his head. "No…, I'm sorry Leanna. If you did, you must have seen a ghost."

Michael smiled and spoke. "Give them one more cup of that tea. I'll bring more herbs when I meet ye at the pub. After the two of them have drunk their tea, ye must leave here.

*   *   *   *   *

Michael turned his horse towards Marcos's estate. It was time to finish what he had started.

In the tunnel Michael made his way to Marcos's bedroom. Ronald had found his journal under his packed clothes. He grabbed the journal and through his packed clothes. He wanted Marcos to believe they were after his journal. When he opened the book. Michael found every name of the women he killed. It explains how he killed them. There were no names of the women Albert had raped. A note saying Albert can't be my son.

He finds what I'm doing is wrong. Michael had seen that it went back to the time he was seventeen. It devastated him, to read the number of women who gave their lives so Marcos could get a son.

Michael could hear someone saying. "You're dead we killed you in the Lowlands of Scotland. How did you get in here MacGregor."

Michael heard his brother's laughter. *"Marcos I'm a spirit; The Lord sent me. I'm here to take ye back with me, The Lord will judge ye."*

Then Ronald stood in front of Michael. *"Are ye having fun with that man brother."*

Ronald smiled *"Aye… that I am. I will get Marcos's men to kill each other. Ye take care of Marcos. Who knows? I may let Marcos kill his own men. Marcos's time has come. Judgment is at hand for what he has done to all those men and women."*

Then Michael showed Ronald the journal. *"Aye… I have met these women. I asked to be the tool to bring Marcos and his son to judgment. Go now to the study, there is more books for ye to find."*

In Marcos's study Michael went through everything. What he found was a great amount of money that was ready to take with him. He found a booklet about how Marcos was able to take everyone's land. Even the land that this house stood on.

Ronald went over to the bookcase. He showed Michael which book to pull down. Doing as Ronald had asked, Michael found a deed to this land. When Michael read the deed. He found out that the house and all its land belonged to Johnny and his wife Dias. It was to go to them after he died.

Ronald said. *"I met this old man. He asked me if ye would give it to Johnny along with the money that's with the deed."*

Michael saw Ronald stop. *"It's time to go. Hide in the tunnel until I come for ye. Ye can watch what I'm doing from the peepholes. Don't come out intel I come to ye. Will ye do this for me Michael."*

He nodded his head yes. *"Aye... ye know I will do as ye ask."*

Outside Michael could hear gunfire. He went to look through the peephole near the hallway. A man ran inside yelling for Gauge. "Gauge, where are you. Marcos has just killed Taft. He thought he saw the MacGregor and shot Taft. I think he's going crazy. Marcos told me that you and I must take care of the women. We are to burn both houses down. He said we can leave the bodies in the houses. We must get out of here; Hawk is here Terror is dead."

The man's hand was shaking. "Adamson you said Marcos saw the MacGregor."

Gauge spoke. "Yes, isn't that what I just said. I too have seen the MacGregor. Where to go with him The Lord had sent him to bring us for judgment day."

Then he took out his knife. "Adamson, I want out of here. The MacGregor is here. He is a ghost, and I saw him. I don't want anything more to do with Marcos and his killing. What are you doing? Stay away from me."

The next thing Michael saw. Adamson had taken his knife to Gauge. He laughed at him. "You are a fool not to believe in ghost; it's your time to be judged Gauge."

He watched Gauge fall limply to the ground. Adamson had stepped over the body and unlocked the door. Michael then went quickly over to that bedroom. There he saw Ronald sitting on the bed. *"Hello Adamson, now who is the fool. Did ye think I would forget about ye? Ye had killed Gauge, would ye think I wouldn't come for ye. I'm here to take all ye back for judgement day. Your reign of terror is over with."*

Ronald smiled at him. "You're dead and can't hurt me, where are the women."

He ran his hand over the blanket. *"I did nothing with the women. They are safe from ye and Marcos."*

Ronald laughed. *"I can see you're not safe. Do ye think he is going to leave ye alive. He doesn't have to pay ye now. Ye have taken care of Gauge for him. Ye said that he killed Taft did ye not. He came to clean up the mess in this house. Your part of this mess is ye not. I'll see ye later Adamson in joy Marcos's rage."*

He tried to move Ronald away. "Get out of my way. I must get out of here before Marcos comes into the house."

Adamson saw Ronald's face change. Then he turned around quickly to find Marcos in the doorway. He had his gun out and trained on Marcos. When Marcos was facing Adamson, he was ready to kill him. At the same time, the two men fired. Adamson shot Marcos in his stomach. Marcos hit Adamson directly in the heart killing him outright.

Ronald smiled at him. *"Well now Marcos, things are not going the way ye thought they would be. Soon ye will see the Lord. He will judge ye for the things ye did. I can see your time is running out. Ye have until the blood runs out of your body. Marcos, ye will watch everything ye killed for, The Lord will take it from ye. Did ye think ye would live forever? An eye for an eye a tooth for a tooth… Before the night is over ye will be dead."*

Marcos was stumbling to his bedroom. He was bleeding out as he walked. There he found his journal was gone. Everything he did was in that journal. Including the names of the women he killed. He thought he was so smart to write everything down. He never thought someone would find his journal, who knew about it.

Then Ronald spoke. *"Ye know that answer. The one who will judge ye for what ye have done. Time is running out. Can't ye see Marcos that ye are bleeding all over your bedding."*

Ronald laughed at him. "Get out of here and leave me be. My time is not up yet, until I say it's up. Do you hear me."

Marcos shook his hand toward the heavens. "You will never get to judged me. I have power over life and death. You'll see."

He tries to hit Ronald with his hand. But it went right through him. *"Marcos ye are not God the Almighty. Ye are just a man who let the power go to his head. He is the only one will say your time is up on this earth."*

Ronald looked at Marcos. "You're still here. I had you killed and enjoyed watching you die. Hawk had no right to stop me from burning you alive. I may be dying but your name will not go on. I killed the MacGregor's name. Those roses will die, even if I die. Next, I will make it because those roses will be dead."

Ronald turned and went out the door. He was leading Marcos to the study, laughing over what he had said. The man didn't know that the bullet had hit an artery. Marcos was following him; each step he took he was swearing at Ronald. This is where he wanted him to die. Michael realizes on that his brother didn't desire for him to kill Marcos. When his time was near the end. Only then did Ronald have Michael come out. When Marcos saw him. He took the gun from the desk drawer and shot Michael.

The bullet just bounds off his vest. "Die… Why won't you just die? I killed you in the Lowlands of Scotland. I saw you die, are you a ghost also."

Marcos shot Michael; he had his gun trained at his heart. His bullet hit Michael and bounced off his vest.

He and his brother laughed at him. "No…, ye killed our cousin Peter who looked like me. He gave up his life because he was dying. I'm Michael MacGregor, brother to Ronald and Thomas MacGregor. I have another name they call me; it's Hawk. Marcos, your name won't live on. Ye have nothing but girls. Now for the MacGregor name, there are two sons left. There is also a grandson to make sure the name goes on. Those magic fairy roses are in the highlands. Our brother takes care of them. We know that ye tried to kill all the roses in Scotland."

Michael watched Marcos's rage spill out of his mouth. Blood was coming out of his mouth and pouring out of his wound. "My son won't let me down."

Michael laughed at what he said. He spoke. "Wow…, That was funny. The words around town, the people speaking about ye. The woman was a witch that curse ye. She made it so ye wouldn't have a son. Albert is not your son, ye took a woman already with child. Ye killed her husband after ye raped his wife.

"I heard that ye are part Fairy and demon. I found out that your name was Marcuse, in the 15th century ye die. The King of the Fairy's and his twin, two hundred years ago. His name was Kenyon MacGregor. His mother was a Fairy, and his father was a Wizard. My brother and his wife went to the valley of the Fairy's. His wife saved all the roses even in the valley. Ye had try to kill the roses in Scotland but ye failed."

Ronald watched him slowly die. *"I know ye are thinking that ye will come back to life with Albert's body. We will stop ye, the roses give us our magic back. I spoke to Albert's mother; the baby was her husband's son. That's how ye were able to get a son."*

Marcos yelled as he spit out blood. "Lies… he is my son."

Michael spoke. "Then why did ye say in your journal. That Albert wasn't your son. That ye were going to use him if this is not true. He will die in Scotland with my brother's hands. Thomas is the best knife thrower and swordsman in Scotland. Marcos, we know where your men is heading."

With the last of his strength Marcos screamed out his anger. He died in a pool of his own blood and his own doings. "I will be back you will see."

Ronald then told Michael. *"I want ye to use your magic. Send these bodies to the small cabin. The woman who had the baby with her child is gone. The people of this town have had enough with these men. The cabin is burning hot, I want ye to clean this house with your magic. Send the blood and bodies to the cabin."*

Then Ronald got on his knees. "Father in heaven bless this house so evil will leave this land. I ask this in Jesus's name Amen."

Michael looked at his brother as he got to his feet. "Ronald, I know that this is not over, I wish it were. I know ye have one more man, who needs to go to The Lord. These men souls I must bring them to the Lord.

"I know Marcos went to see his master. He doesn't want to be judge by The Lord. It's something that Meghalaya said. Two hundred years from now, Tom and Ellen will need these roses. She also said that the roses will be going to the new world."

Ronald looked at his brother. *That man is waiting for Marcos to pay him. He will be in the town just before we cross into the Highlands.*"

*   *   *   *   *

Michael looked around as if the house were clean with holy light. "Ronald if Marcos's mother was a Fairy and his father was a Demon. The Lord will not judge Marcos because his father is Satan, he will punish him. Ronald, I wish that ye didn't have to fight him. With the vest and your weapons that have the rose petals on everything. Ye have your magic with the Lord's blessing.

*   *   *   *   *

Michael had to find more herbal. "I guess I'm not going to get anymore answers. I still have things I must do before I leave England. I got to get more herbs for Leanna and Declan. I need to teach them how to make herbal drinks. After I give Johnny the deed to this place along with the money. Then head to that pub near the crossing.

"I will take care of Marcos's man who will be waiting for him. Ronald ye knew that his men would shoot back at him. Ye didn't want me to be the one to kill him."

Ronald looked at his brother. *"Aye..., ye are right. Marcos was pure evil right to the end of his life. Ye have enough to deal with, as ye said it's not over yet. Be careful that last man could be afraid."*

Michael looked at him. "Aye… I believe his man will be waiting for him at the last town. It will be before we cross into the Highlands. I'll see ye at home brother."

*   *   *   *   *

Michael gathered all the herbs he needed for Leanna and Declan. At the pub everyone was relieved to see Michael was all right. Then the questions started to fly.

Michael took a little time for himself; he had saved the town. It was Johnny then he asked him. "What is your real name. I know it's not Michael McGee."

Michael laughed when he saw Declan and Johnny fighting over who was right. "Declan, I'm called Hawk. My grandfather gave me the nickname when he saw me shoot at night. Both my uncle and grandfather had this gift. I had inherited it from them. Johnny ye were also right, my name is Michael MacGregor. I'm the oldest son now that Ronald has passed away."

Then Michael had to set up a meeting with Gallivan and Mena. "Declan and Leanna ye have a wonderful daughter. I think she would like my cousin Gallivan. He had asked me if I could find a lass for him. My parents would host her coming out party. What do ye say."

Declan looked at Michael. This is his little girl. "Who is this cousin of yours."

Michael smiled, he was wondering if he would be like Declan. When it's his daughter's coming out party happens. "Ye know of the family. Donald McKinnon is my mother's brother. Peter who looked like me he was dying a slow death. He gave me my cover so I could do as my brother asked me.

"Gallivan had asked me to find him someone that he would like. Ye see all his brothers are getting married. Peter had a twin his name is Damian. For a long time, he had his eyes on a girl called Marianne. Before I came home, Marcos went after Marianne. Eleanor had saved her, which is Thomas's wife. Damian got scared, he thought he was going to lose her. She is like your daughter working in the pub.

When I came home with my wife and my children, he started to court Marianne.

"Gallivan is the youngest. The oldest is married with one on the way he is the age of Ronald. Damian finished his home while Duncan was away for two years. Duncan went with Thomas to find their brother's. Damian stayed in his home to look after it. After Gallivan helps my brother Thomas with his home. He likes to build his own place. His land is in the back of us, two miles from us.

"I would like to take her with me. I still must find Marcos other man. Then there is the other four men. I would like for ye to bring her up to the Highlands after this is all done. There are still things my family must do; Marcos is now dead. He is going to use Albert's body somehow. My sister-in-law knows a bit about black magic. She had a dream about a locket going into his chest. That is why ye saw him digging at his chest."

Then Mena spoke. "That make sense of what Albert had said. One day he was in the house. He kept saying that damn locket is trying to go into my chest. I've told him why don't ye take it off. He told me, "I wish I could. That old man who was like a father to Albert. He looks more like him then Marcos."

Michael had everything he needed. "I heard enough of this. I like to hear a little bit about your cousin. How old is he? Is he strong like you Michael? Is Gallivan kind like you and thoughtful. How tall is he? Is he good looking like you? What color hair and eyes does he have."

Michael laughed. "Ye are like my sister-in-law. She likes to get right to the point. Ye know his name is Gallivan McKinnon. He is eighteen and the reason I asked your parents to bring ye. As ye know his older brother just got married a year ago. His other brother has a girlfriend and thinks she is the one for him. He has his land and is looking to build on it. He asked me to keep and I for a young woman that he may like. Ye are very pretty. His hair is reddish brown with green eyes like his mother's. Gallivan built his like his father's and mine. He likes women that keeps their head, ye do just that. Ye are tall but a little smaller than Gallivan. Myself I take after my mother in looks, as he takes after his father. My mother and his father are brother and sister. He is close to my brother Thomas. Gallivan is a strong fighter. He likes to work with wood and Thomas is showing him other things. He is one of the best riders in the land. If he goes up against my brother and his wife, he will lose. With him family comes first. Does that help ye."

Mena smiled. "Yes, thank you I can't wait to meet him. Can ye leave his address with me? Before ye leave I will write him a letter that ye can give him.

Michael was glad that she liked the idea of checking him out now. "Before ye bring your daughter to meet my cousin. If ye agree with this she can stay with my family. My mother would love to show her things; she is a healer and midwife. She could stay for the summer next year to get to know my cousin. His mother would love to have another woman in the house. Right now, it's not safe for her."

Both parents smiled. "That will be fine with us, there is one thing I'd like to know. Michael, could ye tell me who were ye talking to in the back of the pub?"

He took a deep breath. "Declan think about this. Ye and your wife was dying a slow death. Who do ye think would have my back even in death."

Declan closed his eyes and shook his head. "That was your brother Ronald. Are you saying that my wife and I was that close to death."

Michael closed his eyes when he opened them. He spoke. "Aye… if my brother didn't tell me to come here. In two days ye would have died. Ronald came the last time to ease your mind. To let ye know I was the one called Hawk. Johnny and Norward were right about who I am. My brother didn't want ye to blow my cover. He asked to come back here to send these men to the Lord. All the men who died in that house. Michael used his magic to send the bodies to the cabin. Marcos had the cabin burned. There is no blood to be clean up that is gone now. The Lord cleans the house with holy light.

The beginning of the MacGregor

"In the 15th century my great grandfather, his family lived in the Lowlands of Scotland. He was working to buy a castle in the Highlands. He was a bounty hunter; at the time he was hunting down a demon who killed his twin for his magic.

The MacGregor's men was strong wizard. When he killed the demon, he got all his magic. This demon went around killing anyone for their magic.

At the time he was near England, there was a valley of fairies. These fairies was the size of humans; he was having dreams of this beautiful woman. He was hearing a song at the time it was only in his dream. Until he killed the demon, then he heard it all the time.

What he found out this woman was calling for men with magic. She needed a man to get her pregnant to become Queen. To show new life in the valley, the fairy men couldn't do it. The call went out to anyone with strong magic. This MacGregor had done the impossible because he wasn't a fairy. Their race was dying out and they needed new blood to survive. The MacGregor provided just that the Queen made him King. He had given her twins, the oldest was a girl. The second child was a boy, once he was old enough. He went to his father's home in the Lowland of Scotland. This home was near a waterfall that he knew hidden in a valley of the Fairies.

One day she had a dream of a man outside the waterfall. They called him Jonathan D Gregor. He found is love in the valley near his home.

It was his child that made the roses. Their first-born son became king once he was old enough to mate with the Queen's daughter. When his son had their children, he made three rose bushes, when they were older give the roses their magic.

"Before ye ask my family does have the magic from them. Just before they die their magic went to the roses. For a while there weren't any roses in the lowland. Marcos wanted the roses to stay gone. In doing so we don't have our magic. Thomas, my brother, has found the magic fairy roses. The vest I wear has rose petals on it. The magic helps to keep me safe. I can also see my brother because of it. Not everyone can have magic. My sister has magic, because of Marcos. Grana had all the women have a cross with rose petals on it. These crosses with the rose petals gave all the MacGregor's their magic. Now her husband has magic, I have magicked my wife has a bit.

Catherine and her husband have a bit of magic. Her husband is my brother's best friend. When we were children, Eleanor wanted Thomas to teach her how to ride. Catherine wanted William to teach her. So ye see the girls had pick the man they wanted as children. Then William wanted a pack between Thomas and himself to always think of them as their sister. The girls fell in love with each other's brothers."

Johnny then spoke. "Michael, here take this money to help ye get back home. We will use the rest to help the town, and the children Marcos left behind.

Michael smiled. "Thank ye, but I won't need it. Please put aside money for Mena. That way she can come to the Highlands."

*   *   *   *   *

The next day Michael got on his horse. He said his goodbyes to everyone. He waved his hand and thought of where he wanted to be. Just outside of town he appeared. He could ride into town; there he could stop at the pub. This is where the hired killer was to be, he was waiting for Marcos.

Michael kept an eye out for Marcos's last hired killer. The men who have Albert will be making a list of the pretty women for him. Only if Marcos takes over Albert's body. If he does, then evil will go after the women again. His thoughts were sad about these women. *"We can't let this happen again"* He thought.

Eleanor told him about her dreams. Marcos thinks he will have Eleanor first. Thomas had him thinking she was a virgin. He was angry to find out that she was married. All his plans were going up in smoke.

*   *   *   *   *

Michael needed to pray, he had found a place to stop and pray. *"Please Lord helps us with this evil man called Marcos. Lord I'm scared for my brother Ronald soul. Marcos is not going to fight fair; he will have men with him. I give ye everything we must do to ye Lord. In Jesus name. Amen."*

*   *   *   *   *

Michael came to the pub, that man Marcos had hired. He walked into the pub; he made a point to look over every man there. He saw one who fit the description of Taylor. This man had deep scars on his face. He was looking around to make a point that he was looking for someone. He remembered what Johnny told him. When you're a bartender, you must keep your eyes moving. That way nothing would get past you.

Michael went up to the bar. "I will have a pint of ale and do ye serve food also."

The bartender was watching Michael as he looked over the men. "Aye… that we do, would Ye like a menu."

He smiled back at him. "Aye…" The man handed Michael a menu. "I think I will have your fish dinner."

Michael knew what was coming next. "Are ye from around here mister."

He smiled at him again. "No, I'm from the Highlands."

Michael knew the next question. "Ye are a long way from home. Is it business or pleasure."

In a deep voice Michael spoke. "This is business, I've been on the trail of a group of men. One man was always digging at his chest. There are six men all together."

The bartender asked another question. "What did these men do."

Michael answered. "Ye name it, and they have done it. Their leader's name is Marcos Huascaran. His men were taking a young man to die."

The bartender looked at Michael. "Aye… they came in here for food and drink. That man Albert he didn't look to good. He kept rubbing his chest. The old man with him looked worried for him. There was two of the men who felt evil. One of the men stay here after they left. He has been here for a day."

Michael told him why he was here. "Aye… he is looking for the man called Marcos Huascaran."

Michael had talked louder so the man in the back could hear him. "He will have a long wait, for that man is dead. One of his men killed him. He was cleaning house killing all his hire killers. Marcos takes women and gets them with child. If she gives him a girl, she dies. He needs a son. Have ye had any girl come up missing? When was this young woman found? Did they find her dead with a little girl on her."

The bartender looked at him. "Aye… about a year ago. As ye said we found her dead and a baby girl with her. Tell me sir. How would one-man is able to hunt all these men?"

Michael thought about this. "Have ye heard of a man called Hawk."

The bartender smiled at him. "Aye… he is well known around these parts. He took down the group of men that was robbing Scotland."

Michael was tired of all of this. "Did ye know that Marcos was the head of all of those men."

The bartender shook his head no. "No, we do know that the MacGregor's were trying to stop these men. Two years ago, the oldest son they killed him and his brother. He was on his way to the conference. May I ask who ye are."

Michael stood tall as he spoke his name. "They call me Hawk McGee. I'm after one of these men who was waiting for Marcos. I know we're the others are heading."

The bartender looked at him. "Hawk ye must be hungry. I'll get your food for ye."

When the bartender came back, he had the pint of ale and a bowl of nuts. In the bowl was a piece of paper. Michael had turned his back to the man, to read the note. He still could see him in a mirror on the wall. The note said, Hawk the man who's sitting by the fireplace was with five other men. He has been here all day, they call him Taylor, one of the men told him. Tell Marcos we will be at the new place in four days tops. I will see you when you get there. Taylor has a room across the street. He's been watching you from the moment you came into the pub. Be careful Hawk that man has a temper. Your friend David.

Michael placed the note in his sporran. He had picked up his ale and bowl of nuts. He went over to the other side of the fireplace and sat down. Taylor glared as he watched Michael sit across the table from him.

Then Taylor spoke. "Hawk did you really kill Marcos Huascaran."

Michael looked at Taylor. "Ye don't hear to good, do ye. I said one of his men killed him. I heard the names of these men. Ye know Adamson Gauge and Taft?"

The man's eyes showed anger. "I do know them."

When he came into the house. He called for Gauge and spoke. Marcos killed Taft; he saw the ghost of Ronald McGregor."

Taylor looked like he was getting ready for a fight. "I know of them go on."

Michael knew that he was getting scared. "Gauge was also talking about ghosts. Adamson killed Gauge and pushed him aside. He had to unlock the door to the women's room. When Adamson opened the door. He found that the women were gone. Adamson and Gauge were to kill the women. Then burn down the two houses with the bodies inside.

"When he opened the door, the women were gone. Marcos called him; he spoke. Where are the women. He had told him that he didn't know. Then Adamson turned quickly, and Marcos shot him in the heart. Adamson shot Marcos in the stomach. I could hear Marcos talking, he was speaking to the ghost of Ronald MacGregor. Then Marcos went to his room, he was bleeding over everything. I listened to him talk to the ghost of Ronald, as he made his way to the study."

Michael smile at the man. "Tell me this, why were you not shot."

He spoke to Taylor. "Did ye know that the house had tunnels? They have doorways to get into other rooms. I was nowhere near Marcos; there were peepholes to watch from. He yelled that he was cleaning the house. He did it with everyone's blood, even his own. Tell me this, did he pay ye."

Taylor was getting angry; he wanted to start killing. To take his anger out on someone. "No! My orders were to wait for Marcos. Then I was to take him to his son. That son of a bitch was going to kill me."

The people in the pub were clearing out of the pub fast. There was just the bartender and Taylor with Michael.

Michael started to laugh. Then his face changed. Taylor spoke. "Why are you here. You look like one of the men we killed. Have you come to kill me."

Michael had taken a drink of his ale. To cover up his hand going for his dirk. "I've come here to eat and drink. When I leave the pub that is a different story. Ye were with the men who killed Ronald MacGregor, they were cousins of mine. I will let ye have your last meal before I take ye out. I overheard Ronald telling Marcos. He came back to bring him to The Lord. Your time is running out Taylor, eat and drink for tonight ye die."

Taylor went for his gun. He spoke, "Not if I kill you first." He wasn't fast enough; his hand was only on his gun. Michael had his dirk going through the air. Even before Taylor could get a shot off.

Michael turned to David. "I'm sorry David to scare off your customers."

David smiled at Michael. "Don't worry about that, after ye leave they will be back. There will be so many questions, they will drink as they listen to the story I will tell."

Michael nodded then took out his dirk from Taylor's heart. He wiped the blood off his dirk on the man shirt. He had checked his eyes to see if he was a demon. Thank heavens he's just a man. He still took a rose petal and made it into a cross. Then he placed it onto his skin, and a towel went over the blood. Michael put Taylor over his shoulder.

David told him where he could take him. "Hawks take him outback; I will have the corner take him away. Would you like a stronger drink."

Michael told him what he wanted. "Aye…, could I have a Scotch. I think I will eat then I'll leave for the Highlands."

*　*　*　*　*

Michael had called his brother. *"Thomas can ye hear me."*

Thomas was working in his home they had everything like a bed, table, and chairs. Then he heard his brother. *"I hear ye Michael are ye all right."*

Michael called back. *"Aye…, Marcus is dead. The last men are in the Highlands. I will let ye know when to meet me at the pub."*

Thomas then asked how far he was. "They have crossed before me. I'll use my magic to get there just after them."

*　*　*　*　*

Inside the castle Eleanor and Catherin were in the study. They were trying to finish their wedding quilts for their beds. Malinda was upstairs putting her daughter and son down for their naps.

Eleanor had felt that evil was heading there way. "Catherine, check on everyone make sure they have the rose petals on them. I just heard Michael telling Thomas that Marcos is dead. Make sure Briana has the cover over the baby to protect her child."

Catherine nodded with her understanding. "It's time we have to put the spell around the castle." She went to get Grana and her mother and Maryann along with Bridget. Ginny was staying close to her future mother-in-law. Everyone had a cross on their chest. There scarf was on their head and there close had petals on them. The women were coming out of the kitchen, Grana and Franceam had felt that evil was heading their way. Every man had their vest on. There was a cross with a rose petal on them.

Eleanor waved her hand and went to where the children were sleeping. When she appeared, Malinda knew that evil was coming. Her son had his vest on; her daughter had a little scarf on her head. She had also heard her husband talking to Thomas. Quickly she took Eleanor's hand, and they put a bubble around the room. Eleanor then waved her hand to take them downstairs. At the time everyone was getting ready for a wedding. Also, a blessing of three couple's marriages.

Eight women had joined hands. Then they spoke the words to keep evil out. At the end of the spell, they threw up their hands and ended the spell with Amen. Around the castle, a strong bubble is established. Only people with a cross and rose petal on them could get in.

*   *   *   *   *

Michael felt the cold that passed through him, he just finished his food. He could feel evil within the spirit. He knew it was Marcos, Ronald told him to place four rose petals over his heart. It had gone into his skin and around his heart. A spirit can go into the body where there was a small piece of bare skin. The evil spirit tried to freeze his heart but couldn't. *"Marcos, I know ye are here. If ye think ye can stop me think again."*

Then Ronald appeared right in front of Marcos. *"Your fight is with me, do ye think I would let ye hurt my family. Think again Marcos, we have the magic fairy roses. We know how to use them. Ye tried to take down my family two hundred years ago."* Ronald hit Marcus with a bright light. *"Begone Satan. Brother pays your bill and head for home. I will follow ye after I take Taylor to the Lord. Tell Thomas about placing four petals over his heart. That goes for dad to do the same also."*

Quickly Michael called Thomas, he had told him what Marcos tried to do. He spoke. *"He's trying to frieze our hearts so we will die. He also told him to get to dad. Do the same to him also."*

Thomas then called Eleanor. He told her to put four petals on little Ronald heart. Marcus is on his way.

Michael paid his bill and went out to his horse. On his horse he headed out of town. With a quick wave of his hand. He found himself near an old castle. Then he saw his brother.

Michael spoke. *"What the is going on Ronald. Why did ye bring me here."*

Ronald looked at his brother. *"So ye knew it was me to bring ye here. This is the place where they're going to take Albert. They are not here yet, I thought ye like to see where ye are going to fight the demon."*

Ronald took Michael through a tunnel that led to the castle. This way no one will see ye. Ones Inside the castle he could see walls that were half gone. Doorways there wasn't any left but one. Walls were blown-up, there was only one room left with walls and a ceiling. All holes in the wall's vines grew through. It had seemed that the vines were taking over a hundred holes in the castle. Ronald told him *"That they don't know about the tunnel. There is a mountain lion ye will have to get around. This is the cat's home."*

Then Michael saw where they were going to keep Albert. It had a door locked, inside there was a floor and a sealing. It had all its sides and a top. This was the only place that survived the attack long ago.

Ronald then gave him something to think about. *"There will be a young man about nineteen. There is a demon that took over the boy's body a long time ago. This part is hard to believe, the boy still lives inside his body. His name is Garret, the demon doesn't know he's there."*

Michael looked at Ronald. "What are we to do now, does that mean we can't fight the demon."

Ronald then showed Michael the steep hill that the demon would defend. *"Ye must fight him there is no other way. I spoke to my father and mother. They told me that their son has his father's magic. This magic is like a bubble that goes around our son's mind. The demon that took over the lad's body thought when he saw his parents die, he died also. This young boy had a strong faith that his mother taught him. With his faith he prayed to The Lord and with those prayers he built walls with them. He could see everything when he saw what Marcos was going to do to his sister. He made a planned to save her, the boy saw women raped. What he had to do was get closer to his sister. Marcos had him tie her to the bed. As he did so the boy spoke a spell to take his sister's mind from her body. Marcos made the boy watch what he was going to do for his sister. He raped her body until she was with child. He saved his sister's mind; she stayed with her brother inside that bubble made with prayers. They never saw what he had done to her body. Marcos made the boy watch what he was doing. He was the one that had to tie his sister up. That is when he put the demon asleep. He called his sister. When she heard him, he took her mind inside the bubble." His sister stayed with him until the baby was ready to be born. The boy now knew he had gotten the body with child. All they had to do was wait until the baby was ready to be born. That was when the boy took the infant brain from the baby and put it into his sister's body. His sister's mind was place into the baby body. When she was born Marcos saw it was a girl, he slit her throat. The baby and her body where taken to his mother's sister. His mother's sister had the baby evaluated to see if the child was evil. The baby's mind was pure; she went to The Lord. The boy had cast out evil from the baby before he placed his sister in her new body.*

*   *   *   *   *

Ronald tried to give information to Michael. If the demon's body dies, the boy inside the demon is freed. Ye must take down the demon, there is no other way.

Michael was looking around. "Ronald wouldn't he be evil also."

Ronald sat at the top of the hill. *"The boy is of ten years old. His body kept growing but he is still ten in mind and soul. His mother told him to pray to the Lord that the prayers would save him. The demon doesn't know about him or his magic."*

Michael was looking around, taking everything in. "Ronald, we need Thomas to see this. Can I bring him here to us."

He shook his head no. *"This is for ye only."* Then Ronald waved his hand, and he had the layout of this place. *"Ye can show them this. At the pub there is the other demons that goes with the old man. Ye must listen to this man story, about his mother and Albert. Those other men take them down. Don't forget to place across on his chest with the rose petals."*

Then Ronald told him what was happening at the castle. *"Eleanor and the women had to put the magic spell, that Eleanor had found in that room. It's now around the castle. Your children have a bubble around the hole room where they are sleeping in. It goes from top and all the sides, she heard ye telling about the rose petals around the men heart. She put three around your son heart. Now that he knows about your son, along with Thomas. Marcos will try to get to them, he thought he could take ye out at that pub. He will be surprised when he tries to get into the castle. They were going to set up all the party things. But it was Eleanor who told them know. She had felt Marcus when he had crossed over to the Highlands. I thought I sent him away from us."*

* * * * *

"Michael don't worry. Malinda and your children, have been at the castle from the time the horses were giving birth. Along with Briana, Lindy, and Mariann. Also, Grana's there with Bridget. The men have their vest on. As ye know there has been across place on everyone. Father is to be at the castle this afternoon. Everyone knows when ye will be at the pub. It's Damian who will be married tomorrow to Mariann.

"The women are to get ready for tomorrow. All the young men are to keep Damian away for a while. They will be heading to the pub to eat and drink."

Michael was wondering about the time limit they had. He spoke. "When will the demon get here? They are here now. Michael put his horse invisible, at the same time himself. He watched them get Albert down from his horse. The young man was two years older them himself."

The demon checked his chest and saw it wasn't going into his chest fast enough. Michael heard a young boy's voice. *"Get back he will see that you're invisible, the other demon can't. Ronald is this* Hawk. *"*

Ronald looked at the boy. *"Aye... The demon hunter will be with him. Don't gave yourself away."*

Then Ronald told Michael to follow them. But stay invisible, until ye see the pub. I know that Thomas William with Damian and his two brothers, will be heading to the pub.

* * * * *

At the castle Father had come over to eat breakfast. She had to let Father know what was going to happen. Eleanor knew that Father heard the story about the magic roses. His cross had rose petals on it. She had also placed rose petals on his habit. When they were at the roses, she had seen Father bless the roses with holy water. To see if they were evil, what he didn't know. That MacGregor's had magic with the petals on them. That had meant the three brother's and the women they had married. That even meant Catherine and William, being her husband, had the magic.

*　*　*　*　*

Taking a deep breath, she started to tell Father about her visions. She also added what Catherin had seen without using her name. Then she said that Marcos is using a young man for his evil doing. Father Sinclair, she had asked if he could bless the women with holy water. Marcos is now an evil demon with powers.

Father spoke. "I will bless around the castle to help keep him out. I will need help to bless the castle. Eleanor will ye help me with this."

She saw one of the visions had Marcos trying to take her ora. She had her scarf on with the rose petals on it. Everything else she had was to mark him for life. The risk ban had petals, her nails also had petals. The two of them went outside to start blessing the castle.

Eleanor heard loud laughter; this was to make her head hurt. They were about to do when the laughter went to a hi pitch. She had pulled down her scarf to block the sound out. Father spoke. "I'm going in, are ye coming with me."

Eleanor told him in a minute Father. She had heard Marcos telling her to stay. She had gone along with it. Then Marcos pinned her wrist up against the castle wall. She had let him think he was doing this to her. She could see him as he came up to her. When he was close enough to her, she pulled away and scratched his face. Marcos pulled back and he screamed in pain. "I was going to have ye, ones I got my new body. Now I will hurt ye and ye will die a slow death."

Eleanor laughed. "Ye will not get your knew body, anybody ye use will have my mark on your face. This will not go away; no magic will help ye. For I'm the mate to Thomas MacGregor. He is the keeper of the magic roses. His grate grandfather King Kenyon of the Fairy's left his magic for his children after him. He knew ye would be back."

She saw his eyes go to the roses. Eleanor waved her hand to put a bubble over the roses.

Then Marcos pulled back, he looked at her. He waved his hand to try to hurt her. She waved her hand, and he hit a strong wall. "Ye can't hurt me, I was able to hurt ye."

The marks on Marcos's face became a scarred. Eleanor had magic rose petals on her nails, the marks will be there for life. "Ye will not have Albert's body, without his body ye can't come back from the dead."

*   *   *   *   *

Then Thomas felt that she was fighting with Marcus. Michael had felt is brother was scared for Eleanor. Ronald looked at Michael. "Ye follow these men. Tell Thomas, I got this."

Michael called Thomas. *"Little brother, stand down. Ronald will take care of Marcos."*

Thomas called back. *"Michael I can't lose my wife."*

He was following those men. *"Don't ye think Ronald knows this, he knows how ye feels. Tell William to stand down, we have a job to do. I'm following those other men to the pub. We must talk with the old man, remember one or both is a demon. Your wife is a strong woman, she knows what to do. The face of Marcos must be mark by Eleanor a man who rapes women. I know she has all her weapons on her."*

Then Thomas called back. *"I know she is, we will be at the pub."*

Thomas closed his eyes. He called his wife. *"Ronald is coming to help ye, be careful my love. I can't lose ye, I love ye."*

Eleanor had to keep the doors closed. She knew that they wanted to come out. Then she heard Thomas. *"Honey, stay away; it's not your time to fight. I love Ye to, my love. Your brother is here with me. Be careful also."*

Then she saw Ronald. He stood in front of Marcos. *"So ye tried to mess with my sister-in-law. I see she was able to mark ye. Eleanor did the best job on your face. Ye know that it won't come off. With she had done will show in the future. Remember they will have their magic even then.*

"*Your fight is with me. These women are stronger then ye thought. Ye went up against Kenyon and his brother. Ye thought that ye wipe out the MacGregor's. Both times ye fail to do so. We have the magic from Kenyon and Kina. It lives in the rose petals; your tricks are not working. I've had enough of ye we fight in the valley of the dead. No one else, ye killed my mate I have a sore to finish with ye.*" Then Ronald hit Marcos with a bright light. It had sent the evil spirit away from them.

Ronald turned to his sister-in-law. "*I can see that ye and Thomas is so much alike, ye complement each other. He loves Ye very much, your love for him is the same. Now get in the castle let us men do what we must do.*"

Eleanor looked at him as a brother. "I love ye also Ronald, I had to do something for the women in the future. This way he can't cover it up or take it away. Ye couldn't do that only a woman could."

She went up to him and on her finger, she placed a kiss. Then put it on his cheek. "*Only a woman could mark Marcos, as a man that rapes women. Ye been one of my big brothers. Please, I know that Ye are a spirit. If ye fight here is crosses and petals to put on the men that fights with ye. I know he will have help; I saw it in a dream. He will have two men with him.*"

With her magic she placed four rose petals on him. "*Ye have the cross and rose on ye, be careful my brother. I know he will try to vanquish your soul.*"

She took four petals out and placed them over his heart. "*This will protect your heart from being frozen.*"

She took more petals out and placed one on his forehead. "*So, he can't get into your mind. One went on both ears to keep out the evil sounds. The men ye fight with due to them, what I had done to ye. As place everything that they fight with.*"

Also, she placed one on each of his muscles. *So, he can't take your strength away from ye.*"

Eleanor had let Father come outside. "Lass what are ye doing."

She looked at Father. In her hand was a full rose. "Father please bless this with holy water." He had done this for her.

Eleanor whispered a handful of words and ended it. "In Jesus's name Amen." The magic roses were then change into a holy light; it appeared to come down from the heavens. She made a circle around Ronald's body. "There my brother ye are ready to fight evil. Anyone ye touch will have what ye have now. If ye touch evil, it will put him in prison. If ye get to touch Marcos, he will go to The Lord. Good luck my big brother."

Ronald went to her and touched her shoulder. He had seen that it worked. "Marcos will be angry with ye, my little sister needs it too. I love Ye too, I must meet with my brothers. Father, we will need your help also. Make sure everyone gets this. I will do the same."

*   *   *   *   *

Eleanor went into the castle. Father staired at her. "Tell me about this ghost called Marcos." She nodded her head and touched his shoulder. Father had looked at his hands, think ye young lass.

Before she told the story about her visions. It was time for lunch and the men had come into the castle. Everyone she touched had the light. Father had done as she did. At the table as they ate. Eleanor started to talk about her vision. Donald knew that his son Gallivan would be coming to fetch them.

"Right now, Michael is in the Highlands, he is following the men to the pub. Albert is at a castle that set high on a hill. With him, is a demon that has strong magic. There is a locket around Alberts's neck. This locket is very evil it has the hair and blood from the women he killed. The locket is going into Albert's chest. The demon is to keep him safe for Marcos. This is the way to come back from the dead. He will go through the locket. Albert Master will acquire his Soul for the time he was on earth.

"The ones that is heading to the pub there are three men. An old man with a demon and just a higher killer. The one man gets the women for Marcos.

"Now Albert had a dream, he had seen Thomas kill the demon in his dream. Albert knows that I am his mate. He is calling to ask my mate, the demon hunter, to save him from damnation. Marcos

195

is afraid of Thomas, he thought he killed Michael. Albert's dream shows three brothers will take down his future. Marcus at one time was a fairy, a demon raped his mother. Satan his father told him ye can be on earth three time every two hundred years. The first time Marcos had died was in the 15th century. If we can do it again that will be the second time.

"There will always be someone that we will have to fight. Freedom comes at a big price; Freedom is not free. History will always show good and evil. But evil always tries to take history away. It's easy to control people when they don't know the truth. Remember Freedom will always cost to be free. Don't think if there is no history it's no big deal. Wonder why these people hide the past. What is wrong with knowing about the history that the world went through?

These words came from my husband's brother. Remember he lost everything to give us a little bit of freedom.

"Father Sinclair, I know one of your questions. Why did I put myself in danger? I had to mark Marcos's face. The next time he can come back will be two hundred years from now. I need to let the women of the future; know he rapes women. I also need to give our men strong weapons to fight with. I believe in all our men's ability."

When the five men left the castle, they kissed their bride's good-bye. Tonight, they will have a big party for five new married couples. Last night there was a talk about another fight. Duncan felt over-whelmed, being the oldest son of three families. He missed his oldest friend. That's why he left to talk to Ronald. At the time he didn't know that he was helping Eleanor.

*　*　*　*　*

Thomas gave his father a hug. "Thank ye for the help dad. Uncle there is trouble coming. Michael is in the Highlands. The last time I heard from him; he was following those three men to the pub."

Then William Damian along with Theseus was riding up. Thomas walked over to them, as the three men got off their horses. William spoke. "We're done with the two homes, my home is ready for Catherine and I. Along with Damian's home, is now ready to be, lived in."

Then Ronald appeared, Thomas spoke. "Wow brother that is a bright light around ye."

Then he went over to William and Thomas and placed a hand on their shoulders. What Ronald has, they now have. He spoke. "*A gift from my little sister Eleanor. She found a spell to let me fight Marcos without any danger of him taking my soul. That is not all she has done. She helped Father to bless the castle. When Father went into the castle she stayed outside. She knew Marcos was around, Eleanor was ready for him.*

"That demon was always a fool he didn't think it was a trap. With his magic he pinned her to the wall. She had let it happen. When he was close enough that she could touch him. Eleanor marked his face with her nails. Try as he may, he couldn't get her fingernail marks off. She saw that he wanted to destroy the roses. Quickly Eleanor put a bubble around them. Still trying to get that mark off his face. He went after Eleanor and ran into a wall that she had made. I came over and stepped in front of her. What I did was push him away from her and I. I've done that two times to him."

While Ronald spoke, he placed his hand on everyone's shoulder. "*Thomas don't get mad with Eleanor. She knew what she was doing. Her vision shows that he was going to try to take her ora. Then he went after ye. Ye have quite a woman, brother she matched ye perfick. It's time those men are all most to the pub. Where is Duncan.*"

Thomas looked at his brother. "Don't worry, I won't get mad at my wife. She had told me about all her visions. I saw her looking for spells to help us. This has been going on for weeks. I know that I had quite a woman on my hands.

"For Duncan he's going through what Michael, and I have done. When dad said, "My boy takes your brothers to have a drink. Ye may be already married the four of ye. Just enjoy each other's freedom for one day. Ye can have all the ale at the party tonight. I saw it in his eyes, it made him feel strange. It caught him off guard. Now he is trying to figure out why he feels like this."

Then Daniel spoke. "Thomas is right being married and a baby on the way. Now he is the oldest of these three families. It made him feel uncomfortable. Duncan will break it down to see why it had bothered him. It was not having is best friend to talk with. Michael has been married the longest. Thomas and William were married before him. He just can't get over ye three are gone."

Then Thomas spoke. "Brother, he needs ye one more time. Duncan doesn't realize Michael knows how it feels to be the oldest. I think that's why he went to your grave. He wants to talk it over with ye. Ye, two were best friends. We will get to the pub, ye get Duncan straighten out. Send him our way, it's time we end this. Dad, get your weapons ready for us. Uncle, do ye think ye are up to another battle."

Donald looked at his boys. He spoke. "Send Gallivan back here with the two kegs of ale. We will party tomorrow. Now get going your brother will need ye. I remember Eleanor said that Michael will kill one, ye will kill the other man. It's time for a ye boy's ride. I will help with the cleaning of that one barn for tomorrow. I will come to Ye with Father and our weapons. When Gallivan brings the two kegs of ale back to us."

*   *   *   *   *

Duncan stood at Ronald's grave; he needed to talk to his best friend about his feelings. "Ronald, why do I feel lost. I don't like being the oldest of the three families. Of all things to bother me, just the words your father spoke. Take your brothers to have a drink. Enjoy are freedom for one day. There are five new married families and I'm the oldest of them. Why is that making me feel uncomfortable?

Ronald placed a hand on Duncan's shoulder. "It's all new to ye, my two brothers went through it also. Ye been fighting with it for a while now. Ye just figure out what is happening to ye. Your brothers need ye, Michael's in the Highlands. They have Albert soul ready to be Marcos's sacrifice to his master. The locket when it's in his body Marcus can take his body over. Ye must help hold Albert down, it's going to be very painful for him. This fight is for my brothers to finish. All the women are safe inside the castle, Marcos found this out the hard way.

*   *   *   *   *

Michael had just arrived at the pub; he had let them go ahead of him. With a wave of his hand, he reappeared. He noticed two men that Declan had described to him. Slowly he pulled his horse up to the hitching post and got off. He had tied his horse away from them. Michael walked toward them determined to finish this once in for all. He had his dirk ready to throw if they made any wrong move. "Where is your master, Marcos, I know ye have Albert. Ye are not welcome here in the Highlands."

The older man spoke. "Mister I don't know who you are. We don't work for anyone who's called Marcos."

Michael stood tall. "Then let me introduce myself to ye. They call me Hawk, I know ye work for Huascaran."

Right then the two men went for their guns. Michael had killed one man with his dirk. The other man followed him to the ground with a dirk in his chest. It had flown passed his head; it found its mark in the man's heart.

Michael turned to see where the dirk came from. He smiled at his brother. He should have known that Thomas was the one who threw that dirk.

Thomas got off his horse and ran to his brother's side. He gave his brother a well deserve bear hug. "Michael are ye all right,"

He looked at his hands. They were glowing with bright light. "Aye… I am now. There was only one man who could take a shot with is dirk like that. At the same time, giving me a close shave doing it. I should have known that ye would be around when I needed ye the most. Well done my brother… well done. Ronald said ye would deal with it, anything that came your way. Now tell me where this light came from."

Thomas took a breath and spoke. "A gift from my wife. This bright light will keep Ronald soul safe. Marcos can't take his soul now. Here put four petals over your heart. This way he can't freeze your heart. Now we must take care of these bodies."

Michael had holy water with him, both men took a rose petal out. They put a drop on the rose petal. With their magic they turned it into a cross and placed it on their chest. Then they took their dirk, from their body. They wiped the blood off on the man shirt. Thomas spoke. "Now touch their shoulder. This will in closed their bodies and send their souls to the Lord."

With the wave of Thomas's hand. The undertaker had received two dead men. Then they saw four men riding up. They saw the extra horse had a sled behind.

William got off his horse. "Damian, take care of the horses and tied them up for us. Gallivan ye bring the sled to the back of the pub. Find out what is going on in there. Damian goes in the front door and back your brother."

William knew Thomas was upset with Duncan. He went over to Michael and gave him a hug. The two men watch what Thomas was going to do.

Duncan staired at Thomas. "Ye had said there were three men not two."

Thomas looked right at him. "Now how do ye even know what I had said. Ye were off to talk with Ronald. If ye had stayed ye could have talked to him there. The other man is inside the pub."

Duncan then spoke. "I sure hope so. Then that means there is only one man with Albert."

Thomas was a little upset with him. He was running through his mouth without even knowing that Michael had the information. "Will ye stop talking, I don't care if ye are older than us. Damn it, ye are full of yourself. Ye don't act your age, grow up and deal with your responsibility."

Then Michael bellowed. "Stop it right now Thomas. Duncan didn't understand why he couldn't go with us. We always let him know what was going on. His younger brother was going with us. He didn't know that they were going to die in battle. It made him feel like he was a kid, which isn't true.

CHAPTER TWELVE

Albert is in the Highland's

THOMAS RAN A hand through his hair; he looked at his brother Michael. "Duncan is acting like a scared deer. When we were in the Lowlands do ye think he would come and check on us. Hell, no we were supposed to have talks on the history of the Lowlands. Do ye think he did his job? No, we had to ask the old-timers about different things about their town.

"Don't take this the wrong way. I'm happy he found his love. We found out the young women we been with all are life, we were in love with them. Before we left the Highlands, we married them. William and I had a job to do. We couldn't be with our brides, but William and I had to deal with it. We had to pretend we were looking for a wife.

"Duncan, I had to figure out everything from Eleanor to why Ronald was going back to the talks. I didn't have Michael to tell me what was going on. William had the same problem as I did. I was also dealing with the chance I was going to be the oldest. I had to believe that Michael was dead, that I was now the oldest.

"As the night went on, I realize Ronald wanted Michael to hunt down all those hired killers. After I took everything apart, I figured out why Ronald talked to Jonathan and Peter and why he was leaving. They knew this would be the end of their life, to fight in battle was better than dyeing a slow death."

"Duncan, grow-up, we need men to do this job. Not one that is winy, about being the oldest of three families. If ye worried that we will come to ye for advice stop worrying. If I need advice I will go to Michael or my father. Michael has been married longer than the ye, I don't know why ye are acting like this. Ye been worrying over nothing, we have a job to do we must work together. Michael is in charge he has the information about where we must go."

*　*　*　*　*

Right at that moment Gallivan opened the pub door. "Hawk, ye are home."

Then Gallivan shouted to Nutley the bartender. "Set up a Scotch for Hawk."

He quickly closed the door behind him and ran over to us. "Gallivan what was that all about."

He spoke. "Nutley said he been asking questions about Eleanor. He is one of Huascaran men. Michael would ye, like to talk with him. He's sitting at the back of the pub. Damian is near the front door. "That man has been asking about Eleanor by name. He knew her age was about nineteen. Then he went on to say what color hair Eleanor had. Nutley knew this man worked for Huascaran. This man was telling stories that happened when Eleanor and Catherin went to the Lowlands."

Thomas spoke. "Did he say if ye knew of any women that fit that description."

Gallivan shook his head no. "He just stopped talking when Nutley got upset. I'm sorry that we weren't any help to ye."

William spoke. "There ye are wrong Gallivan. Ye were able to set it up so that we could take him down. Gallivan, I want ye to go out back, to make sure he doesn't sneak out the back. I'll send Damian when we have everything locked down, ye can take the two kegs and scotch back to the castle.

Then bring Father and Donald here with everything we need. Damian ye can come back with them. While we take care of that man in the pub. Thomas give us a bit of time. Let him hear of the stories of Hawk's hunt for Marcos and his son. Then ye come on into the pub. If he makes it to the door, don't let him out. Grab him or lay him out cold if ye like."

Thomas didn't know why he was with this group. "Can I have some fun with him."

Michael shook his head. "Ye can do what ye like, if ye don't kill him or scare him to death."

* * * * *

Inside the pub Nutley, was watching the old man. He was making his way to the front door. Gallivan was right, he did look old and feeble. How did an old man get himself into a mess like this.

Michael looked around then his eyes landed on the old man. "Nutley, could I have a Scotch and one for my cousin.

Nutley started the conversation. "How was your trip Hawk, were ye able to kill Marcos."

Michael then answered. "If ye mean, is he dead. Aye… one of his men shot him. I watched him bleed to death. He killed all his men but one. I killed the last one on the way home. Along with the two here in the Highlands. There are only two men including Albert."

Michael knew that the old man was carefully listening to every word he said. "I don't want to be the man who has been finding these women for Marcos."

Duncan had gotten into the story. "Aye…, our fathers would enjoy getting their hands, on his scrawny little neck." Michael nodded to Damian; he came over to the bar and spoke. "If ye find him I like to have a piece of him. He took my wife to be for his master."

Michael pat Damian on the back. "Take it easy she is safe now. Go with your brother in a bit. Ye know there are ten men who would help our fathers string him up. They would let him hang until he is dead. Just for the part he played in the deaths of all those women. I know all about those women. Marcos killed them because they didn't give him a son. That man who found these women for him, should also paid for what he did."

Michael went on to say. "I know this young lass just over the line of Scotland. Her name is Mena; she has just turned sixteen. She's a sweet thing, with the heart of a fighter and can ride. She almost lost her parents because of Marcos."

*   *   *   *   *

Right then Nutley touched Michael's hand. He gave a nod toward the old man. They did it, the old man was scared. He was trying to make his way over to the front door. When he reached the door handle. That's when Thomas opened the door. The momentum threw the old man into Thomas muscular body.

The impression Thomas received when the older man slammed into his chest. This man wasn't evil. His age was around his father's age, maybe a little older. Thomas took out his dirk and placed it under the man's chin. Slowly he backed the man up to the bar where Michael and Duncan were sitting. "Sit down and tell us do ye work for the family of Huascaran."

Thomas watched the man try to sit a little taller. He knew that they had him by right, so he bent his head and spoke. "I'm ashamed to say I do. Outside there was two men, I saw Hawk kill the man that gets the women for Marcos. The other man is a demon; I saw that dirk go pass your cheek. Are ye the man called the demon hunter."

He looked right at Thomas. Without saying a word, he went over to the bar and asked for two scotches. He handed one of the scotches to William. He went and sat near the man, the old man saw he was box in. "May I have a Scotch please sir."

Thomas took his money out and paid for all the drinks. He then handed the Scotch to the old man. The man took and tossed the drink back. He closed his eyes and took two deep breaths. "I will tell you I'm glad those men are gone. Ye said that Marcos is dead, then we don't have time to waste. I would like to tell ye that Albert, is being utilize for his face and body. Marcos found out that Albert is not his son. There is a locket that is going into his chest. Due to that fact, Marcos is dead. Albert, is fighting for his life; Marcos has put a locket around his neck. This locket is now going into his chest. The demon has been keeping him sleeping but Albert is still fighting to dig out that locket. When he's awake, he told me about his dream. This young woman helps him a bit she must have magic. She was able to pull the locket out so Albert could grab it again.

"I need to tell ye about the demon, who took over a young boy's body. This demon has black magic. What I understand is that the boy had magic to start with. When the demon took over the boy's body, he was around ten at the time."

*　*　*　*　*

Then Michael spoke. "I know right where they have him. I saw Albert, he is still trying to dig the locket out. Then I followed ye three here. What makes ye think this boy is all evil. Did ye see the demon take over the boy's body."

The old man looked at Michael. "No, I didn't join them back then. I watched him thrust his hand into the man's chest and pull out his heart. There were other things like giving Marcos a glass of blood to drink. Marcos told me it was wine; I know what wine smells like. That was no wine but warm blood from the woman Marcos had just killed. Albert wasn't the one who raped or killed those women. It was Marcos who did those things."

Then their brother Ronald appeared to them. *"Hello my brother's. Have ye figured out that he is telling the truth yet."*

Thomas and Michael nodded their heads yes. *"Ronald, he had said that Marcos drank the blood of the dead women. That is part of black magic."*

They saw Ronald nodded his head yes. The old man was scared that the men wouldn't help him. "You don't believe me, that a man would do that. Marcos drinks the women's blood after he kills them. He had this demon to cut the blonde hair from each of the women. He dipped the hair in their blood them placed it in the locket.

"I found out why Marcos drinks the blood. He believes he is taking their life force. One of these times he tried to get Albert to drink the blood. He quickly rejected the glass; he knew that wasn't wine. The smell made him sick when he realized it was blood. After that day every time they had these rituals, they had to drug him. When he woke up, they told him that he raped the woman then killed her. Marcos thought that Albert was his son. Believing that, he thought he would act just like him.

"The older Albert got, the more Marcos knew he wasn't his son. The woman Marcos took was already with child. The things that they have said about Albert are not true. I've been with him since the day he was two days old. My wife and I raised him, he is my grandson. Marcos doesn't know this. After the death of my son, I found where Marcos had taken Malinda."

Duncan spoke. "Hold on! Did ye say Albert is your grandson? Now it's making sense. My dad told me that an old woman cursed him. For him to not have any son, no woman could give him a son. She did that because he raped her daughter. Marcos killed them both, I think ye better start this story at the beginning."

*　*　*　*　*

The old man looked over the four young men. "My name is Timothy McWaters. Twenty-four years ago, Marcos came to my son's home. He took my son's wife who was pregnant with Dan's child. Ginny just found out the week before Marcos came to their home. My son and I had gone hunting. Ginny was alone that day, she was doing her canning for winter. My wife was bringing more vegetables from our garden later that day. On our way home Dan arrived at the house. At first, he had a bad feeling that something was wrong at home. He walked right in while Marcos was… damn it. All these years and it still hurts to talk about it."

Tears rolled down Timothy's cheeks and he quickly wiped them away and kept on talking. "One man had his hand over Lindy's mouth. The others two men held her while Marcos raped her. My son Dan didn't see the beast come up behind him. He thrust his knife into Dan's back. It didn't kill him outright. Dan had to play dead so he could save his wife. One of the men called Marcos Duke Huascaran.

"I wasn't far away when I saw what the beast had done to my boy. I couldn't do anything to help my son right then. I thought they had killed Dan and Ginny, the man must get done raping Ginny. He through her over his shoulder and carried her out. I still can hear her scream when she saw her husband lying on the floor."

William quickly passed Timothy another Scotch drink. Timothy downed the Scotch in one gulp. "Thank you, I needed that."

William asked. "When Marcos and his men left, did ye get to talk to your son for very long."

Timothy eyes had tears in them. "Just long enough to find out Marcos's name and what he had done to Ginny."

Thomas asked. "How did ye find Marcos. Did ye leave your son to follow Marcos and his men."

Timothy looked at him. There was anger in his voice. "No, I wasn't going to leave my son so my wife would find him dead. Right when I was giving up hope, The Lord sent my son's friend to me. Mike had come over to see my boy. He wanted to know how we did when we went hunting. Dan was still alive, and he asked his friend to follow Marcos. Mike was one that could track anything. He had discovered where Marcos had brought Ginny. When Mike returned, he told us where to find Ginny. My wife and I went there and kept watching for a chance to save my daughter-in-law. That man kept raping Ginny until he knew she was with child. Nine months later Marcos thought he had himself a son. My daughter in law… she died giving birth to my grandson. Marcos's wife didn't want anything to do with the child. My wife and I made friends with someone in Marcos's house. I found out that Marcos was looking for an older couple to raise the boy. He had a house in the Lowlands of Scotland."

Duncan spoke. "Tell us when Marcos's start drinking the blood from his victims."

Timothy spoke. "It was two years ago. He was in a battle and almost died. His servant took him to this place deep in the woods."

Michael slammed down his fist. "I knew my arrow hit him; it had to be when Marcos tried to wipe out the MacGregor men. I should have followed him and finished the job."

Thomas bellowed at Michael. "Stop it! Ye knew that ye couldn't let Ronald die without a family member being with him. Your mind wasn't on killing Marcos. Ye knew our brother was still alive, Ye didn't want him to die alone. I would have done the same thing. We are not evil; we care about life and family. I don't want ye to think about that again, my brother. Timothy, I'm sorry to but in like that please go on with ye story."

Now he knew that these two men had to be MacGregor's. "One day Marcos had gotten drunk. He was laughing about the people coming after him. Then he started to talk about the brotherhood. Marcos said that the brotherhood gave him powers. If he were to die, there was a way he could come back. His manservant knows just what to do. Do any of you know about black magic."

Michael spoke. "Aye… why do ye want to know about black magic. Do ye know this magic is evil? It comes from the dark side."

The man shook his head no. "I don't want to know about black magic, just how to stop it. This young man across from me. He killed Marcos's man who had an evil spell put on him. He was to be unstoppable. Standing here with you four men, I can feel the power of good within you. I know how it feels when you are in the presence of evil. I'm hoping you can save my grandson before it's too late."

Duncan spoke. "I don't like where this is going. Ye are talking about black magic and stopping Marcos. Ye are saying he is trying to take over Albert's body, know man should be able to do such a thing. Then again Marcos was part Fairy and Demon."

Thomas looked right at Ronald. *"Damn it! Ronald ye are going to fight Marcos are ye not."*

Ronald smiled at his little brother. *"Thomas ye knew that I was going to fight him in the valley of the dead. Ye have a strong wife and determine woman. She had found a spell to keep are souls safe. Marcos will not have the upper hand. I already know he will have demons with him. I will also have family members who have magic. They have fought Marcos once before; one is the keeper of the roses for he gave his magic to the roses. Ye wife has taken care of them they have what I have. Remember little brother, now I have more protection."*

Timothy was looking at the men. "Yes! That is just what I'm talking about. I'm scared now that Hawk is here, the beast will wait only two days. This demon would carry out any orders his master would give him. I must find someone with the opposite power."

Timothy looked right at Thomas. "You are the man I've been looking for. The man you killed… he was the strongest of the four. That man was the one who takes the women. The demon has magical powers. I don't know how Marcos received his powers that he has. All I know is his servant and two of his men have demon's living inside them. I need to find the one called Eleanor."

Thomas spoke. "Why do ye ask about this woman Eleanor. Is she to be one of his women he will rape to give him a son."

Timothy shook his head. "No. Heavens no. Marcos believes her betrothed could stop the plans he has put in motion. I'm looking for her betrothed. I need him to help me save Albert."

William spoke. "How could Marcos know about Eleanor and her betrothed…and where to find her."

Timothy spoke. "Marcos used his magic to take on Albert's face. Whatever Marcos can see Albert can see and feel everything he does. That night Albert had a dream about Eleanor. The look that she gave Marcos. Told him she knew that Marcos was evil. She must have seen that the eyes didn't match his face. This had happened in the Lowlands of Scotland. She was at a party he attended. Before he left the party. Marcos found out what her name was and where she came from. In Albert's dream when Marcos eyes met hers.

"Albert had a feeling she could free him. He called her one day, he couldn't dig at it. This Eleanor used her magic and pulled it out more to give him more time. The demon had felt her magic and pushed her back. He felt that she knew someone who could stop Marcos. This scared him to high heavens. Albert didn't feel as if he was the one doing those awful things to these women. In the dream his mind was slipping away. Albert told me he felt as if Marcos's mind was in his head. The dream showed him who could stop Marcos. He was a tall Scottish man with black hair and golden-brown eyes like yours. She called her savior who rescued her Thomas.

"Albert saw this Thomas that he has strong magic. There was this magic that was on his knife. There is a spirit that helps him at times. He tells him were Hawk or Marcos is."

Timothy looked at Michael then at each one at the table. "You all have the same powers. It keeps you save. You're all brothers and fought the demons together. Hawk one of those men that Marco had killed was your brother. Albert said in his dream he saw Marcos fighting with him. While you two was fighting with the demon."

Timothy had pointed to Thomas and Michael. "You two are the ones along with the spirit of your brother. Thomas could kill my grandson, or he could save him. I need to convince him to help me save him. Albert is all we have left of our son."

Thomas then asked. "Did Marcos know about these dreams."

Timothy answered. "Yes…, Marcos can see what he is dreaming about. That's why Marcos has men out looking for this Eleanor along with her betrothed."

Michael spoke. "That explains why those men asked if my name was Thomas, and if I knew of a woman called Eleanor. I told them the name is Hawk."

"Timothy ye know what happened to these men. Now it's your turn to tell me the number of men is with Albert. Don't lie to me when I left England. The townspeople told me who was with Albert. They even told me what each of them looked like. Tell me the number of men ye are traveling with?"

Michael watched him swallow. "Albert had four men with him. You took down two of them. We should do something before it's too late. The beast may wait the two days, I really don't know."

Michael picked up his meal and spoke. "I believe we should sit at a table. I'm going to eat my meal in a more comfortable chair."

* * * * *

The five men moved to sit at around table. Thomas didn't know if he could trust or believe Timothy's story. When he looked over at Michael, he saw Ronald standing behind him. Ronald placed his hands right on Michael's shoulders. Thomas smiled, took a deep breath, and spoke. "Timothy, take this coin and get yourself a drink. I need to speak with my kinsmen. We need to decide what we are going to do."

Ronald appeared next to Thomas. He spoke in a soft tone. "Does everyone see Ronald."

The three men chimed in, "Aye."

Michael spoke. "Thank heavens ye are here Ronald. Is everything Timothy has told us true."

Ronald smiled at his brothers. *"Aye… ye can trust Timothy. The time is going quickly we won't have enough time left if we stand here any longer. So be quick about your decision for the demon of Marcos is nearby. I can't help ye in this fight, The Lord has tied my hands. This fight is for the living. Ye all must understand that Marcos can't come back, he will be more ruthless then before. His goal is to take Albert soul and sacrifice it to the dark side. If he can do so, it will be hard to stop him. The dark side owns Marcos, not Albert. Albert is still fighting the evil spell. His strength is going. Ye can do this Thomas with Michael's help. I can fight Marcos in the spirit world. I can't help to kill the beast."*

Then Thomas looked at his brother. "How do we stop Marcos and the beast."

Ronald looked at his brother's. *"The same way ye stop the last one."*

Duncan spoke. "Ronald what do ye mean the last one. Are ye talking about the man that Thomas killed?"

Ronald shook his head. *"Look old friend. Get your head out of the clouds. Thomas killed a man under the power of black magic. What I had found out about the magic of the roses. Marcos tries to kill all the roses in Scotland. When ye took Eleanor to where the roses were. She found that the power would help your weapons. He knew how strong our great grandfather was. Marcos knew when Kina had mated, with him, her powers matched his. Remember Marcos's mother was a Fairy; Satan is his father.*

"The Fairy Magic was strong enough to cut through the black magic. Eleanor's visions told her more then she had told ye. Now she has place on your bodies the shield from the Lord. Marcus can't get into my mind, heart, or soul. I can't hear him when he tries to take over me.

Father Sinclair blessed the vest with holy water. Damian has holy water and rose petals that is if ye need it."

Thomas was tired of all of this. *"Brother when will this be over with. Aye…, Michael, and I have magic. William also has magic; he is our sister's mate. Ye are saying with are skills and the magic, we can take down this demon."*

Ronald went over and put his hands directly on Thomas, shoulders. *"Breathe little brother ye will do fine. Don't worry about these things. There is more help on the way."*

Michael looked around at his brothers. "Ye have heard everything that Timothy and Ronald have said. I would like to hear more about this locket. Timothy, ye can come back to the table. We'd like to know more about the locket. Where is the locket kept and is there a symbol on the locket."

Ronald moved to stand behind Michael. Timothy came back to the table and sat down in his seat. "Albert's locket is around his neck always; it's hidden under his clothing. The symbol on the locket is a circle with a star in the middle of the circle. Marcos's ordered Albert never to take the locket off. At first, he could move it. Now it's become part of his skin. He's unable to take it off or move it around. Each day Albert's acting more like Marcos.

"I see the good in him is still trying to fight the evil within this locket. As the days go by, I'm slowly losing my grandson to him. Marcos took my son and his wife. He's trying to take my grandson away from me.

"Please help me save Albert from Marcos. If he must die let it be before He takes over his body. At least his soul will be with his mother and father. I pray that we can save Albert. He was a good man until Marcos's step into the picture. He has a sweet loving wife and beautiful little girl. His wife had a baby nine months later. My wife sent me a message that it was a boy. Marcos doesn't know anything about her being pregnant. Albert don't know that he has a son."

Michael spoke. "I saw how Marcos died; everything is making sense now. His death was too quick and easy. Marcos ignored everything that happened to him. He didn't care that he was bleeding out to his death. He laughed and said he would die when he was ready to die. Ye said that he had ye raise Albert. When did Marcos come to see him?"

Timothy laughed. "About three times in his lifetime. This last time was on his twenty-fourth birthday. Marcos played as a loving father and grandfather. The gift he gave Albert was a locket. From the moment he placed it around his neck. Albert started changing in little ways. He didn't know what was happening to him. The third visit was late at night. The devil's helper took Albert from his bed. Marcos must have put a sleeping spell on everyone. I was outside taking care of one of the horses. I saw what was happening and went to follow them.

William then spoke. "Why did they let ye come with them."

Timothy answered. "It was the Lord who helped me. With his help I was able to convince him. I told him I'd take care of Albert. It worked. He took us to England to a house deep in the woods. You must know the rest of their story."

Michael spoke. "Aye… the townspeople didn't paint a pretty picture of Albert. They made him out to be a monster. Before I left, I showed them the book that Marcos kept. It told how Marcos killed all those women. Albert's name wasn't in the book until the last page. At the end of the book, he said that Albert wasn't his son. That he was going to use his body and soul to come back from the dead."

Timothy nodded his head yes. "Marcos did a number on Albert's reputation. He had his men tell stories about him. The men would talk about him when the townspeople were in ear shot of them."

Michael then spoke. "With that book everyone came to the pub. In Marcos own words, said that Albert is not his son. That he was weak when he saw me rape these women. That he would get sick of the things that he done to these women.

Timothy looked at Michael. "You are telling me that the towns people know that he's not like Marcos. Thank you for doing that for us. His poor wife what she was hearing about her husband. The people were talking about it made it hard on her. My wife took them to where his father and mother lived. That helped her and the children. These stories were so bad that they told. About Albert and Marcos would take turns raping the women. Marcos was the only one who touched them.

"My poor grandson would get sick when Marcos made him watch what he did. He put all of this in writing. That's when Marcos found out that Albert wasn't his son. From then on, he would drug his drink. He used black magic on him. Marcos's trying to make Albert; into himself. Soon that locket will be inside his chest.

"Before we left England, I overheard Marcos giving the devil's helper orders. Just in case Marcos doesn't show up, take it that he is dead. He told the beast to start the last part of the spell. The black magic will allow Marcos to take over Albert's body. He will take Albert's soul and sacrifice it to the dark side. When that happens, we will lose Albert for good."

Right then the door opened Damian came in. "Thomas, can I have a word with ye and Hawk outside."

Timothy looked at the four men. "There is a Thomas in the mix of you, why didn't you tell me. I know two of your names. The two youngest are keeping their names a secret. Why do you not believe what I have told you? Oh my God you are Thomas, I was right. You were the one to kill the man who was under the spell of the black magic. I saw Marcos take a knife and stab that man, there was no blood or hole in his chest. Do you know if Marcos had the demon take his soul."

Thomas looked at Ronald. *"Brother touch Timothy and see if he has any evil in him.* William ye come with us. *Ronald, keep an eye on Duncan and Timothy."*

Timothy found that his hands were all light. "What is going on."

Thomas smiled at him and went out with Michael. They followed Damian outside the pub.

Damian spoke. "I'm sorry Thomas. I didn't know what was happening inside the pub. When we got to the castle Eleanor and Grana had a vision. Father Sinclair and Dad's with me, and I have all your weapons. There are three bottles of holy water. Father had Uncle make two big crosses for him. Ye have two bags of rose petals,

Father Sinclair had blessed them. The holy water, ye must pour it around the locket on his chest.

"Grana said not to touch this object with your bare hands. It is pure evil; here are gloves with holy water that Father blessed. Wear them when ye take off the locket.

"With these weapons, Michael and ye will be able to kill the beast. After the beast is dead, ye must burn him with what was around Albert's neck.

*   *   *   *   *

Thomas was about to unload his fear on Damian. Michael saw two riders coming toward them. "Breathe…little brother. The Lord answered your prayers. I saw Uncle Donald and Father Sinclair. Father can take care of the locket while we try to kill that beast. Now there will be eight of us. I see that they also have the heavenly glow also."

Donald and Father Sinclair rode up to the men. Damian went over to his father. "Dad, I tried to tell them what everyone told me. I forgot parts in the excitement. I'm sorry Thomas will ye forgive me?"

Thomas went over to him. "All this has me anxious, things with Eleanor's involvement had scare me for her life. Ye did nothing wrong Damian."

Donald spoke. "What excitement son."

Michael told the story. "They saw us kill the two men here. It was Marcos's men that we had killed when we got here. The one Thomas killed was under a spell. Timothy said that man couldn't die they used black magic on him. If that is so he gave his soul to the devil. After they were dead, we took a rose petal and made it into a cross. We put holy water on the cross and we placed it on their chest. Then Thomas told me to touch the man's body as he did. I thought I had seen their souls went to be judge."

Damian spoke. "When they found out whom Michael was, they tried to kill him. I saw Thomas make a difficult shot with his dirk. Ye should have seen that dirk just miss Michael's cheek. Thomas, I wish ye could teach me how to do that."

Father Sinclair got down from his horse. "Tell me where the bodies are now."

*   *   *   *   *

Father went over to Thomas. "Will done, both of ye did just what ye should do. I just like to give them absolution. Could ye show me where they are? Ye did everything right, my son. I just want to add the blessing. The one that wasn't a demon, may need a little more help."

I went to bless the roses, as the holy water touched them. The Lord sent the petals to my cross. I saw the moonlight made them glow brighter. The rose bushes have the blessing of The Lord. May I see your dirk."

Thomas took out the dirk. Father blessed the knife, and he put three more rose petals on the dirk. Then he poured a bit of holy water over it. "The petals are inside the man. It will hole the man for a bit."

"There, your dirk is ready. Ye will come with me for ye may have to kill him again. My boy ye have been dealing with this. For myself I haven't got to deal with any of this. A man made this cross with his magic. Will see if it is the same when The Lord makes it."

Thomas went with Father while the others headed toward the pub and went inside. Ye could have heard a pin drop when Donald stepped into the pub.

Duncan was surprised when he spoke. "Dad what are ye doing here?"

Donald wanted to laugh, with the look on his son's face. He spoke. "The people will keep high hopes in their thoughts, for ye to get this job done. Father Sinclair and I thought ye could use a hand with the black magic."

*   *   *   *   *

Father was walking along the path with Thomas. He spoke. "My son ye have quite a woman as your mate. She was determined, to mark

Marcos as a man who rapes women. She watched as he tried to rid himself of the mark.

Thomas was so proud of his wife. He spoke. "When we were children, she tried to do as I did. She is the best rider on horseback in the Highlands. I showed her everything my father and brother showed me. I never thought she was my mate. Father all I want is to be with my wife."

*　*　*　*　*

Thomas was looking at all the beauty around them. Today the sky was a deep blue. The sun was a deep red and orange. It was a muggy day in the highlands. The birds were singing to the once they wanted to mate with. Why does he feel cold inside right to his bones?

Thomas watched Father Sinclair place rose petals on the cross. The rose petals would function as if they were nails holding the cross down on the man's chest. He noticed strange things that were happening to him. There it was again, from nowhere came a freezing wind. He looked around and he couldn't see any wind blowing, still he felt cold inside. The two men were talking about what they had seen. Thomas heard loud laughter.

Then Ronald appeared to Father and Thomas. He had turned to Marcos and spoke. *"Enough Marcos, I see ye are scared that my brother will defeat the demon. Ye look so old with those marks on your face. Too bad it will turn women off. Leve my brother alone. Can ye feel the holy water on my brother's body. I can see where it burned ye. Try going through my brother slowly. Then I will take ye to The Lord. Marcos ye can see, your men are ready for me to bring them to The Lord. Be gone son of Satan."*

Like before, Ronald sent Marcos away from the living. Thomas looked at his brother. "Has Marcos tried to take us down with the cold."

His brother smiled at him. *"Little brother he's been trying to frieze your heart. What Eleanor did for all of us. She was the one to save ye. I'll be back after I take them to The Lord. Thomas uses your magic to get back to the pub. Father blessed his mind and lips and his ears. Marcos will keep trying everything he can to take all ye down."*

*   *   *   *   *

Father was a maze of what Eleanor and Thomas could do. When they opened the door, he saw Ronald was back. He watched as he put a loving hand on Michael's shoulder.

"Now that Thomas is back, I think I'll look at the beast. Then I will look in on Albert. I will try this magic that Eleanor gave me. I will see if I can frieze the locket, so it can't go farther into his chest. I'll be back."

Thomas stared at Ronald while he drank his Scotch. *"Ronald, can Marcos hurt ye when the two of ye are fighting."*

Ronald looked at his brother. *"I will tell ye this. Your wife saved me along with yourself and anyone that has the light from The Lord. We are lucky to have her in our family."*

Ronald went over and placed a hand on Thomas's shoulder. It felt cold in that spot where he touched him. Just knowing it was Ronald who touched him warmed his heart. His brother loved him and Michael. *"The Lord sent me to take them for judgment. Marcos believes he will get away without being judge. He has been doing this for longer than ye know. Ye take care of Michael. I know he will take care of ye little brother. Be careful I don't want to see ye there in heaven yet. See ye in a bit little brother."*

Thomas looked at his brother. *"Ronald, have I told ye that I'm proud to be your brother and that I love ye. We will be careful, ye must be careful also."*

*   *   *   *   *

Michael touch Thomas on the shoulder. "It's time we have to get ready for this fight."

Thomas nodded his head. They followed Michael into the backroom of the pub. There the others were making plans with Donald and Timothy. The outline that Ronald gave Michael was on the table. It had shown where Albert was.

Donald walked over to Thomas and gave him a hug. "Are ye all right my boy."

He had nodded his head. "I was glad Ronald was with us. He said what's going into Albert's chest is pure evil. Make sure that Father has those gloves with him. Have Damian, keep Father Albert and Timothy in the tunnel with Duncan. I pray that we can take this beast down quickly."

Outside the men loaded the horses with their weapons. Donald saw his family looking toward the castle. He suspected that he knew what they were thinking. He had the same thoughts about being at home with his wife and children. It's one thing to go up against a man to fight with weapons. It's a whole different story when the man knows black magic.

Father then spoke. "Dear Heavenly Father, please keep all of us save. Let us help Albert so he can go home to his wife and children. Help us bring down the beast and send him to Ye Lord, so that he will be judged. In Jesus name Amen.

CHAPTER THIRTEEN

The battle of good and evil.

ONALD WENT OVER to his family. "My sons, I love ye five. We must watch out for other demons. I don't want anyone of us to die tonight. We won't bring any bodies home just to tell our women their men are dead."

Duncan spoke. "Dad that goes for ye also. Ye are still young and need to see your grandchildren grow up."

Donald nodded his head and spoke. "Saddle up we ride to defeat the demon. Let's ride."

The eight men mounted their horses and headed out of town. They were riding through the hillside enjoying the sights. It made the men relax to hear the birds singing in the trees. To feel the warmth of the sun at their backs as they rode. When they came to a field of wildflowers that was all in bloom. They could smell the sweet scent all around them.

All these things we will fight for in life and for freedom. In a while they will be in a battle fighting for their lives. The place they were heading had a battle long ago. Once again that place will see another battle. Until then they will enjoy the new leaves on the trees and flowers in bloom. There was a soft wind blowing through the treetops. Ye would think they were out just for a ride through the countryside. At the hillside, the men would start there climb to the ruined castle. The eight of them were about through the clearing. These trees gave cover for the eight men. Just before they got to the castle, they saw three men. One of them he knew, the other two looked like his father.

*　*　*　*　*

Thomas and Michael moved closer to these men. "Ronald is that ye."

Both men got off their horses. Ronald moved up to them. *"Michael and Thomas come here and meet our uncle's. Uncle Donald ye should know one of these men."*

Donald got off his horse and went to stand with his nephews. "Oh my God, it can't be them. Joseph, is that ye."

The spirit of Joseph came over to his friend. *"Hello old friend. I wish we all didn't meet this way. How's my brother doing."*

He looked at the other two young men. Joseph looked at Michael and Thomas. *"Are these young men, my brothers' son's."*

Donald nodded yes. "Aye… This is Michael, they call him Hawk. This is Thomas, they call him eagle eye and now he is known as the demon hunter."

Thomas and Michael already knew who these men were. Both brothers walked over to the men. Thomas spoke. "Ronald ye brought are uncles to us. But why."

Then he knew why. "It's because Marcos is not going to play fair."

Thomas then called Eleanor. *"Honey, I need two more vests right now. Make sure that it comes from the deer's hide. Ye can use magic on the hide. Place rose petals on it and give them to my father, have dad call me when it's done. I love ye honey."*

Then Thomas heard his father's voice. He waved his hand, and his father appeared to them. "Thomas what is going on son. Here are the vest ye ask for."

Thomas took them from him. "Dad, turn around and say hello to your brother."

Daniel hadn't felt his brother in a while. The two men functioned as if they never went away from each other. He went over and gave his brother a bear hug. The heavenly light surrounded the two men.

Thomas placed the names in the vests Raymond and Joseph. He went into his sporran to get his brother's weapons. Then he waved his hand and there were three sets of weapons. "Father could ye come here and bless these men and their weapons."

Father got down from his horse. In his pocket he had two crosses. When the men hugged, he saw the heavenly light. "My sons ye are here to help Ronald. Ye comes from The Lord, it's true. I felt the power from ye. Then Father placed a cross on the men and two rose petals on the crosses. He blessed them afterwards, with holy water.

Joseph went over to Raymond. *"Daniel, I like ye to meet* Raymond *are great grandfather. He fought with his brother as I did with ye. I didn't think I would see ye until it was your time. How is Franceam."*

Daniel had to wipe his eyes. "She is more beautiful than before. Use men can't get away with anything." Then he turned to Ronald. "Son, can they come back one last time to see everyone if possible."

He smiled at his father. *"If The Lord tells us we can. We will see ye again."*

Daniel went over to the two men. "It was wonderful to meet ye grandfather. He had told his brother. "It was hard without ye here. I will pray that ye can come back to meet everyone. God speed son, ye have two powerful men with ye."

This time Daniel waved his hand, and the vests were on the men. He gave his brother his weapons. Michael gave Ronald his. Then Thomas gave his grandfather his weapons. "Ronald is this just to keep Marcos away from us."

Ronald looked at Thomas. *"So ye figured it out, I knew ye would. Now do ye know what to do with the locket."*

Thomas smiled at his brother. "Is this another puzzle for me to figure out again."

Ronald then laughed. "Brother ye got this. Ye four men will take Marcos's man down. They will send Marcos back to his father. Ye do know that his father is Satan. We three will keep him busy until ye call him to the locket."

Thomas saw William talking to his uncle. He went over to them. "Uncle this is Theseus son. He married my sister, and I married William's sister." They heard him laugh. "Well done."

Thomas felt it was time to get this done. "I pray we will see all ye tomorrow night. Ronald ye are going to the valley of the dead are ye."

He saw the three men nodded their heads. Raymond was watching Thomas as he got ready to send them there. "Father would ye place holy water over my hands. This is a holy place; my magic must be pure to send them there."

He then did what he asked. Thomas bent his head and said a prayer. "May The Lord be with ye. Michael sends dad home."

Thomas then gathered his magic. He spoke. "Whole on to your weapons and I will send ye there. To the last point were Raymond and his brother who fought Marcuse."

Thomas closed his eyes and pictured that place from his nightmare. With both hands he made a circle gathering his power. Then he brought his hands back together. He felt the power he had inside him. Then he pushed all his power at them to send them into the valley of the dead. "Good luck my family."

Father saw the men disappear. "This needed to happen. The Lord sent me here in order that I could help Albert and your family."

Thomas called Ronald. "Brother are the three of ye there and safe." Then he heard them say. "Well done, Marcos is not happy to see us. He thought I wouldn't bring anyone with me. Good luck little brother, and the battle starts."

*　*　*　*　*

Thomas then looked at everyone. "All right men we have a job to do. I need the four of ye to take care of Albert. When the locket is off Albert's neck. Duncan will bring it to me in this box, along with the gloves. Father ye must stay in the tunnel with Damian and Timothy. We all know what we need to do. Good luck to all of us."

Father then spoke. "May The Lord be with us all, Amen."

Thomas looked at his brother. Michael knew what Thomas wanted. He took out the map from his sporran. "Where would Ye like us to be at."

Donald looked at the map. Then spoke. "About halfway up this hillside. We need cover about here."

Thomas looked at the hillside. There was a wall not far away from where uncle wanted to be. With a wave of his hand there was a wall of dirt cut into the hillside. It was the size of four men across. There was grass all on it, the bottom was flat. "Will this do uncle?"

Donald was pleased with that. "Aye… now we have cover."

Thomas waved his hand, and they were in position on the hillside.

The battle spot

While Duncan's party of four went to the other side of the hill. They made their way through small trees and rocks. Just in front of the cave there are large rocks and great amount of long vines. Duncan and William had to clean the rocks and vines away from the cave. Then Duncan lit the torches that he had brought along with them. Inside the cave it was very damp. They worked their way down the long tunnel. Duncan noticed there were traces of bones.

He spoke. "Ronald was right, there's a mountain lion living in here. Damian ye come with me."

He followed his brother through the cave side. He had left his sord with Father. Damian remembered the story about the war in which he had fought. "Father, here take my sord if the cat comes back. Timothy here is one of the torches. There seems to be a good amount of wood. They could build a small fire. I'll give ye the go ahead to make one when we check out the rest of this tunnel. If I yell to ye. Get out of the way. For a lion will be coming down the tunnel."

Father then spoke. "Hurry back before that cat comes back."

Not far ahead was the end of the tunnel. There was no mountain lion inside. Duncan sent Damian back to have Timothy make a small fire near the entrance. This should keep out the lion for now. While Damian was gone, he left his torch in the tunnel. He went to find the location where Albert was.

Inside the castle he could see walls that were half gone. Doorways were kick in as the vines grew through and over them. It had seemed that the vines were taking over parts of the castle. Duncan then saw a doorway that wasn't damaged. He looked around before he tried the door.

Outside the castle, voices had echo through the castle. The fight had started; his job was to get to Albert while the beast was fighting. Then he saw his brother and motioned for him to come over to him. Duncan asked is everything was all right."

Damian smiled as he spoke. "When I got back Father and Timothy were fighting off the mountain lion. Father told me he fought in the war. Wow he could manage my sword. The two of them scared off the mountain lion. They were getting a fire going to keep the lion out of the tunnel. Father is not weak as he appears to be. That man can fight when he must."

Duncan nodded his head. "I didn't think he was. Those robes hide his body strength from people. Come on brother, we have a job to do the fighting has started. I need ye to help me get Albert back in the tunnel. It will take time to get that locket out from under his skin."

Duncan had tried the doorknob and found it locked. He had to get into that room right now. Then Damian saw a set of keys and went over to fetch them. With the door unlock they moved quickly inside. The men had found Albert moving all over the floor. The poor man had ripped his shirt wide open. They saw pain in Albert's face. His hands were trying to dig out the locket from his chest. He had blood and skin on his fingernails. Damian and Duncan grabbed both of Albert's arms and legs. It would have been faster if Duncan could throw him over his shoulder. It had to be this way as they carried him back to the tunnel. Father had a blanket down for him. His prayer book was on the blanket. A fire was also nearby. The torches were hanging over their heads, to give them more-light.

Duncan and his brother place Albert's body on the blanket. He spoke. "Father he's losing the battle with the locket."

Father Sinclair went right to work on him. He needed to clean the blood off his chest, as the men hell Albert down. He spoke. "My son ye prayers answered, I'm sorry this is going to be very painful."

Father had the gloves on, and he started to pour the holy water around the locket. Albert screamed as it burned into his skin.

His eyes flew open, the demon's spell broken. He looked into Timothy's eyes. "Bite down on this my brave grandson. Ye are just like your father, he was a brave and a good man as ye are. Ye are not this demon son."

Timothy told his grandson all about his real father and mother. As Father worked on the locket. The three men held down Albert as Father prayed and poured the holy water onto the locket.

**They found out that the demon was a strong fighter. **

Outside Donald was running towards the demon. As the demon breathed fire at him. Donald raised his shield to block the fire the moment it hit the shield it died. The men were coming at the demon from all sides. The demon had sent each of them a whirlwind to blow them away from him. They had cut them in half with their swords. The wind died as their swords went through the whirlwind.

On the other side of the castle, Michael was coming up fast on the demon's right side. The demon waved his hand; he hurled large rocks that were on fire and came at them. Thomas waved his hand, and all the rocks went right back at the beast. Then he through bigger rocks, this time the men use their swords to cut them in half.

Michael waved his hand; his shield got larger. To send the rocks back to the demon. Quickly the beast waved his hand to stop them. Everything the demon tried didn't work. This time he shot arrows from his fingertips.

Thomas and Michael waved their hands to send the arrows back at the beast. It looked that the beast was running out of ideas. Now he tried sending large trees rolling down the hill to them.

Donald yelled. *"Get into the shelter, make our shield bigger and rounder to make the trees roll back at him."*

The demon tried heaving rocks and trees on fire to them. They had to stay in their shelter.

Thomas had an idea; he called Michael. *"How about we put holds. That the beast could fall into them?"*

Michael called back. *"It must be that he doesn't see them. A grass cover, he won't see it."*

Thomas called back. *"The beast realize that Timothy and his helper isn't coming back."*

William had an idea. *"Try fire balls the size of him, coming at him from all sides."*

Then Michael spoke. *"I'll take the left side and back. Thomas ye take the right side and back. William ye have all the front. We do it on three. One, two, three."*

The magic poured from their fingertips; there was so much smoke it made it difficult to see where the beast was. Until the beast turned himself into three large bulls and hit the fire balls at them. Quickly they made the shield bigger and in front of them. These bulls could breathe fire.

Thomas had made a waterfall that put out the fire behind them. They had to kill each of these bulls. One by one their swords slashed through each of these bulls. When the bulls were gone.

Thomas spoke to his uncle through his mind. *"Uncle what happened, did we kill it."*

Donald replied. *"No… keep an eye out for anything to happen. I don't believe the demon is dead."*

When the demon disappeared. The ground shook violently and opened a deep crack in the earth, the men thrown to the ground.

Donald cried out. *"Get ready to fight, here it comes."*

The men jumped to their feet. They were going to rush the demon and cut his head off. When it was out of the crack fire was pouring out. It was cover for the demon to be able to climb out of the hole. He turned into a large devil with two long horns on his head. Once on the ground he was as tall as the castle walls. When the ground closed back up the devil breathed fire. His skin was as red as the fire in his eyes. The waterfall stopped the fire from taking down the trees behind the waterfall.

They all went back to the shelter. William then spoke. "I know what Ronald meant when he talked about are two skills. That's what is going to take down that fire breathing devil.

Thomas and Michael do ye remember when ye had that contest. Ye threw your dirk, and he had to push it into the target.

Thomas spoke. "Aye… I remember. We must time it for it to work. We have only one chance to get this done."

William then told them what each of them needed to do. "Michael takeout his sight first. Thomas can ye throw your dirk that high up."

He looked at his best friend. "Hell no…ye know I can't throw it that high not from where we are standing. The wind is too strong."

He quickly looked around and saw where he needed to be. "I found where I could throw from. You're going to have to keep that devil busy. I can make us invisible, so we can get to the wall and up it. I can do it with magic; I can't pinpoint us onto that wall. Ye go first, make your shield small to put it into your sporran.

Michael we're going to climb up to one of the walls nearest to the devil. When I do, I'll tell ye when I'm going to throw the dirk. It will be up to ye to push the dirk into the devil's heart."

Donald spoke. "Thomas whatever you're going to do. Do it right now. We're running out of time."

The fireballs were coming at Thomas and William as fast as the devil could throw them.

"Damn it he can see us even invisible. That one was too close; the demon aim was getting better. He could pick us off that wall not even trying."

Thomas called him. *"Michael can ye take out the devil's sight where ye are standing?"*

Michael replied. *"Aye… give me a minute. Keep on running. Don't stop if ye know what's good for ye."*

Thomas then said. *"That's very funny brother. We our laughing all the way in between fireballs. Now takeout that damn devil's sight and be quick about it. That's if ye are thinking on becoming an uncle any time soon."*

The devil threw a big fireball right at them. It had just missed their heads.

Michael replied. *"Hang on. Ye two are going to have that chance to make me an uncle."*

While Michael got ready. Donald covered for Michael. He had to use both of their shields for another fireball, hit them.

Michael yelled. *"Uncles tell me when to shoot. Then ye drop to your knees at the same time."*

Michael taken a quick peek. Where was that devil standing? "All right… I'm ready."

Donald spoke. *"Hold your fire my boy."* As another fireball came at them. Donald looked quickly. *"Ye are clear Michael. Fire…"*

Donald dropped, and Michael shot two arrows at the devil. The devil's hands quickly went to his eyes. There was a loud scream that the four men heard all the way inside the tunnel.

Timothy spoke. "What was that."

Duncan replied. "They just took out the demon's eyes. Thomas and William are going on to the wall. When Thomas throws his dirk. Michael will push the dirk into the heart."

Timothy asked. "How do ye know this?"

All Duncan said was. "It's the magic I'm wearing. Thomas and Michael have done it before in a contest."

He had left it as that. Father quickly said a prayer for them. As the locket was about to get out of Albert's chest.

The two men were all most to the spot where they had to be. The demon was breathing fire, at the last direction that the men had stood at.

Donald yelled. *"Move everyone ye got to move quickly! Don't say anything aloud he has good hearing."*

Thomas and William made it to the wall and climbed to the top. Donald and Michael moved closer to where Thomas and William were. They had to make this shot perfect for it to work. *"William ye go first. I'll get my shield out and make it bigger."*

Thomas spoke. *"Not to big that it will block my shot."*

William spoke. "Relax old friend I got your back. Ye and Michael are the best around."

*　　*　　*　　*　　*

In the valley of the dead. The three men could feel the war in Thomas's mind. Ronald called Thomas. *"Hay little brother what is the matter with ye. I can feel your doubt."*

Donald and Michael knew they had to get closer to the devil. They had to be next to the wall, to make this work. This shot the two of them will make will be one in a million.

Michael could feel the doubt in his brother. What was he thinking about?

*　　*　　*　　*　　*

Even in the castle Eleanor felt, it wasn't doubt. She had felt more emotional problems. She went to their room. There she called him. *"Honey, I know ye are not doubting yourself. Can ye feel my kisses on the back of your neck."*

For a minute he let the feeling take hold of him. *"Aye…, I want this over with. Your kisses are making me relax, thank ye I can think now."*

She knew everyone heard her. *"Ye are having trouble with which way the wind is blowing. Take three rose petals and make yourself a dirk. Then throw it at the devil and see what it takes, to get the dirk to his heart. Two more kisses I gave ye. You're ready to do this. Honey, I love ye and believe in ye. Do this and come home with everyone with ye."*

*　　*　　*　　*　　*

Inside the tunnel Duncan also heard Eleanor. He thought it was doubt; this wasn't like him to doubt himself. It was Satan messing with him.

Father heard Eleanor's voice. She was blocking Satan magic. He was the one to mess with his emotion. Telling him it was his emotion to figure out which way the wind was blowing and how strong it was.

Father spoke. "Let us pray for them to fine the strength to make this shot work."

Then Duncan thought of something. "Father ye have the rose petals with ye. In your mind let them hear your prayer for them."

Father had cleared his mind. *"Dear heavenly Father. Please help Thomas Michael make this shot. Help them to take down this demon. Then we can crush evil. We give this to ye heavenly Father. In Jesuses name Amen."*

Then Father heard. Everyone saying, *"Amen."*

They would need all their strength to make that shot count. It would take the two of them to take down the devil. The smoke was making it hard to see through the wet grass. The devil was making long sweeps to try to burn them in a grass fire. Then a cool mist of rain came from nowhere. The smoke started to clear. On the wall, William and Thomas were as close as they could get to the devil.

Michael, was now in position to fire his arrows. He called out to his brother. *"Thomas this is as good as it's going to get for us. Let me know when ye are ready."*

Thomas did what his wife had told him. He through the dirk that he made. He now knows he must use all his strength. Now he was ready. He called his brother Michael. *"Ready…, let's kill this damn devil and send him back to hell."*

Michael, end it with. *"Amen to that. Ye take the lead little brother. Let me know and I'll be right behind ye."*

Thomas took out his dirk and said a prayer. Ones done he called Michael. *"Are ye ready brother. Let's end this for ourselves and for Ronald."*

Michael readied his Bow. *"Aye…, ready, make it a good one."*

Thomas was ready to shoot. *"I'll do my best. For all of us past and present. For the ones who fought and died fighting against Marcos and his killers. Let it end here today."*

Outside the men said. *"Amen."*

Inside the tunnel the locket came out of Albert's chest. At the same time the men in the tunnel said "Amen."

*   *   *   *   *

The young boy.

THOMAS CLEARED HIS mind and let his dirk fly. Michael's arrow left his bow just after Thomas threw his dirk. This time his dirk went right into the demon's heart. The arrow hit the end of the handle pushing the dirk farther into the demon. He didn't know what happened to him. The demon just fell to the ground, face first.

Thomas waved his hand, and the four men where farther away from the devil. When he hit the ground. They felt the ground shook violently.

They all dropped everything and ran over to the body. Thomas waved his hand, and the devil was on his back. Donald quickly placed a cross on his chest. They saw it burn into his skin then the red devil was gone. It was as if there were two demons in this large body.

Slowly the demon grew smaller. Donald was able to place the chain around his neck. He had opened the beast shirt. The beast appeared as the cross burned into his skin. Even then he started to change again. The four men watched the beast, and the burn mark disappear. There before them appeared a young man still had the cross around his neck. This young man looked to be around sixteen. Three rose petals placed on the cross. This time there were two bodies. The burn mark was on the first body; his eyes were gone. The second body was much younger looking.

Thomas spoke. "Ronald told me about this young man. He was ten years old when Marcos had a demon take over his body. After that he taken him just outside of England.

Thomas retrieved his knife. Father Sinclair and Duncan were already heading to the end of the tunnel, when they had felt the earth shake. They knew the beast turned into a devil. They were wondering what was happening in the courtyard.

Duncan then heard his father call him. *"I hear ye dad what is happening now."*

Donald spoke. *"We're all right. Can ye ask Father to come out here with ye? We are ready for the locket. Were ye able to save Albert from that terrible fate."*

Duncan was happy to say. *"Aye…, that we did. He is sleeping with his grandfather watching over him. Dad, we felt the earth shake what happened?"*

Donald went on to say. *"Son as ye know the beast had turn into a devil. We were able to bring him down."*

Duncan went on to say. *"Father like to know why he must come out."*

Donald then spoke. *"We have a young man for ye to bless. At one time, this poor soul had two demons in this body. Now we have a young man here."*

*   *   *   *   *

Duncan told his father he would be right out. The two men came out of the tunnel and headed toward the outer gate. It was Father Sinclair who was carrying the box with the locket inside. On the ground two young men laid. They surrounded by the four men who ended his nightmares of horror. One body looked to have gone through hell. He had the burn mark on his chest, was there three demons in his body? Could this boy be willing to give himself to the dark side?

The other one had a cross around his neck. This boy had three demons inside him. Could he be innocent of all wrong doings? Father made his way over to the boy's bodies. He knelt to not a man but a teenager.

His thought was that this young man was too young. Didn't Thomas say that the boy was ten years old? He couldn't know what he was getting himself into with Marcos. A vision hit him, a family of four taken. The mother and father tried to get them away. A ghost was standing next to the boy. The father gave the boy a shield around his mine. His father stabbed in the back and killed in front of his son. The word spoken between the boy and man. *"Son ye have my powers protecting ye. If there is any way to save your sister do so. Pray to the Lord and he will keep ye safe."*

Then he found out what Marcos wanted. He tried to take his magic from the man. But the man gave his powers to the boy. The boy didn't know how to use his father's magic. When the demon came into the body there was nothing there. The boy was gone.

Donald spoke. "Father what we saw at first, he was a devil. I put the cross on him then he disappeared. When the beast appeared. He also disappeared after the cross hit his skin. Those demons didn't come out of the body. It looked as if they went into the ground. Afterward these two young boys left. One boy looks evil the other looks to be an angel."

Thomas spoke. "Father when I touched the devil and took our knifes out of them. I felt evil within them. Ones the devil and demon were gone. Here were two teenagers. One had a burn mark, and the other was wearing a cross. I didn't feel that this young man was evil, he was too young."

Father then spoke. "Marcos had the whole family. What I saw in a vision was that father gave the boy his magic. By putting it around his mind and soul. When the demon went inside the boy was gone. Aye… his soul is free. The body that looks evil is just the shall of the other. This body is free; he wears the cross. This young man I will bless. Ye can put the locket on the other body, put the cross on his back. The locket can go on the front. We will take this young body back to the tunnel.

Father blessed and prayed over the young man's body. He lifted his head to the heavens. "I give ye this young man's soul. I pray ye will be merciful and save him from the life of damnation. Amen. This is all I can do for him. I can only pray that we have saved two men souls today. Only the Lord knows about this young man. I can put that locket around the other body neck with a cross in the back. Put on clothes that are like Albert. I'm going back to the tunnel, and I will bring this young man with me."

Donald spoke. "That is all right Father ye save souls. Ye don't have to catch demons."

Father Sinclair nodded his head and handed the gloves to Donald. He left the box on the ground. Then he headed for the courtyard with the young teenager. "I'll wait in the tunnel and pray for all of us."

Father headed toward the outer gate then into the tunnel. When he was out of sight.

Donald spoke. "Whatever happens we must stop Marcos here today. Thomas could ye wait here with the body. I need to walk a bit. We all saw the cross burn his skin. It was as if by magic the burn mark kept the evil part of this body and freed the good part. Allowing the young man's body to appear."

Thomas had stayed with the body. "I pray ye this is what the Lord wanted."

He cleaned the body, then he placed clothes like Albert's. The last thing he did with his magic placed the locket on the body.

Thomas could almost picture this young man at ten years old. "I swear that we will get Marcos and make him pay."

The young man was walking over to him. His spirit was glowing when Father touched him. *"Hello Thomas. I hope it's all right to call you Thomas."*

He felt a powerful jolt that ran up his arm. That's when he snapped out of it. It brought him back to the present. There in front of him was that young man who looked to be sixteen. The teenager went over to him. *"I'm sorry… sir."*

Thomas's head popped up. The teenager jumped back when he spoke. "Ye don't have to call me sir, it's Thomas."

He knew he was talking to the spirit of the young man. *"Thomas, you seem to be somewhere else in thought."*

He gave the young man a smile. "Aye…, ye could say that I was. Tell me what your name is."

The young man stood tall. He had given Thomas a big smile. *"My name is Garret."*

Thomas was wondering if he knew what had happened to him. "Garret do ye know how ye got here?"

He turned and looked at the evil part of his body. *"The demons that lived inside me. At last, they are dead. I see that the Lord freed my soul and gave me the good part of my body. Ronald said his two brothers would free me from Marcos."*

Thomas wanted him to know what part he had in bringing him down. "Aye…, ye are free from Marcos. Do ye understand that I was the one to kill ye."

Garret just looked at his body. *"No Thomas! You didn't kill me. Marcos killed me. I was ten years old when he took and killed my father. Marcos, raped my older sister. He made me watch as he had his way with her and his mother. After he had fun with them. He slid his mother neck and watched her bleed to death."* Then he laughed. *"There is one thing I did for the women. It started with my sister. I took her mind and soul into my little room. Marcos was a coward the women, he had them tied down. I would all ways take the next woman and free her mind. We talked all through the nine months. After the baby was ready to be born. I switched my mind and soul so she would have another chance in life. I liked talking with all the women. My mother she stays with me until she was ready to die."*

Thomas watched as this young man was growing up quickly in front of him. *"I remember everything he did. Just before they killed my father. Daddy poured his magic into me. I was in a little room. Daddy gave me his magic; it surrounded me I could see everything. The demon couldn't see or hear me. My spirit trapped inside my body; I thought I was dead. The three demons who shared my body with me. They couldn't take my soul. This demon was more than just a demon. He had powers to do black magic, but he failed to take my soul. I watched the demon do his magic and learned to use his power. Thomas, I know you have magic, it's strong. There was magic on your knife. It broke through the demon magic, then the two of you was able to kill the body. It started with the one who blinded me. That magic was pure not black magic. I know too much about black magic. You freed me. Without your help, I would still be trapped in that body with the demons. Thank you for freeing me."*

Thomas looked at this teenager. I wish that he could stay with us. It would be good to have someone under me. "Garret ye could be dead. I may have freed ye but at the cost of your life."

Garret looked at him and he wished he could stay here with Thomas. *"Thomas No…! I told you; I was dead, you freed my soul not my body. Could you tell me what those men are doing over there."*

Thomas had to tell him. That they must use his old body. "This may sound harsh to ye. The men down at the bottom of the hill is getting wood. Marcos is now dead. He was going to use Albert's body. There is this locket he placed on him that was going into his skin. Father Sinclair was able to get the locket out of his chest. We will use this body to catch Marcos, then we will burn the body with him inside."

Garret then understood what Marcos told the beast. *"Marcos needed his first soul before he could take over his new body. The locket inside the body would trap the soul of Albert. Then Marcos could give Albert's soul to his master. This would have been Marcos first payment to stay on earth. He must give the devil twenty souls by the end of this year. Were you able to free Albert."*

Thomas smiled. "Aye…, I understood it wasn't easy. Now that we have the locket, we can call Marcos with this old spell."

Garret was shaking his head no. *"Thomas it won't work. The one who has Marcos's soul gave the spell to the demon. He will only answer, to that spell. It's funny, Marcos thinks he will continue his life here on earth with Albert's body. I just thought of something. He thought all those women soul went to his master. The babies had the women's soul; the babies went to the Lord. He got nothing."*

Thomas watched as he did a little dance. *"Marcos doesn't know that the demons failed him. You see he thinks he sent Albert to hell. Tell me what your plan to trap him. I could help you. You see while I was inside with the demons. Without him knowing I learned how to do magic.*

"For the longest time that wall my father had between us. I saw and heard everything the demon did and spoke. Being outside my body I

remember. If we don't stop Marcos from coming back alive. He will keep on killing and raping these women. I won't be there to give the woman a chance to live again, he will kill anyone that gets in his way."

Thomas smiled at him. "Garret did ye know that 200 years ago Marcos was a fairy."

Garret laughed. *"Are you saying that he was a little fairy."*

Thomas smiled and shook his head no. "These fairies are like humans. Our family is part fairy, are magic comes from the fairies and the man was a wizard."

Thomas had got everything done, the hill was fix and the water-fall was gone. There was a place for the body with wood inside it.

Garret looked at his hands. *"My sister went to my father sister. Do ye know my sister is six years old? I wish I could see her and the other women that got a second chance."*

CHAPTER FIFTEEN

Garret helped Albert.

THOMAS HAD A thought. "Garret, have ye thought that The Lord gave ye your body back to ye. Think about this. The Lord wants ye to decide what ye like to do. To die or to live."

Garret didn't know what to do. *"I Guess I better think about this. Thomas where would I live. I always had someone to feed me. A place to sleep."*

Thomas looked at the boy. "My father could use help around the ranch. Like are magic it comes from the rose."

Then he looked at Thomas. *"I know my magic is extraordinarily strong. I would give my magic to these roses. You had placed three rose petals on my cross. Why did you do that?"*

Thomas looked at this young man. "This way no one could take the cross off ye."

*   *   *   *   *

Thomas heard thunder way off in the distance. The thunder was coming from the location of the valley of the dead. In the sky the clouds were black over the Lowlands. There was lightning coming out of them. Marcos was using the lightning to try to take out his family. It looked like the battlefield that they fought on. That night when the six of us fought those evil men. When it was raining each time sword hit, they saw lightning. Has Marcos brook away from the valley of the dead? That's why we can see the lightning in the sky.

Then he heard Ronald calling for him. *"Ronald what's happening with ye three?"*

He then heard his brother say that Marcos is breaking away from here. He's almost free and will be heading back to Ye. Get us out of here, he knew how to get out of the valley."

Thomas cleared his mind. Once again, he made the circle. Before he put his hands together, he let the power build. He closed his eyes and picture the three men as he closed his hands. When he opened his hands, he pushed the magic out as he pulled his family to him.

*   *   *   *   *

Everything was moving too fast. When his family appeared, Thomas spoke. "What happen how is Marcos getting out of the valley?"

The three men looked at him. Joseph spoke. *"It, was a trap for us, he thought he could beat us there. Like always he had too many men there. What he didn't know was that we had power from the magic roses. He tried everything to vanquish are souls. Marcos is extremely angry with us three right now."*

Then Ronald saw Garret. *"We may still have a chance to set Marcos up. Garret is free, I knew that boy would figure out how to help us. He's going to use black magic to heal Albert and call Marcos.*

Then Thomas understood what he was talking about. In his mind's eye he saw Garret, entering Albert's body. Thomas knew that Garret needed the black magic from him. To help Albert he was going to take the last bet of black magic from his body. He knew then what Garret was about to do.

The darkness was coming on them fast. Everything was almost ready. Thomas spoke. "Ronald what are ye three going to do?"

Joseph looked at the three of them. "How about we try to vanquish Marcos. While we keep him busy until we hear Garret calling him."

Then Raymond spoke. *"Grandson, it will take the six of us, to put a shield around the land. Marcos will try to damage the land and homes that ye worked so hard for."*

Then one by one the once who had magic appeared in front of Thomas. William was the first one, then Michael appeared. Both men went over to Thomas. It was Michael who spoke. "Thomas what the hell is going on here?"

Then Garret also appeared. Along with Donald and Duncan. Raymond spoke. *"All right we need your help now. Marcos is determined to destroy everything ye work for. We need to use your bodies so we can put a big enough bubble around the castle to the town. Will ye help us to do this?"*

Joseph spoke. *"Donald, my I use your body to assist with the spell?"*

Raymond spoke. *"Michael with your magic and mine we can do this."*

Ronald spoke, *"what say ye old friend, ye will have the answers ye been looking for."* Duncan nodded his head yes.

Garret looked at Thomas. *"What shall I do?"*

Thomas spoke. "Ye are with me. The Lord might let ye stay here on earth with my family. Will see what happens. Come with me, we have work to do. I can feel Marcos is almost free."

With that done. The men who stood there had quite power. They started the spell. Thomas could feel Garret's power; it matched his own magic. They all felt when Marcos, brook free from the valley. The bubble was set the four men came out from there host.

Ronald spoke. *"All right we will keep Marcus busy for now. At twilight I hope ye will be able to call Marcos. I don't know what it will take to get rid of Marcos for good. At lease we won't destroy the Highland. Good luck Garret, which is a great idea to help Albert.*

Raymond spoke. *"I see that his grandfather is still helping him. Marcos is going to find out that Garret helped the women to live again. All the babies' souls went to heaven. There was no evil left in the body. The women were able to live so the evil would die. Come on, I would like to tell him that. This is going to be fun if we get to stop him again. Marcos will have one more time to come back in two hundred years. He will have to take down the rose by preventing the next Thomas from having a son."* The three lefts to do their best, to try to vanquish Marcos.

All the men who felt the power was standing on the hill. Thomas introduced Garret to everyone. It was Garret that asked if he could help Albert. He spoke. *"I must get the black magic out of him; it still could kill him. Please, Thomas, let me do this. Ye are the only one who could stop me now.*

"I just need to enter Albert's body. Then I'll bring him out here to use magic. I will say the spell through him to push the last of the magic out of him. It will help to clean his body out of the black magic. I want Marcos to believe Albert is now with his master. This way he won't detect me he will think I will be getting things ready to leave. Ones he has taken over my evil part of my body."

*   *   *   *   *

Garret came out of the tunnel with Albert. They watched him open his eyes. The eyes looked to have fire burning in them. His body started to glow with a bright golden light. Out of Albert's mouth, pour black magic. The voice that sounded just like the demon. He spoke in a language that none of them could understand. The golden light that surrounded Albert moved up his legs to his hips. It went into his chest and stayed there for a minute. It made its way to his head. There it cleared every bad thought that Albert heard. The black stream of energy moved through his arms and out of his fingertips. It poured out as a beacon to call Marcos to his new body. The golden light finely pushed every bit of black magic out of Albert's body.

Afterward Albert fell backwards into Thomas's and William's arms. Donald and Duncan saw what happened and came over quickly to stand next to Thomas and William. "Uncle, do ye have any more crosses? If ye do, may I have one?" He took the cross and placed it around Albert's neck. "Duncan, I need ye to take Albert to the tunnel. To tell the truth all ye need to go there. Marcos will be coming. I don't need ye all here to scare him away."

Donald wasn't going to take this. "See here ye are not going to fight Marcos by yourself."

Thomas looked at his uncle. "I'm not playing games with my life. Ye, don't have magic I do. Michael has magic and so does William. I need William to host Garret."

Then Garret spoke. *"I need my other body, just to stand there so Marcos can see me."*

Thomas had a thought he spoke. "Garret what do ye want to do after this is done?"

Garret stood there, he hadn't thought about that. When he was in Thomas's body, he saw all the things he did as a teenager. Would he be able to have someone to love him? He knew The Lord gave him the good part of his body. That he wears a cross around his neck. Didn't he talk with all those teenage women. They told him they wished he could fall in love and have a family with someone. Father had blessed him and his body. It was time to ask The Lord if he could live again. *"Thomas give me a minute I have to do something."*

Quickly he went into the tunnel. *"Father will ye pray with me?"*

He looked at the young man before him. "My son I will be happy to pray with ye. Garret, have ye seen your hands? There is a holy light that surrounded your body."

Then he got down on his knees. Father did the same. *"Heavenly Father ye know what I have done after the demons came into my body. Does this holy light mean that I could live, or does it mean that I will see my family. Lord, I wish I could live to find a love like Thomas has. I will do as ye ask of me. In Jesus name Amen."*

Father had added "In Jesus name Amen. All right my boy. Why don't Ye go into your body? The Lord will answer your prayer."

Garret went inside his body. "Father them place holy water on his four head his eyes then his ears. He blessed his mouth then his heart. Two drops on the cross and three rose petals to hold it in place. He touched his two shoulders to give him protection from the demons.

He then made the sign of the cross over Garret's heart. The moment Father Sinclair finished blessing all of Garret's body with holy water. The golden light got brighter; it was as if there was an explosion in his body.

Then Garret took a deep breath. "Father does this mean I'm alive."

He took another breath; tears filled his eyes. He got to his knees and praised The Lord. Then he spoke. "Thank you, Father Sinclair. I know after we take down Marcos. I will give my magic to the roses. I want to find love and have a family of my own. I will have a cross with rose petals to go on them. That will be the spell I will have for them. With this shield around me. Anyone I touch will have it." Joy filled Garret. He remembered what his mother said. "My Mother always told me to say a prayer. Even when it looked to be hopeless. I know why the demons couldn't get to me. With my father's magic and with the wall of prayers kept the demons out. Pray for us that we can take Marcos down."

*　*　*　*　*

When Garret came out, they saw a strong man stand before them. He spoke. "Michael ye and Thomas will need your weapons." With a wave of his hand, both men received their weapons. "Show me your swords." The men gave Garret their swords. His power moved through his arms into the swords. With these swords, if I'm here on this earth you will have the power to take down demons. To be Judge, we must burn his body. In less his father pulls him down to him. Thomas, I know that the two rose bushes at your place feed the one with it magic. Can I give my magic to the roses? The cross and rose's petals is what gives us our powers."

Thomas looked at his brother. *"Do ye think dad will mine if we have another brother? I think we must ask Ronald."*

Garret felt the power that Thomas has. "Let me have your shields, I like the way they protected you. This time it will protect your whole body from black magic. The rose petals will be able to do more. The shield can hide you from Marcos now. I send the power to Ronald and the other men he fights with, through your shield and sword Thomas. Garret laughed. I know that Marcos is not going to like this part. I have waited for this day, for a long time. My mother father will rest in peace along with the people Marcos killed. I know that there will always be people like him. I just pray that there will be people like yourselves that will take them down."

Garret, got right to work. He made his body look like Albert. Thomas was watching him work. "Garret I'm proud of ye."

He looked at Thomas. "Thank you for helping me."

Michael heard a big thank ye from the three men. "Garret, they love the new shield. But Marcos doesn't. They said that they were disappearing from him. Joseph said he almost touched him. Thomas are ye going to let me fight by your side?"

Thomas spoke. "Michael ye win, I knew I couldn't keep ye away from me. The three of us always cooperated with each other. Ye can tell the three of them, they can start herding him this way. We are ready for Marcos.

Michael walked toward Garret. "Ronald and the others are heading back here. He likes what ye have done to the sword and shield. Marcos was surprised that he couldn't hit them anymore. He said it made him angry when we almost touched him."

They could see that the black clouds were now moving. The winds were like a hurricane that made the long grass ripple. The limbs of the trees were now moving violently back and forth. Sand was blowing in their faces. As a small twister started to form. Garret had yelled their coming this way.

* * * * *

Michael spoke. "Aye..., I can see the difference with the weapons that they all have. They are using them to drive Marcos here."

Thomas saw the wind pushing everything. Even with the bubble a good amount got through. He spoke. "Aye..., the wind is pushing the trees to their breaking points. They are getting Marcos extremely angry. He doesn't like them trying to vanquish him. I think we had better get ourselves in place. Michael where would you like to have your perch?"

He looked around. "How about up there on the wall. I could get Marcos in a crossfire with Thomas. Do ye know how far the magic of the sword could reach?

Garret then spoke. "It can reach to the middle of this area. Michael, I know how to get Marcos inside the locket."

He made Michael's bow and arrow appear in his hands. "Take these weapons. Shoot this arrow into Marcos's body. Yes, I know it will go right through him. I'm going to put a spell on the locket. What the arrow will do is activate the spell. If Marcos doesn't go into the locket by himself. Then you shoot this arrow at him. I will also make sure you can get down from there."

Quickly Garret went and took care of everything that needed to be set up. He made sure the spell worked with the arrow. Then he made Michael a place from where he could climb up or down. Garret made the spot where Michael was going to stand extra strong. Now where to place Thomas…?"

Thomas didn't like Garret exposed; now that he was human they could kill him. "Garret, where are ye going to be standing?"

He hasn't had anyone to worry about him. "Thomas, don't you worry about me. I will be where Marcos expects me to be. Right in front or on the side of this body? Yes, that is where I must be."

Both brothers got on the defense of protecting their new brother. "No, ye put something there that looks like the beast. Marcos will know that ye are not the beast anymore. To do what ye must do. Ye will have to cross back over to the dark side."

Garret hadn't felt love for a long time. "I understand and you are right. I think your idea will work. I'll do it right now."

Next to the body he placed the beast he made. It was able to move around the body. This made it look as if he was guarding the body for Marcos.

Thomas and Garret were near a bunch of boulders. "Garret, ye better make yourself a shield? Remember ye are human, he will see you now."

He looked at his hands. "All right thank you for having my back. Will you teach me all the things you know? You have great ideas; I hope that I can learn from the two of you. Now I have a shield like you do.

"Thomas, what is it like to be alive? When I had these girls with me. I like talking with them. Are there girls around the Highlands?"

Thomas thought a bit then spoke. "Garret ye have time if I know my wife's mother. She will set ye up with a young lass. Gallivan is closer to your age, he is a diligent worker. There is one thing ye will have to do, give your magic to the roses. Ye will always have the roses with ye. My wife went out of her way to find a spell to keep Ronald save. All my family has the protection, ye have it right now."

*   *   *   *   *

Once they were at their places. The battle between Marcos and Ronald and our family got intense. They could now feel the outcome of their blows to each other. Big rocks thrown by Marcos, hit the barrier as smaller flying objects. Without the barrier the wind blew so violently, that the debris could kill them.

Thomas spoke. "Where did Marcos get that magic from."

Garret looked at all the rocks that could have hit them. "The demon that lived inside me. Took him to this place, they prayed to Satan his father. They called themselves the brotherhood. "Aye…, I found out that day that his father was Satan himself. He found out who had stronger magic. He had killed the last demon, who had gathered large amount of magic throughout time. Even with the barrier, this fighting is getting out of hand. The spell of the barrier could break at any time."

Then Thomas called Ronald. *"Brother hear me, it's time for all ye break away from this battle. The barrier is getting weak; it won't hold for much longer."*

Then Thomas heard Ronald call back. *"We need a place to go, like the host of before. All right, this time ye can go inside Garret. The Lord is letting him stay on earth, he is now alive he will understand what it means to be brothers."*

Ronald spoke. *"I'm happy for him. I know he wants to have a family of his own one day."*

Thomas then called his uncle. *"Uncle Joseph can ye hear me. I need ye to come to me. I will be your host."*

247

Michael had heard his brother talking. Then he called his grandfather. *"Grandfather come to me. I will be your host. Together we will take down Marcos."*

Raymond then called back. *"I hear ye Grandson. We will head there together on the count of three."* At the same time, they disappeared and went right to their host.

*　*　*　*　*

Garret waved his hand toward the body and the rope disappeared. Then he heard Marcos telling him that this was a trap. Garret spoke. He's called Thomas a Michael. *"There is trouble Marcos will not come here; he thinks it's a trap. He believes once he gets inside his new body. We will kill him before he has a chance to come back from the dead."*

Michael then had an idea how to fix this problem. *"Aye…, I had a feeling this would happen. Tie up the beast black-out his eyes, he's captured and can't use his magic. Have the beast called him, tell him he failed him. They're going to burn me and Albert's body. When Marcos gets here, we can surround him. I will shoot the arrow threw him so the locket can pull him into the body.*

Thomas spoke. *"Before we start let me call home first. Eleanor my love is everything set at home?"*

She was doing some more reading. *"We are all fine here at the castle. Why are ye asking this?"*

Thomas spoke. *"Ye remember the dream I had that Marcos took your ora from your body?"*

Eleanor, looked around at everyone. *"Everyone is in the castle safe. Because of your dream that's why I set Marcos up. I had all my protection with me. I marked him as a man that rapes women. Ronald came to my defense. I gave him that protection for his soul."*

Thomas looked around. "I hope we will be home soon. Do ye feel any of the battle?"

Eleanor looked outside. *"She could see that the horses were getting a little restless. There spooked a bit, ye better wrap this up soon. The horses don't like what is going on."*

Thomas answered. *"All right honey, tell everyone to stay inside. We're trying to do just that."*

Then he called William. *"Get your shield out put it in front of ye. Tell the others and please pray this works."*

William called back. *"We can hear what everyone says. Good luck old friend."*

With everything gone over again. The three of them hoped that it was right this time. The three spirits stepped inside their host. It was now or never. In the blink of an eye. Ronald then saw Garret as a young boy of ten. There was a birthday party going on when he was turning eleven. That's when Marcos came into their lives. He knew that the family had powers. If he kills the father, he could get his powers.

*   *   *   *   *

The night before Garret had a dream. He saw bad men kill his father. "My son the man must fight me. Not to be a coward and stab me in the back. If ye are around me my powers, will go to ye my son. If that happens, I will give Ye, a magical wall inside your body. That demon will not know ye are there. As your mother has always said. Say prayers to The Lord, he will keep ye save my son. Ye will not be able to save your mother. For your sister with my magic pull her mind and spirit from her body. After the baby is ready to be born, switch their mind and spirit. This will let your sister live again. If this happens, save yourself bide your time. Men like him will fall in time with good men to take them down."

Ronald could see why Garret thought he was evil. The demon did a great amount of terrible things to others. He knew his own body was pure evil.

Ones again in the blink of an eye. Garret was able to see everything Ronald had done in his life. He could also see who he loved. She was pretty like his sister. Her name was Marian. She's the one Marcos had killed. The pain he felt, Garret knew pain like that.

He saw the fighting that the four of them had done. Then he saw the killings that Ronald had done. He stopped the evil men in what they were doing. He saw Michael fighting to save their bodies from being thrown into the fire alive. He remembered that day, what he didn't see what his brother did for him. The words between them were touching. He saw Michael and his wife clean their bodies. Then she had given birth to their son.

As boys the three worked together helping with the horses. They brought in hay to feed them. Even helped with the birth of the babies. He saw his two brothers running to Thomas's side. It was the day the bear had attacked Eleanor. Gerret felt the pain that Thomas's brothers felt. There were deep cuts, and blood was over his arms. His shirt cut half off his body. He saw his father trying to take Eleanor from him. Thomas didn't let anyone take his love from him.

All three men, when they love they love with all there being. Then there was the time their father told them to assess Thomas in washing. He saw Ronald and Michael hogtying Thomas. Wow! Even as a young man Thomas could hold his own. But there was love between them. It was funny that the three brothers had a bath along with their clothes.

*　*　*　*　*

Everything was set up and ready for Marcos. Then the beast called out. "Master, I failed you their going to burn the beast and Albert's body."

Then Garret laid the beast down with his magic. Marcos appeared he was near the campfire. Michael watched him move closer to the body. He was acting as if something wasn't quite right. He was right to think that way.

Michael smiled. He was ready with his bow and arrow. He knew he would only get one shot at Marcos. Then the shot came, he had moved into the right spot. He thought. *"Just a little more. That's it, ye are mine Marcos. Now kiss ye new life goodbye."*

Michael let his arrow fly, at the last moment Marcos turned. He watched the arrow past through him.

As he started to laugh at the man who shot it. *"Are you a fool to think you could kill me? You were wrong, but I can kill you."*

The fire light aloud Michael to see Marcos. The whirlwind swirled with high winds. Whatever caught inside the whirlwind vanished into the locket. Out in the heavens... came a lightning bolt. It struck the body of Albert; they went up in a ball of fire along with the beast.

* * * * *

With magic everything was back as it was before. Thomas spoke. "Grana is at the castle we will take Albert and his grandfather with us. Albert, Ye, must have a checkup. I think Garret could send ye home. Ye look so much better then ye did."

Albert nodded then spoke. "All these years I thought he was my father. Granddad, I'm glad that ye stayed with me. The only thing I want around my neck is this cross. I didn't like the feeling that locket and black magic was making my body feel like."

Timothy looked at his grandson. Then he spoke. "I think it's time to change your name to Albert McWaters. Your father would be so happy to know that your son will continue his name on."

Then Thomas called his wife. *"Honey, asks mamma if we can bring Albert McWaters home with us. Along with his wife and two children, girls, and a boy. With his grandparents he is free from Marcos. There will be another couple, who will have their name change."*

Then Eleanor spoke. *"Bring them here tonight we will have a feast. For tomorrow we will party. Tonight, we will rest and just eat and drink a bit."*

* * * * *

Once everyone was together, the ones who had magic. Waved their hands and thoughts, of the MacGregor castle. They all landed in the clearing near the barn. Thomas then waved his hand, and the horses were all taken care of. As they walked up the hill to the castle their family was coming out. Garret smiled and waved his hand. There off to the side was Albert's wife and grandmother with the two children. Everyone was greeting their family.

The three spirits went over to Garret. Ronald spoke. *"If I know my sister-in-law and William, they will take ye into their family. In the future the ones that go to the new world, the Heart's name will be change to Angel-Heart. Ye will have two families, come on let's Thomas tell who ye are."*

Thomas went over to his father and mother. "This is Garret, he was the one who lived in the beast. For six years, The Lord let him live for what he had done for all those women. The souls Marcos thought he had were not so. Garret saved them by switching their mind and souls with the baby's. The children went right to The Lord. They didn't have a chance to become evil."

The castle was full. There was just enough room when Thomas, Michael, and William went to their home. Uncle Donald and their family went home to rest. Garret slept in Thomas's old room. Tonight, they rest after Grana checked over Albert. She had given him something to clean out anything left from the magic. His wife and children, had a checked, even his grandparents. Along with Garret who had a checkup.

*   *   *   *   *

After having a drink and food. They all headed to where they were to sleep. Thomas and Michael had sent William's parents' home. Thomas sent his uncle and his family home they had their horse with them. Who had their home got to go home.

*   *   *   *   *

Downstairs in the study. Theseus and his wife were talking with Garret. "So do ye want to stay in the Highlands?"

Garret thought about it. "I like this place; I have the ones that save my life. They worried about me and made sure I was safe. They told me that one of the Heart's and MacGregor males will go to the new world. They will bring the Magic Fairy Roses with them.

"When I had to live with those three demons, I was never alone. I always had a young woman to talk with. When Marcos got another woman. I would take the young woman's mind and soul from her body. They would tell me about their life. I made sure they never experienced what Marcos did to them. I did what my mother and father told me to do for my sister. I did it also for all those women too.

"I got to see what Ronald's did with his life. I felt love, anger, and pleasure. I saw what it was like to have brothers. I know what friendship is like, I saw what demanding work. To have magic is privilege, ye don't use magic to do everything. Building things with your own hands is wonderful. I had fun when I was a boy. But now I want to learn to do things with my hands. I want to find a young woman that I could start my life with. I know that killing is not right to do. Ye only do that when it's to save your life or someone else's life. Ye, don't do it for money, which is evil.

"Thomas told me that I could have two families. The MacGregor family and the Heart's. I don't know what to do yet. For my magic I will give to the roses. The part of my body that was evil went with Marcos. The Lord gave me the other half that was good.

"I don't need to be a young boy of ten. When I was talking to all those women I found out. I like being with them, it makes me happy. I think it's time to find my place. Then find someone to love me. Thomas and William told me I have two families. I just want to find my place in life."

*   *   *   *   *

At home Theseus was talking with his wife. "Now Daniel has two sons. We have one son, if it is true that his children will go into the new world. We should adopt Garret."

Then Bridget spoke. "Honey I would love to have another child. I know I can't have any more children. Could we keep this teenager? He needs us, as much as we need him."

Theseus spoke. "Aye... William said his name is Garret. He is three years older than our grandson. I think he could be a big brother to him. William will have his hands full with his new bride."

Bridget then spoke. "Garret that is a nice name… He is also one year older than my sister's daughter. Have I told ye that I've heard my sister is moving closer to us?"

Theseus just looked at her. "Is she now… when will she be here? Tell me how long have ye known about this?"

She smiled at her husband then said. "I found out yesterday. When this letter arrives, they will be here in the morning. My sister had a dream. In her dream she saw the man her daughter was to marry. This young man, was going to be at the party of the newly married couples."

Theseus smack his forehead. "So ye and your sister are going to see, if ye could get the two of them to fall in love."

She gave him a pretty smile. "Why not…? My sister and her husband bought the ranch close to us. He's a good-looking young man; our niece is a beautiful young woman. It could happen we have time."

Theseus looked at his wife. "Honey, I like ye this way. Please don't go off what Franceam gave ye. Right now, ye have been more like yourself. I don't want to go through that again."

Bridget gave her husband a nod then went to kiss him. "I do feel much better; I didn't like myself ether. My mind couldn't get around what the kids were saying." The light went out and the two of them kissed.

*　*　*　*　*

Up in Thomas's old room the spirit of Ronald came to Garret. *"Hello Garret, so how do ye like life so far?"*

Garret sat up in bed. "I like this bed for one thing. I got to talk with Theseus and his wife. I told them all about the things I have learn so far."

Then Ronald wanted to know more about the magic Marcos had. *"Can ye tell me where Marcos's magic came from?"*

Garret then yond. "A year ago, he found the demon he been looking for as far back as 13th century. This demon knew of the old magic. Marcos was able to kill him before he could find another body for himself. To get the magic he had to fight that demon. He couldn't get my father's magic because he stabbed him in the back. That's how I got my father's magic. Did you know that Marcos had met Eleanor? Not once but twice he came across Eleanor's path."

Ronald was watching the young man. *"Did ye know about this before I came to ye?"*

Garret found out he was getting sleepy. "No! I didn't know the name of the woman he picked out for himself. His plan once he took over Albert's body. He was going back for her. Eleanor was going to be his first taste of young blood. She was the one to give him a son, so he thought. Marcos painted a colorful plan for her. After he had his way with her and got her with his child. He was going to give her to his master. That plan went out the window. She was married and he wouldn't be her first. I saw his face; Eleanor got him good. She told me she had the rose petals on her nails."

He saw the young man couldn't keep his eyes open. *"Garret why didn't Marcos take over your powers?"*

Garret yawn again. "Ye see I was too young at the time; my magic was weak. He needed magic that came from long ago. Marcos didn't know I learned the old magic from him. He was so pleased with himself that he did all these magical tricks right in front of me. He forgot to keep it from the demon who kept me prisoner. While he was using his magic, the demon watched, and I learned. The magic my father gave me was the wall between the beast and me. When Thomas killed the beast. My father's magic became part of me.

"Ronald when I placed the locket on my body, I sealed it with the old magic. I knew he would think he could get out of the locket, so I put a twist on it. I made it so he can't use his magic in the locket. I sealed it with the old magic and added a part that my parents taught me. He couldn't say the last part of the spell."

Ronald smiled at the boy. *"What was the last part?"*

Garret smiled back at him. "I made it as a prayer."

Ronald laughed. *"Aye… he wouldn't dare to speak those words. Well done, Garret how did Marcos become Albert?"*

He smiled. "It was with his newfound powers. Marcos learned how to change himself, for anyone he liked to become. He wanted everyone to think his son Albert was just like him. It was the end of winter when Marcos started to be Albert. He went to a party that Eleanor's cousin was giving. It was in the Lowlands of Scotland. He had brought Eleanor's cousin home; the baby was her cousin. How would ye tell a mother that your daughter is not there, she is inside the baby. Ye know about Eleanor saving a young woman from Albert."

Ronald knew of the story. "Aye…, she had call to Thomas. William and Thomas came to her side. That's when he stopped him from raping anymore women. Eleanor couldn't get to the bridge in time."

"Ye see no one knew it was Marcos playing the part of Albert. At the party Eleanor knew something wasn't right with him. She saw the evil in his eyes. Ones Thomas placed the rose petals on her hair that he carried with him. She could see through Marcos. He had to show everyone that Albert was just like him. He even had Eleanor dream that Albert was coming after her. When Thomas saved her, and place rose petals inside Marcos body. He knew he was going to die soon. The rose petals stop him from having sex with the women. Since that happened, he knew he was going to die. His horse was dead, that was another sign that the end was near. Ronald being in my body by myself. I get tired fast. I'm the one that made my body work. The demons take turns controlling my body. I want to go to sleep now. Can we take this up tomorrow please?"

Ronald started to laugh. "I'm sorry I remember Thomas wanting to stay up late. A friend of my father was coming over to see him. He had taken a trip and just got back."

Garret didn't hear a word he said. "He was out."

Good night my half-brother. The other half will be William's.

CHAPTER SIXTEEN

Meeting the women.

THE NEXT DAY was beautiful; Michael's children were awake. He thought he had time to make love to his wife. "Honey I'll go and get her for ye." Getting out of bed he went and checked to see if their son was up, he was.

He was playing quietly with the toy Uncle Gunkel gave him. Leaving the room, he went to get his daughter. "Come on daughter mamma is waiting for ye. Daughter ye stink I better get ye clean up." No way was he going to change her. With the wave of his hand, she was clean. His wife looked at him. "She nice and clean. Thank ye honey."

Michael was getting his clothes on. "Honey ye remember I told ye about this family. That I was thinking of bringing their daughter here to the Highlands. I want to see if Mina would like Gallivan. She is sixteen and now we have two young men. We will see. I overheard Bridget saying that her sister is moving to the Highlands. They will be at the party. She has a daughter a year younger than Garret."

Malinda laughed. "Michael when did ye become a match maker. I thought that was Bridget thing."

He looked at his wife. "Very funny, I'll be right back. I also wanted to see how her parents were doing."

Then little Ronald was up. "Daddy, me want to go with ye."

Michael went and picked his son up. "Ye, stink son not ye two. Come on let's get ye clean up." Ones again he gave a wave of his hand, and he was clean, and dressed. Michael then fed his son before leaving the house. With his face clean he went to give his wife and daughter a kiss. "I'll be back I will take Ronald with me."

She saw he had his vest on. Malinda thought differently about it. Honey, "Ye, have your vest on and so does Ronald. Is there any reason for it?"

Michael had to think about that. "It feels right when I'm leaving the Highlands. I believe all Marcos men are dead. What I did will take time, for me not to look over my shoulder. I love ye honey."

Malinda got up and gave him and their son a kiss. "I'm going over to the castle. I'll see ye there."

*　*　*　*　*

In the Lowlands he went to the pub. It was breakfast time. There were many families having their breakfast, the pub was humming. With Marcos gone people were coming out again. Everyone was there, no one wanted to cook. Michael then walked into the pub with his son. "Michael your back."

Then he saw Mina. "There she is. Son, this is Mina. Mina this is my son Ronald."

Then she looked at Michael. "Does this mean that I can come to the Highlands?"

Michael gave her a big smile. "Aye… he is gone. The Lord came after him. Now that he is dead, he can't come back for two hundred years. Where your parents I need to ask if I can bring ye to the Highlands?"

Mamma and dad are out back. "Mamma look who I found."

Michael step inside the room. Everyone was having breakfast. "Michael your back and ye have your son with ye. Is the fighting over with? Tell me are all those men gone?"

He took a deep breath and spoke. "Aye…, it's all over with. Marcos is gone and Albert is free from the locket. The old man that was with him. He was Albert's grandfather; Marcos killed his son and his wife. His daughter-in-law was pregnant with his son's child. Could I take Mina to the Highlands?"

Her parents nodded yes. "Her bags are packed she been ready to go since you left."

Mina had run home to get change and to get her things. She was back before his son could finish what they gave him. "I'm already to go."

Michael wondered if she was excited. Just to get away from here for a while. Then again it could be Gallivan. We also have another young man who is a year older then ye. One thing is my sister-in-law mother has plans for him. Her sister is moving to the Highlands. So, we will see. Now can she go with me and my son? I must get back to the castle."

They looked at him as if he had grown horns. "Can she go?"

Then Michael took out something. He had many petals on it. "Hold this in your hand and think of me. Then say where ready to go. Ye can bring your horses to have something to get around on. Then I will do the rest."

They walked outside. He then told his son to hang on to daddy's neck. He took Mina hand then close his eyes and thought of the castle. As he waved his hand. In the blink of an eye, they were at the castle. Then he heard her parents say. "You have magic, I wish we could do that. Daughter, are you there now?"

Michael gave Mina something to hold so she could talk with her parents. "I'm here mamma." He had pointed to Gallivan. "Wow!" Her parents heard. "He is handsome, will see if he is the one for me. Michael was right he is strong looking."

* * * * *

Just at that moment, Gallivan was walking down the walkway. That was who she saw first. She gave him the sweetest smile. Michael took one look at the two of them. "Mina this is Gallivan the young man I told ye about. Gallivan, I would like ye to meet Mina, she is the one I told Ye about last night. Later I will get her a horse and ye can show her around."

Then little Ronald wanted to see Mina. "I want Mina, to take me to my bed, me sleepy." As he laid his head on her shoulder. He went right to sleep.

Michael smiled. "I think ye can stay with us. Gallivan show her where to lay my son down."

Gallivan was looking at her. Michael placed his hands directly on her shoulders. He kissed his son then placed his hand on his son's head. Then he went to Gallivan and placed a gentle hand on his shoulder. "There now ye have the magic of the roses. From here out know demons could hurt ye. Don't be scared if ye see three spirits around here. Later tonight after the blessing of the five married couples. The spirit of Raymond is going to tell the story of how the MacGregor's got their magic. Ye see Raymond is a twin, it was his brother who married the Queen of the Fairy's.

We had found the book but couldn't read it, the story had a magical spell place on it.

Why don't ye take my son in, ye can place him in his bed upstairs."

*   *   *   *   *

Michael saw that Garret was down by Eleanor and Thomas. Her mother and sister were taking Marianne to the party. He spoke. "It looked to be Garret's time, to be matched up with Marianne. Mina don't think that Garret is the beast."

He saw her step backwards into Gallivan's arms. "Why is he here, my parents won't like him to be here."

Michael looked into her eyes. "Listen to me when Garret was ten. Marcos killed his family; on the day he turned eleven years old. He wanted Garret's father's magic. But he had to fight him not stab him in the back. So, the magic went to his son. It put a bubble around his mind and soul.

"When we killed the beast there was three demons inside his body. When the three demons were gone there were two bodies left. One had the last beast who was dead. The other body was Garret. Father had come out to bless the two bodies. It was as if Garret was a twin. Father took the one body back to the tunnel with him. That's when the spirit of Garret appeared to Thomas. He had walked back to Thomas. It looks like he will have a chance to find someone to love him. He is a good man; he saved all the young women by taking their mind and soul into his bubble. When the baby was ready to be born, he switched the baby's mind and soul. They could live again; the three demons didn't know anything about it. Garret's father told him to save his sister. He couldn't save his mother, all he could do was take her memory away. She went to her husband that day. Garret made the beast stay and watch him rape these women. He just closed the window and talked with the woman he saved. The babies' souls went to the Lord not to Marcos's boss. The woman went to the baby.

"Now go and put my son to bed. Then ye two can bring food down to the tables. In less the women who has the magic sends it themselves. Ones Garret give his magic to the roses. The cross with rose petals on it will help him to use his magic the right way."

Then Michael waved his hand and across was around her neck. Then he placed three petals on the cross.

*　*　*　*　*

Father had gone around to bless all the new homes. Then before it was dark, the five couples.

had their marriage blessed. They had to fill out paperwork to show they were married.

Garret with the three brothers and Father went with him to the roses, on Thomas land. He had uncovered these magical rose bushes. Father had blessed his hands with holy water and place across and three rose petals in his hands. Then Garret spoke. "Before I give all my magic to the roses. To all the women, who is now a baby. I give ye the cross and rose on your chest. Ye will always have it with ye, once ye become women again. Ye will see the cross and rose in the moonlight.

Tonight, was the full moon. Garret sends his spell out to the Highlands and to the Lowlands of Scotland. In his mind he called out. "To all the young women who I help save here me, remember the time with me. Praise the Lord for he was the one to safe ye. To my sister hear me, who is now six years old. I give ye the cross and rose so ye can be safe. Ye will know if evil is around ye. Ye will also have your powers, only when ye are twenty-one. The magic rose will give ye the power if ye need it. When ye take a mate gave him the cross and rose. Sister, ye will remember our mother and father. Ye were born from love, not evil. Ye will know right off they are evil or not."

Then Garret took two roses and sent them to his sister. "Wave your hand the rose will disappear, wave your hand and they will reappear when ye need them."

For a moment he heard a young voice. *"My brother, I hear ye. I remember. One day I will see you again. Thank you for the roses."*

There were tears in his eyes. It was time to give the roses his magic. When he needs it, he will have it through the roses. He could only use it for good not evil. He pointed his fingers at the roses and gave the roses his magic. At that moment, anyone with the cross and roses on them. They had felt a burning sensation on their chest even though Father had felt it. All the children had a cross and rose on them also.

* * * * *

Back at the party they dance and enjoy who they were with. Little by little the people that live in town packed up and headed home. They went together many was fox, they couldn't stand that well. When they were on their horses, Thomas waved his hand to send them over the bridge into town. Even Grana didn't notice that they got there too fast. They were all safe and, in their homes, that was all that mattered.

The eight couples were the only ones left. The three spirits were there. It was time for the tale of the King of the fairies. Blankets were on the hillside. Everyone had their mates with them. Even Gallivan was with Mina and Garret was with Marianne. Everything was all right in the world.

Eleanor had the story book; she opened it up. Raymond waved his hand over the book; the pages appeared.

Thomas's grandfather read the story. "It was a long time ago; my grandfather was hunting for the demon who killed his twin. Aye…, we have twins in are family history."

He saw two young women looking at Gallivan. The poor boy was turning red. But Mina smiled and went closer to him. He looked at her, "would she want that to happen to them." He had heard her say. *"Aye…, That's if ye want me."*

Gallivan looked at her. His hand went to the back of her neck. He had bent and kissed her. *"Then we must get to know each other before that even happens. I need to build my home. Ye must get to know what we like and don't like. Will ye work with me on my land?"* She smiled and nodded her head.

The story of the King of the Fairies

My grandfather found the demon. His magic was of a wizard; the demon had all kinds of magic. But this wasn't the fight of magic. It was the fight of who was the better sword fighter. My grandfather was the best swordman of all Scotland. This fight was in the Highlands, the demon wanted to use magic.

However, my grandfather prevented him from using his magic. His twin brother killed by the demon's magic. This time it would be different; the demon wasn't that bad of a fighter. He had moved one way, and our grandfather took the opening and killed the demon. After the demon dropped all his magic went rushing to my grandfather. The battle was fought in this very place; he had stayed inside this very castle.

The people had been watching the fight. When the demon disappeared, they all knew he had been a demon. That night as he slept, he heard a beautiful song. This song sounded desperate, he had thought she was crying. With his eyes close he saw her, outside her castle men with magic. They were lined up all the way around the castle. The song told him she must be with the child to become the next queen. Her magic would tell her if she was with a child.

* * * * *

My grandfather looked at where the song came from. In the morning, he said his goodbye to these kind people. He knew one day, one of his children would buy this castle. It was time to ride, that woman will be his. Once out of sight he waved his hand and appeared in this small town. There was an old man who watched, men go into the fog. Every one of them was a fairy, the old man shook his head. Then he saw our grandfather. He had ridden up to talk with him. "Hello sir."

Our grandfather walked up to him. He bowed to him, for under his magic he looked like a King. "Sire why do ye make yourself look like a popper."

*   *   *   *   *

The old man smiled at him. "Ye are the first to see who I was. Come let us eat and ye rest, for tomorrow ye will meet our daughter. These men just want to be king; all these fairy's will rape our daughter. Ye must understand these men can't get her with child. I know ye can, for ye are human. I want ye to get your horse and put him out back. We will know when she is with child."

Then his wife came into the room. Our grandfather bowed to her. She had put the food down and went over to him. She touched his face and ran her hands over his armes. She left his kilt and touched his bag of jewels and looked up into his eyes. "Aye…, this one will take her virginity all these fairies can't reach that spot. I want ye to close your eyes and listen to the song she sings. Can ye see her now."

The queen saw his heat grow before her. "Aye…, ye are the one, just looking at her. Ye are hard and ye wants her. She ran a finger over his heat, husband he hasn't been with anyone."

*   *   *   *   *

He had eaten and they showed him to his room. What he didn't know, he had visited her room. She was crying and he could feel she felt dirty. He had waved his hand, and she was in a tub. She did know what was happening to her. She couldn't see who was doing all of this to her. She only saw his hands on her body. She watched his finger slip inside her.

About Kenyon
and Raiman

ELEANOR STOOD UP. "Hold on, we have four teenagers here, don't go on with this story. What happen in the new world?"

He looked right at Thomas. "Come here and tell them about your dream. Thomass ye had a dream about Tom and Ellen."

Thomas didn't want to talk about it. "Wow…, Dad ye are so right that being friends is important before love making. When we cross over a kiss can light the two of ye. Why do I say that ye four should get to know each other first?

"In my dream I saw two people that looked like Eleanor and me. What I had gathered Tom with going to Scotland. He was told that he wouldn't remember Ellen. The two of them were under some kind of light. Tom had loved Ellen all his life, he had fought Marcos at the age of two. The boy would do anything for her. At this time of their lives, he felt scared of losing her.

"What I understand is that there, in the new world called America. This place was called Vermont and came about in the 17th century. This place had a waterfall behind Tom's home. Now let's get to the story. Tom was going away from Ellen; she was two years behind him. But like my Eleanor she was smarter and much older acting than she was. Tom never kissed her, or crossover. She was of the age of fourteen, he thought he would start to date her when she turned sixteen. Marcos wasn't in the picture yet. He had other people there to give them grief. These people produced the idea of sending them to a school who would take their names away from them. They will push all memories back; they will go under the nicknames Tom will be Mick and Ellen will be Angel.

"Tonight, he must know if she loves him. Will she fear him kissing her? He felt would he go beyond that, like touching her. Tom didn't know that Ellen could hear his thoughts.

Ellen looked at him and she knew there was a battle going on in his mind. "Tom what do you want to know?"

He looked at her and swallowed hard. Taking her hand he brough her over to where it was dark. "I need to find out if you love me."

Ellen knew her own mind; she had loved him for a long time. It was dark and he didn't want to scare her. "Ellen, will you let me kiss you."

She had been waiting for him to do just that. "What took you so long."

Ellen through her arms around his neck. It had surprised him; she had closed her eyes, and he bent to kiss her. It had been a quick kiss. She looked at him, to her that was a peck. "I thought you were going to kiss. That's right, I'm just a young girl to you. Not a woman who loves you."

That did it. "One question that kiss you want it could make me want you."

She had heard his voice was getting husky. "Tom I'm not afraid of you. Mamma took me to the doctor two months ago. I'm on something to regulate my period. It means I can't get with child."

It took his brain time to catch up on what she had said. "Your saying."

He didn't notice she was backing him up against the building. "I'm saying give me a kiss how you feel about me."

Tom pulled her into him. She wanted him when he moved his tongue over her lips. Ellen opened to taste a kiss, which was part of love making. She was against the building; her hands went under his shirt. He had followed her suggestion and went for her breast. Ellen blouse was up then her bra; she felt his lips on her nipple.

Her body wanted more, one leg between hers. He rubbed her heat as he sucked her nipple. Ellen cried. "What's those butterflies in the lower part of my stomach. It's making it's aching all most to the point of hurting."

He never thought she would want him in that way. "Do ye know why these feelings are happening."

She looked into his eyes as her hand went to find his heat. "Ellen, I don't know if I'm strong enough to stop."

She waved her hand, and they were behind the big rock were no one could see what they were doing. Their pants were down, and she moved over his heat. "Tom stop those butterflies."

He moved over and his hand went down to her flower. Moved between her wet kips, his hand waved. He had made his finger get big each time she came. His finger slipped inside her pussy. When she came, he came, a quick wave of his hand and they were clean. "Tom don't stop."

She wanted more. "I want your cross and rose. So, I can find my mate. Take want is yours, I don't want anyone else but you. I want you to make love to me this summer."

Toms never dreamed of going this far. He took his finger out and tasted her sweetness. I need to give you my cross and rose. I want your cross and rose."

The four teenagers then spoke together. "Did they go all the way."

Thomas shrugged his shoulders. "I don't know what happened. My uncle had woken me up. Ye four, this is your time to see if ye can be mates. One think, I want the young women to know, that a man has two brains. He takes over and makes him do things that would get the two of ye in trouble. Her mother was smart she took her draught to get on something. Remember this is your courting day's work with him. She if ye can work together without fighting. Take care of each other, and young women watch out for his little friend."

The End

It was 18th century evil was in Scotland more families had left. Meghalaya, told us that Magic Fairy Rose will go to the new world. Marcos will have to wait until two hundred years have passed. A young Heart and a MacGregor will go to America. Find out the number of families that came before Thomas. They will call him Tom MacGregor. Eleanor who will be known as Ellen Angel-Heart. Discover why their fathers became Navy Seals. Learn about the two schools they went to. See why the school pushed back the children's names, to the back of their memories. Seek out what names they went by in school.

Learn why the children think their school looks like a jail to them. Fine out if they have magic?

DICTIONARY: GAELIC WORDS

Aye: - a Scottish or northeastern English way of saying 'yes.' Scottish and Geordie people mostly say "Aye."

Biodag: - Dirk, a knife, a dagger a Highland Weapons.

Dee: - a Scot word for die.

Dirk: - "Knife." The word Dirk is a Scottish word for a long dagger; sometimes a cut-down sword blade mounted on a dagger hilt, rather than a knife blade.

Ye: is for the word you.

History

Clan: Popular history has painted this to mean that every member of a clan was related to its chief of the clan. Only the higher echelons of the clan were related to the chief and his immediate family. The majority were simply ordinary men not necessarily related to the chief. Who looked to him as their leader and most importantly their father?

"Brosnachadh Bhruis:" Is a patriotic song of Scotland written in the Scots language.

Biodag or Dirk; was a long stabbing knife. Ideal for close-quarter fighting. After uprising in 1745 the broadswords took on a new look. An enormous number of broadswords were ordered to be cut down and made into dirks.

Broadsword: From the mid-16th century, basket hilt swords were in common use in Scotland. The idea of a basket to protect the hand first came to England and then Scotland from

Scandinavian and German sword makers. By the mid-17th century, ribbon baskets. They made them in massive quantities; to save their hands and by the turn of the 18th century, the Highland basket was reaching its full pattern.

Scottish slang for "do not." "Say sorry, you do nothing wrong.

Frog: When worn, the dirk (knife) normally hangs by a leather strap known as a "frog" from a dirk belt, which is a wide leather belt having a large, usually ornate, buckle that's worn around the waist with a kilt.

Sporran: A pouch of skin with hair or fur on that's worn in front of the kilt.

The word "Aye..., for yes." The USN also used this in the navy, the response would be "Aye-aye, Sir."

www.ingramcontent.com/pod-product-compliance
Lightning Source LLC
Chambersburg PA
CBHW041043310726
48978CB00011BA/419